Illegal

Joyce Larrabee

To Ron and Anne

Best wishes!

Joyce Larrabee

Illegal

By Joyce Larrabee

Cover design by Todd Engel, Engel Creative

Published by BookLocker.com, Inc., St. Petersburg, Florida.

Printed on acid-free paper.

BookLocker.com, Inc.
2018

First Edition

Author Information: www.joycelarrabee.com

Dedication

To Albert Buice, my father and forever friend, who wanted to see this book in print before he went to Heaven. Unfortunately, he will only be able to see it from Above.

Introduction

It's not going away. We rant about it, blog about it, call in to talk shows about it, write letters to editors and politicians about it, whine to our neighbors and friends about it... or just try to ignore it. The truth is that the problem of immigrants, legal and illegal, in the United States is here to stay. These people, who have come to our country in search of a better life—or perhaps for more nefarious purposes—have become a very colorful thread in the tapestry of our society.

This book is not a political commentary. It is a novel. All characters and circumstances are figments of the author's imagination. It is the story of a teacher and her husband, a family of undocumented Mexicans, the residents in the small town of Perkins Grove, Georgia—and of choices.

Chapter 1

Pow! Whop, whop, whop!

"No! Not this morning," she groaned as she wrestled her white minivan over to the narrow shoulder beside a field of strawberries that had been harvested last spring. She got out and walked around the car. Back right tire. Blowout. Now what?

Lynn Bartholomew watched as cars zoomed past her on the highway, her shoulder length salt-and-pepper hair whipping around her face.

Sure am glad I got every hair in place for my first day on the job, she thought grimly.

Cars of every shape and size zipped past her. A bright green motorcycle roared by. A tractor-trailer blasted his air horn, and she could actually feel the road grit bouncing off her face as the big truck thundered past. August is hot in middle Georgia, and even at this early hour of the morning, the air was humid and oppressive. Lynn tried to brush the sand off her face and clothes, but she was already sweating, and the grime stuck fast.

For heaven's sake, she thought, I've lived in this area for years. Surely one of these cars is carrying somebody who knows me.

But she was not yet to the tiny town of Perkins Grove. Her house was a few miles east of the city limits, and she was currently sitting on the side of the main state highway.

Lynn searched the face of every driver that passed. Most of them refused to make eye contact, and those who did actually look at her didn't seem to care.

OK. Sam's in Connecticut, she reasoned with herself. I don't have time to call AAA and wait for them to send someone, so now what? She pulled out her cell phone and scrolled down the list of contacts. It seemed that everyone was either at work or at home with kids. So…

Exchanging her helpless-little-old-lady face for a determined I-can-do-this face, she reached a decision: I know how to change a tire. I'll do it myself!

She raised the back hatch of the van to get the jack and the spare. She found the jack in the side compartment. "Good grief," she grunted, unscrewing the thing-a-ma-jig. "Gotta have a master's in engineering just to get it out!"

She explored every nook and cranny of the back compartment but couldn't find the spare. Surely not… but when she looked under the car, there was the donut securely fastened to the frame. Marvelous, just marvelous!

She decided to figure out the jack first and then deal with the tire. When Lynn was a little girl, her daddy had owned a gas station. He used to let her "help" him change tires, and that's where she learned how it was done. But the jack he had taught her to use bore little resemblance to the thing she was looking at now. *That* jack had little teeth that clickety-clacked as you pumped the handle up and down, raising the car off the ground. *This* jack kind of folded in on itself and had a skinny little handle thing that, according to the instructions, you cranked in circles instead of pumping up and down. Sheesh!

She was on her hands and knees reaching under the van trying to dislodge the donut without getting totally filthy, when an old, dilapidated Ford pickup pulled over some distance behind her car. No telling what color the truck had been in its prime. Now it was just a faded bluish mass of metal with one red fender. She peered out from under the bumper to see a dark-skinned Hispanic man emerging from the wreck. He looked clean enough, but his jeans were worn and faded, and his lightweight long-sleeved shirt was thin from use. It was impossible to tell his age. He jammed his wide-brimmed straw hat lower on his head when a truck swooshed by and almost sent it flying. Probably a migrant worker on his way to the peach orchards, Lynn thought.

"I help?" he called cautiously before approaching.

"Please!" begged Lynn. How ironic, she thought, I might be teaching this man's kids this morning—*if* I get to school in time. She stood up and brushed off her jeans skirt. It never occurred to her to be mistrusting of the man. He was the only hope she had of getting out of this mess.

The man made quick work of changing the tire. Then threw the bad tire and the tools into the van, and with a nod, started back to his pickup.

"Wait!" Lynn said. "Thank you so much." She tried to hand him a $20, but he refused. She dug a $10 out of her wallet and added it to the $20.

"No! No!" He laughed, pointing to the sky. "*Dios* say help."

"Well, thank *Dios*, then."

"OK. *Si*. Yes." He grinned, as he headed to his pickup.

He pulled out first and then she followed him back onto the highway. When he came to his turnoff, he honked and waved, and Lynn tooted her horn in grateful reply.

"Yes, thank You, God," she breathed.

* * * *

Mrs. Bartholomew, brand new English for Speakers of Other Languages teacher at Flanders County Consolidated Middle and High Schools, threw her bookbag across her shoulder, grabbed her purse and set a fast pace for the hike across the parking lot to the door nearest her classroom. She checked her watch. Good! In spite of the flat, she would still make it to her room before the bulk of the students arrived. This was it—first day of the new school year, first day in a new school.

She unlocked her door, quickly scanned her room, and smiled. She had spent more than the required week on preparation, and it showed. The focal point was the large Wheel-of-Fortune-type wheel her husband Sam had made for her. Its sparkly paint glistened in the sunlight streaming through the bank of windows. Colorful pictures depicting different aspects of American culture filled every wall. Student desks stood at attention in perfect rows; the alphabet marched across the front of the room above the board with military precision. Brightly colored cards labeled important items in the room: shelf, book, desk, wall, window, and door, among others. Her desk was clean—for the moment. The apple mug sprouted pens and pencils, and the placement tests were stacked neatly on the corner, ready for distribution.

Now she was nervous, but her nervousness was overshadowed by the thrill that this was actually happening. She wasn't kidding herself. She knew that this year would hold challenges she couldn't even imagine. There would be kids who "already ehspeek the Englis'," so why should they be in an English as a second language course? Thrown together with them would be those who knew next to nothing. And then there would be the kids who were just plain rebellious. But she loved working with teens and was up for the challenge.

The tumult in the hall was getting louder.

Mrs. Bartholomew had a love/hate relationship with the hallways between classes. She loved watching the kids dodging each other, stopping at lockers to pick up books and slam doors, calling out to friends. But she hated being in the hallways at those times. When she was younger, she had jostled and yelled with the best of them, but she was 61 years old now, for crying out loud—too old to be bumped by some football player twice her size and walk away unscathed.

Every once in a while someone would raise a hand or speak in greeting. She had taught many of these kids in kindergarten in the next town. The high school/middle school was situated between the county seat and Perkins Grove, and kids were bused in from all over the area. She had tried to retire after 25 years of teaching kindergarten but had discovered that thumb-twiddling and rocking-chair-sitting were just not in her DNA. When this position opened up, she jumped at it. It was easy to spot the ESOL students: the newly arrived foreigners, the ones who didn't quite fit the scene. They kind of migrated toward each other, quieter than the general throngs, always reluctant to call attention to themselves. Those were *her* kids, and she was anxious to get to know them.

There was no real reason for Lynn to venture into the hall this morning, so she hovered in the doorway to watch the river of teenagers flowing toward their respective homerooms. Since she was only part-time, there was no homeroom for her, and she was fine with that. She had twenty minutes before her first-hour class would descend upon her, and she wanted everything to be perfect—no time to allow this morning's flat to slow her down.

The bell rang. In seconds the halls were full of scurrying, shouting kids again, but this time some of them were heading her way. This is it, she thought.

"Good morning!" She smiled as the first students came timidly into her room. "Sit anywhere. We'll assign seats later."

Some of the students returned her greeting. *Fog* was the only word that came to mind when she looked into the faces of others. She felt for them. When they had settled themselves and their gear, she stood before them, again smiling.

"My name is Mrs. Bartholomew, your English teacher. Repeat please: Mrs. Bartholomew."

A few of the students tried her name. Pretty bad.

"Let's try it again. Mrs. Bartholomew."

A few more tried. Her smile widened to a grin as she said, "Most of my students call me Mrs. B."

At that announcement, some of the students returned her smile and repeated the shortened version.

"When I call your name, please raise your hand so I can see who you are. How many of you understand what I am saying?"

About half the hands went up, a few kids looked around and then raised their hands a little, and the rest of them just gave her a blank stare.

"Good! I might have to call on some of you to help translate if I get into trouble."

Only one girl returned her smile this time.

"Antonio Alvarez."

A hand went up on a nice-looking, muscular teen in the back.

"Isabel Benita."

No hand.

"Isabel Benita," she repeated.

Finally, the girl who had smiled said in Spanish for Isabel to raise her hand. The hand went up shyly. Isabel turned beet red, in spite of her dark skin, and looked down at her hands. Mrs. B smiled at the girl with the too heavy make-up, too tight blouse, and too short skirt.

Soon she came to the student she'd noticed when he came in. He was wearing jeans and a heavy hooded sweatshirt zipped all the way up, his left arm held close to his body.

"Diego Lopez."

The right hand went up slightly, almost fearfully. He still seemed to be cradling his left arm almost as if it were in a sling, and he still had on his sweatshirt. Mercy, this was August in central Georgia, and it was HOT! The air conditioning worked fine, but even Mrs. B, who was always cold in the building, had taken off her sweater when the room filled with teenagers. She gave Diego what she hoped was a reassuring smile.

The roll call continued. She knew she had students from Mexico, Angola, Brazil, and even one from Japan.

The girl from Angola was wearing a *hijab*. That would make her a Portuguese-speaking Muslim. The Brazilian boy was obviously upper-middle class, well dressed and neatly groomed. He would also speak Portuguese, possibly a little English. The pretty, petite Asian girl, who fairly dripped high class, was the one from Japan. Although Perkins Grove was a little town in the middle of nowhere, their families had all come here for reasons of their own. Most of the Spanish speakers were probably migrant workers, and she had no idea what had brought the others. She had her work cut out for her.

Finally, there were only two names left in her book.

"Anita Vasquez."

Her translator at last raised her hand.

"Thank you for your help, Anita."

"Reiko Yakomoto."

The Japanese girl right in front of her respectfully raised her hand.

"Welcome, Reiko."

"Thank you, Mrs. Bartholomew," said Reiko in perfect English.

Hmm, she really might not need to be in here, but she could be a real asset, thought Lynn. Reiko was impeccably groomed, hair in the traditional Japanese style, understated make-up, and what appeared to be an authentic emerald ring glittering on her finger.

Mrs. B held up a pen and a pencil. "Please take out a pen or a pencil. I am going to give you a test so I can see how much English you know."

She showed them the test. Most of the students complied, and the others looked around and followed their neighbors' lead.

"Just do your best. This is not a part of your grade, but..." Lynn paused until she had everyone's attention, "... I have zero tolerance for cheating." She acted out looking at someone else's paper and made it clear that this was not to be. The seriousness in her voice and on her face seemed to convince them. No translation necessary. She handed the papers out and went over the instructions. Then everyone got to work.

The bell rang, and the students laid their tests on the teacher's desk as they filed out. Diego was the last to go. He looked sad and discouraged—almost a haunted or pursued expression. Although his jeans and sweatshirt were far from new, they were spotless. She noticed he was sweating profusely, but still the sweatshirt stayed in place. He gave her a slight nod and then ducked out the door.

Lynn's next class was with the middle school kids. She loved this age. It was easy to get them excited about almost anything. She discovered that many of her first hour students had brothers or sisters in this class, including Diego's pretty, petite younger sister Ana. Like her brother, she was well groomed and clean. Her jeans and cute, feminine T-shirt had even been ironed. She didn't seem as sad as her brother, but the exuberance of the other girls her age just wasn't there. She and Gloria, another sad looking girl, clung to each other like beans and rice.

As a part-time teacher, Mrs. B was free to leave early. Today she chose to stick around to straighten her room for tomorrow and finish grading the tests, classifying her students according to their scores. As she was stacking the papers, she was surprised to hear the bell ring signaling the end of fourth hour. Where had the time gone? Well, she wasn't about to head for her car until the dust settled from the class change, so she packed up and stood just inside the door waiting.

"Hey, what's with that wetback?" she overheard a masculine voice ask. "What's he hidin' inside that sweatshirt? He couldn' be cold."

"Ain't cold. I saw 'im wipin' sweat durin' hist'ry," answered another voice.

"Well, cold or not, he waxed us in math," said yet another guy. "Mr. Philips asked three people that review question from last year, and the only one who could answer was Sweatshirt, and he wad'n even here last year."

"Bet 'e's hidin' drugs," said speaker number one. "All 'em fer'ners take drugs."

"So they're not too differ'nt from us," snickered a fourth voice.

Lynn just barely heard this last remark as the group drifted away. She stole a peek out the door and saw four burly, athletic types meandering down the hall. What she had just heard alarmed her. She was sure Diego was in for trouble if he kept wearing that sweatshirt.

Why was he wearing it anyway?

* * * *

Later that afternoon Lynn settled into the rocking chair on her front porch.

Aaaah, she thought, laying her head back and allowing the peace to seep into her being. She loved her home out here in the country. The roomy ranch-style three-bedroom house where she and Sam had raised their two children sat on the site of the "big house" of an antebellum plantation. The Bartholomew "mansion" boasted a wrap-around covered porch on three sides and a double carport on the fourth. The house had been various colors over the years, but now it sported simple white aluminum siding with forest green trim. The field in front of the house that sloped gently down to the creek had once nurtured row upon row of cotton, and the crumbling foundation below and behind the mansion had supported the carriage house for the fancy rides drawn by sleek horses. Behind the house was a narrow strip of grass that dissolved into the woods that stretched up to the lane. Two beautiful giant oaks stood as sentinels at the entrance to the driveway.

The original barn had been rebuilt long before the Bartholomews bought the place. Now Sam parked his small tractor in what was once the pony's stall, and the other stalls had become storage areas, the largest becoming his workshop. The tack room had morphed into a tool shed. Sam and Lynn kept the picnic tables and benches used for their frequent gatherings in the large open space in the middle of the barn, and the loft was still the best place for kids to play hide and seek.

Sweat ran down the outside of Lynn's tall glass of iced tea. Bees buzzed in the flowers along the front of the porch. Shep, the Bartholomews' super-sized German Shepherd, chased something through the trees that bordered the creek. Lynn was glad they lived here in the country where he could run free without restriction of fence or chain. He never wandered far, especially when Sam was out of town.

The minutes ticked by as she slowly relaxed, her thoughts meandering from one subject to another, finally settling on her students. Most of them seemed to respond well to "Mrs. B," but there were always those who resisted any effort to befriend them. She considered it a personal challenge to win those kids over and transfuse into them a love of learning. Perhaps they were reacting to the rejection they felt by being invisible to the Americans. Most places in the US had learned to get along with the immigrants, but for some reason, Perkins Grove still held them at arm's length.

Lynn's thoughts turned to Diego. She wanted to discuss him—as well as the conversation she had overheard—with Sam, who was in Connecticut presenting seminars for his management consulting firm. He tried to call home every evening around 6:00. When Sam began to travel for his company, he bought Shep and trained him to take care of Lynn. He also bought a .38 revolver and taught his wife to use it. Both Shep and Lynn had learned their lessons well.

* * * *

On Monday the students who had scored high enough on the placement tests were transferred to other classes. After that, there were seven students in first hour and nine in second hour—perfect for lots of personal attention and help. Reiko had made a hundred on her placement test. But her mother had petitioned Mr. Cline, the principal, to allow her to stay in the class to learn the ins and outs of American culture, and he had consented. Lynn was happy that Diego and Ana were both still with her. The boy still seemed like a cornered rabbit, but she thought he might be learning to trust her a little.

Lynn stood at her classroom door, mesmerized by the parade of youthful, multiracial humanity making its way to homeroom. When she shifted to look the other direction, she discovered that the guys she had heard talking about Diego last week had lockers right outside her room.

"Hey," the pimply-faced one was saying, "look who's here." He nodded toward Diego who was creeping along the wall on the other side of the hall.

"Man, he looks rough," said the tall one, a touch of concern in his voice.

"Must 'a been quite th' high this weeken'," grinned the boy in the basketball jersey. Same snickering voice she had heard last week. He leaned in and spoke quietly, "Reckon he's a dealer?"

"Maybe," said a quieter voice, "and one of these days we might even have to persuade him to let us in on the action. We'll just find out what's under that sweatshirt!"

Although he was the smallest and quietest of the bunch, he seemed to speak with the authority of a leader. Lynn hadn't seen or heard him last week. He was well dressed and neat, not the type that you would cast as a bully or a gang leader. At that instant Basketball Jersey glanced up and saw her watching them.

"Psst!" he hissed, signaling the others.

All conversation immediately ceased, but they knew she had heard them. What they did not know was that Diego was one of her brood and that she would go to battle for him, if she had to. The only one who defiantly met her gaze was the leader. He was the first to look away, but she knew it was only because he had to get to class.

She also knew that this was not over.

Lynn was shaken. She was afraid for Diego, but she had to pull herself together before her first hour students arrived twenty minutes later. She knew she was not imagining that everyone filed in a little more somber than usual this morning. What on earth had happened over the weekend? Whatever it was, the only ones that appeared to be unaffected by it were the non-Hispanic students, and even they could tell that something wasn't right. The classroom was deathly silent.

Diego and Antonio were the last ones in. Antonio set Diego's backpack down and turned to check on his friend. Diego made it to his desk and gingerly slid in. He really did look awful. Lynn wanted to go to him, but Antonio gently waved her away. She noticed that all the Hispanic kids were looking either down or out the window. No one wanted to notice that anything was wrong.

Something *was* wrong, though—terribly wrong—but she, along with everyone else, was powerless to do anything.

She bowed her head. "Lord..." she whispered, but she didn't know how to pray in this situation. Lynn struggled again to get hold of herself. How should she proceed?

After a moment she raised her head—and saw six sets of eyes watching her. They silently begged for normalcy. OK, then, normalcy it would be. She grabbed her yardstick and slapped it against the alphabet letters above the board.

"A!"

"A!" her students fairly shouted.

"B!"

"B!" they repeated.

They continued through the alphabet, repeating each letter until everyone got it right. The normalcy did seem to calm them.

When the bell rang, Antonio let everyone else leave before he again shouldered Diego's backpack and headed for the door, where he waited for his friend to catch up. Diego struggled from his desk, shuffled toward the door, and was soon swallowed up in the sea of teenagers, with Antonio shielding him from as much jostling as possible.

The next class poured through the door, boys punching each other and girls giggling. Why did tween boys always punch each other and tween girls always giggle? Who knew? Hormones, she guessed.

In this class the only ones that seemed affected by Diego's plight were his sister Ana, who had obviously been crying—a lot—and her friend Gloria. Some of the others may have noticed there was a problem but were doing their best to ignore it. Taking her cue from her first hour students, Lynn conducted a normal class. As Ana was walking out, the teacher gave the girl's shoulder a quick squeeze. Ana responded with a sad little smile, her lip trembling.

Lynn made the decision to stay at school all day, just to keep an eye on things. She went to the lunchroom and bought something to take back to her room. On Tuesday she would bring lunch because she knew she had to stay for the weekly after-school faculty meeting.

There were two lunch periods. The kids who weren't eating could choose from various enrichment activities like chess club, crafts, debate, or even yoga. She wasn't sure what the other offerings were. Students had until the Friday after Labor Day to choose an activity. Right now there seemed to be a lot of milling around as everyone visited this or that club or class. Lynn made sure she was a presence in the hall until everyone was settled in a classroom.

The rest of the day passed quietly, and although she stationed herself just inside the door every time the bell rang, she heard no more talk among the guys. They were being more careful now. Not a good sign.

After she had unobtrusively watched Diego, Ana, Antonio and Gloria get on the bus, the tired, tense ESOL teacher went home. She longed to talk things over with her husband when he called. He would be in the Northeast for three full weeks this time. Thank the Lord for cell phones!

* * * *

Lynn was resting in her porch swing, a glass of iced tea at her side. Shep, her black-and-tan gentle giant, came crashing out of the underbrush where he had been chasing who-knows-what ever since she'd let him out when she got home. She appreciated his watchfulness and companionship. He was devoted to both Sam and Lynn, and in return, they considered him part of the family. He stopped to say hello and receive a pat on the head and then was off again on his quest to traumatize yet another woodland creature. Lynn relished sitting on the front porch during these last fleeting days of summer. She was sipping her tea when her phone finally rang.

"Hi!" she said, knowing it was the man she loved.

"Hi!" came the familiar voice, "How're you?"

"I'm fine. Tell me about your meetings."

Lynn listened for several minutes, making comments at the appropriate times. She could picture her tall, distinguished looking silver-haired husband behind the podium in some auditorium or seated at a long conference table. He would be "telling it like it is" to a group of department heads, his well-modulated southern drawl resonating around the room. Although Sam was as mild-mannered as they come, he pulled no punches when dealing with company business. He was well respected and had made many friends among the higher-ups in the companies he helped—as well as a few enemies.

"Sounds like your evaluations and presentations are going to make a huge difference," she said when he was winding down.

"Hope so. We've only just begun—four more days of hard labor to go. Now tell me what's going on in your neck of the woods. What's happening with the kid we were talking about over the weekend?"

She told him, punctuating the telling with a few tears, which surprised her. Her husband had always had a sympathetic ear, and he grieved with her over Diego's plight. She told of his obvious pain and distress. She also shared her suspicions.

"What do you plan to do about it?" he asked.

"I don't know. You know we can't move ahead without evidence, so I don't know what I can do. What do you think?"

Sam was silent for a minute. "Have you spoken to any of the other teachers about it?"

"No, but they have to have noticed he was in bad shape. Tomorrow afternoon is faculty meeting, so maybe someone will bring it up then."

"If he's as bad as you say, maybe you should go talk to the principal before the meeting. Maybe no one has made him aware of the problem. Does he have much personal contact with the kids?"

"I really don't know. My room is at the end of the hall, about as far away from the office as you can get. But that's a good idea. I'll see how Diego is in the morning and go see Mr. Cline."

After they had said good-bye, Lynn sat on the porch thinking.

Shep finally satisfied himself that his home was safe from attack by any furry little invaders and was ready to call it a day. After he had lapped up about a gallon of water and thoroughly scratched and shaken himself, he came and sat down beside her, panting, slobbering, and looking intently into her green eyes with his big brown ones. He was a mess, and she knew what had to be done before they went back inside.

"OK, Goofus, I can take a hint. Go get your brush."

Shep didn't have to be told twice. He shot across the porch, stretched up to his full height, and got the dog brush off the shelf.

"Uh-oh, you've been to the carriage house again, haven't you?" She didn't know what he found so irresistible in that old stone foundation, but he always came back filthy when he had been down there. He dipped his head in mock shame at being found out. She brushed all the burrs, sticks, and spider webs out of his coat, checking carefully for ticks as she went.

"There! Now go put your brush away and let's find some supper."

The only word Shep liked better than "brush" was "supper," so before Lynn could pick up her tea glass, the brush was in its place and he was in the carport at the back door, wagging that great big tail of his.

After supper Lynn cleaned the kitchen and practiced the piano for a while. She was trying her best to concentrate on the choir piece she was to accompany on Sunday—instead of what she would face tomorrow morning.

Chapter 2

For more years than she could remember, Lynn had begun her day with Bible study and prayer. Today was no exception. If anything, she felt she needed God's direction for this day more than at any other time in her life. She was legally obligated to bring Diego's situation to the principal's attention, but she was really nervous about it. If her suspicions were correct, the next twenty-four hours were going to indelibly mark the future of several people.

"Help me, Father," she prayed. What else could she say?

Shep was outside, and she was finishing her breakfast when it dawned on her that before school might be the best time to catch Mr. Cline. She quickly put her dishes into the dishwasher, called Shep, grabbed her stuff, remembered the lunch she had packed the night before, and headed for the door. Miracle of miracles, her keys were actually hanging where they belonged.

Mrs. B dropped her things in her classroom and headed for the office.

"Good morning, Sheila. Is Mr. Cline in?"

"Good morning!" Sheila flashed her a cheery smile. "He's coming in right behind you."

Sheila Vaughn was the attractive, mocha-colored epitome of secretarial efficiency. If Sheila didn't know what was going on around school, nobody did.

"Good morning!" said Lynn to the principal. "Do you have a minute?"

"Sure," said Mr. Cline. "Shall we step into my office?" He closed the door behind them. "What can I do for you?"

"I'm going to come right to the point," she said when they were seated. "Do you know Diego Lopez? He's a sophomore, Hispanic, has a younger sister Ana."

"Should I know him? Has he been giving you trouble?"

"No, no. He's not giving me trouble. He seems to be a good kid. I believe he's in some sort of trouble himself. He's the one who wears a sweatshirt zipped up all the time. Have any of the other teachers mentioned anything to you about him?"

He ignored her last question. "OK, I think I know who you're talking about. What seems to be the problem?"

"Last week I overheard some boys talking outside my classroom. They think he might be hiding drugs inside his sweatshirt. Yesterday they were chatting each other up to get his sweatshirt off of him."

"Hmm, I see. Anything else? I can alert security, but other than that, I don't know what I can do."

"Actually there is something else. Yesterday when Diego got to my class he could hardly walk. He seemed to be in tremendous pain, but it was as if he had to keep going."

"Did you notice any marks on him?"

"Well, with jeans and that shirt zipped all the way up, the only skin showing was on his head and his hands, and no, there were no marks. I looked as quickly as I could without letting on."

"Thank you, Mrs. Bartholomew. You have fulfilled your obligation, but we need more to go on. I will consult with the school counselor and take it from here."

"OK, I'll be here all day today because of faculty meeting."

"Fine," said Mr. Cline, standing. "Thank you for coming to me, Mrs. Bartholomew. We'll do what we can."

"Thank you."

Lynn left the office no more comforted than when she came in. She got to the hallway in front of the main entrance just as the buses spilled out their passengers. Her room seemed to be five miles down the hall, and she was destined to be jostled the whole way.

Lynn made it to her room more or less intact and only slightly more deaf than when she woke up that morning. She was surprised to find Diego leaning against her door and Antonio pacing nervously in front of him. If possible, Diego looked worse than he had the day before. Now he looked flushed and feverish.

"Mrs. B!" began Antonio, "please no mad. Diego no... walk... homeroom. We... this one hour class... He sit, yes?"

She quickly unlocked the door. "Of course he can stay here! I'll write a note to his homeroom teacher, and hopefully, she'll accept it. Are you in the same homeroom?"

The boy nodded. She scribbled a note, signed it and passed it to Antonio as he sprinted out the door.

Diego had his head on his desk, moaning quietly. She brushed the damp hair back and felt his forehead. He was burning up.

"Diego," she said softly, "What can I do? Won't you let me help you down to the school nurse?"

"No!" he whispered. "More bad."

She thought a minute, and then asked, "Are you allergic to aspirin or Tylenol?"

She knew that giving unauthorized medication to a student could not only cause her to lose her job, but could also land her in jail.

He shook his head no. "Take-ed."

The boy must be badly hurt if he had already taken something for pain and was still like this. What should she do?

She left him with his head down on his desk and hurried to glance quickly at her lesson plan. In only a few minutes she had to be ready to act as if nothing had happened. She knew she must be pale, so she pinched her cheeks and quickly put on more lipstick. Thank goodness she had prepared a review worksheet! For class she would have the kids do that first to give herself a little more time to calm down.

When the bell rang, Mrs. B forced herself to walk calmly to the door to greet her students. Anita was first.

"Good morning!" said the teacher enthusiastically.

Anita only glanced at her and then at Diego as she made her way to her desk.

Lynn stayed at her station, greeting all the students as they came in. She stood before her class soberly, pasting on a smile.

"First thing this morning we are going to find out how much you remember. Please finish this worksheet, and then we will do it together."

They weren't buying it, and she knew it. Diego couldn't be ignored, but no one could deal with it openly, either. She longed to talk it all out as badly as they did. That simply could not happen.

Lynn wasn't sure how she filled the rest of the class time, but somehow they all got through it. Maybe she could bluff her way through the next hour with the younger kids. Then she would be home free—at least for today. She was relieved when the bell rang. She sighed and turned to greet her punching, giggling younger class as they came through the door. Ah yes, 'twas good to have a bit of normalcy.

* * * *

It was near the end of the second lunch/enrichment rotation. Mrs. Bartholomew was sitting at her desk eating when she heard the scuffle begin outside her door. Instantly she was in the hall.

"Stop it! Get away from him!"

Diego was on the floor and four boys were struggling with him. She grabbed a double handful of basketball jersey and jerked with all her might. Where the strength came from she would never know. The guy fell backward and landed against the wall. She snagged the next kid by the arm and shoved him back. He collided with Pimple Face before she could get to him, and both boys went down. The fourth boy suddenly stood and started backing up, hands raised, a look of horror on his blanched white face. She noticed the leader of the pack leaning against the wall with his arms folded across his chest. He had obviously given the order for the attack but could not be accused of actually taking part in it. He silently turned and glided away. Out of the corner of her eye, she saw Antonio skid to a stop, kneeling at his friend's head. Mr. Philips had run out of his room when he heard her yell. After the boys picked themselves up off the floor, he corralled them into a corner.

She turned around to check on Diego and was sickened by what she saw. They had gotten his sweatshirt open, all right. Under a thin white T-shirt she saw a torso so badly injured that it was a wonder the boy was able to stand up, let alone walk. Along with the bruising, there were cuts and abrasions, many of them infected, bleeding through his T-shirt. He probably had some broken ribs and possibly even internal injuries.

"Diego! Diego!" Antonio pleaded.

Mercifully, Diego had passed out.

Mrs. B started barking orders. Mr. Philips was still standing with the boys, but she had taken charge, and he knew enough not to interfere. She pointed to a girl with a lunch bag in her hand.

"You! Go get the school nurse down here as fast as you can. Tell her we need a blanket."

She pointed to various students as she singled them out. "You! Go to the office and have Mrs. Vaughn call 9-1-1. Tell them we need an ambulance ASAP or faster. You! Go get Mr. Cline. You! Go outside and wait for the ambulance. Direct them around to this outside door. Mr. Philips! Get these other kids back to class. You boys that attacked him, form a circle around him so the other kids can't see what you've done."

"Hey! We didn't beat 'im up! We just…" protested one of the boys.

Mrs. B's icy glare froze the end of his sentence in mid-air.

She dropped to her knees beside Diego and checked his pulse and respiration. His pulse was weak, and his breathing shallow and uneven, but at least he wasn't thrashing around.

"Talk to him, Antonio! Talk to him in Spanish and tell him everything will be all right. Keep talking until the EMTs get here." Where was the ambulance?

She stood and looked around as she thought of something else. Anita had paused in the hall on her way to lunch.

"Anita! Please go to the office, find out where Ana is and bring her here. Tell her to bring her things. Understand?" Anita nodded and took off down the hall.

The school nurse arrived at a run with a blanket and some other equipment. Lynn helped her spread the blanket over the boy and reported on his pulse and respiration. Where was that ambulance? Why on earth was it taking so long?

Lynn heard the siren enter the parking lot at the same time she saw Mr. Cline and a security guard hurrying toward the group in the hall. Quickly she gave him the abbreviated version of what had happened and left Mr. Philips to fill in the details later. She and Mr. Cline looked each other briefly in the eye. "Now we have evidence," she said quietly.

"Yes," he responded. "You can stop by the office and fill out the forms. I'll contact the authorities at once."

"Mr. Cline, you, the security guard, Mr. Philips, and the nurse have all seen the wounds. You can sign the papers and call the police. I'm going to take Ana to find her mother and take them both to the hospital. Please sign her out for me. Thank you."

He knew she wasn't asking.

The EMTs burst through the outside door as Ana and Anita came running from the other direction. They all reached Diego at the same time. Ana gasped when she saw her brother.

"Let's move back!" commanded Mrs. B. "And give the gentlemen room to work."

She knew Diego would be better off with the professionals working on him without interference. The school nurse quickly filled them in on the boy's condition.

"Mr. Cline, would you like security to escort these boys to your office?" Mrs. B asked, indicating the four wide-eyed attackers standing against the wall.

Mr. Cline nodded, and the security guard herded four very sober boys down the hall.

Ana had been clinging to Anita crying quietly, but when the EMTs pulled back the blanket, she collapsed against the older girl sobbing. Mrs. B instantly moved to her side. "Let's go to my room."

The three sat in student desks facing each other. "Ana, I need you to tell me what is going on, and I need you to tell me now," Lynn said quietly and distinctly, but authoritatively. "Who did this to Diego?"

Anita translated Mrs. B's urgent question and asked Ana who had beaten her brother so severely.

Ana was sobbing almost hysterically, so Lynn gave her a drink from her own water bottle. Then the girl started speaking in rapid-fire Spanish, interrupted by sobs and hiccups. Lynn was glad Anita had stayed to translate. Although Ana could usually make herself understood in English, she was just too upset right now.

At first Ana kept saying he would kill them if they told. Finally, Anita convinced her that it was time to deal with this thing. It had gone on long enough. If she didn't tell, her father would eventually kill Diego anyway, and she knew it. Ana looked at her teacher, took a deep breath and started talking.

The abuse had been going on her whole life but had escalated significantly when the family came to America. Her mother and Diego had vowed to protect Ana from her father. Sometimes Armando Lopez would come home drunk and start toward his daughter. Mother and son would intervene, keeping the father at bay until Ana could sneak out of the house and hide in the woods. When Armando discovered that his daughter had escaped yet again, he would fly into an uncontrollable rage. Diego always received the brunt of his father's fury when he tried to protect his mother as well.

Armando Lopez was a violent man from a violent family, but he was no fool. He knew better than to leave marks on the boy where they could be seen. When Armando's wrath was finally spent, Diego would creep outside until his mother could calm her husband. After Armando was asleep, Ana would help Diego back inside and she and Maria would clean up his wounds. The kids would make it a point to be gone before their father woke up the following morning.

Lynn needed to know more, but she could hear the EMTs loading Diego onto a gurney for transport to the hospital. She went out to the hall to talk to them.

"Tell me what to do. Should I follow you to the hospital now to get him checked in, or should I go get his mother? Can you treat him as a minor without her consent?"

"She signed a consent form before school started, so treating him shouldn't be a problem," said Mr. Cline.

"Do you have translators at the hospital, or should I bring one of the kids to translate?"

"We have a translator. She works in the finance office, but she speaks Spanish fluently. You go get the mom. Mr. Cline, could you get us that consent form? That will have all the necessary information to do a preliminary check-in. We'll meet you at the front door of the school after we get him loaded."

Mr. Cline headed for the office. The EMTs started for the outside door with Diego. Mrs. B gave both Antonio and Anita a quick hug, thanking them for their help, and sent them back to class. She went back into her room with Ana and quickly grabbed her purse.

Before she backed out of the parking space, she turned to Ana. "We have to get your mother and take her to the hospital. Will your father be at home now?"

"No, he... come night. The mother... she... home... only she."

"OK. Where do you live?"

"On trailer park. Go..." Ana pointed left. "Very road bad."

"While we are driving, Ana, I want to ask you more questions. I guess the most important is, why didn't you and your mother and Diego leave when the abuse got bad?"

Ana almost started crying again but managed to keep herself in check. "Go...?" She shrugged. "No have family. No money go Mexico."

"What about a shelter, a government place for abused families?"

Ana smiled wryly. "The law, she say can go... very difficult... how you say... of my peoples. Womans *Americanas* no like."

"For my people," corrected Lynn absentmindedly. "I see. If you had a safe place, would you go?"

She was skating on thin ice here, knowing that often abused women and children choose to stay in an abusive situation over going into the unknown.

"Yes!" said Ana with no hesitation. "We talk many... have afraid. He find... he keel us." Lynn heard the fear in her voice.

They drove out of town, and then Ana pointed out several back roads. Finally, they arrived at a run-down trailer park. On both sides of the rutted, muddy dirt road were old dilapidated trailers. The yards were unkempt and somewhat junky; weeds sparsely covered the bare, hard-packed clay. Every now and then she could tell that someone had tried to fix things up a bit, but there was only so much a person could do, given the general run-down state of things. Shame on the owner of this 'park,' thought Lynn.

"That," said Ana pointing to the last trailer.

It was a 1970s vintage faded yellow and tan singlewide with a cracked picture window in the front. Rickety stairs led to a small, cockeyed wooden stoop at the door. Lynn couldn't help but notice that the yard around this particular trailer had been swept and the weeds cut back. Clean laundry waved gently in the breeze on the clothesline out back. It was obvious that the woman of this house did not work in the fields, but stayed home and kept house for her family.

Ana jumped from the car before it even stopped rolling. "*¡Mamita! ¡Mamita!*" she called.

The door flew open, and a small, pretty, but very much alarmed woman ran out. She was an older version of her daughter, neatly dressed in a cool, print summer dress. Her feet were bare—no air-conditioning here. It was impossible to tell how old she was. She looked worn, but Lynn figured it was more because of her home life than her age. Ana explained everything in a rapid flood of Spanish.

By this time Lynn was at the door, and Ana hurriedly introduced her to her mother Maria. The woman was reaching for her purse and shoes when Lynn held up her hand to stop her. She spoke slowly to the girl.

"Ana, I want you and your mother to get all your things and Diego's and come with me. It will not be safe for you to come back here. It will be a long time before we can see Diego, so if we move quickly, I think we can get everything out now. Do you understand?"

"Yes," said Ana with wide eyes. She translated for her mother, and, although Lynn could see the poor lady's uncertainty, she nodded her agreement and immediately went to comply.

There were no suitcases or even boxes, so everything was quickly put into plastic grocery bags and stowed in the van. Maria's cleanliness and organization made it quick and easy to get the job done. They almost forgot the clothes on the line, but Ana noticed them at the last minute and gathered them into her arms, leaving her father's.

Maria took one last look around the trailer and the yard and got into the car. Slowly and silently the three women left the trailer park. Only God knew what the future held for this family.

Chapter 3

No one tried to speak on the ride to the hospital. When they reached the emergency room, they were taken directly to the cubicle where a still unconscious Diego lay hooked up to various tubes and monitors. His torso and right arm were swathed in bandages. His left arm was splinted and bandaged. Antiseptic smells permeated the room. Maria stopped short, letting the flimsy privacy curtain drop against her shoulder. Visibly shaken by what she saw, she covered her mouth with her hand, and tears pooled in her eyes. She and Ana clung to each other as they advanced to the bedside.

"A doctor will be in shortly to talk to you," said the nurse who had ushered them in. She checked Diego and his monitors. "We're still waiting for the results of the tests, x-rays and MRI. We've started antibiotics and pain medication in his IV."

"The EMTs said the hospital had a translator," said Mrs. B. "Could you please make sure that person is here when the doctor comes in?"

The nurse nodded and hustled out to deliver the message and tend to her other patients.

Lynn simplified what the nurse had said for Ana, who then translated for her mother. She noticed that Diego's respiration, heart rate and blood pressure had improved since he had arrived at the hospital and breathed a sigh of relief. She encouraged Maria to talk to her son and let him know she was there and that he would be fine. Maria dried her eyes and cleared her throat, knowing instinctively that she needed to be brave for Diego's sake. She took his hand, smoothed his feverish brow and crooned to him as only a mother can.

"Ana," said Lynn, holding up her phone, "is there anyone we should call? A relative or close friend? Maybe your priest?"

Ana relayed the question to her mother, who responded quickly and eagerly.

"*Mamita*, she say call to *Pastor Juan.*"

"Do you know his number?" asked Lynn. She handed the phone to Maria, who just looked at it in her hand.

"She no… cell phone," said Ana, "I, yes. Friends teach."

She took the phone and slowly punched in the numbers as her mother called them out to her. It took three or four tries, but they finally did it. Maria listened to the ring coming from the other end, but as soon as she heard her pastor's voice, she broke down. Although no sound of crying came from the poor lady, she found it impossible to form any words as the tears streamed down her face. As soon as Ana saw her mother, she began sobbing as well. Lynn took the phone.

"Hello?"

"Hello?" came a male voice. "May I help you? Who's speaking, please?" Lynn could tell that the man was Hispanic, but his accent was very light. Then he spoke in Spanish, and she assumed he was repeating the questions.

"My name is Lynn Bartholomew, and I'm calling on behalf of Maria and Ana Lopez. Is this Pastor Juan?"

"Yes, it is," said the pastor. "What's wrong? Is Maria there?"

By this time, Maria had composed herself for the most part and was reaching for the phone.

"Yes, I'm going to let you talk to her," answered Lynn.

Maria told Pastor Juan what had happened, still struggling to speak through her tears.

"He come," said Ana when the call ended.

It seemed that the doctor was taking an awfully long time to get to Diego's cubicle. The ladies tried to talk a little but soon just sat quietly. The waiting seemed interminable.

A tall, good-looking, 40-something Hispanic man came through the curtain. Ana jumped up and threw her arms around him, sobbing yet again. Pastor Juan. He held the girl, letting her cry it out. When her sobs at last turned to hiccups, he made his way to Maria and simply put his hand on her shoulder as he looked down on the boy. She broke down again.

A small, round, middle-aged lady stepped through the curtain.

"*¡Buenas tardes! ¿Doña Maria? Soy Lola.*"

Maria nodded her head, and the lady continued to speak to her in Spanish. This must be the translator. Lynn couldn't tell if she was American or from some other country, but she spoke Spanish fluently and had no trouble understanding what Maria or Ana said, even though they were often talking through tears.

It seemed that mother and daughter were telling Lola the whole sordid tale. Pastor Juan listened quietly, pain and regret clearly showing on his face. What kind of pastor would let this go on without intervening? Thought Lynn. He had not only a moral obligation but also a legal one.

When it seemed that Maria and Ana were calming down, Lola showed them some paperwork that needed to be completed. Lynn motioned Pastor Juan out into the hall.

"Do you know of any place Maria and Ana could go? They simply cannot be at their trailer when Armando gets home. No telling what he might do. We already got their things out."

"I agree," said the pastor, "but, honestly, I can't think of any place. One of our men owns a construction company, but he and his wife are out of town right now. Many of our church families are migrant workers who live in tiny, inadequate apartments or trailers like the Lopez's. Most of them would squeeze Maria and the children into their home in a heartbeat, but I can't ask them to unless there is simply no alternative.

"The Lopez family has been here only a few months. I have never even met Armando. Maria is a Christian; the children are not. Armando allows Maria and Ana to come to church occasionally, but Diego has been just a couple of times. Armando made it clear that I am not welcome in the home. I knew there were problems within the family, but I had no idea the man was so violent."

"I see," said Lynn, thinking hard. "Would you have any reservations about having them in your own home?"

The pastor swallowed hard. "No reservations whatsoever, but... uh... unfortunately... that's not possible at this time. I'm sorry."

He looked like he was ready to break down himself, but didn't offer an explanation. Lynn wondered, but of course, she didn't ask. She stepped down the hall to the restroom where she stood deep in thought for several minutes—weighing personal security against peace of mind, the Lopez family's needs against her means to meet those needs, and praying for wisdom. She could usually tell when people were faking it, but she had not picked up the slightest bit of duplicity from the Lopez family. Finally, she sent a quick text to Sam.

When Lynn got back to the room, Lola was nowhere to be seen, and Maria, Ana and Pastor Juan were gathered around Diego's bed, talking softly. She handed them all a vending machine juice and opened the water she had gotten for herself.

Ana came to stand beside her. "*Mamita* and me, we talk. Want know... go...?" She shrugged, palms out.

"You will come to my house," Lynn said simply.

Ana stopped short, her mouth open. "You house, *Señora*! No can..."

The girl looked at Pastor Juan and rattled off something in Spanish. Relief and concern battled for predominance on the man's face, but he said nothing.

"Maybe... how you say...

"Dangerous," inserted Pastor Juan.

"Dang... danger..." she gave up. "You... man?"

"Husband. He is in another state. I texted him and just received his answer."

She turned her phone around to show it to the girl. "Whatever it takes," it read.

"No understand," said Ana.

"He says it will be good for you to come home with me. He won't be back for two more weeks and will be happy for me to have the company." She spoke as simply as she could so that Ana would understand.

"*¿Ana?*" questioned Maria. "*¿Pastor?*"

Ana translated for her mother in that machine-gun Spanish of hers. Pastor Juan added a comment here or there. Lynn expected Maria to object. Instead, the Hispanic lady held her gaze for a long moment, and then looked at Pastor Juan. She turned back to Lynn and simply said, "*Gracias.*"

A slender, graying-around-the-temples doctor stepped through the curtain, Lola and a nurse in his wake.

"I'm Dr. Benjamin." He addressed Maria. "Are you the mother?"

Lola quickly translated.

"*Si,*" answered Maria.

"And who are you?" he asked Pastor Juan.

"Juan Garcia, the family's pastor. This is Mrs. Bartholomew, Diego's ESOL teacher. "

"Hi, Mrs. B. You taught my kids in kindergarten. You signed the abuse papers?"

"Will sign, if someone else hasn't already done so." She answered, racking her brain to try to remember this man's children. "I was there when the boys attacked Diego. His sister and I picked up their mother and came directly to the hospital. I will sign the papers as soon as possible, if necessary."

"Boys that attacked Diego? I thought we were looking at a domestic abuse case," said the confused doctor.

He adjusted the reading glasses that had been perched on top of his head and examined Diego's chart.

Lynn gave the condensed version of the attack at school and the abuse that it revealed. The tears again trickled down Maria's face as Lola translated.

"What have you found?" asked Lynn.

"Well, we have good news and bad news," replied the doctor.

He tried to address the whole group, but mostly he looked at Lynn. Lola was translating quietly for Maria and Ana.

"The good news is that there are no severe internal injuries. His organs are bruised but not permanently damaged. He doesn't seem to have a severe head injury—responds to touch, no swelling or anything. Four fractured ribs—they will heal without surgery. No spinal damage."

Everyone breathed a sigh of relief.

"And the bad news?" asked Lynn.

"His left arm has been broken three times in the past but was never set properly. We'll have to re-break it in the two spots where it knit improperly. Then we'll set the bones correctly and put in pins or plates where necessary, as well as repair the break from the most recent incident," answered the doctor with earnest sympathy.

"Can you set all of them at the same time, or will it take a series of treatments and surgeries?" asked Lynn.

"My colleagues and I were discussing that. It would be more painful to do them at once, but it would keep him from going through more surgeries. Our opinion is that it would be better for him to have them done all at once. When he wakes up, we'll keep him for a day or two to see if he's strong enough for the procedure. If not, we'll send him home to recover before we repair his arm."

"What about the infection?" asked Pastor Juan.

"We caught it before it became systemic," said the doctor. He turned to Maria, "You did a good job caring for your son, Mrs. Lopez. The infection would have been much worse without it."

When Lola translated this last statement, Maria colored slightly and looked at her son.

"When do you think he'll wake up?" asked Lynn

"There is no way to anticipate that, but his vitals have stabilized, and he doesn't seem to be in a deep coma."

As if on cue, Diego moaned. The doctor leaped to his side.

"Talk to him, Mrs. Lopez!" he commanded.

Lola didn't need to translate. Maria was already bending over her son, talking to him quietly.

"Talk louder, Mrs. Lopez. Call his name!" insisted the doctor.

Lola translated and Maria began calling her son's name and using their personal terms of endearment.

Diego moved his hand, and his mother took it and squeezed it, still talking. He moved his head. Then finally opened his eyes.

"*Mamita*," he whispered.

His mother was crying in earnest now, still calling to her son.

"Diego!" called Dr. Benjamin. "Can you hear me?"

Diego turned his head slowly in the doctor's direction.

"You are in the hospital, but you will be fine."

The doctor then proceeded to poke poor Diego with a needle in several locations. The nurse noted his responses on a chart. Then Dr. Benjamin asked the boy to move various parts of his body, the nurse again making notes.

When the doctor finished his exam, he turned to the little group and smiled. "He's going to be fine. He can hear. There does not appear to be nerve damage, and he can move his extremities on demand."

Lola translated and told Maria to tell her son where he was and that he was going to be OK.

"*¿Papá?*" said Diego.

Again Maria assured her son that they were all safe and that his father could not hurt them. Diego was to rest and get well. The doctors and nurses were all there to help him. She told him they would be going home with Mrs. B, so he should not worry.

Pastor Juan nodded to Lynn, so she stepped up to the bed and gave Diego a big smile.

"Hi, Diego! Look who else is here."

She stepped back and let Ana take her brother's hand. True to form, Ana cut loose with a stream of her turbo-boost Spanish. No one knew if Diego got it all or not, but one side of his mouth lifted in a weak, crooked smile. The pastor spoke quietly to Ana when she had said enough. Then he took the boy's hand and greeted him.

Diego closed his eyes again, and immediately the doctor moved in to examine him. He stepped back smiling.

"I think he's asleep," he said. "That's a good thing."

Lola translated and everyone relaxed a little.

Maria moved a chair up close to her son's head and sat down, again taking his hand. Ana sat in a chair in one corner of the curtained area. The pastor stood reflectively on the side of the bed opposite Maria. He didn't want to wake Diego, so he began to pray just loud enough for the boy's mother and sister to hear. Lola went back to her other work. The doctor motioned Lynn outside with him.

Dr. Benjamin spoke in a quiet voice. "Have the authorities been notified? That boy might not survive another beating like this."

"My principal at school said he was going to call and that I could sign the paperwork tomorrow." said Lynn. "Should I call and see if he's turned it in?"

"Yes. If the father comes home and finds them gone, he might figure it out and come here. If he hasn't been arrested, I'm going to need a 24-hour guard on Diego until his father's in custody." He paused a moment, thinking. "Lola told me you're taking Ana and Maria to your house. You know you're taking a tremendous risk, don't you? Not only is the father a factor, but there are folks in this town that won't like it a bit."

"I know, but what else can I do? My husband and I have been taking in needy people almost since our wedding day. The Lopezes have nowhere else to go. I wouldn't take in just anybody, but I think Maria is OK."

"I admire your courage," said the doctor. "Now call the principal."

It was almost 4:00. Faculty meeting should be over any minute now. She had the number in her speed dial, so she hit the button and listened to the phone ring. Finally, the secretary picked up.

"Sheila, I need to speak to Mr. Cline right away. Is he still there?"

"Hi, Mrs. B. We've all been hoping you'd call. Mr. Cline is still in faculty meeting, but they should be wrapping up any minute. He told me to give you his cell phone number, if you called. How's the boy?"

"He'll be fine. What's the number?"

Sheila gave it to her, and she wrote it on her palm with the red pen from her pocket. She punched in the number and almost immediately Mr. Cline answered. She wasted no time with niceties.

"Mr. Cline, did you call DFCS to report the abuse or the police to pick up Mr. Lopez?"

"Well… no, not yet. I have to wait for you to sign the papers."

"Mr. Cline, you or the nurse or even the security guard or Mr. Philips could have signed those papers. You all saw his bruises as well as I did," said Lynn through clenched teeth. It had been a long time since her ire had risen this fast. "You have left the whole family, not to mention me and everyone at this hospital in mortal danger, and that's not an exaggeration. The man is vicious. Make the call *now!*"

She pushed the button to end the call. She had never spoken to a principal like that in her life, but she was too stressed to care. She turned to look for Dr. Benjamin to report that nothing had been done with respect to Mr. Lopez and to ask what they should do next. Her face was white with anger, and she was close to tears.

"Mrs. Bartholomew? Are you OK?" queried the doctor. "I take it he didn't make the call."

Lynn just wagged her head.

"You need to calm down," he said as he took her hand and checked her pulse. "You really do need to calm down. I'll call the Division of Family and Children Services immediately. They will contact the police. Do you know where they can find Mr. Lopez?"

Lynn took a deep breath, trying to do as the doctor ordered.

"I don't know where he's working, but according to the family, he won't be home 'til dark. If he sees police cars there waiting for him, he'll probably run. Like you said, if he comes home and finds his family gone, we're all in trouble."

"Maybe they can catch him on the way home. Do you know what kind of car he drives?"

"Let me go ask the family," replied Lynn.

She ducked back inside the curtain and asked Pastor Juan to ask Maria. The poor lady wasn't sure where her husband worked, but she described the car as well as she could. She also gave a description of Armando Lopez. The pastor wrote it all down in English as Maria gave it to him in Spanish.

Lynn gave the information to Dr. Benjamin, who turned immediately to go to his office and make the call. Before he got around the corner, she ran after him.

"Doctor, when will you be moving Diego to a room?"

"Probably within the next hour. You have no idea how much paperwork and documentation we have to have for a case like this. Let me call this in, and I'll get back to you. By the way, DFCS will want to question Mrs. Lopez. They will have to be assured that she was not involved in the abuse in order for the children to stay with her. I'm not sure what their posture will be concerning your taking them home with you."

"Thanks for the warning. I'll have Pastor Juan talk to Maria before he leaves."

Lynn needed to get home and let Shep out and be there when her husband called. She texted Sam the good news that Diego had come to and that she hoped to be home soon. Shep, poor fella, would just have to hold it a little longer.

Maria was torn. She didn't want to leave her son, but she didn't want to send her daughter home with a stranger either. She asked about staying overnight at the hospital, but since Armando Lopez had still not been arrested, Dr. Benjamin felt it would be better for her and Ana to go home with Mrs. Bartholomew. He assured them that Diego would sleep all night and that the hospital staff would take good care of him. Reluctantly, Maria and Ana agreed.

On the way home Lynn told them about Shep, trying her best to make them understand that he would not hurt them. In Mexico dogs were something to be feared, as they were usually either street dogs that ran in packs, or guard dogs. She decided to leave Maria and Ana in the car while she went into her house first, and then she would introduce them to Shep, after the big dog had settled down from being in the house all day.

Shep greeted her as exuberantly as she had expected and then streaked into the yard to relieve himself. Ana and Maria sat in the car, not moving a muscle. The dog's size was enough to scare anybody.

Lynn called Shep before he had a chance to go rambling off through the bushes. She really wasn't in the mood for the brushing thing tonight. Besides, it was time for him to meet the Lopez ladies. She hoped he would behave himself.

"Here, boy. I want you to meet somebody! Come on!"

She whistled, and Shep came bounding up, tail wagging, tongue hanging out the side of his face, just happy to be in the presence of his beloved person. Lynn ruffled his fur and grabbed his collar.

"Shep, I'd like you to meet Maria."

She opened the front passenger door. Shep stiffened when he saw the stranger. Then, when Maria shyly extended her hand, he cautiously sniffed and then licked it, tail wagging slowly. Maria smiled and timidly reached to pet the big head. As she eased from the protection of the car, she continued to pet him, talking quietly in Spanish. Shep tilted his head, trying to understand. She said something to Ana, and Lynn slid open the back door. Ana was a little more reluctant to surrender her hand to the big dog, so he nudged her bare forearm with his wet nose. Ana jumped, and Lynn and Maria giggled, encouraging her to pet him.

When Ana finally got out of the car, Shep adopted the girl as his own. He velcroed himself to her side and refused to leave it. Lynn could see Ana slowly relax. Like it or not, Shep was going to help heal this family.

The three ladies unloaded the car, even giving Shep a bag to carry. The guests looked around curiously as they went through the house. Lynn couldn't help but notice the look of interest with a hint of longing that crossed Ana's face when she saw the piano. She led them to the guest room and showed them their bathroom. Diego would have the daybed in the office at the end of the hall, right next to Maria and Ana's room. In the closet she pushed some winter clothes out of the way and quickly emptied four dresser drawers. She would find a place for the extra tablecloths and sheets later. Then she left her guests to get settled. Her phone rang. Was it already 6:00?

"Tell me what's happening," said Sam without preamble.

She could hear the concern in his voice. Cradling the phone on her shoulder, she grabbed a handful of ice from the freezer and poured a glass of tea. She opened the door for Shep and headed out to her spot on the porch. It had started to rain, and once again, she was thankful for the peacefulness of her special place.

Starting with her meeting with Mr. Cline, she recounted her day. As she was telling her story, the weariness began to creep into her very bones. It was so good to be able to share with her husband, to let him carry some of her burden. He was so wise. Sam trusted his wife and knew she had thought through the ramifications of having the ladies in their home. He was not really worried about her but was glad that Shep was on site to handle anything that came up, knowing that the dog would lay down his life for Lynn.

When she had finished telling him everything, there was little time for Sam to talk about his day. He had an evening meeting at 7:30, so they said goodbye and hung up. Lynn stayed on the porch for a few more minutes, head back on the chair, eyes closed.

Goodness! Had she fallen asleep? She woke up with a start when Shep nuzzled her with his cold nose. Wow! And what was that smell? How long had she been out there? It was evening, and the rain was still falling, harder now.

She stood up stiffly, stretching. Was that smell coming from her kitchen? Now she understood Shep's urgency. She suddenly realized that lunch had been a really long time ago.

Shep beat her to the back door, of course. When she opened it, the pungent aroma of Mexican spices about knocked her over. She grabbed a towel from the cabinet by the back door and dried her dog.

"Ana? Maria?" she called as she came into the kitchen.

The two appeared from the dining room in aprons, smiling shyly.

"Make food," said Ana.

When they saw that Lynn had fallen asleep on the porch, they'd somewhat timidly taken the liberty of exploring her kitchen. Whatever they had put together smelled amazing. Having the Lopez family with her could have some real advantages!

When they were seated at the table, Lynn took both their hands.

"In our home, we always thank God for the food before we eat," she explained. Ana translated, and then they bowed their heads.

"Lord," she began, taking a deep breath, "thank You. Thank You for the food and for bringing Ana and Maria and Diego into my life. Thank You that Diego is getting such good care and that he is going to be OK. Now, Father, we bring the situation of Mr. Lopez before You. We ask for Your wisdom and for Your protection in the days ahead. Thank You, for Jesus' sake, Amen."

Lynn opened her eyes to see Maria wiping hers. She would be glad when the two of them could communicate a little better. The only words of the prayer the Hispanic lady could understand had been her families' names, so she knew Lynn had prayed for them and was touched.

The food tasted as amazing as its aroma had promised. Maria had taken the leftover chicken and added a mixture of chili powder and cocoa. Wow! Lynn had never tasted anything like it. Served with rice, it was perfect. Caramelized bananas were for dessert, utilizing the bananas that were a little past their prime. Delicious!

Before they got up from the table, Lynn brought up a plan for the time that Diego would be in the hospital. It would mean leaving home a little earlier than normal, dropping Maria at the hospital, and taking Ana to school. Hopefully, he would be released in a few days, and from there, they would play it by ear.

The phone rang. The three ladies looked at each other, and then Lynn answered. Had Armando Lopez been apprehended?

"Hello," she said tentatively.

"Hello. Is this Mrs. Bartholomew?" asked a voice she did not recognize.

"Yes. May I ask who's calling?"

"This is Michael Taylor from the Division of Family and Children Services. I understand you have a Maria Lopez at your house with her daughter Ana. Is that correct?"

"Yes."

The man went on to question Lynn about the details of the attack on Diego and about her own background and family. She thought he would *never* finish.

Then he asked to speak to Ana. He obviously questioned her in Spanish, and most of her answers were short and concise. He was on the phone with her for only a few minutes.

Ana handed the phone to her mother, explaining who the man was. Another long grilling session ensued. At last, the phone went back to Lynn.

"This is highly unusual, Mrs. Bartholomew," said Mr. Taylor, "but I am acting on the recommendation of Dr. Benjamin and allowing the Lopezes to stay with you tonight. Tomorrow we'll interview them further and go from there."

All Lynn could think of to say was, "Thank you."

Tomorrow, the man had said. What would tomorrow hold for the Lopez family?

Chapter 4

Because of the rain, it was darker than usual when Armando Lopez made his way home from work. Wrapped in a couple of sleeping bags in the trunk of his beat up 1981 Malibu was a shipment of marijuana and cocaine from Mexico. The drugs had just arrived from his brothers in the Cartel via a string of mules. His job was to set up a new distribution network in central Georgia. Since 2008, there had been a big increase in drug use in that area, and his people wanted a piece of the action. This was his first delivery, and he was confident. His dealers were all in place. In the morning he would get them all set up, and soon he would be on easy street. A smile played around the corners of his mouth. He ran his hand over his oily black hair. All was good with his world.

He rounded the curve just before the cutoff to the trailer park and, through the pouring rain, saw a police roadblock. What...? How…?

No! They couldn't know what he had! How could they? Questions flashed through Armando's brain without his even forming them.

The police had chosen their spot well. Once around the curve, there was no way to turn back without drawing attention. If he was caught and lost all those drugs, he was a dead man. His brothers would see to that.

At first he panicked, but almost immediately willed himself to think straight. Lopez knew what was under his hood. He drove a Mexican-made Chevy Malibu with a 350 V8. A little tweaking had given him more than 400 horses, raring to be let loose. He punched it and spun the wheel hard. The car fishtailed around. A silver Mercedes that had passed through the roadblock from the other direction was coming toward him. He clipped its sleek front fender, sending it crashing into the ditch. Armando let fly a string of profanity as he fought to get his car under control on the wet pavement.

"Hey!" yelled the officer who was checking out the drivers of each car. Rain was dripping from his hat and running down his slicker. "Go get 'im, Sarge!" he hollered to the cruiser idling on the shoulder.

The police car shot after Armando, radioing ahead for the State Patrol to intercept him.

It didn't take long for Armando to leave the police behind.

"What on earth has he got in that thing?" commented Ike, the driver.

"Wouldn' ya' know it—a sleeper," muttered Sergeant Johnson. "Just my luck."

"Sleeper? What on earth's a sleeper?"

"A junker body with a muscle car engine. Used by drug runners. But I don't care what he's got under the hood," growled Sarge. "I wanna see what he's got in the trunk! He ain't runnin' like that from no child abuse charge."

Sarge would love nothing better than to send this guy back to wherever he came from. One less beaner in his jurisdiction would be a good thing. His frown deepened. He'd be glad when the politicians finally got around to deporting the whole lot of 'em. Even if he didn't get this guy on a drug charge, he could send him up for the child abuse. Whatever.

Armando glanced in the mirror and grinned. The flashing lights were getting smaller. Then through the pouring rain, he saw flashing blue lights coming at him from the other direction. He could hear the siren. Between him and the blue lights was a crossroads with a blinking red light. An intersecting state highway. Good! He didn't care where it went, as long as it took him away from *la policia.*

He would just have time to make the turn. Now! A hard right. He hydroplaned into the watery ditch, but his momentum bounced him back up onto the other highway. The oncoming Georgia State Patrol car made the turn behind him. More bitter cursing, but he still wasn't worried. He could outrun anything these *gringos* had. He saw the police cruiser make the turn behind the GSP car, and then punched it.

He looked in the mirror again. "*¡Caramba!*"

The blue lights were not dropping behind; the siren was still wailing. He let a few more horses out. It was *loco* to drive like this in this weather, but what choice did he have?

Now he was worried. That other car was actually staying with him, possibly even gaining a little. He couldn't believe it! Nor could he think what to do. He'd never been on this road before. Eyes wide, he began desperately scanning left and right for a side road he could turn into and disappear. Mile after mile the cars sped. Suddenly he came upon a small, dark road on the left. There was a sign, but he was so intent on escaping that he never even saw it. He swerved, again hydroplaning, but managed to make the turn. Too late, he realized it was the entrance to something. He veered around the metal bar blocking the road, knocking the unattended guard shack off its foundation as he squeezed through. So what if there were a few more dents in his car.

That oughta stop 'em! he thought.

"He turned into the park!" yelled the trooper to his partner. "Doesn't he know where that road goes? That's Perkins Gorge! Didn' he see the sign?"

The State Patrol car performed the same maneuver around the bar, the little guard shack becoming kindling for somebody's campfire. Armando swore. More police cars followed around the bar.

A portion of the park road runs along the edge of the gorge. The scenery is breathtaking, and there are several scenic overlooks marked along the way. But as Armando Lopez was running way too fast on that wet, curvy, narrow road, scenery was the last thing on his mind. He had no idea where he was or where he was going, and it was pouring so hard that he couldn't have seen the scenery even if he had been walking.

The signs warning of the sharp curve ahead were obscured, his one remaining headlight doing little to penetrate the rain and darkness.

The officers slowed way down when they followed Armando onto the road that ran just a few yards from the precipice.

"That guy might be stupid enough to drive on this road like that, but I ain't," said the trooper.

His partner radioed for another Patrol car to be waiting at the other park entrance. They could barely see Armando's taillights as he went this way and that around the curves.

Suddenly, the guardrail loomed directly in front of Armando. He yanked the wheel! But on the wet pavement...

The speeding car flipped over the rail. The poor man screamed as his car tumbled end over end, all the way to the bottom of the deep gorge.

But there was nobody around to hear him.

The troopers saw two red glows plunge over the edge. "He's gone over!" yelled the officer, straining against his seat belt. "He's gone over!" He grabbed the radio mike "Sarge, he's gone over the edge! Get an ambulance! Get a rescue squad! He's gone over!"

The emergency vehicles came, but there was nothing they could do at night in that heavy rain. They had no choice but to wait until morning. Besides, they reasoned, there was no way Armando Lopez could have survived that crash.

As the ladies were saying good night, Lynn lifted the kitchen curtain and looked out at the rain. It was pouring.

The phone rang. The three of them froze, looking at each other. They were still waiting to hear that Armando Lopez had been captured. Could this be the call?

"Hello," said Lynn. "This is Mrs. Bartholomew. Yes... Yes..." She swallowed hard. "I see..." Her hand went involuntarily to her mouth. How much more could this poor family stand in one day? "Uh... OK. Thank you."

She put the phone down and just stood staring at it.

"Mrs. B?" said Ana. "My father?"

"Yes... Ana, Maria, let's sit down in the living room."

Ana translated for her mother, and they all sat down.

"Lord, help me," prayed Lynn silently.

When they were settled, she took Maria's hand. "Armando was on the way home from work when the police saw him." Lynn was talking very slowly and simply so that Ana could get every word and translate. "When the police tried to stop him, Armando tried to run away in his car." Pause. "He went faster and faster with the police behind him." She waited again for the translation. "He went up by the gorge—a gorge is like a deep canyon. The road was bad because of the rain." Pause. "On a big curve, he lost control of the car. He crashed through the guardrail... uh... fence... the barrier." Pause. "His car turned over and over and went to the bottom." She used her hands to illustrate the car tumbling into the gorge.

Ana's voice dropped to a whisper as she translated.

"*¿Y Armando?*" asked Maria breathlessly.

Lynn looked her in the eye sympathetically. "I'm so sorry, Maria. The rescuers could not get to him tonight because of the storm, but they assume that your husband died in the accident."

Ana sucked in her breath sharply before she translated. Maria really didn't need to hear it in Spanish to know what had happened. The blood drained from her face.

"*Armando,*" she whispered.

"I'm so sorry," Lynn repeated to both of them. What more could she say?

Ana just sat on the edge of the couch. Her expression showed pain, shock and sadness—mingled with a hint of relief. She began to cry quietly, and her mother pulled her into her arms and held her close. Maria had not shed a tear, and her face, though pale, was void of expression.

Lynn wasn't sure how the three of them got through the evening, but eventually, they decided to get ready for bed. They were exhausted from the events of the day but were still in too much of a state of shock to fall asleep. She needed to talk to her husband, so she texted, asking him to call. He would find the message after his meeting.

Maria stayed with Ana until she finally fell into a fitful sleep. Lynn fixed a cup of Sleepytime Tea for herself and Maria, and they sat together at the table. She could tell Maria wanted to talk but was frustrated because she couldn't. Lynn didn't know what to do, so she just sat silently with her new friend, hoping her presence would bring a little comfort.

After they had put their cups into the dishwasher, Maria took Lynn's hands in her own. Their eyes met.

"*Gracias, Señora, muchas gracias.*" With that, she went to her bedroom, shoulders sagging, head down.

Lynn's weariness was setting in again.

Shep had just gone outside for the last time that night when her phone rang. Lynn answered it quickly as she waited by the back door for her dog.

"What's wrong?" asked Sam as soon as she had said hello. "Are you OK? What's happening?"

Her text had obviously worried him.

She hardly knew where to start. "I'm fine," she said. "I just wanted to bring you up to date on things here. How was the meeting?"

"Forget the meeting! What happened?"

She opened the door for Shep and then closed and locked it. She turned on the speakerphone and talked while she dried the dog.

"Diego's father was killed tonight in an accident when he tried to run from the police."

"Wow!" Sam was shocked and saddened. "Do you need me to come home?"

Lynn had already thought about it. She would give anything to have her wise, strong husband by her side through all this.

"No," she said slowly, "I think having a man in the house right now would make Maria and the kids uncomfortable, maybe even afraid. They don't know you are the gentlest man on the planet. The only man in their home was cruel and abusive. We're fine for now. If the situation changes, I know you'll be on the first plane home."

She turned off the lights and headed for her bedroom. Sam was reluctant to say goodbye but finally hung up. Lynn didn't know if she had even told him good night. She dragged herself to the bathroom and glanced at her toothbrush. Forget it. Her teeth could rot and fall out, for all she cared tonight. Though she didn't usually have to set a clock to wake up, it occurred to her that tonight it might not be a bad idea.

No clock was set.

Chapter 5

Lynn awoke with a start to the smell of coffee. Where was she? Who made coffee? Was Sam home? What time was it?

Oh, yeah, she was at home in her own bed. Yesterday... She took a deep breath and let it out slowly. That's when she noticed she had slept in her clothes. Good grief! She took another deep breath and reluctantly put her feet on the floor.

Maria must have gotten up early and made coffee. What time was it, anyway? She squinted at the clock. Good. Only about 10 minutes behind schedule. She could make that up somewhere. Then she remembered that they had to leave early to take Maria to the hospital and began to move a little faster. Class? Ha! She had no idea what she was supposed to do in class this morning. For once she was glad the school required her to turn in the next week's lesson plan every Friday.

Lynn stumbled out to the kitchen, stale clothes and all. Coffee! She usually drank decaf, but this morning she could use a shot of high octane. Grabbing her favorite mug and her Bible, she headed for the dining room table to read and pray.

Oh, well, she thought, when she discovered that she couldn't bring the words into focus, even with her glasses. Have to wait 'til later.

She sat with her head down, waiting for the caffeine to motivate her to move.

Maria must have let Shep out. Lynn hadn't seen or heard him, nor had a wet nose been placed anywhere on her exposed skin. There he was, scratching at the back door. He said good morning in his happy dog fashion. She was almost mad at him for not being tired.

As Lynn was going back into her bedroom to get dressed, Ana came slowly out of hers, blinking at the light.

"Good morning," smiled her teacher. She gave the girl a sympathetic hug.

Shep pushed his way in to hand out his own brand of affection and comfort.

Maria came to the kitchen and immediately started getting breakfast on the table.

"*Gracias*, Maria," said Lynn holding up her coffee mug. "It's wonderful."

Maria smiled, but her eyes were sunken and empty.

"I... *Mamita*," started Ana, "we talk. I no... school. Go hospital... Diego and *Mamita*."

Lynn thought that would be a good idea, in case the translator was not available. Besides, the family needed time alone together to process everything.

"I'll come back to the hospital about 11:00. There will be things to take care of for Armando."

Ana translated for her mother. "*No!*" said Maria emphatically. Lynn looked at her in surprise. Maria explained to Ana, who then turned to Lynn.

"*Mamita* say no... hospital. Home. Sleep. You *mucho* tired."

Lynn smiled gratefully at Maria. She was, indeed, *mucho* tired, and she appreciated the younger woman's consideration. She would run in quickly at the hospital this morning and talk to Dr. Benjamin. Maybe he could help the family take care of things—at least he could point them in the right direction. She got a pen and a piece of paper from the desk and wrote her cell phone number.

"I'm going to leave my phone on all day. If you need anything, please call me."

After getting dressed in record time, Lynn and the others piled into the van. She bowed her head over the steering wheel.

"Lord," she prayed, "guide us this day. Give us wisdom in everything that must be done. Thank You, Father. In Jesus' name, Amen."

When the three got to the hospital, Lynn parked as close to the door as possible, and they walked quickly into the lobby. They padded down the hall as quietly as possible. Maria peeked into her son's room and stepped back quickly to check the number on the door. There he was, sitting up in bed eating breakfast. He looked like a different person! Ana squealed and flew to his side. She slowed only slightly to dodge the tubes and then gingerly gave her big brother a hug. Maria was beaming! She kissed Diego and smoothed his hair.

While the family talked, Lynn went out to find Dr. Benjamin. She wanted to be gone before Maria told Diego about his father.

"Is Dr. Benjamin here today?" she asked at the nurses' station.

"Let me check," said the lady at the computer. "Yes, would you like me to page him?"

"Yes, please," said Lynn, looking at her watch. She was cutting it close. She would not get to school before homeroom, if she didn't leave right then. That meant she would not have time to go over her lesson plan.

"Mrs. Bartholomew?"

Lynn jumped, as Dr. Benjamin came up behind her.

"Sorry. Didn't mean to startle you. I was right around the corner when they paged me. You wanted to see me?"

Lynn told him about Armando Lopez. The doctor whistled softly.

"That's good news and bad news, isn't it?" he asked.

She only nodded.

"I have no idea what arrangements have to be made for him... or whatever... or how Diego will react to the news," said Lynn, checking her watch, "but I do know that if I don't leave right now, I'm going to be late for work. I think Maria will tell Diego about his dad when he finishes breakfast."

"Thank you for filling me in," said the kind doctor. "I'll give them a little time, and then I'll stop by the room. Do they have a number where you can be reached, if necessary?"

She started for the door. "Yes, I gave it to them just a few minutes ago."

She stopped. "Thanks for recommending me to DFCS. They called last night and interviewed all three of us. From the way the guy talked, there is a long way to go before they finish their investigation."

She walked quickly through the drizzle to her car and called Pastor Juan on the way to school.

Of course, all the parking spaces near the building had been taken by the time she got there. She grabbed for her bookbag but then remembered it was still in her classroom from the day before. It was raining lightly, so, purse tucked under her arm like a football, she sprinted toward the school, dodging puddles as she went. She hit the front door just as kids came pouring from their homerooms on the way to first hour. For the second time in as many days, she faced the challenge of getting to her classroom against the tide. The boys that had attacked Diego were visibly missing from in front of their lockers. She wondered what kind of punishment they'd received.

As Lynn made her way down the hall, she noticed that some of the kids looked at her with new respect in their eyes. Maybe slamming that guy against the wall had earned her that much. When she got to her door, there were already several students waiting.

While everyone was getting settled, she jerked out her lesson plan and looked it over. It would take her a few minutes to get organized, but she could let them work in pairs on something until she was ready.

"Good morning!" She hoped her smile was convincing.

"Please take out your vocabulary list. I want you to divide into pairs and work on it together for a few minutes." That should keep them busy until she got her act together. Antonio raised his hand.

"Please, Mrs. B, Diego is OK?"

Several of the other students nodded and looked at her questioningly.

They wanted to talk. Good. Lesson plans could always be revised.

"Diego will be fine," she began.

She then went on to explain about his condition as much as possible, while still maintaining his privacy.

"*¿Y Doña Maria y Ana?*" Isabel asked.

"They are staying with me for a while."

Why not tell them? she reasoned. Number 1, none of these kids knew where she lived. Number 2, the danger was past. And number 3, it might gain her a few points with the Hispanic community. She certainly hoped so.

Some of the kids looked at each other, but no one commented.

"The *policia* shoot father of Diego?" said another student. "Armando Lopez, he is die?"

"No," said Mrs. B, "he was not shot, but yes, he died. Most of you know the situation in their home. In this country child abuse is against the law. When the police tried to arrest Mr. Lopez, he did not stop but tried to get away from them. His car slid on the wet road and he died in an accident."

Reiko's eyes were wide. The other kids were quiet after Anita translated.

"Mrs. B," Isabel said, her hand about halfway up. She turned to Anita and asked a question.

"Why the fathers… hits the childrens?" Anita translated.

Where was Sam? This was a question for him; he was much better at this kind of thing than she was. Why on earth had she told him not to come? In the meantime these kids were waiting for an answer. Was this an opportunity to bring up something from the Bible? Legally she could not take the initiative to promote her faith, but if asked, she could answer.

"Listen carefully," said Mrs. B. "I am a Christian. I choose to live my life based on the Bible, *La Bíblia*, and I believe it has the answers to questions like the one you just asked me. Would you like to hear what the Bible says?"

When Anita repeated the question, several of the students looked at each other uncertainly.

Finally, Isabel raised her hand.

"I, *si...* yes," she said.

Some of the other kids raised their hands. Lynn wondered if any of them were from abusive situations. Her heart went out to them.

Reiko raised her hand. "Please, Mrs. B, tell us what the Bible says."

Lynn couldn't help but notice the tears in her eyes. Could Reiko be living with abuse? Did that sort of thing happen in respectable Asian families? She had to admit that she had kind of overlooked Reiko with everything else going on. Not being a part of the Hispanic community like most of the other kids isolated her enough. So did her perfect English. I must make it a point to reach out to her, she thought.

Antonio raised his hand, "I, yes."

"Why *La Bíblia*?" Ramon interrupted. "Why no Koran or book of... how you say... p-sychlo... spyclo..."

"Psychology?" asked Reiko.

"Hmpf!" said someone else, "This guys not know *nada*. One say this... other ones sayes no... different."

"There are many reasons why I believe the Bible, but I would rather tell you what it says and let you form your own opinion," answered Mrs. B.

"Are there any of you who would object or be offended if I opened my Bible to answer?"

Lynn knew she needed to protect herself as much as possible so that she could keep working with these kids. Anita translated, and everyone looked around. No one raised a hand or indicated that they would be offended.

"Cecilia?" she looked at the Angolan girl. "Do you understand?"

"*Sim*, yes," said Cecilia. Uncertainty, fear, and curiosity were all evident on the Muslim girl's face.

"What do you think?" She could see the girl struggling, not only with her thoughts, but also with how to express them.

"Imam... say... Bible *and* Koran... Koran... good."

"So, it is OK for me to answer the questions from the Bible?"

"Yes," she said.

"First of all, do any of you know where the Bible came from?"

Again, everyone looked around.

Lord, give me the words, she thought. She spoke slowly. "God, the Creator of the universe, loves us. Because He loves us, He wants mankind, us, to know Him. He gave us the Bible so we could know Him."

She looked at Anita, who seemed to be fascinated by what she was saying.

"Anita, could you translate please?"

Antonio jumped in and translated. Good.

"As we look for the answer to your question in the Bible, let's keep that thought in mind." She looked at the clock.

"We cannot study more of the Bible right now. We must study at least a little English, but I promise we will come back to the Bible tomorrow. OK?"

They weren't really happy about it, but they agreed.

Because it was so near the end of the hour, she did a little review, worked on pronunciation, and then divided them into pairs to work on vocabulary, as she had planned to do at the beginning.

The bell rang and the class filed out. A few minutes later her next class swarmed in. Ana's was the only empty seat.

"Where Ana?" asked Miguel.

"She's with her family. Her father was killed in an automobile accident last night, and the family is together."

Even these kids were subdued by the news. She didn't think they were ready for the things she was sharing with her first-hour class.

"Get out your books, please, and turn to page 11." She pushed through the rest of the hour, and the kids responded well.

They're a good bunch, she thought.

Mrs. B sat at her desk, staring at the back wall, thinking. She decided to call Sam and run an idea by him. According to the published schedule, he should be on a coffee break.

After Lynn had spoken to her husband, she made her way to the office. On the way, her phone beeped. Mr. Cline wanted to meet with her. Good! She wanted to meet with him too.

"Hi, Sheila."

The secretary just waved a pen at her as she answered the phone.

"Is Mr. Cline here?" she asked Sheila, when she was free.

"Yes, I think he is. Let me tell him you're here."

Sheila punched a button, spoke into her headset, and then waved Mrs. B into the principal's office as the phone rang once again.

Mr. Cline stood when she entered.

"Good morning, Mrs. Bartholomew. You had quite a day yesterday."

He smiled sympathetically and indicated a chair.

"I hope you can get some rest this afternoon."

"Yes, thank you," she said, settling into the chair. "I hope so too."

"You took Ana and her mother to the hospital, and...?"

She filled him in as quickly as she could, including Armando's death.

"I see," he said noncommittally. "Do you think it is wise for them to stay with you? What about the Division of Family and Children Services?"

"My husband and I agree that there is no alternative right now. Besides, so far, we're getting along beautifully, in spite of the stress. We're still getting things worked out with DFCS, but I think they can stay with us because Maria is the mother and had nothing to do with Armando's illegal activities. Besides, we have a big German Shepherd that is already helping Ana heal." She paused. "What about the boys that jumped Diego?"

"They are suspended until we decide what to do with them. Has anything been mentioned about filing criminal charges against them?" asked Mr. Cline.

"That never crossed my mind, actually. We had a few other things to worry about yesterday. What would you recommend?" Again she paused. "You know, I just remembered something. There was another boy there. In fact, I think he was the ringleader who gave the order to jump Diego. He didn't actually take part, just watched, and then disappeared before you got there. Is there anything we can do about him?"

"Do you know his name?"

"I don't know any of their names, but their lockers are right outside my classroom door. I can point him out, but then what?"

"Well, I'm not sure we can do anything about him if he didn't actually participate in the attack."

"What if the other guys testified against him?" asked Lynn.

"I'll check with our lawyer on that. I'm scheduled to meet with the boys and their parents this afternoon after school. The lawyer will be here then."

"I don't even know how to approach the subject of pressing charges with Maria, Diego's mother. She's had so much on her plate these two days, and we still don't know how long Diego will be in the hospital."

"Why don't you hold off until after I talk with the boys and their parents?"

"I can do that."

Mr. Cline stood up. "Is there anything else?"

"Well, actually, there is," said Mrs. B, staying seated.

"How can I help you?" asked Mr. Cline, sitting back down.

She was suddenly nervous. "Mr. Cline, there's an enrichment period in the schedule, right?"

"Yes, during the lunch rotations. Why?"

"Well, today some of the kids were asking questions in class. I told them I believe the Bible has the answers. They said they wanted to know what the Bible said. I asked if anyone would object or be offended and no one objected."

"Are you sure they all understood?" interrupted Mr. Cline, frowning.

"I tried to make sure of that."

"What about the Muslim girl?"

"I'm sure she understood. She said her Imam encouraged them to study the Bible and the Koran to see that the Koran is better. I'm aware of the problems in taking class time for something like this, so I was wondering if maybe we could offer a Bible class, or call it a club, if you like, during the enrichment period."

Mr. Cline was silent for a minute, thinking.

"Who would sponsor this club?" he asked. "Most of the teachers are already involved in other activities during that time."

"I would do it as a volunteer, if you would allow it. We could meet in my room, and I would stay during both lunch periods to make sure everyone who wanted to could participate."

Again he considered her request.

"Sounds like a good idea to me. Let me do some checking and get back to you."

"Thank you," said Mrs. B. "I really appreciate your consideration."

Chapter 6

That afternoon, following a quick lunch of leftovers and a nice, long nap, Lynn felt like a new woman. Around 3:00 she went to the hospital to pick up Maria and Ana. She also wanted to see what had been decided about Diego's surgery.

Wow! When Lynn walked into Diego's room, she saw someone she almost didn't recognize sitting in a chair beside the bed. He was still hooked up to a few machines, but the improvement in the boy was remarkable.

"Hi, Mrs. B!" said Diego.

It was as if a huge burden had been taken from his shoulders—like he could be a 15-year-old kid instead of the family defender.

"Diego? Diego! You look great! When can you come home?"

She took the boy's hand, wanting to give him a hug. She noticed for the first time how skinny he was. He was short—a lot of Mexicans are—but he was way too skinny.

Of course, thought Lynn, how could he look robust with all he's been going through? She would make sure he took vitamins and ate a healthy diet when he came home.

"Doctor break arm tomorrow," said Diego only a little less happy.

"Yes. Dr. Benj…Benj…doctor say… home in Saturday, if good," said Ana, smiling.

"Great! Someone else to play with Shep!" From the glance that passed between them, it looked as if Ana had told Diego about her new canine friend.

Maria stood by the window, thrilled to see her son doing so well. She spoke to Ana, who then turned to Lynn.

"*Mamita*… you go *Doña* Lola… talk. No want…" she indicated herself and Diego and put a hand to her ear as if listening.

Lynn and Maria went in search of the translator. They found her on her way out the door with a stack of papers, but she graciously agreed to return to her office.

When they were seated, Maria began the conversation. Lola listened, and then spoke to Lynn.

"Maria wants to know what will happen to the boys that jumped Diego."

"Mr. Cline is meeting with them and their parents even as we speak," Lynn responded, glancing at her watch. "He and I will talk tomorrow morning."

Lola translated for Maria, who then gave a long response.

Lola turned back to Lynn with a strange look on her face.

"Maria doesn't want the boys punished. She would like to go to school with you tomorrow and speak to the boys. She wants to tell them thank you and that they are forgiven."

Lynn was shocked, to say the least. Yes, the thought had crossed her mind that they should be grateful that everything had come to light when it did. Dr. Benjamin had already said that Diego might not have survived another beating by his father. She wasn't sure how she felt about actually thanking the boys for attacking him, though. But if that's what Maria wanted…

After thinking it over for a minute, Lynn asked if she should call right then and set up a meeting for tomorrow morning with Mr. Cline, Maria, the boys and their parents, if they could come. She wanted to call with Maria and Lola present to verify that what she said was what Maria wanted to communicate.

"Do you want me there also?"

"Of course!" emphasized Maria through Lola. "You saw the whole thing."

She dialed Mr. Cline's cell phone number. "Mr. Cline, are you still with the boys and their parents?"

"We're just finishing up," answered the principal. "Why?"

"I'm at the hospital with Maria, Diego's mom. She would like to come to the school tomorrow and talk with the boys and their parents, if possible. We will need a translator."

Mr. Cline hesitated. "This is highly unusual," he said. "Just a minute."

Lynn overheard him excuse himself from the group in the conference room.

Once he was alone, he asked, "What's this all about? What does Diego's mother want to say to them? Two of the boys' parents are embarrassed and apologetic and very supportive. One of the other dads has been pretty aggressive, even threatening to sue you for assault. I think the fourth family is waiting to see which way the wind will blow. From what these guys are saying, you must be Wonder Woman, or something. After watching the security video, I tend to agree with them."

Lynn ignored his last remark.

"Maria wants to thank them and tell them they are forgiven."

There was a very loud silence.

"Did I hear you right?" asked a shocked Mr. Cline. "She wants to *thank* them?"

"Yes. You see, the doctor told us that Diego would possibly not have survived another beating from his father. If those boys had not jumped him and revealed what had been going on, Diego might even be dead by now. Instead, he and his family are no longer in the abusive situation."

"I see," said Mr. Cline slowly. "Let me talk to the families, and I'll get back to you in a little while. Our school attorney speaks Spanish, and I'd feel a whole lot better if we also had him in the meeting."

"Good. I have class first and second hours. Our meeting could be before or after that. Diego is scheduled for surgery tomorrow afternoon at 2:00."

Lynn relayed what Mr. Cline had said to Lola and Maria. Mr. Cline returned to the waiting families and finally arranged a time before school when the boys and at least one parent could be present. He called Lynn, and everything was set.

When Maria and Lynn returned to Diego's room, he was back in bed, looking worn out. They quickly said their good-byes and headed home. The boy needed a good night's sleep before his surgery.

Shep was so happy to see Ana that, after dancing around her until she couldn't walk, he again became glued to her side and finally went to lie in her room when she went to bed. Later, however, after Ana was asleep, he crept back to Lynn's room.

Dogs didn't come any more loyal than her Shep.

* * * *

The next day dawned clear and beautiful. The three in the Bartholomew household were up and dressed early. Ana would go to Mrs. B's classroom and try to catch up on the schoolwork she had missed while Lynn and Maria went to their conference with the boys and their parents. The principal and the school's attorney were waiting for them.

"Mr. Cline," began Mrs. B, "I'd like you to meet Mrs. Lopez. Maria, Mr. Cline."

"*Mucho gusto,*" said Maria.

"Nice to meet you," responded Mr. Cline. "This is our lawyer Mr. Weston."

Mr. Cline wanted to interview Maria before the others arrived, as they had planned. When they had taken their places around the conference table, Mr. Weston, the stocky, sandy-haired lawyer began. "Please explain what you want to say to the boys, Mrs. Lopez."

"I want to tell them thank you for saving Diego's life. What they did in attacking him was very wrong, especially four against one, but by allowing everyone to see what his father had done to him, they saved his life, and I am thankful. That is all. They are forgiven."

After Mr. Weston had translated, he and Mr. Cline just looked at each other. They had never encountered anything like this before.

"So you're not going to press charges?" asked the lawyer.

"No," answered Maria. "If the school must punish them, that is between you and them, but I have forgiven them. There will be no charges."

"OK, thank you, Mrs. Lopez," said the lawyer after he had translated.

"Now, Mrs. Bartholomew, we need to talk about the attack itself. Could you explain exactly what happened and exactly what you did?"

Lynn took a deep breath. She had dreaded this moment. "Well, the boys' lockers are right outside my door. I'd overheard them talking about Diego on two occasions. I talked to you about it, Mr. Cline."

Mr. Cline nodded.

"The second time, they were talking about forcing him to show them what was under his sweatshirt. They thought it was drugs, but what he was really hiding were the bruises from his beatings. I was sitting at my desk finishing lunch when I heard a commotion in the hall. The next thing I knew, I was throwing the first guy off Diego. He stumbled into the wall. I pushed another, who fell against number three, and they both went down. The fourth boy was already backing away."

She thought a minute.

"Then I started sending people to get you and the nurse and to call 9-1-1," she continued, addressing Mr. Cline. "I checked on Diego—you know, heart rate, respiration and such. The nurse came, and then you with Security, and Ana and Anita, then the EMTs... and you know the rest."

"Thank you," said Mr. Cline. "Your statement matches exactly what the security cameras show."

"How tall are you?" asked Mr. Weston after a moment.

"5'2''", answered Lynn, puzzled.

"Weight about 125 to 130?"

"More or less."

"And would you mind telling me your age?"

"Not nearly as much as telling you my weight!" she laughed. "I'm 61."

"From what I understand, the guys that jumped Diego are pretty big. How did you manhandle them like you described?"

"I really don't have a clue," said Lynn, smiling a little sheepishly. "I guess it was the adrenal 'fight or flight' response."

Mr. Cline looked at his watch. "They should be here any minute. Are we ready for this?"

"*Si*," said Maria simply after the translation.

Everyone stood when the families came in. Mrs. B stationed herself by the door, extended her hand as she was introduced to each boy and his parent, and tried not to look as nervous as she felt. It was easy to spot the one who wanted to sue her. He was the guy who swaggered in, sneering at her outstretched hand. The one whose bitter scowl was reflected in his son's face.

Lynn felt sorry for the boy.

Mr. Cline sat at the head of the long conference table. Mrs. B took her place on his right, between him and Maria. The lawyer was on Maria's other side, providing a buffer between her and the others in the room. Most of the boys and their parents were seated on the opposite side of the table. The only places left for the Prickly Pair were beside the lawyer. There was a bottle of water in front of each participant.

"OK," began Mr. Cline. "We're here this morning because Mrs. Lopez wanted to address the boys who attacked her son. Mrs. Lopez…"

Mr. Gibson, the pimply-faced boy's father interrupted. "Excuse me, Mr. Cline. Before Mrs. Lopez says anything, I want her to know how sorry Ben's mother and I are that our son was involved in this."

Ben looked thoroughly miserable.

Then Mrs. Aimes, who was dressed like a corporate executive, glanced disapprovingly at her son. "And embarrassed," she added.

Daniel Aimes looked even more miserable than Ben, if that was possible.

There was a brief silence. Maria opened her mouth to speak...

"Well, I ain't sorry, or embarrassed," spat Mr. Barrett. The man reeked of stale cigarette smoke. His dark blue work uniform was stained and wrinkled.

"I say good enough fer 'im. These people sneak acrost the border, steal our jo—"

"Just a minute, Mr. Barrett," interrupted Mr. Cline, holding up a hand but speaking in a quiet, yet commanding voice. "I think you need to hear what Mrs. Lopez has to say."

Barrett glared at Mr. Cline, folded his arms across his chest, and slouched in his chair.

Frank, the fourth boy, and his mother Mrs. Walenski sat in total silence.

Mr. Weston had been translating quietly.

Mr. Cline nodded to Maria. She gulped, cleared her throat and began. Everyone looked at her as she spoke, and then at the lawyer as he translated.

"First of all, I want to thank you all for coming to meet with me. I don't know how many of you are aware of what was happening in our home, but let's just say that my husband was a very violent man. My son Diego always tried to protect his sister and me when my husband would come home drunk and would become abusive. Because of his intervention, Diego was severely beaten many times. Armando only hit him where nobody could see his bruises, if he wore a long-sleeved shirt. That is why Diego always used that sweatshirt zipped all the way up. It was thick and no one could see through it."

Maria paused for a moment, took a drink of water and then continued.

"The police were called after Diego was taken to the hospital. When they tried to arrest Armando, he ran away in his car, slid on the wet pavement, had an accident and died."

She paused again, this time needing several swallows of water.

"We're sorry for your loss, Mrs. Lopez," inserted Mr. Cline sympathetically.

Lynn glanced around the room. Mrs. Aimes and Mr. Gibson nodded. The boys looked as if they might burst into tears. Mrs. Walenski still sat stiff as a board. Mr. Barrett had turned white as a sheet, a look of realization and disbelief spreading across his face.

What's that all about? thought Lynn.

"When your sons attacked Diego and opened his sweatshirt," continued Maria, "they revealed the abuse and probably saved his life."

She looked each boy in the eye. "What you did was very wrong, boys, especially since there were four of you against one. The doctor at the hospital said Diego could possibly not have survived another beating from his father."

She paused once again, looking at her hands.

"I wanted to thank you boys for saving my son's life and to let you know that I have forgiven you and so has Diego. We will not press charges."

Lynn noticed that several mouths were hanging open. Mr. Barrett shook his head, as if trying to clear the cobwebs.

Mrs. Aimes began wiping tears, trying not to smudge her makeup.

"I don't know what to say, but—"

"Just a minute, Mom," said Daniel. "Before I can accept Mrs. Lopez's forgiveness, I need to apologize. I'm sorry,

Ma'am. Even if what we did saved Diego's life, we were wrong to do it. I intend to apologize to Diego too, as soon as I can. Thank you for your forgiveness."

Maria smiled at him with tears in her eyes.

"Uh, me too," said Ben. "I'm… uh… sorry too."

"Thank you, Mrs. Lopez," said Ben's father. "I don't know what else to say. Thank you."

Maria nodded.

There was a short silence.

"Well, that's just ducky," sneered Mr. Barrett, who had returned to his normal nasty self. "It's gettin' a little too gushy in here fer me. But I ain't buyin' it. I really don't care whether you fergive Jack or not."

His face had gone from white to scarlet in a matter of seconds.

"Are you saying you would rather Mrs. Lopez press charges against your son?" asked Mr. Weston.

"Press away," said Mr. Barrett, beginning to shout. "No judge in this county's gonna find anybody guilty for beatin' up a spic."

Jack looked embarrassed underneath his belligerent exterior.

"And speakin' of charges," Mr. Barrett ranted, "I inten' to sue Mizz Bartholomew fer assault on a minor an' this school for hirin' somebody like her in the firs' place."

The man was on his feet now, still shouting, his anger totally out of proportion to the situation at hand.

"Well," said Mr. Weston calmly, "I've been in this business a long time, been in lots of courtrooms, and I've never seen a case like this go the way you're imagining."

"Well, you're about to see yer first," snarled Barrett.

Lynn spoke for the first time. She decided to make the move Sam had suggested last night on the phone.

"May I say something?"

The lawyer held up his hand.

"Let me just mention one thing first," he said.

"Please sit down for one more minute, Mr. Barrett." Mr. Barrett flopped back in his chair. "Mr. Barrett, I'm sure you realize that a case such as this would be very well publicized, possibly a media circus, if you will."

"You're dead right, it will be! I inten' t' contac' ever' newspaper and TV station from here t' Atlanna. I'll see to it that you never work again in this state, Lady!" he shouted, wagging his finger at Lynn.

"The thing is, Mr. Barrett," said Mr. Weston, still maintaining a conversational tone of voice, "the fact will come out that your big, strapping, letterman son was whipped by a 5′2″, 125 pound, 61-year-old woman. That he was, in fact, slammed against the wall by this little old lady. Are you sure you want that bit of information to come out?"

Jack's mouth fell open again. "Dad…" he pleaded.

Mr. Barrett was fuming, sputtering, in fact. He grabbed his son by the arm and jerked him out of his chair.

"Let's get outta here!" he managed to choke out.

He turned and gestured at the whole assembly as if to say more but apparently couldn't get it out, and so charged through the door.

Everyone breathed an audible sigh of relief when they were gone.

Then Lynn began to grin.

"Nicely done, Mr. Weston," she chuckled. "Couldn't have said it better myself."

Her remark eased the tension in the room.

Mr. Cline stood up. "I know you folks need to get to work, and so do I," he said. "We'll let you know what the consequences from the school will be for your boys. I'm sure you understand that as an institution we cannot let this sort of thing go unpunished. They will not be allowed back in class until something is decided. Thank you very much for coming."

Mrs. Aimes immediately made her way to Maria. Mr. Weston continued translating.

"Thank you so much, Mrs. Lopez. Thank you!"

Maria gave her a hug, and both women teared up.

Daniel was next in line. He extended his hand. Maria held it and looked him in the eye while she spoke.

"I think you have good character, Daniel. You made a mistake, but you owned up to it. You appear to have leadership potential, and your parents should be proud of you. Just be careful who you choose as friends and use your leadership abilities for good."

She gave the boy a big smile, and Daniel returned it gratefully, pumping her hand enthusiastically.

"Thank you!" he exclaimed.

Mr. Gibson shook her hand and thanked her, and then it was Ben's turn.

Maria spoke again. "Ben, be careful. You seem to be easily led, so you, too, must choose your friends wisely."

The Walenskis simply walked out without looking back.

Chapter 7

Lynn felt drained, and her day hadn't even started yet. She knew Maria must feel the same way. Her new friend would sit in on her classes today, and then they and Ana would go to the hospital to be there during Diego's surgery.

Rats! She hadn't had the opportunity to ask Mr. Cline about the Bible club. What could she do with her class today? She couldn't just not say anything about the Bible. She had given her word.

Whoa! Now that's a thought. Might just work. Lynn turned to her friend as they walked down the hall.

"Maria, would you be willing to tell my first hour class what you told the boys? Most of them know about the abuse that Diego was enduring, and I think it would be good for them to hear your reaction to what happened."

Maria just looked at her.

Oh, for goodness sake! thought Lynn. Simultaneously she and Maria burst out laughing. She couldn't believe she had forgotten that Maria couldn't understand a word she was saying. There was no way she could communicate her request without a translator. They would have to wait for Anita.

Just before the ladies made it to the ESOL room, the bell rang. Maria watched, fascinated, as students poured into the hallway from every direction. The ladies ducked into Lynn's classroom before the cacophony reached its climax.

As soon as Anita walked in, Lynn snagged her and drew her aside to translate her question to Maria.

"You mean I have to stand in front of the class and talk?" asked Maria nervously.

"You may sit down, if you like." Lynn reassured her. "Just pretend you are talking to friends. You know some of the kids already."

With a little urging from Anita, Maria finally agreed. Lynn said she would call on her during the last few minutes of class.

The kids were on their best behavior for the visitor, and Maria seemed to enjoy herself. She participated along with the students.

Then it was time for her to speak.

This time Anita had to translate into English, which was harder. Mrs. B helped make the meaning clear to the non-Spanish speakers.

While Maria was repeating what she had said earlier, Lynn was watching her students' faces. She saw quite a variety of responses.

Some of the kids showed total disbelief. Was this woman crazy? Forgive the guys that jumped her son, four against one? Didn't she even love him?

Other kids looked at her with a total lack of understanding. Deer-in-the-headlights. Huh? What was she talking about?

There were one or two, however, who got it. They knew exactly where she was coming from and what she was doing. Yes!

One minute before the bell, Mrs. B again addressed the class.

"I felt it would be important for you to hear what Mrs. Lopez had to say this morning in light of our discussion yesterday. For this reason I asked her to speak to you instead of telling you any more from the Bible."

Riiiiiiiing!

The next class came in punching and giggling as usual. Lynn noticed that Maria was quite amused watching them. Ana ran to give her mother a hug and asked if she could sit in the back with Maria during class.

"Of course! You can explain anything she doesn't understand."

Class went very well. Mrs. B always tried to make class interesting, but this week had been a little... uh... unusual, and she was having to draw on her years of experience to come up with creative ways to present the material. She was sure Mr. Philips next door did not share her students' enthusiasm when they sang "The Alphabet Song" at the top of their lungs.

About the middle of the hour, she received a note from the office.

"Bible class a go," it read. "You may announce it to your students, and we will post it on the school web page. Begin Tuesday. You will have a slot during both lunch periods on Tuesdays and Thursdays. Please stop by the office to discuss details. Mr. Cline."

She felt like woo-hooing but managed to stifle it.

Mr. Cline met her in the hallway as she was on the way to his office.

"Mrs. B! Do you have a few minutes? I talked with our lawyer, and I think you'll like what he had to say."

"Sure," she said.

They stepped into his office and sat down.

"Actually, I learned a lot talking to Mr. Weston this morning. Believe it or not, there are hundreds of Bible study groups in public schools all across America, and Georgia has more freedom in this area than many of the other states. All the hype back in the '60s that made people think that prayer and Bible reading in schools were against the law was just that—media hype."

"Wow! That's amazing!" said Lynn. "I've heard rumblings on both sides of the question for the last 50 years, but nothing ever really definitive. So, where do we go from here?"

"Well, in the first place, it cannot be a club. A club must be student originated and student run. In light of how this idea came about, I think you need to be in charge. It will be a class just like any other, but without grades or credit for this year.

After we see how it goes, it might become a regular part of the curriculum.

"I just need to make sure that during your study of the Bible you won't be pressuring any of the kids to become part of a movement or denomination or to make any decisions against what they've been taught in their homes. I need you to get some details on paper that will demonstrate your goals and how you plan to attain them."

"Terrific! I told the kids when we were talking yesterday that I would tell them what the Bible says and let them draw their own conclusions."

"Good," said Mr. Cline. "I'm interested to see if a religious study will have any significant impact on our student body. We've never had anything like this before."

"Thank you!" responded Mrs. B with a smile. "I can't wait to see the results either."

Maria and Ana were waiting for Lynn when she came out of the office. They hurriedly left for the hospital, stopping at the drive-thru on the highway for burgers and fries. The trio reached Diego's room at the same time the nurses came to take him to surgery. Lynn hadn't realized they would be taking him so early. The boy looked greatly relieved to see his mother and sister.

Maria said something to Ana, and she turned to the nurses.

"Uh... the mother want... a time... Diego first he go." She held her fingers about an inch apart to illustrate that they wanted only a few minutes with the boy.

The nurses looked at each other, knowing the schedule was tight.

"Will five minutes be enough?" asked the older of the two, holding up five fingers.

"*Cinco minutos*," agreed Maria, copying the nurse's gesture.

Maria took her son's hand and spoke to him quietly. The boy instantly looked less anxious. Lynn was pleased to see the three of them bow their heads while Maria prayed with Diego. She bowed her head along with them. It didn't matter whether she could understand or not. Maria wasn't talking to her. She was talking to God.

When the nurses returned, they found a much calmer boy than the one they had left only minutes before. They quickly whisked him away, telling the ladies they could wait there in the room.

During the first hour Maria, Ana, and Lynn ate their lunch. Then a second hour went by. The third hour seemed endless. Lynn and Ana were studying, but both finished their work far too soon. Poor Maria had nothing to keep her mind occupied. They tried watching TV, but there was so much garbage on, they gave up on that also.

They were approaching the end of the fourth hour, when suddenly the gurney with Diego on board burst into the room, accompanied by his entourage of nurses, orderlies, and machines. He was obviously heavily sedated, and his left arm was in a cast from the shoulder all the way to his hand, bent at the elbow. He would be able to move his arm at the shoulder and wiggle his fingers, but nothing more.

"How did it go?" asked Lynn.

"We really can't say, but Dr. Benjamin will be right up to talk to you," responded one of the nurses.

They positioned Diego's bed, arranged all the tubes and wires, checked his vitals once more, and left. In a few minutes Dr. Benjamin came in, still dressed in his surgical scrubs. He smiled tiredly at the ladies and flopped into a chair.

"Forgive me if I sit down a minute."

Lola came into the room, and the doctor continued.

"It was a rough surgery, but it went well, and I think we got everything all straightened up in there." He indicated the boy's arm. "I'm confident that it will heal correctly and that he'll regain full use of it. He'll have to have therapy to retrain the muscles, but he'll be fine."

"When can he come home?" asked Lynn.

"Before I answer that, I need to ask if there will be someone there to care for him twenty-four hours a day for at least the first week. If so, and if there are no complications and if he continues to do as well as he has so far, he should be released Saturday. We'll make sure he has plenty of pain medication, and we'll explain his care before he goes."

"Great!" said Lynn, "And yes, there will be someone there all the time when he comes home. When will he come out of the anesthesia?"

"Should be just a few minutes now," answered the doctor.

"Excuse me, Doctor," inserted Lola. "Mrs. Lopez wants to know if she can sleep here tonight." She indicated the recliner beside Diego's bed.

"Of course!" said the doctor, smiling. "She can sleep right here in the room. We welcome all the help we can get."

He checked his pager.

"Duty calls," he said, getting up wearily from the chair. "I'll see you ladies again."

"Thank you," Lynn called as the doctor disappeared out the door.

Dr. Benjamin had been gone only a few seconds when Pastor Juan appeared in the doorway.

"*¡Buenas tardes!*" he said.

The worry lines on Maria and Ana's faces were replaced with happy smiles.

"*¡Pastor Juan!*" Ana almost screamed, as she ran to give the man a hug.

Maria shook his hand warmly.

He addressed Maria in Spanish, "Looks like I missed the surgery," he said, moving to the bed. "I'm sorry. I had to go to Atlanta this morning. I haven't even been home yet. How's Diego?"

Maria updated him, with comments from Ana.

"Hi, Mrs. B," he said, turning to her and shaking hands. "We didn't get to talk much when we met before, but my niece has been telling me all about you."

Uh-oh, thought Lynn. Who was his niece, and what on earth had he heard? She smiled a little uncertainly.

"Don't worry," said the pastor with a smile. "It was all good. My niece is Gloria in your middle-school class. The U.S. government allowed my wife and me to adopt her when her parents died of hepatitis last year. We finally got through all the bureaucracy and she got here about three months ago."

Gloria was the shy girl in her second-hour class, Ana's BFF. She always giggled along with the others, but there also seemed to be an underlying sadness in her. Now Lynn understood.

"Gloria! She's a good student."

"Thank you," said the pastor.

There was the sorrow in his eyes again.

"I'll go down to the cafeteria and get supper for Maria. She's going to stay here with Diego tonight," said Lynn.

Ana asked her mother something but seemed disappointed with the answer.

"Ana wants to sleep here too, but her mother said it would be better for her to go with you," Pastor Juan explained.

"Shep would be heartbroken if you didn't come home with me today," said Lynn, hoping to cheer the girl.

Ana gave her a teary little smile. Lynn really couldn't blame her. They were still almost strangers.

She picked up her purse and started for the door.

"I'll be back in a few minutes."

Lynn kind of meandered down the hospital corridor, wanting to give the folks in Diego's room as much time as possible. In the cafeteria line she picked out things she thought Maria would enjoy.

When she returned to Pediatrics, Room 2, she discovered a beehive of activity. Diego was awake, and nurses and other medical people were rushing in and out, checking various things.

"Is he OK?" she managed to ask someone as he zoomed by.

"He's doing great! Having his family and the pastor here is good medicine, but you mustn't stay too long. He needs to rest."

"OK, thanks." She found a spot in the corner of the room and waited for the traffic to clear.

After things had settled down a little, Lynn gave Maria her supper, greeted a groggy Diego, and suggested to Ana that they needed to go. Ana was reluctant to leave until Pastor Juan said he would walk them out. He prayed with Diego before they left.

They were in the lobby when the pastor turned to Lynn.

"I'd like to invite you to our services Sunday, if you are free. Antonio goes to our church, as do some of your other students. You might not be able to understand much, but we would love to have you."

"Why, thank you," she said, pleased to be asked. "I teach a Sunday school class in the morning at my church. Do you have an evening service?"

"Yes. In fact, our evening service is usually larger than our morning service during the harvest season. Employers are not too quick to give their seasonal workers time off for church when every minute counts at this time of year."

"OK, then. I'll bring Ana, and we'll be there Sunday night."

On the way home Ana explained to Mrs. B that the pastor's wife had died about three weeks ago from complications of a miscarriage. Aha! thought Lynn. That explains the sadness in Pastor Juan. And poor Gloria—losing a second mom! Lynn's heart broke for them.

"Are there any other children?" she asked.

"Yes, three. Carlos have eight year, Lucas have six year, and the baby, she have two year." The girl paused. "They... how you say... sad for the *mamá*."

"They miss their mother," supplied Lynn. "I am so sorry. It must be very hard for Pastor Juan."

"Yes, very."

Shep was elated to see Lynn and Ana. He couldn't seem to make up his mind whether to stay with two of his favorite people in the whole wide world or run around outside. Finally, the issue was settled when Lynn suggested that they sit on the porch for a while. That way Shep could chase some rabbits, visit with the ladies for a few minutes, and then he could terrorize the squirrels. Ana soon tired of sitting, so she threw the tennis balls for Shep. Crazy dog would chase them until he succeeded in bringing all three back in his mouth at the same time. It was good to hear the girl laugh. He really did look funny with his lips spread over three bright green balls. By the time Ana tired of the game, Shep's tongue was hanging out and he was panting. He lapped up all the water in his bowl and brought it to Lynn to refill. Ana jumped up to do it before her teacher could drag herself out of the chair. It felt so good to relax a little after all that had happened these last few days.

The phone rang.

"Hi, Mr. Wonderful!" she said into the receiver.

"Hi!" said Sam. "Tell me about your day."

She started with the meeting with the boys and their parents and ended with a report on Diego's surgery. Had she ever lived through another week like this one? She certainly couldn't remember one.

"Just be careful. Barrett sounds like a bitter man looking for someone to take it out on. I don't want you to be that one."

"I'll be careful," she assured him. "What's on your plate?"

"Just another dull, boring seminar," said Sam with a sigh.

Lynn laughed out loud. "What are you talking about? You're the speaker, and you've never been dull or boring... uh... well, maybe once or twice."

It was Sam's turn to laugh. "OK, I'll try to liven things up a bit. Good night, my dear. I love you and wish I were there."

"I love you too, Sam. I'll talk to you tomorrow. Good night."

Shep had been sitting patiently by her side, brush on the floor in front of him. As soon as she hung up the phone, he picked up the brush and laid it in her lap.

"OK, I can take a hint," she said.

Neither Lynn nor Ana nor even Shep noticed the young man crouched in the woods down by the creek. He didn't move a muscle. Just watched.

Lynn brushed the dog's coat until it shone, and then they went inside for supper. Ana had already heated up some leftovers and what they couldn't finish, Shep gobbled down in two gulps. So what if it was spicy Mexican food? She didn't think it even touched his tongue. Only time would tell what it would do to his stomach.

Ana and Lynn had both finished studying at the hospital, so they spent the evening arranging the office for Diego. They made up the daybed and moved the computer to the small desk in the Bartholomews' bedroom. There was no mirror, so they rambled around in the attic until they found the one Lynn knew was there somewhere. After hanging it above the desk, they moved on to the problem of what to do with the boy's clothes. There was no chest of drawers, so they rearranged some of the books on the bookcase, and Ana neatly put his folded clothes on the now empty shelf. There was a small closet in the room, so again Lynn did some shuffling and found a little space for the few hanging clothes he owned.

When everything was in place, the girl and her teacher stood back to survey their handiwork.

"Thank you," said Ana. "Is good. Diego like."

"Good! Now I think it's time for bed, don't you?"

"Yes! Is... how you say... uh... no is hour. I very tired."

"It's early, but you are tired," supplied Lynn.

"Yes, thank you. I... clothes of Diego come home?"

"Good idea, and get some for your mother too. She can take a shower in Diego's bathroom at the hospital."

After the clothes were ready, Lynn gave Ana a hug and left the girl to get herself in bed. Shep needed to be let out one more time. While he was on his evening romp, she fixed lunches for the next day and got everything ready for yet another early departure.

As Shep was coming in, he stiffened, one paw on the step. He turned, ears pricked, testing the breeze from the direction of the creek with his sensitive nose.

"What is it, Boy?" Lynn whispered, grabbing his collar. He whimpered, then growled. She dragged him into the house, but not before he let loose a series of deep-throated, don't-come-any-closer barks. She tried to continue her preparations for the next day while Shep pranced nervously around the house. He bristled when he heard a motorcycle in the distance. Lynn stopped to listen too. She didn't know of anyone around there who had a bike, but dismissed it as being some kid out for a joy ride.

"Come on, Shep. Let's go to bed. Tomorrow's a big day."

Lynn knew she could prepare for tomorrow—it was always good to have a plan. But she also realized that only God knew what tomorrow would hold.

Chapter 8

The next morning at the hospital while Ana ran up to see her brother and give Maria the clothes, Lynn called Sam. She needed to talk to him before he went to his seminar.

"'Lo," came his sleepy voice.

"Good morning, Handsome! This is your wake-up call!"

"What's wrong?" asked Sam, instantly awake.

"Nothing. Sorry I scared you. I just need your help on something."

"Well, give me a minute for my blood pressure to come back down, and I'm at your service. In light of all that's gone on this week, you can't blame me for jumping to conclusions."

He took a deep breath and let it out slowly. "OK, shoot."

"I forgot to mention yesterday that Mr. Cline has given the go-ahead on the Bible class, and it's all legal. We start Tuesday. He's putting it on the school web page."

"That's great!" exclaimed Sam. "How can I help?"

"Well, he wants something in writing explaining my goals and how I plan to achieve them. He—"

"A mission statement," interrupted Sam.

"Well, yes, I guess so. He wants me to assure him that I won't push the kids for any kind of decision that would go against their families' beliefs and that I won't be endorsing any particular denomination over another. I told him I would just share what the Bible says and let each student draw his own conclusions. So, where do I start? You do this kind of thing for a living, and you're *so* good at it. Alas, I am but a humble teacher."

"Flattery will get you everywhere, my dear. Let me get some coffee, take a shower, and think it over. I'll get back to you. When can I call?"

"Well, I'm in class from 8:30 'til 10:35, but you'll be at work then. Maybe you can shoot me a quick email with some sort of outline or something. I know you're busy, but..."

"You know I will always find time for anything you need. If I can't call before 8:30, I'll email you."

"Thank you so much, I really appreciate it," said Lynn. "I'd better go. I'm in the hospital parking lot, and I see Ana coming out the door. She ran in to check on Diego and take him and Maria some clothes. If everything goes well, he should be coming home tomorrow."

"Great! I'll be in touch."

Ana went to her homeroom and Lynn to her classroom. She could hardly believe there was no crisis to deal with this morning. She took her time reviewing her lesson plans and was ready when her first hour students arrived.

"Good morning!" she greeted them as they came in.

Class went well, and most of the students seemed to have learned something during the week, in spite of everything. Was it really only four days ago that Diego had been attacked?

At the end of the hour, Lynn announced the Bible class. Although no one wanted to commit to anything in front of everybody, she felt sure that most of them would come. Second hour also went well. She announced the Bible class to them, but this time she went a little more in depth to explain what she was talking about. Ana was the only one to show any real interest, but Gloria would probably come too. She didn't know if the others in this group would show up or not.

Of course, the Bible class was not limited to foreign students, but she had not had the opportunity to interact with many of the kids outside her realm. Maybe the celebrity that her run-in with the boys had earned her would be enough to interest some of them.

At the end of second hour Lynn opened her email and found that Sam had done her work for her. She knew he would come through, but this was more than she had expected. Just a little tweaking, and the document was ready to take to Mr. Cline. Actually, these days she guessed she just had to email it. Would she ever catch up to the Technology Age? Not in this lifetime, she thought, as she hit the print button.

The afternoon stretched before her. She couldn't go home because she had to take Ana to the hospital and pick up Maria. But there was always work to be done. She touched up her lesson plans for the next week and set up the Wheel to do review on Monday... uh... Tuesday. Monday was Labor Day. After lunch she turned off the lights, locked the world out, went to the least visible corner of her room, put her head down on one of the student desks, and took a nap. She longed to stretch out, but this would have to do.

Flanders County Consolidated High School's dignified ESOL teacher awoke with a start when the bell rang, signaling the end of fifth hour. Her eyes were swollen, her neck stiff, her face creased and her hair a rat's nest. And she didn't even feel rested. Maybe a desk nap was not such a good idea, after all.

Ana greeted her after school. She was a different girl since her father was no longer a threat and her brother and mother were safe. When she and Lynn got to the hospital, Diego was awake, but obviously still under the influence of the pain medication. He smiled crookedly when he saw them, and said something to Ana.

She turned to Mrs. B and said, "He sorry no speak English. The head no is good."

Lynn laughed. "Sometimes my head is not good, either. You just get better, Diego. We will worry about English later."

Maria and Ana talked for a few minutes, and then Ana spoke to Lynn. "*Mamita*, she think sleep in hospital this night. Diego come tomorrow. She want... teach help him in home. No have *Doña* Lola... all times."

"OK," said Lynn. "Does your mother know what time he can leave tomorrow? Does she need to ask the nurses anything while you are here to translate?"

Ana and Maria talked again.

"What time?" Ana shrugged, not knowing how to answer. "You ask."

Lynn poked her head out the door but didn't see a nurse anywhere.

"Let's wait until someone comes to check him again, and then we can ask anything you want."

The family visited together, and Ana tried to catch Diego up on what was happening at school. Her brother kept falling asleep, which was a little frustrating for the girl, but her mother said Diego probably wouldn't remember anything anyway.

In a few minutes a nurse came in to do a routine check on her patient. Diego woke up a little with all her poking and prodding.

"How's he doing?" asked Lynn.

"He looks great! Of course, he'll be groggy from the pain medication, but that'll diminish."

"Mrs. B," interjected Ana. "What is…'groggy?'"

"Sorry," said the nurse. "Sleepy. He will want to sleep all the time."

"Thank you," said Ana, passing along the information to her mother.

"Can you tell us if the doctor is still planning to release him tomorrow?" asked Lynn.

"Let me check the computer," The nurse referred to the rolling laptop that accompanied her from room to room.

"If he has a good night, he'll be released tomorrow."

"Do you know what time he should be ready to go?"

"I would guess around three," replied the nurse.

"Will we need a wheelchair at home to get him into the house? There's one story with two steps up to the house, maybe fifty feet from the back door to his bed."

The nurse thought a minute.

"He should be able to walk that far with someone on each side. We've had him up a little already and will walk him around more today, so he should be fine. Just make sure someone is holding on to him in case he stumbles."

Ana had been translating for her mother all this time. Maria spoke, and Ana turned to Lynn.

"*Mamita* sleep… night?" She indicated the recliner. "The nurse, she say… Diego?" Ana pointed to her brother and pretended to change the boy's bandages.

The nurse intercepted the questions.

"I don't think she'll need to stay. Diego is stable and will probably sleep through the night. You'll get a printed page of care instructions in English and in Spanish tomorrow. We'll go over them with you and answer any questions before you leave."

Ana didn't understand.

"Great!" interjected Lynn, smiling. "I'm sure he will be spoiled rotten when he comes home." She held up her hand to quiet Ana. "I'll explain later," she told her quietly.

"Any more questions?" asked the nurse.

No one had any, so the nurse said goodbye and wheeled her computer down the hall.

Dr. Benjamin came in.

"Hi!" he said. "How's our patient this afternoon?"

"Well, the nurse that just left said he was doing fine. What do you think?" asked Lynn.

"Looks great to me!" answered the doctor, listening to Diego's heart. "As long as he behaves himself tonight, he should be able to go home tomorrow."

"We're counting on it," said Lynn, adding sincerely, "Thank you so much for all you've done."

"You're most welcome. Could I have a word with you, Mrs. B?"

The two stepped out into the corridor.

"What are your plans?" he asked. "I know Mrs. Lopez and her daughter have been staying with you, but what about when Diego leaves the hospital?"

"For the foreseeable future they'll continue to stay with me. They have no means of support and nowhere else to go. Our home is theirs for as long as they need it. Only the Lord knows the next step, and He will show us what that step should be when the time comes."

"Thank you for your attitude. I must admit that I've been impressed by this young man. Diego has suffered tremendously, but the suffering seems to have made him stronger instead of defeating him. I haven't had a lot of opportunity to talk with him because he's been on strong pain medication ever since we met, but I believe he has the capacity to become a leader, and I want to do what I can to help."

"I've known the family only a few days longer than you, but I, too, have been impressed by them. This has been an unbelievably rough week for Maria, but she has not crumbled under the burden. Ana has been a little more emotional, but that's to be expected. She's a great kid. I've grown to love them all in this short time."

The doctor looked at his watch. "I need to go now. Please call my office and make an appointment for Diego in about three weeks. His cast will be on for at least six, but I just want to check and make sure everything is OK at the three-week mark. Besides, I like him and want to meet the real Diego when he's not medicated."

"Good! My husband will be back by then, so you can meet him too. Does your family like Mexican food? Maria's a sensational cook. Since you seem to have taken a personal interest in this family, maybe we can have your family over for dinner some evening."

"Sounds great," said the doctor.

As Lynn was turning to go back into Diego's room, she caught sight of some familiar faces headed her direction.

"Antonio! Gloria! Pastor Juan! Hi! Come on in and see Diego." She quickly became lost in the flood of Spanish and decided it was time for a break. Signaling Maria, she stepped back into the hall, but not before she'd noted Diego's happy smile. The visit from his friends was obviously good medicine.

* * * *

Shep didn't wag his tail when he discovered that all three of his charges were safely home; he wagged the whole back half of his body! He ran outside for a few minutes while the ladies were bringing in things from the car. Then he proudly led the way to Diego's new room as if he had transformed the office all by himself, instead of getting underfoot every time Lynn or Ana tried to move.

After dinner, the three ladies went their own ways to spend the rest of the evening doing what each needed to do. Ana did her homework so she would be free to spend the weekend with her brother; Maria did laundry; Lynn studied her Sunday school lesson. She also needed to think about her Bible class on Tuesday. She had to do something this week that would grab the kids' attention—

Food! That was it! Teens were always up for food, even if they had just finished lunch.

* * * *

In the little house on a dead-end alley behind the last block of shops in town, Jack Barrett, one of Diego's attackers, the one whose dad wanted to sue Mrs. B, was sitting in front of his dinosaur desktop scrolling through the school's web page. His father was sprawled on the couch watching TV, beer in one hand, cigarette in the other.

They had moved to this "dump," as Jack called it, a few years ago when his mother had run off with another man—a Mexican migrant worker. She had taken all the neglect and mental and physical abuse she could handle. For the first couple of years, she had tried to talk Jack into joining her, but he had refused to leave his dad. Eventually, she gave up, and Jack had not heard from her since.

When Jack's mother left, his father had sunk even lower into the unfathomable depths of alcohol. Oh, he never drank the hard stuff; that was too rich for his blood; but beer was his constant companion. He managed to leave it alone when he was at work at the chicken processing plant, but from the time he hit the back door of his house each evening until he finally fell asleep on the couch, he had a can in his hand.

The only housework that was ever done was what Jack did, and that wasn't much. The house was situated right next to the dumpster behind the Mexican restaurant. The smell of spicy, rotting garbage combined with that of stale beer, cigarette smoke, and filth was almost unbearable, but the Barretts had gotten used to it. Occasionally, Jack's stomach would roll for a few minutes after he got home, but he knew it would eventually settle down and he would stop noticing the stench.

A couple of weeks ago Mr. Barrett had swaggered in from work with a smile on his face and promises of soon living "high on the hog." He had been jovial and had even joined Jack at the table for their usual supper of Ramen noodles. Jack had no idea why his dad had been so happy, but he had no intention of asking. He'd take it, no matter what the reason!

Then, after the meeting with Mrs. Lopez, Mr. Barrett had fallen into a depression that even his beer couldn't dispel, and he had begun slapping Jack around even more than usual.

"Wha'd I do?" Jack would cry.

But Mr. Barrett would never say.

What Jack did not know was that Wayne Barrett had been recruited as one of Armando Lopez's dealers. He'd never done anything like that before, but Armando had convinced him that he would soon become richer than he'd ever imagined.

Then when he'd gone to that meeting at the school and realized that Jack was partially responsible for the death of Armando—as well as the death of his dreams—his anger had become almost unbearable.

"Whoa! Dad, get a load o' this!" said Jack from in front of the computer.

Jack had begun to talk to his dad only when absolutely necessary in order to keep from being hit again. He knew, however, that his dad would want to know about this.

His father ignored him and turned up the volume on the TV. Jack took the hint and waited for a commercial.

"I think you'll wanna see this, Dad," said Jack.

"Why?" growled his dad. "You got some girly picture there?"

"Naw, ain't nothin' like that. I'm lookin' at the school site. Looks like Mizz B is startin' a *Bible* class durin' activity period." He snickered derisively.

Mr. Barrett sat up slowly. "Oh, she is, is she? Don't them people know that's agin the law?"

Jack turned in his chair to look at his dad, being careful not to snag his pants on the torn vinyl. "Whatcha gonna do 'bout it?"

Mr. Barrett took a long drag on his cigarette and blew the smoke out his nose. He took the last swallow of beer and threw the can at the pile in the corner. "I think NAIL'd like t' know that li'l bit o' news, don't you?" He grinned at Jack sardonically.

"What on earth is NAIL?" asked Jack, confused.

"The National Association for Individual Liberties. This is the kind o' thing they love t' git their hands on. Maybe we won't have t' sue Mizz B. When NAIL gets aholt o' this, they'll do it for us." His lips were smiling; his eyes were not.

Jack mirrored his father's expression.

Their revenge would be sweet.

Chapter 9

Oh! It was nice to be able to sleep in Saturday morning. Of course, for Lynn, sleeping in meant forcing herself to stay in bed until at least 7:00, but it was a luxury she rarely had. She stretched lazily as she got up and tiptoed to the back door to let Shep out. Then she headed for a long soak in the shower.

When she came out of the bathroom, she smelled the coffee. So, Maria was up too, and Ana was talking with her mother. She guessed they were too excited about Diego's homecoming to sleep any later.

"Good morning!" said Lynn, stepping into the kitchen.

"Good morning!" Ana returned and then looked at her mother expectantly.

"Goo' morny!" Maria blushed as she spoke her heavily accented greeting, the first English words Lynn had ever heard her attempt.

"Wow! Good morning, indeed!" she said, laughing and rushing to give her friend a hug.

Shep was scratching at the back door, not wanting to be left out of the excitement. He was one happy dog because his people were here instead of rushing out the door to who-knew-where.

When the three got to Diego's room after lunch, they were surprised to find Pastor Juan and Antonio there. Diego was dressed but resting in bed until time to go.

"We thought you might need some help getting him into the house," said the pastor, "so we came."

"See where is you house for visit," added Antonio with a grin. The prior worry over his friend's condition had given way to a youthful, carefree spirit.

A nurse and Lola came in, along with an orderly pushing a wheelchair.

"Wow!" exclaimed the nurse, "looks like the homecoming party's already begun!" She gave Lynn a folder and told her that inside she would find the instructions for Diego's care. Lola gave the same thing to Maria in Spanish. The ladies went over the points carefully in their respective languages.

"Any questions?" asked the nurse when they were finished.

Four voices translated at the same time.

"*No,*" said Maria, laughing along with the others. "*Gracias.*"

While an orderly helped Diego into the wheelchair, Lynn and Pastor Juan went downstairs to bring the cars to the main entrance. After the jovial group had piled into the vehicles, Mrs. B gave Pastor Juan directions in case they got separated, and they headed for home.

No one had seen the motorcycle hidden around the corner of the hospital. The rider had heard everything and now knew that Diego was out of the hospital and where he was going. He calmly got on his bike and turned the other way.

Lynn could hear Shep barking as she pulled into the carport—his happy bark of recognition at hearing her car, a pause, and then his deep-throated, protective bark when the pastor's car pulled into Sam's spot.

She had planned to take hold of the dog before anyone else opened the car doors, but of course, Ana didn't wait. She jumped out, grabbed his collar when he came to greet her and took him around to meet Diego. The dog was uncertain when all the strange hospital smells assaulted his nostrils, but then he slowly approached the boy and was finally satisfied that Ana's brother was OK. A couple of Shep's well-placed licks and a wagging tail confirmed his approval. Then Ana introduced him to Antonio and Pastor Juan.

After the dog issue was settled, the men supported a rather shaky Diego up the steps and down the hall to his bedroom. Maria and Ana followed with a load of stuff, while Lynn and Shep brought up the rear.

"Welcome home!" she said. "If you need anything, please tell me."

She thought Diego was probably too tired to understand, so she excused herself and Ana by asking the girl to help prepare a snack to serve the guests. While Pastor Juan and Maria got Diego undressed and into bed, Ana and Lynn cut the cake and put ice into the glasses.

"This is a beautiful area," declared the pastor, when they were seated on the porch.

"Thank you," said Lynn. "We love it here. Our twenty acres are enough to keep us busy and out of trouble, and we have lots of room for youth activities or whatever. By the way, if you ever want to bring your teens or any other groups from your church here, please let me know. We have a little creek to splash around in, and—"

"Creek?" said Antonio. "Is little river, yes?" He turned to Ana and spoke excitedly in Spanish. He then asked Lynn, "May we can go creek?"

"Of course! Yes!"

The two kids ran across the yard, stopped, and then ran back with Shep barking at their heels.

"Where creek?" shouted Antonio, laughing.

"That way!" laughed Lynn, pointing toward the row of trees. "Shep will show you."

The kids and the dog raced across the field.

After a few minutes of silence, Lynn approached a subject she had been avoiding all week.

"Pastor," she began, "what do we need to do about Armando? I should have asked before now, but I kept forgetting, and I really didn't want to bring the subject up to Maria and have Ana translate. That would have been too painful for everyone. We also need to do something with their belongings in the trailer. I'm sure the owner will want to rent it out again as soon as he can."

"Everything has already been done for Armando, answered the pastor. Maria and her kids and I held a short memorial service for him at the hospital the day that you were gone. His remains were too badly damaged in the accident to even donate to science. The city paid for cremation.

"I guess you haven't had much opportunity to watch the news this week. Armando's accident and death were major stories for a while. They even had camera crews out at the gorge when the car was hoisted up. As far as the media were concerned, it was all drug related. They made a big deal out of the cocaine and marijuana the police found at the accident scene."

"He was a drug runner?" asked an incredulous Lynn. No wonder he was so violent.

"Yes, though he was new to our area. The police confiscated a lot of marijuana and cocaine. Miraculously, the abuse angle was never discovered, nor was the attack at school. I think God protected us all from a very ugly situation. The talk shows have again been flooded with callers commenting on the problem of "illegal aliens." Things were a little tense around town, but now it's old news, and everyone has settled down.

"As far as the family's belongings are concerned, they have until the end of September to clear out the trailer. They had paid through August, and our church pitched in to pay another month to take some of the pressure off Maria."

Lynn said no more, but she felt a great sense of relief and gratitude.

Maria joined the adults on the porch when Diego was asleep. Pastor Juan pulled up a chair that one of the kids had abandoned, and Lynn poured a glass of soda. The three adults sat in a comfortable silence, listening to the shouts, squeals, and barks coming from the creek. Behind Maria's smiles and chuckles, Lynn saw the lines of weariness around her eyes and knew this week was taking its toll.

Poor thing! How can I ease her load? she asked herself.

"Antonio and I really should be going soon," said Pastor Juan. "Gloria is taking care of the younger ones, and I don't like leaving them too long. I'll walk down and get the kids."

"Oh, you don't need to go all the way down to the creek. I'll call them."

With that Lynn stood at the edge of the porch and let fly a yodel that made the leaves quake. In the startled silence that followed, she cut loose with another. Shep barked in return, and the group on the porch watched as he streaked across the field, danced in a circle, and streaked back to herd the kids home.

"I'm glad Diego's medicated," said Pastor Juan, laughing.

"Oops," said Lynn sheepishly. "I forgot."

The trio reached the porch wet to the knees, mud-spattered and breathless. Lynn handed the kids a glass of soda and listened without understanding a word as they excitedly relayed their adventures. She knew that wet teens always equals hungry teens, so she went inside and quickly threw together a couple of sandwiches. Grabbing a treat for Shep, she headed back outside with her napkin-wrapped treasures. She figured Antonio could eat his on the way home, if Pastor Juan was ready to go.

Ha! That sandwich barely made it out of her hand before it was gone!

As they were standing around the car, Pastor Juan said to Lynn, "Maria tells me that Dr. Benjamin said it would be good for Diego to get out a little each day before he tries to go back to school. What do you think about bringing the whole family to church with you tomorrow night? Being around her friends at church would be good for Maria as well."

"That sounds great!" said Lynn. "I had no idea he would be ready to go out so soon."

The pastor closed the car door and spoke to her through the window.

"Plan to arrive a few minutes late so he won't get worn out greeting people before the service starts, and you can leave a little early, if he's tired."

"Good! We'll be there."

They waved goodbye and then the ladies started straightening the porch and carrying the dirty dishes inside. Shep sat patiently with his brush in his mouth, waiting his turn.

"Ana," said Lynn, taking the dirty dishes from the girl. "I think Shep might be trying to tell you something. We can finish the cleanup while you do the honors."

The rest of the afternoon passed quietly, and when Sam called, Lynn updated him on everything that had gone on. He seemed pleased with the plans for Sunday night, but he sounded terribly tired and a little hoarse. She assumed it was because of another week of talking all day and all evening and urged him to go to bed early.

Maria had insisted on making dinner, so after Lynn had talked to Sam, she went into the kitchen to see how she could help. They got everything on the table and then Maria arranged a tray for Diego. As she was putting the rice onto his plate, she looked up to see Ana escorting her brother to the table.

"He say no bed," said the smiling girl.

Diego, as well as everyone else, dug in to Maria's wonderful home-cooked meal. It wouldn't take long for the boy to regain his health with food like this on the table, and Lynn would have to be careful not to get downright plump before her husband got home.

Lynn and Ana cleaned up the kitchen while Maria got Diego back to his room. Ana watched TV for a while and then went to bed. The ladies sat at the table drinking a cup of Sleepytime Tea and quietly enjoying each other's company.

Maria continued to stare into her empty cup long after the tea was gone. She began quietly to relate something to Lynn, knowing that her new friend couldn't understand. Lynn let her talk. She heard Armando's name, as well as Diego's and Ana's. Soon Maria's tears began mixing with the dregs of her tea.

Although Lynn had no idea what the poor lady was saying, she took Maria's hand and cried along with her friend, even with knowing what this man had done still fresh in her mind.

Chapter 10

Jack Barrett still didn't know why his dad was always so mad at him. He just knew it had something to do with Diego Lopez and so he vowed to get even with the little jerk when he came back to school. Jack was fast becoming as bitter as his father and had even taken up drinking beer—something he had sworn he would never do after he saw how it was sucking the life out of his father.

Saturday night after Wayne Barrett had fallen asleep on the couch, Jack quietly took his dad's car keys from the table and closed the door silently behind him. He picked up some buddies and went out on the town. There's not a lot to do in Perkins Grove, so they drove the ten miles to the county seat, took in a movie, and hung out at the mall until closing time. Then one of the older guys bought a case of beer, and they sat in the car in front of a closed gas station swapping stories and downing the brew. By midnight the beer was gone and so was their good sense. They dared Jack to go back to the mall and cut donuts in the parking lot and get out before the cops showed up.

Tires squealing, Jack took off out of the gas station, careening wildly down the street and into the empty lot. He revved the engine a few times, and then, with the wheel cranked as far to the left as it would go, laid rubber in great black circles on the asphalt. After three dizzying spins, he squealed back out of the lot and headed for home, the guys in the back seat hooting with laughter.

"Yeah, I see 'im," said the state trooper into the radio. "We'll pick 'im up."

The GSP cruiser pulled out onto the highway and, with lights flashing and siren blaring, chased down Jack Barrett.

When Mr. Barrett was jolted out of a deep sleep at 2:30 a.m. by a phone call from the city jail, he was not a happy camper.

"Let 'im sleep it off in the slammer," he told the officer. "I'll deal with 'im in the mornin'."

Then he lay back on the couch fuming. He lit a cigarette and sat up, trying to think of a suitable punishment—one that Jack would never forget. He'd beat the snot out of him if he thought it would help, but beating had never gotten through to the boy before, and he doubted it would this time either.

He was into his third cigarette when the idea began to form.

That was it. That'd fix him. Mrs. B's Bible class would be the perfect punishment. He'd meekly ask Mr. Cline if someone could make sure his boy was there for every class.

He grinned, snuffed out his cigarette on the end table and flopped over to go to sleep.

NAIL would have to find itself another stoolie.

There was a junior college between Perkins Grove and the county seat, just two miles north of the high school. The Bartholomews' church had sprouted from an on-campus ministry there, and Sam and Lynn team-taught the college age class in Sunday school. The couple had worked with the ministry since its inception, and the kids loved them.

Sunday morning Ana opted to stay at home rather than brave a new church crowd without her family, especially since everything would be in English. That was fine. Some down time would probably be a good thing for the three of them.

As soon as she entered her Sunday school room, Lynn knew the lesson would not go as planned. She was accosted on every side by students with questions about the past week.

Word travels fast in a small town, she thought.

The more they asked, the more she realized it really was a miracle that the media hadn't gotten wind of what had happened at school.

"OK, Lord," she prayed silently, "if you want me to deal with this, please give me the words."

When everyone had finally settled down, she said, "Please open your Bibles to the book of Esther." They had been studying in Second Timothy so were a little surprised by the reference.

"We're going to read the whole book, and then I'll answer your questions. Allen, would you begin?"

"Now it came to pass in the days of Ahasuerus..." read Allen.

The reading continued with other people participating until the last verse, which Lynn read.

"... and speaking peace to all his seed."

The classroom was reverently silent until someone quietly said, "Wow!"

"Wow is right. Does anyone notice anything missing from this book?" asked Lynn.

Everyone started flipping pages, looking blankly at one another and finally at her.

"Maybe I should say 'anyone' missing—a name."

"How can we know what's missing if it's not there?" Robert grumbled.

She didn't answer.

More page flipping.

"I don't see anything about a priest," ventured Stephen. "Is that it?"

"That's good, Stephen. You're on the right track. Anyone else?"

Tanya shyly raised her hand.

"I didn't see God mentioned anywhere in the book," she said so softly Lynn had to strain to hear. "Is that it?"

"You're absolutely right, Tanya! Although the name of God does not appear in the book of Esther a single time, does anyone doubt that He was at work in the circumstances that saved the entire Jewish nation? Several students nodded their understanding.

"God was at work this week in our town just as He was in Persia all those centuries ago."

With that, she gave a quick summary of all that had transpired in the past week and pointed out how God had demonstrated over and over that He was in control.

She ended with, "... and I don't think God is finished with this situation yet."

At that instant the buzzer sounded to end the Sunday school hour. A very pensive group of young people filed out of the room.

Maria had helped Diego dress early in the afternoon. Then he had lain down to rest very carefully so as not to muss his church clothes. When he walked out of the bedroom with Maria and Ana on either side, he looked better than Lynn had ever seen him. His empty left sleeve was pinned up, and the shirt was buttoned around the bulky cast. The sling kept his arm at the right angle and close to his body.

"Wow! You look great!" said Lynn. "You all do!"

Lynn followed Pastor Juan's directions to the old abandoned farm implement store on the outskirts of town. The folks had done a great job of cleaning up around the outside of the building and of converting the inside into a small auditorium. Everything was sparkling clean. There was no platform; folding chairs stood in rows facing a small podium. Artificial flowers, arranged in ways that Lynn would never think of, adorned the front of the church, which had been the back of the store. The only window was the big plate glass display window, a remnant from the building's former life.

Antonio was waiting to help Diego out of the car and into the last row of chairs. The congregation was on its feet singing lustily. Lynn wanted to sing along but couldn't. She decided then and there that she had to learn Spanish. Period.

Pastor Juan was smiling at the family from behind the song leader. When the hymn ended, he stepped to the pulpit and announced that Diego and his family had just come in. The cultural difference was quite evident when everyone turned around to smile at Diego, Ana, and Maria and wave or shout a greeting. At one point Ana told Lynn to wave because Pastor Juan had just introduced her. She timidly raised her hand, and many again waved or shouted a greeting.

Diego's eyes were glued to the pastor during the message and he seemed to drink in the words like a thirsty man drinks water. As the sermon drew to a close, Lynn noticed that he was beginning to droop. Maria also noticed and started preparing to go.

Antonio slipped out and spoke to a man near him. The two of them helped Diego to the car and buckled him in. Lynn hoped that this trip hadn't been too much for him physically but knew that what it had done for him spiritually and emotionally would contribute to his healing far more than staying in bed would have.

"I… father go you house. Help Diego. Is very… how you say…" He flexed the muscle in his arm and then let it wilt.

"Weak. Thank you. That would be great."

Shep didn't even raise a ruckus when the strange man entered his home.

Maria rushed ahead to pull back the covers and Diego lay down, clothes and all. His mother got his shoes off and covered her son. Everyone came out of the room with a communal sigh.

Lynn offered the men a snack, but they refused saying they had to go pick up the rest of the family at church and get home. After they had gone, she, Maria, and Ana sat around the table with sandwiches and the last pieces of cake, not counting the one they had saved for Diego.

Again the guy with the motorcycle observed silently and patiently from his position down by the creek.

Chapter 11

Monday was Labor Day. No school. Lynn woke up at her normal time but then snuggled back under the covers. Alas, she just wasn't programmed to lie around. She tiptoed to the kitchen to start breakfast before Maria got up but was surprised to find her already dressed and spooning coffee into the basket. Shep came over for some lovin', his damp feet signaling that he had already been out.

"You're getting more spoiled by the day, Fella," said Lynn, ruffling his coat. "There are just too many people around here to coddle you."

She smiled at Maria and sat at the counter, waiting for the coffee to brew. Oh, how she wished she could talk to her friend. Nothing earth shaking, just chitchat.

Taking her coffee and her dog, Lynn went to her room to read her Bible.

Later, as she was finishing breakfast with Maria and Ana, she heard Shep whine. He got up and went to the office door, wagging his big tail slowly.

The door opened and Diego came out, supporting himself on the doorpost. This was the first time he had tried to walk on his own. Maria made a beeline for her son as Lynn quickly went to retrieve a cane she had found in the attic.

With the help of the cane and with his mother nearby, the boy made it to the table without incident. The look on his face was victorious—one more step toward recovery. Ana's praise was a bit over the top, but Diego seemed to like it.

"What shall we do today? We have a whole day with nothing pressing," said Lynn.

When the kids told Maria what she had said, Maria pointed to the dog and held her nose.

"OK, I can take a hint. Ana, wanna help? And we can wash the car at the same time. I have a hammock I put on the porch sometimes. Maybe Diego would like to lie in it and watch the show. Shep does *not* like a bath, and sometimes trying to give him one can be better than *I Love Lucy*! Uh... that's a really funny old TV program.

"Oh, and it's my turn to cook, Maria. It's the law in the United States—all families must cook out on Labor Day," she said with total sincerity.

The others looked at her, question marks all over their faces. Lynn couldn't help but laugh.

"Just kidding. But I will fix hamburgers on the grill today, OK?"

"OK!" they chorused—after she had explained.

Steve Cooper was the owner/proprietor of The Corner Store, the only grocery store in town, which was usually just called The Store. It had been in his family for four generations and was the oldest continuing institution in Perkins Grove. Besides being a general store, it had once housed the Post Office, which now had a building of its own. Court had been held there, merchandise being shoved out of the way and benches set up in its place, and the first church in town had begun in The Store. It had been the original train depot, and large pictures of mule-drawn wagons delivering watermelons, peanuts, peaches and cotton occupied the walls above the shelves. One half of the original building was cordoned off as a museum where spittoons, washboards, butter churns, and plows were displayed. The old balance scale that had been used to weigh flour, beans, corn, and whatever stood in the corner. The new, modern part, that had been added over 30 years ago, had been constructed to blend almost seamlessly with the old building. The Store had somehow managed to keep its old South personality while reaching into the twenty-first century.

A plaque by the front door declared The Corner Store an official Historical Site, but it was still open for business six days a week. Steve considered himself an expert on local history.

The Store was closing at noon because of Labor Day, so after the car and the dog were clean, Lynn went and bought everything she needed for the cookout. Then she picked out apples, bananas, peaches, strawberries, blueberries and two fresh pineapples, a rare find in Perkins Grove, for Bible class. Considering the fact that she would have two consecutive classes with unknown numbers of students, she added a few oranges and two watermelons.

"Goodness!" said Steve as he watched her clean out his produce section. "You plannin' some big goat ropin' out at your place tonight?"

"Nope. This is for class tomorrow."

"Class! Can I come?"

"Sure! Bring the wife and kids... oh, and Sandy." They both looked fondly at the old beagle that was a permanent fixture in the museum part of the store. Upon hearing her name, Sandy thumped the floor with her tail, not even bothering to open her eyes.

"Don't be so enthusiastic, Sandy," said Lynn.

Steve looked around the store while ringing up her purchases. He lowered his voice. "You still got them folks out at your place?"

Lynn wasn't sure how to read his question, so she decided to be positive.

"Sure do," she said with a cheerful smile. "The boy just got out of the hospital Saturday, so they'll be there at least until he's on his feet again."

Steve leaned over the counter and lowered his voice even more. "Historically," he said, "fer'ners ain't exactly been welcomed with open arms 'round here, you know."

Lynn leaned over and met him eye-to-eye. "Maybe it's time to write a new chapter in the history book."

Steve raised his eyebrows, but he wasn't offended. He kept his voice low. "You watch yersef, now, Mizz B. Some folks are talkin' mighty big."

"Thanks, Steve. I appreciate your concern."

She piled her bags into the shopping cart and headed for the exit. As she was reaching for the old-fashioned handle, the door suddenly opened. In walked Jack Barrett, Frank Walenski, and Ben Gibson, three of the boys that had jumped Diego, causing the situation Steve was just mentioning.

"Mornin', boys!" she greeted them cheerily as she pushed the shopping cart by them. "Thanks for getting the door."

Lynn fixed hamburgers with all the trimmings, baked beans and chips. After a late picnic lunch on the porch, everyone went back to his or her chosen activity. Lynn prepared the fruit and arranged her other visuals. She then attended to paying bills and several other little chores. Diego was resting. Ana was outside somewhere with Shep. Maria was by the window in the dining room with a needle and thread working on Diego's shirts so the sleeves would fit over his cast.

Sam will be here a week from tomorrow, thought Lynn. *Maybe it's time to prepare Maria and the kids for his homecoming.*

"Lord," she prayed, "please give me the words that will help this family, especially Diego, to accept Sam and learn to love him. He'll be such a blessing to them."

Lynn decided to start very low key. She showed Maria the new dark green shirt she had bought for her husband.

"Sam will be here next week!" she said, happily pointing to the dates on the calendar.

She wasn't expecting the reaction she got.

"*Si, Señora,*" said Maria. She looked down at her hands and sat very still.

Lynn could see her struggling. She noticed tears begin to roll down her cheeks. "Maria!" she cried. "What's wrong? What did I say to hurt you?"

Maria stood up, got a cardboard box from the pantry and took it to the laundry room. With tears still falling, she began to take her family's clothes from the dryer, fold them carefully and put them into the box.

"Maria, what are you doing?" asked Lynn with tears forming in her own eyes.

Maria turned to her, "Diego, Ana, *y yo... salimos.*" She said these words with a gesture that Lynn could interpret only as leaving.

Suddenly she understood. Maria thought that since Sam was coming home, she and her kids would have to leave. No wonder she was crying! After having her family traumatized and uprooted just last week, they would soon have to leave this haven where they had been happy and secure. Poor thing!

Lynn held the sobbing lady in her arms. When the torrent of tears had passed, she took her friend by the shoulders and looked her in the eye.

"No," she said, "you no *salimos.* You are part of my family now. This is your home. You and Diego and Ana will stay as long as you need to."

Maria just looked at her.

The ladies heard a movement behind them and saw Diego standing in the doorway. He had heard his mother sobbing and had come as quickly as his condition and his cane would allow. The boy had been protecting his mother for most of his life, and even though their circumstances had changed, his response to her distress was automatic. He didn't know what was going on, but he had overheard Lynn's last statement.

He went to his mother and put his good arm around her. "*Mamita, Mamita,*" he said soothingly.

This young man is mature far beyond his years, thought Lynn. He spoke to his mother softly, calming her as she had probably calmed him throughout the years in a dysfunctional, abusive home. Maria responded with more tears, sobbing out her woes in Spanish. Finally, she calmed down.

Diego turned to Lynn. "What happen?" He wasn't asking as a child or as a defender—he had heard what she'd said— nor was he being belligerent. He was asking as a man seeking information, taking responsibility for his family.

Lynn explained that she had told Maria that Sam was coming home next week, and Maria had thought she meant that the family had to leave. "Diego, I am so sorry," she said. "I should have waited until someone was here to translate. I love your mother so much that I forget she can't understand English. Your family is my family now; my home is your home. I want you to stay here with me as long as you need to or want to. Do you understand?"

Diego nodded and then turned to his mother and related what Lynn had said. Yet again, Maria was overcome by tears, but this time they were tears of relief. Her son held her for a moment, and then she looked at Lynn.

"*Gracias, Señora, gracias,*" she said, managing to hold the tears back this time. Both ladies sighed deeply and then giggled a little when they realized they had done so as one.

"I think it's time for a break and a snack," said Lynn.

She led the group back to the kitchen and opened the fridge. When she turned around, Maria was holding a plate of cookies. Ana and Shep joined them, the dog doing his usual begging routine.

"Shall we give Diego some exercise and walk to the top of the driveway and back?" suggested Lynn.

Diego used his cane and seemed to be fine on the walk, though he was a little shaky by the time they got back. His sister was beside him, chattering about who-knew-what. Shep ran from one person to another, generally impeding progress and being happy. Lynn noticed how careful he was when he was close to Diego. He seemed to sense that the boy needed extra care and was always gentle around him. Good dog!

When she talked to Sam that evening, she told him about the incident with Maria.

"We'll have to go slowly," he said. "I think you were very wise not to have me come home right away. Like you said, all they've ever known is abuse, and that image is not going to fade overnight."

At supper Lynn mentioned again that her husband would soon be coming home. Ana's head jerked up and she looked at her mother with fear. "Sh-sh-sh," soothed her mother, "*Es OK.*"

Lynn continued talking about Sam's homecoming, saying that he'd heard so much about the Lopez family that he felt he knew them already and that he was anxious to meet them in person. She went on to describe him, hoping that she wasn't building him up so much that they would be disappointed when they met him and discovered he was human, after all. The kids were giving Maria the condensed version of what she said.

There were pictures of the man more than a foot taller than his wife giving her a smothering bear hug, playing basketball with their kids, dressed up as Superman with bulging fake muscles. She was trying to assure them that there was no way on earth that her gentle husband would harm any of them. Again trying to make them feel secure, she restated the fact that they would be welcome in the Bartholomew household for as long as they wanted or needed to stay.

Later that evening Shep got up and walked over to the picture window, easing behind the curtain to peer into the darkness. A low growl formed in his throat.

"What is it, Fella?" asked Lynn, not really concerned. Even when she again heard a motorcycle start up somewhere in the distance, she just figured someone nearby had bought a new toy. Shep begged to go out and went barking loudly down to the creek. The scent of the guy who had been crouched there lingered, but Shep had no way to tell Lynn about it. When he had finally checked out the whole area, he went back to the house to sleep lightly beside Lynn's bed.

Chapter 12

The ladies were finishing up in the kitchen, and Diego was sitting at the kitchen table watching.

"Mrs. B," said Diego carefully, "May I can ask...?"

"Of course," she said with a smile.

"In... uh... room... I sleep..."

"Your room," interrupted Lynn. "Go on."

"In you room, see a little... how you say... soupcase."

She smiled inwardly at his incorrect possessive.

"Suitcase," said Lynn, trying to remember a suitcase in the office closet. She thought they were all in the attic. "What does it look like?"

"Is black. Is..." answered Diego, showing the size with his hands. Maria was trying to shush her son, thinking it very rude to ask about something he had not been given permission to see.

Lynn waved the woman to silence. "We're family, remember?" she said.

No translation necessary. Maria got the point.

Lynn thought the "soupcase" might be a briefcase, although she couldn't remember one being in the closet, and the thing he was describing was not the right shape. She thought for a moment.

"Ana, do you know what he is talking about?"

"*Si*," Ana said without thinking. "Yes, I think yes."

"Could you show me?"

The whole lot of them traipsed into the office/bedroom, a curious Shep nosing his way through their legs. From the closet, Ana retrieved Sam's trumpet case.

"Aha!" laughed Lynn. "What do you think it is, Diego?"

"I not know."

"Shall we have a look?"

She laid the case on the bed and opened the latches. There shone the newly refinished trumpet that her husband had played since high school.

She asked Diego, "Do you know how to play?"

The boy just shook his head no, continuing to stare at the instrument.

"Would you like to learn?"

He raised his head and searched her face.

"You...?" He roughly acted out someone playing the trumpet.

"No, but Sam plays beautifully. He has played this horn for almost fifty years, and he would be happy to teach you."

She adjusted the mouthpiece and handed the trumpet to Diego.

"Here, try it."

Diego blew, and of course, nothing happened. He looked questioningly at Lynn and handed her the trumpet. She showed him how to buzz his lips, and he and Ana both buzzed. She held the instrument to her lips and buzzed into it. Behold, a sound—an ugly sound, to be sure, but a sound. Shep fled, and the trumpet went back to Diego.

"You try it. I'm sure you can do better than I did."

With his one good hand the boy awkwardly put the trumpet to his lips and buzzed. He looked surprised when a note came out, and it actually did sound better than his teacher's. Hearty applause from his audience. He tried it again with a little more confidence and sounded even better.

"I! I!" pestered Ana as Diego continued making "music," pressing the different valves as he blew.

When she finally got her turn, Ana produced a blat that made everyone jump and Shep bark from behind the couch in the living room, where he had taken refuge.

Eureka! Sam would be welcomed home eagerly now.

Diego went back to bed, his eyes on the trumpet case. Lynn wondered where her son's old cornet was. Maybe Diego could use it to learn on. She would call immediately.

"Hey, Son," greeted Lynn when Ken picked up the phone. "It's been a while since we talked. How are you and Marj? And my wonderful granddaughter, has she shown the superior intelligence and beauty she inherited from her paternal grandmother yet? I know she must be growing like a weed. We need pictures. When will we see you again?"

Out of breath, she finally paused.

Ken laughed heartily at his mother's rambling.

"Hi, Mom. How are you? What do you hear from Dad?"

"Your father's fine, coming home next week."

Mother and son continued to chat, Ken catching her up on all the recent antics of his ten-month-old baby girl. Baby Lisa was pulling up on the coffee table now and usually babbling happily in her own language. Lynn talked to Marj for a few minutes, the two of them comparing notes on motherhood. Grandma's heart was smitten when they put the phone on speaker so that she could hear the baby's giggles and squeals as her daddy tickled her.

"When was the last time you opened your email?" asked Ken when he got back on the line. He and Marj were both in their thirties, part of the generation that knew about computers and other electronic gadgets that simply baffled Lynn. Social media? Wouldn't even consider it.

"It's been a few days," she confessed, thinking about the events of the last week.

"Well, when you do, you'll find those pictures you were asking for. But you haven't said anything about what's going on at home. How's Shep? Is he still doing the puppy thing, or has he outgrown the shoe chewing and carpet soiling?"

Lynn laughed, and then took a deep breath. Her son would not like being left out of the loop this long with all that had been happening.

"Shep's fine. I think he's reached the teen years."

Then she started at the beginning and told him all about the last week, ending meekly with, "So, do you know where your old cornet is?"

For the most part Ken listened quietly, only making a comment or asking a question here or there. He knew his mother. She and Dad had been taking in needy people for as long as he could remember. He never knew whose feet would be under the supper table, or how long he might be sharing his bedroom.

What could he say? He and his family lived about five hours away, so it was not like he could rescue her if she got into trouble. But he would not give in to worry. Mom was a big girl and a good judge of character, and he knew she did not make decisions lightly.

And there was Shep.

"Well, Mom, what can I say? You know we'll be praying for you, but please be careful. I'll look for the horn. Last time I saw it, I think it was in the basement somewhere. How can I get it to you?"

"Of course, I'd love for you and the family to bring it down, but I know you have to work. And since I'm working too, our coming to pick it up is out. Guess you'll just have to mail it. We'll pay you back for the postage. Will that work?"

"Sounds good. I'll dig it out in the next couple of days and pack it up. Marj can run it to the UPS place when she goes out. Have you talked to Liz about all this?" Ken's older sister and her family lived in Wisconsin.

"No, she usually calls every Saturday, but she was on some kind of a church retreat with her family this past weekend."

"Have you thought about email?" asked Ken.

"Son, I'm sorry, but I have just barely been keeping my head above water here. You know how well I get along with computers, and even though I know I should check my emails, every time I walk by the silly thing, I cringe. I'm just not up to the technological challenge right now."

It sounded like an excuse, but it was the absolute truth. Computers hated her. From his hotel room, Sam had walked her through preparing a slide show for Bible class. By the time they were finished, they were both exhausted and irritable.

"I'll call Liz tomorrow night. If you want to email her and—"

"Gotta go, Mom. Lisa's landed on her nose again."

"OK, bye," said Lynn to the dead line.

She sat thinking. It probably wasn't a good idea for Diego to blat on the trumpet much before Sam could teach him proper technique—wouldn't want him to develop bad habits before he even got started.

She wondered if Ana had any interest in music.

If she looked a little, she thought she could find the recorders her kids had played in third grade. She poked around her closet, but the instruments weren't there. OK, that meant a trip to the attic. Wait. There they were! What on earth was she thinking when she put them there? So much for organization. Great! Their old *Having Fun on the Recorder* books were there too.

"Ana," she called, "could you come here a minute?"

The girl responded immediately.

"Would you like to learn to play an instrument, too?"

A look of disbelief crossed the girl's face, and her eyes sparkled.

"You… piano?" she asked. "I… piano?"

"Yes, I play the piano, but I was thinking of something a little easier to start with. It would help prepare Diego, too, for his trumpet lessons with Sam."

When he heard his name, Diego came out and joined them. It might be a little awkward with his cast, but she thought he could get it. At least it would help him learn timing and note names and give him a leg up when his lessons started.

She handed the kids the recorders.

"We buzz?" asked Ana.

Lynn took one of the recorders and played a scale and "Mary Had a Little Lamb."

It didn't take much for these kids. They were thrilled! Shep was not. She let him out and showed the kids where to place their fingers. Diego just couldn't finagle the fingers of his left hand over the holes, but he could play from G up to C by putting his right hand in the left hand position. At least he could learn a little before Sam came.

The rest of the evening was filled with squeaks and squawks as the kids "practiced."

Maria took refuge outside with Shep.

Chapter 13

Lynn hopped out of bed, took her shower and got dressed even before she went to the kitchen for coffee. She was too excited to follow her normal routine. Today was the first day of Bible club... uh... class, and she had everything by the back door except the fruit, which would stay in the fridge until time to go.

When she walked into the kitchen, she was surprised to see Diego dressed and ready for school. He had worked very hard on his make-up work over the long weekend.

"Good morning! What's this?" she said.

"I go... lunch. Want... how you say... Bible class. Is OK?" asked the boy hopefully.

Huh? "Huh? You mean you want to go to school until lunch, right?"

"Yes. I want go Bible class."

"Well, of course it's OK, if you feel strong enough. Maria?"

"*Si, si,* yes!" said Maria.

She spoke to Diego, who grinned.

"She say please go. She think I (and here he made recorder squeaks) all today."

"I see. Shep will probably be equally glad."

Ana made her just-crawled-out-of-bed entrance into the kitchen, but when she saw her brother dressed for school, she woke up with a whoop. She cut loose with a stream of Spanish, gave him a quick hug and disappeared into her room on the run. When she reappeared a little later, she was scrubbed and ready for school.

Unfortunately, when it came time to leave, Diego was already exhausted. Even he could see that it was not wise for him to try to go so soon after surgery. Ana promised to listen very carefully during Bible class and tell him everything. Diego laughed.

"Or talk teacher," he said. "She live this house."

Ana looked embarrassed and punched him in his good arm.

When they got to school, Ana helped carry everything. Even then, it took two trips to get it all. Looked like they were moving in for a month!

"See you in class," said Lynn, struggling with the last load.

Ana waved as she disappeared down the nearly deserted hall. Arriving early had its advantages.

First hour went well. The students finally got to use the Wheel, winning pennies instead of thousands of dollars. The pennies could be redeemed later for miniature Tootsie Rolls. The special wedges won the players gag gifts like dirty socks or a Mickey Mouse hat to wear in class.

Second hour was its usual enthusiastic self. The younger kids got into the Wheel game even more than the older ones. She knew she might be giving the local dentists a lot of business by using Tootsie Rolls, but the kids loved them and would work to earn them.

She used her free hour to arrange her room for Bible class and prepare her visuals.

The first class filed in quietly and somewhat timidly. Some of her second hour students were scattered throughout the almost full room. The kids seemed to enjoy it, especially the fruit, and promised to come back the next time.

In flowed the second bunch. All of her first hour class was there, and it seemed that half the high school followed them in. Every seat was taken, some of the girls even squeezing two to a desk. Some of the guys sat on the floor at the front, and after that it was standing room only. She sincerely hoped the fire marshal didn't come by right then. Even Mr. Cline and Mr. Philips showed up. She thought they might have come for crowd control, just in case.

And last but not least, in swaggered Jack Barrett, followed by Ben Gibson and Frank Walenski. Their "fearless" leader brought up the rear. Daniel Aimes was not hanging out with them anymore. He was in the class, but he no longer considered himself part of the gang that had attacked Diego.

"Lord…" Lynn pled silently.

"We won't take time for introductions, but I think most of you already know each other. I'm Mrs. Bartholomew, Mrs. B for short, and I'm glad you all came today.

"Who can tell me what Book I am holding?

"That's right, the Bible."

Then she asked, "Does anyone know how we got the Bible?"

The room was silent for a couple of seconds, and then she answered her own question.

"God used about forty men who believed in Him as His secretaries to write down, word for word, everything He wanted us to know. God told them what to write, and they wrote exactly what He said.

"The Bible took about 1,500 years to write, and it was written in three different languages, each man writing in the language that he spoke. But with all that, there is not one contradiction or mistake from beginning to end."

She was speaking slowly and pausing every few phrases to make sure most of them got it. She could deal with those who didn't later.

"Wait a minute," someone said, "How did those men talk to each other so they wouldn't disagree? Did they all speak the three languages? Why didn't they just write in one language?"

"Come on," someone else scoffed. "1500 years? Gimme a break! Nobody lives that long."

"Of course not!" exclaimed Lynn. "That's why the Bible is a miracle and one of the reasons I believe it.

"Most of those men never talked to each other because they lived and died at different times and in different parts of the world. God told them what to write. That's why there are no mistakes or disagreements. The Bible is what God says, not what men say; that's why it is referred to as 'God's Word.'

"Does anyone have a Spanish Bible at home?" Three students raised their hands. "Could—"

"Why the Spanish Bible?" someone interrupted. "Did those guys write the Bible in Spanish?"

"Actually, the Bible was written many years before Spanish existed, before English existed. The first parts were written almost 4,000 years ago. Over the centuries, it has been translated into many languages. English, Spanish, French, Portuguese, Japanese," she said, smiling at Reiko, "and many others."

"How can you know the Bible says today the same thing it said 4,000 years ago?" asked one of the girls.

"These are all very good questions," responded Lynn. "Thank you for asking them.

"The Bible was copied by hand for hundreds of years before Mr. Gutenberg invented the printing press in 1440. The men who copied it counted the words, and even the letters, to make sure they copied exactly what was written. The translations were checked and rechecked with the oldest manuscripts to make sure they were accurate."

She paused to look around.

"In 1946 some ancient copies were discovered in a cave in Israel. When they were compared to the Bible we have today, they were the same.

"Did you get that? Manuscripts from before the time of Christ are the same as the Scriptures we have today. God has preserved the Bible from the time it was written until now."

She took her Bible and held it up.

"The Bible is divided into two main parts."

She turned on the video projector to the first slide that she and Sam had prepared.

"We call them the Old and New Testaments. Those big parts are divided into books, which those 40 men wrote. The books have been divided into chapters and verses to make it easier for us to find what we are looking for. If I wanted you to look up the Bible reference, Psalm 23:4, you would open to the book of Psalms."

She showed them how in her Bible.

"Find chapter 23 and go down to verse 4.

"How many of you have a Bible at home?"

Most of the hands went up; a few did not. Frank Walenski jerked his hand back down when Jack Barrett shot him a withering look. Ben Gibson snickered, and Frank turned beet red.

"Good! Then you can review what we say in class when you get home."

She didn't know if they could bring their Bibles to school—

"Mr. Cline?"

She knew he was here somewhere, but he had been lost in the crowd.

"Yes?" came a voice from the back.

"May the kids bring their Bibles to school?"

"If that's what we are studying, then it's their textbook. Of course they can bring their book."

She didn't know that Bibles were allowed in public schools, but apparently Mr. Cline had done his homework.

"Great! Then everybody bring a Bible in your own language, and we will study together.

"Now, I need your undivided attention for a minute."

Lynn waited until all eyes were on hers. Her voice was serious.

"Starting now, I am going to teach you exactly what the Bible says.

"I have made the choice to believe the Bible. Whether you do or not is entirely up to you. Fair enough?"

Some of the kids nodded; some looked at their neighbors; others just sat there.

"Let's look at the first verse in the Bible, Genesis 1:1. 'In the beginning God created the heaven and the earth.'

"What can we learn about God from this verse?"

No one spoke.

"Think about it? What kind of being would it take to create everything we see around us?"

"Uh... somebody with a lot of power?"

She gave up trying to locate the speaker. She glanced at the clock. Goodness! The time was flying!

"You got it!" she said. "God is all-powerful. There is nothing He cannot do. What else?"

She wrote the first point on the board and waited.

"Well, He must be pretty smart to know how to make everything," someone else ventured.

"Great! God knows everything. The Bible teaches that there is nothing hidden from Him. Anything else?" She again wrote on the board.

"Can we ask questions?" asked one student.

"Of course! I welcome questions. I never want you to believe something or accept something because I said it. We are here to find out what the Bible says."

"Um... where was God when He... uh... created the Earth? I mean, if there was nothin' to stand on, where did He... uh... stand... or... whatever?"

"Excellent question. In fact, it demonstrates two more characteristics of God: First, God is a spirit, so He doesn't need a place to stand since He doesn't have a body. Second, the Bible teaches that God is everywhere all the time."

She noticed some of the students glancing at each other.

"Anything else?"

"Seems to me," said the overweight guy about mid-way back, "that if God created the world, He would have had to already exist."

"You're absolutely right! The Bible teaches that God is eternal. He had no beginning and will have no end."

She saw the smirks and heard the "no ways" that circulated around the room.

"Can you understand what I'm saying?"

"Yeah, we understand what you're sayin'," said one of the smirkers, "but we're havin' a hard time buyin' it."

"Well, it's like this. I don't understand it either; don't know anybody who does. Think about it. If we could understand everything about God, He wouldn't be God, would He?"

She wished she had more time to let that sink in.

"Let's keep going." Lynn summarized verses 2-10, which give the progression of God's creation of the world, and then put verse 11 on a slide.

"'And God said, Let the earth bring forth grass, the herb yielding seed, and the fruit tree yielding fruit after his kind, whose seed is in itself, upon the earth: and it was so.'

"We see from these verses that God is a God of order and purpose and love. He created all the fruits and vegetables to reproduce in their own way. Do any of you have gardens or work in the fields?"

Most of the hands went up.

"How would it be if you planted strawberries, and zucchini came up? When we plant apple seeds, we expect to pick apples, not oranges.

"God created the world so that everything would reproduce only its own kind.

"I brought some fruit for you to examine and tell me how it reproduces."

She held up the fruits one at a time, and the kids noted the seeds of each kind, commenting on the different modes of reproduction.

One minute.

"We don't have time to pass the fruit around, so... let's see... will you and you and you help me out?"

She positioned the chosen students by the door with napkins and trays of cut fruit.

"You can grab two or three pieces on your way out," she said.

"We'll see you Thursday!" she yelled over the bell and the general hubbub of kids on the move.

"Thank you, Mrs. B," said Mr. Cline on the way out. "I thoroughly enjoyed your lesson and will try to be back as often as I can."

"Me, too," said Mr. Philips, swiping at fresh pineapple juice running down his arm, "especially if you have more fruit."

"Thank you," said Lynn.

She was exhausted. At home she said hi to Maria and Diego, gave Shep a pat on the head, had a quick bite of lunch, and crashed.

What...? Who...? Where was she, and what on earth was that racket? She jumped out of bed and ran smack dab into the bedroom door before she realized it was closed.

Shep had been snoozing on his blanket but had set up a ruckus at the sound that had startled them both out of a deep sleep.

Rubbing her head, she finally had the door partway open when she heard it again, this time accompanied by running footsteps and Maria's whispered warnings to be quiet. Diego and the trumpet! Good grief! She had lost ten years off her life. She flopped onto a kitchen chair, still rubbing her head.

Shep was whimpering, not sure what to do.

Maria came rushing out of Diego's room apologizing, but at the same time, trying to suppress a giggle.

"It's OK, Maria. I'm awake now. Tell him to go ahead and blat."

She looked at Maria and couldn't help a giggle, then a full-blown laugh.

Diego stuck his head out the door, apologized, and then laughed along with the ladies. The more they laughed, the funnier it became, until their sides hurt and their mouth muscles felt like they would never go back to normal.

They were laughing so hard that they didn't hear the motorcycle cruise by on the lane as the school bus pulled away. The biker was getting bolder.

The back door opened, and Shep made a dive for freedom, not even pausing to greet his beloved Ana. They tried to explain what had happened, but Ana didn't find it funny at all.

The evening passed quietly, and before she knew it, the kids were saying good night. Lynn and Maria sat down at the table for their usual cup of Sleepytime Tea. Maria acted like she wanted to say or ask something but couldn't screw up enough courage to do so.

"What is it, Maria? What can I do for you?" Lynn finally asked.

She knew the lady couldn't understand her words, but tone of voice and gestures seemed to convey the message.

The Mexican lady responded, "*Yo. ¿El inglés?*"

She pointed back and forth between Lynn and herself. It didn't take a rocket scientist to figure out that she wanted to study English.

Of course, thought Lynn. Why not?

"I'll teach you English if you teach me Spanish. *Yo. Espanish.*" She used the same gestures Maria had used to indicate teacher/learner.

Maria was shocked by the idea, but seemed pleased. She thought a minute.

"*Está bien,*" she said and held out her hand to shake on it.

Lynn took that as a yes and shook the offered hand with a big smile.

Chapter 14

Lynn stopped by to talk to Mr. Cline.

"You do make some of the most off-the-wall requests," he said when she had told him what she wanted to do for the next day's Bible class. "If you're sure it's safe, you can bring him to my office to wait until you're ready for him. I'll enjoy meeting him.

"By the way," continued the principal, "We're moving your class to the music room. We might get in trouble for having a Bible study on campus, but it won't be because the fire marshal caught us in an overcrowded room."

"Great!" she said. "Thanks!"

When Sam called, he also thought her idea for a visual was a little unusual, but he approved.

On the way to school the next day, Ana sat in the back seat with the visual.

When she had parked the car, Lynn went around, leash in hand, to let Ana and Shep out of the back seat. The dog about jerked her arm out of socket, trying to explore this new place. Ana went ahead to the classroom, taking as much stuff as she could. Lynn took Shep to the hedge and let him sniff around before she reined him in and headed to Mr. Cline's office.

"Well, hello, Shep," greeted Mr. Cline warmly, giving the dog the opportunity to sniff his hands and both pant cuffs. "I've heard a lot about you. Come on into my office, and we'll get to work."

Lynn had to admit she was a little surprised by the greeting.

By way of explanation, Mr. Cline said, "I have two Shepherds at home. Shep is beautiful and way bigger than either of my dogs. We'll have to let them get acquainted some day."

English classes went well. During third hour Lynn hauled all her Bible study materials to the music room. She couldn't set up, though, because the high school band was raising the roof on some jazz number they were rehearsing for the new half-time show. The first home football game was Friday night so they were working really hard to be ready.

While the band was wrapping up, Lynn went to get Shep. Maybe she could sneak him in while the kids were putting their instruments away. She knew better. Nobody could sneak in a dog as big as a pony or as excitable as Shep. But this was the only opportunity she would have to get him before the halls filled with students.

When she was almost to the office, she met Mr. Cline bringing Shep to the music room.

"Why, thank you! I was just on the way to get him."

Shep was beside himself at seeing her again in this strange place. She tried unsuccessfully to calm him.

"You'd better take refuge in the broom closet across the hall from the music room when the bell rings," said Mr. Cline.

"Good idea," responded Lynn, "but I have a slight problem. I need to get my computer set up. The band is still going strong, so I can't do it until they leave."

"OK. So I'll hide out in the broom closet until the halls clear," said Mr. Cline as the bell rang.

Lynn couldn't help but grin at the thought of her dignified principal squashed into the broom closet with her excited dog.

"Cut it out," he said, closing the door. "Just remember, this was your idea."

She scurried into the band room, and amidst fifty students trying to put their instruments away, got all her wires plugged in and the right slide pulled up. Whew!

The kids slowly began filing in after they had gone to her room and seen the sign on the door, or else heard the announcement over the public address system, directing them to the music room. Lynn tried to greet them from behind the computer, but mostly they just made their own way in and sat down.

After the tardy bell rang, Mr. Cline came in with Shep. The kids laughed as Shep dragged the average-sized man over to Mrs. B and gave her a greeting as though he hadn't seen her in weeks. She returned the greeting and then tied his leash to the leg of the teacher's desk.

Shep went berserk when he saw Ana, his high-pitched barks echoing down the hall. The girl felt like a teen rock star in front of her one-dog fan club! She gave him lots of hugs and love and introduced him to several of her friends. Although he was polite, Shep had eyes for Ana only.

When Mr. Randolph, the band director, came from the instrument closet to get his lunch out of the desk drawer, he stopped short. That dog was not there a minute ago!

"He won't hurt you," said Lynn sincerely, "unless of course you have beef, chicken or fish in your lunch bag."

The students cracked up.

"Just kidding. Here, I'll hold him."

"Good morning, everyone," she greeted the students while trying to quiet her hyper dog. "I'm so glad to see you back. Hope you plan to eat a good lunch 'cause I don't have any fruit today."

Murmurs of dissatisfaction.

"Who can remember what we studied on Tuesday?" she asked.

"Fruit!" hollered one guy. "It was goooood!" General laughter and chuckles.

Then some more serious answers started coming in. Lynn was impressed with how much they remembered.

Shep's constant whimpering for Ana didn't help, though, and finally she told the girl to come and sit with her four-legged friend. Lynn taught the day's lesson, and Shep did his part well. He sat there, behaved himself, and looked handsome.

Later, as the high schoolers were coming in, Shep suddenly stiffened. A low, almost imperceptible growl came from his throat. Lynn noticed and went over to see what was upsetting him. The boys that had attacked Diego had come in, but why should Shep react to them? He'd never met them. If only he could tell her that one of those boys had left his scent down by the creek just the other night! That guy! Right over there! That one!

Lunch must have slowed the mental processes of this group because they didn't remember nearly as much as the first. Maybe the review would stick.

"What principle were we illustrating with the fruit on Tuesday?"

"That all the fruits and vegetables reproduce from their own seeds," several kids answered.

"Good! What are some of the things that we learned about God through the Bible's account of creation?"

One after another the answers came: knows everything, all-powerful, everywhere at the same time, organized and orderly, a spirit, eternal.

"One more thing we can learn about God through the creation... well, let me give you an illustration. If I make a cake, to whom does that cake belong? Me. Right. I am its owner. I can do whatever I want to with that cake. I can eat it all myself; I can share it with my family; I can let Shep have some of it; I can sell it or give it away, or even bring it to school and share it with all of you."

Applause. Cheers.

"I am the supreme authority over that cake because I made it.

"God is the creator of the universe. He is supreme. He is sovereign. No one is over Him. No one has more authority than He does. He's God."

She paused, looking the students in the eye, willing them to get the point of God's supremacy and sovereignty in their own lives.

"After God created the plants, He created the sun, moon, stars, and all the other heavenly bodies and then the birds and fish."

She read the verses from the screen as she explained each one.

"Whoa! Hold on a minute," said a voice.

"I'm sorry," said Lynn. "Did you have a question?"

"The verse you read said that God put the stars and all in the firmament. What on earth is a firmament? You've used that word before, but I never heard of it."

"Think about it. Where are the sun, moon and stars?"

"In the sky," said one.

"In space," said another.

"Right," said Lynn. "Now, we don't know how big space is, but the verse says the 'firmament of the heavens.' That literally means the expanse of the heavens. So all those things out there that scientists are always discovering have really been there since God created the earth about 6000 to 8000 years ago."

She paused, waiting for the response she knew would come.

"Wait a minute, Mrs. B," said the same overweight boy that had asked a question on Tuesday. "Did you say 6000 to 8000 years? Are you saying the Earth has existed for just 8000 years or less?"

Mrs. B nodded.

"How is that possible, since it took billions of years for everything to evolve?" the boy continued.

"Thank you for asking that question... What's your name?"

"Bill."

"Bill. No one doubts that mutations within a species, called microevolution, have occurred and continue to occur. But the idea of one species changing into another, the theory of macroevolution, is a different matter. The 'theory of evolution,' as we know it today was popularized by Charles

Darwin about 150 years ago, and before his death, even he expressed doubts about it. You see, if you study the evidence carefully, there is no way, absolutely no way, that cross-species evolution could have taken place. Scientists have been looking for the so-called 'missing link' for decades but have never found it. Why do you think that is?"

She waited.

"We can't answer that, Mrs. B," someone said. "Some people say they have found the missing link."

"Every few years some archeologist or paleontologist says he's discovered it, but most of those 'discoveries' have been proven hoaxes. The ones that weren't totally fabricated really don't prove anything. There simply is NO PROOF that evolution happened the way Darwin described."

Again the students looked at each other.

"Next week I would like to show a film that I think will amaze you and make you think. The reason most people, students your age as well as scientists, accept the theory of evolution is that evolution is the only thing they've ever heard. Is that true of many of you?"

Lots of hands went up.

"Except for my preacher," said the skinny kid on her right. "He says God created everything. But he's just a preacher. What does he know?"

"I think you'd be surprised to find that hundreds of scientists and science teachers in the world reject, *reject* Darwin's theory of evolution.

"For now, let's keep going. In verses 24 and 25 the Bible says that God made the land animals and that He made them to reproduce after their own kind, which brings us to Shep."

She looked over at her dog, who was halfway snoozing, but still alert to *The* Scent—the one he had caught at the creek and now in this classroom.

"Shep!" she called.

He jumped up with a bark as if he had been shot, ready to defend his family.

Laughter.

Then Shep looked sheepishly in her direction, dropped his head in embarrassment, and slowly wagged his tail. She walked over and petted him as she continued speaking.

"Take Shep, for example," she said. "Does he look like his great-great-great-great-grandpa was a hippopotamus?"

Giggles.

"Of course not. Or before that even, an alligator? Or before that a fish, or an amoeba or a cloud of gas that exploded? And before that, who knows?

"Where did that whatever-it-was that exploded come from anyhow? When you think it through, evolution simply does not make sense.

"But back to Shep. Some day this dog is going to make a wonderful dad. Will he sire a cat? Or maybe a chicken?"

Snorts and rolled eyes.

"Right! Shep's son or daughter will be a ____.

"Yes! A dog. Everything was created to reproduce its own kind. And not only will Shep's offspring be dogs, but his grandpuppies will be dogs and his great-grandpuppies will be dogs and his great-great-grandpuppies will be dogs and... you get the point. Everything reproduces its own kind. His descendants will always be dogs; they will never turn into anything else."

She looked at the clock.

"Just one more thing before the bell. Look at verse 31. 'And God saw all that he had made, and, behold, it was very good.'

"Why did God say it was very good?"

No time to wait for a response.

"Because God is perfect, and everything He does is perfect. God is holy. Nothing He does is wrong. Remember, He is supreme and sovereign, the One Who says what's right and wrong. God is God."

Chapter 15

She had no idea what time it was or how long she had been sleeping. Whatever it was that had awakened her had Shep on his feet too. He was standing perfectly still, a low growl rumbling in his throat.

There! She heard it again.

Shep broke into his full-fledged intruder bark and flew to the back door. Lynn grabbed the pistol from her nightstand drawer and followed more cautiously than her dog.

Again the noise came, and this time she called out.

"Identify yourself or I'm letting the dog out!"

No response, but she and Shep both heard footsteps running across the porch. Before she could get the door open, a motorcycle started and roared out of the driveway.

Shep shot out the door and chased the bike until it disappeared around the curve. He came back panting, excited and victorious—he'd showed 'em!

"What is...?" asked Diego.

He had a poker from the fireplace in his good hand, still in the role of protector. His mother and Ana both appeared behind him, the same question shining in their eyes.

"I don't know," said Lynn. "It sounded like someone was trying to break in. They're gone now."

She looked down and realized she was in the fancy red silk pajamas with white trim that her daughter Liz had given her for Christmas last year—pistol in hand. She quickly dialed 9-1-1 and escaped to her bedroom for a robe.

The dog was still casting around outside barking his head off, reluctant to abandon his search.

"Here, Shep!" she called.

Finally, he came to the back door and Lynn dragged him in by the collar. He stood at his post as stiffly as a palace guard, listening for anything unusual.

When the officers arrived, Shep was ready to take their heads off. Lynn finally made him understand that they were the good guys, and he calmed down. But he kept an eye on them, just in case.

"Hey, Sully," said Lynn to the older officer. He and the Bartholomews attended the same church, and they had known each other forever.

"Hey, Lynn. What's goin' on? Y'all OK? Sam on the road?"

"We're fine, and yes, Sam's gone. Had a visitor tonight."

Then everyone said basically the same thing—they had all been awakened by a strange noise, and Shep had sounded the alarm. Sully's Spanish was far less than perfect, but he got the gist of what was said.

While they were inside being interviewed by Officer Sully, the other officer, who was new in town, was outside investigating.

He stuck his head in the door.

"Hey, Sully! Y'all need to come see this!"

What he had found was frightening at first, but then it just made Lynn furious.

Someone had taken red paint and sprayed threats and obscenities all over the front of her lovely, green-shuttered white house. Her blood pressure began to rise, and she had to struggle to control herself as they all trooped back inside.

Maria made coffee and, with trembling hands, went around filling mugs as everyone sat at the kitchen table.

Sully started writing up the report. The younger officer glanced at the gun and then at Lynn. She took a deep breath and spoke quietly but forcefully.

"You need to understand that I am trained to use that gun. I will not shoot to protect things, but I will shoot to kill if those I love are threatened."

At first the officer appeared amused. Then he looked at her and saw that she was dead serious. He glanced at Sully.

Sully nodded. He knew Lynn Bartholomew—knew that he
would not want to be on the barrel end of that gun.

"Wait a minute," said the officer, who Sully had
introduced as Banks. "Ain't you the teacher that took care of
that gang o' boys at the high school?"

"The very one," said Lynn without smiling.

"Well, I'll be," said the officer. "You've become quite th'
legend down at th' station."

The older officer paused but then finished writing. "If
you'll just sign here, we'll be on our way."

"Sully, did you know who we're talkin' to?" said the
young man with obvious admiration.

"Yeah, I heard ya," said Officer Sully. "I'd forgotten
about that. Kinda sheds a new light on things."

He ran his hand through his stubby hair.

"I just wrote this incident up as vandalism, but now I
think it could fall under hate crimes. There are a lot o' people
in this town that're not happy about you takin' in these folks,
Lynn."

"I know. So where do we go from here?"

Sully took a deep breath as he wadded up the paper.

"I'll write another report and you can sign it. Then it
would probably be a good idea for you to request more police
protection. You're kinda off the beaten path out here in the
boonies, so it won't be easy for us to watch you every
minute."

"We'll appreciate anything you can do. Now, where do I
sign?"

Before he went home to sleep, Sully briefed his day-shift
replacement and stopped by Sergeant Johnson's office. "Had
a little excitement out at the Bartholomew place last night,
Sarge."

"What happened?"

"Aw, nothin' serious, just some spray paint on the house."

"Any idea who it was?"

"Nope. Me and Banks snooped around a little, but the guy was long gone. Pretty sure it's 'cause o' those Mexicans they got over there, so I wrote it up as a hate crime. That sends it to the Feds. Hope we catch 'em before it gets worse. The Bartholomews are good folks. Here's my report. See ya."

Johnson skimmed over the page and then shuffled the stack of reports on his desk. Sully's just happened to land on the bottom. Let the do-gooders and the spics take care of themselves. After all, he reasoned with himself, they didn't *know* that it was a hate crime. Could be simple vandalism. He'd heard about the new Bible class. Probably some kid upset because his parents were making him go.

Diego had planned to go to school with Lynn until after third hour on Friday, but after what happened, he decided to stay with his mother. He might be weak, but he would do whatever it took to protect Maria. Besides, he had been up half the night and needed rest.

Ana went to school, but she wasn't happy about it. Maria almost let her stay home, but decided it would be better for her daughter to keep her mind occupied at school rather than stay home and stew over the incident.

What on earth should I tell Sam? thought Lynn on the way home from school. She'd been thinking about it all day, but 6:00 was drawing ever nearer. If she mentioned last night's vandalism, she knew he would be at the airport in a heartbeat. If she didn't, he would want to kill her when he found out.

Oh, she knew she had to tell him, but the question would be how to do it without sending him into a tizzy and bringing him home on the run. After all, he had bought Shep and taught her to use the gun precisely for such a time as this. She really didn't expect to hear anything more out of the vandals. They'd made their point.

As she pulled onto the lane that passed her driveway, she began steeling herself for the sight of her lovely home desecrated by that awful paint.

What she saw instead were several cars parked in her yard.

Now what? she thought.

Then she saw the house. No more red paint!

Wait a minute. Last night hadn't been just a nightmare, had it? She looked again and saw Pastor Juan and some other men putting away ladders and equipment.

"What's all this?" she asked when the pastor opened the door for her.

"Well, when Maria called and told me what had happened, I got on the Internet and looked for a way to remove the paint without harming your siding. Fortunately, you have aluminum instead of vinyl, so the process was pretty simple. I called some of the men from the church who are out of work right now, and... Well, I think it looks pretty good."

"It looks terrific! How can I ever thank you? I will be happy to pay the going rate to you and your men. A new paint job... or new siding... or whatever, would have cost a whole lot more."

"No way," said Pastor Juan. "You are taking care of one of our own, and this is our way of saying thank you. Please accept our gift."

"I don't know what to say..."

She had to stop because the tears were about to take control.

"Thank you," she managed.

Just then Maria called everyone together for refreshments. Seemed like lately they were having snacks every time she turned around. She had definitely put on a few pounds.

Lynn enjoyed trying to talk to the men to express her gratitude. Some of them spoke a little English and helped her with the others. Their good job would definitely make it easier to tell her husband about the whole thing.

Before he left, Pastor Juan called her over and spoke to her privately.

"I understand your husband will be home Tuesday. Is that correct?"

"Yes, unless he hops a plane tonight when I tell him what happened."

"He won't need to do that," said the pastor. "I have spoken with the police and with our men. I don't want you here at night by yourselves, and I especially don't want Maria here alone during the day. We are setting up a 24-hour guard until your husband comes home."

Again Lynn had trouble expressing her gratitude. She hadn't realized how stressed she was over this thing until Pastor Juan had stepped in. She just reached over and gave the tall man a hug, trying not to break down completely. As soon as the men had gone, she went to take a much-needed nap.

Lynn had been awake a little over an hour when Sam called.

"Hi!" she said, "What's new in your world?"

She listened as Sam told of a power outage that had ended the morning session, which meant that he would have to have a Saturday meeting.

"Now tell me about the latest on your end," said Sam.

"We're all fine. Diego will start back to school on Monday."

She stopped.

"But..." said Sam. He could hear in her voice that something was going on.

She told him about last night, and as she knew he would, he began looking up flights on the Internet before she could even finish.

"Sam, hold on a minute. You don't need to come charging home. Pastor Juan and some men from his church have already cleaned up the mess and are working together with the police to put a 24-hour guard around the house."

That slowed him down a little, but she still had to talk hard and fast to persuade him that they were OK for the present. She reminded him of Shep and the gun.

He calmed down some but was still not convinced that he didn't need to come home immediately.

"Besides," Lynn said, "Sully came out to investigate, and you know he won't let anything happen to us."

"I'm going to call and talk to him, and I'll make a decision after that. What's the pastor's name?"

"Juan Garcia."

"Yes, give me his number too. He speaks English, right? I want to know what he has in mind."

They prayed together and hung up.

After they had talked, she sat on the porch thinking. She needed a diversion. What could...? A party! That would take their minds off things, a welcome home party for Sam. She would put Maria to work planning the meal and cooking, and the kids could decorate and make a poster. It would be fun and keep them busy. She would bring up the idea at supper.

"*Piñata!*" said Ana. "We have *piñata*?" The girl's eyes shone with excitement.

"I make," said Diego. "Must have *piñata* in *fiesta Mexicana*."

"I help!" Ana pointed to his cast. He nodded.

"Perfect!" Lynn said happily. "Maria, will you make a special cake? We'll put sparklers on it."

"Spah-kahs?" said Diego. "What is spah-kahs?"

"Sparklers," Lynn corrected.

How on earth do I describe sparklers? she asked herself.

Then she remembered she had some in the junk drawer that had been missed during last year's 4th of July celebration. She retrieved them and lit one for all to see.

"*Bengalas!*" all three shouted at once when the fireworks started.

"On cake?" asked Diego, seeing his mother's dubious look.

"Why not? We're celebrating, right?"

"Yes!" exclaimed Ana. "I like!"

As Lynn was turning out her bedside lamp later that night, she got a text from Sam. "Talkt w Sully and Juan. Going w plan A 4 now. Luv u." As an English teacher she despised texting shorthand, but at least her husband was staying put for now.

The weekend was exceptional. The weather was hot, but not unbearable. Lynn showed Ana what she needed to do to help clean up the yard and the carport in preparation for Sam's arrival. Diego used his good hand to wash a couple of windows on the outside while Maria did the inside. He was getting stronger every day and wanted to help.

Sunday night Lynn again took the family to the Spanish church and enjoyed it more than she had the week before. Two guitars accompanied the hymns. She noticed an old upright piano at the front of the church, but no one played it. Hmm, she thought.

After church Pastor Juan introduced Lynn to his children, Carlos, Lucas and little Melissa. They were all adorable and seemed especially fond of Maria, who held them and cuddled them and generally gave them a good dose of TLC. Ana explained that Maria had often cared for the children during their mother's difficult pregnancy before she died.

"Only when my father work," she said.

Lynn watched Maria and the children.

Hmm, she thought again. She glanced at Pastor Juan and hid a smile. He seemed to be doing a little hmming of his own, as he watched Maria with his children.

All was quiet over the weekend, and so Monday morning Diego went to school with Mrs. B and Ana. By the end of third hour he was exhausted and dragged himself out to the van. Lynn carried his backpack, helped him climb into the passenger seat, and buckled him in. She reclined the seat for him, and he was asleep before they got out of the parking lot.

Tomorrow was the big day. Sam was coming home! Diego put the finishing touches on the *piñata*. Maria made a luscious-looking two-tier chocolate cake that Sam would be tempted to polish off in one sitting, and Ana decorated the house Mexican style. Shep didn't know what was going on, but he was loving it. Ana got upset with him when he grabbed the streamers and took off, but she chased him down, retrieved the streamers, and hung them up higher. Everyone worked together to fill the *piñata*, and then Lynn found a rope and a suitable spot outside to hang it. In the meantime, it sat regally in Sam's recliner. Sam would retrieve his car at the Atlanta airport and arrive home about 5:00. Perfect! They went to bed anticipating the grand event.

"Thank You, Lord," mumbled Lynn sleepily as she snuggled down under the covers, "for whoever is sitting in that pick-up across the road. Bless him and the others from Pastor Juan's church that are looking out for us."

Chapter 16

Lynn was sleeping soundly when Shep's low growl woke her. She put her hand on the dog's head to keep him quiet and slowly sat up, reaching for the pistol that now resided on top of the night stand instead of in the drawer. She still hadn't heard anything, but the hair was up on Shep's back.

She tiptoed to the back door, grabbing the cordless phone on the way through the kitchen. She unlocked the door silently and dialed 9-1—

CRASH! The picture window in the living room shattered!

She threw open the door and Shep flew out, barking with startled fury.

"Go get 'im, boy!"

… -1. The others ran out of their rooms.

"Careful!" she warned. "Broken glass!"

"9-1-1," came the operator's voice. "Wha—"

"Intruder!" Lynn yelled into the phone.

She heard a scream as Shep attacked.

"Get 'im off! Get 'im off me! Help! Get 'im off!"

She dropped the phone and ran outside toward the ruckus, pistol ready. A car skidded into the driveway, followed by a pick-up. Lynn spun around, pistol now pointed at the cars. A police car, lights flashing and siren blaring, was a few yards behind on the lane. The door of the first car flew open.

"Lynn!" called a voice she recognized, but her brain refused to process.

Shep froze. He knew that voice!

"Sam!" screamed Lynn, dropping the gun to her side.

The intruder groped around for anything he could use as a defense against the dog. His hand closed around a decorative post of wrought iron, the last hitching post from the site's former life. It had been loosened by the recent rains and came easily when the guy frantically tugged. He took advantage of Shep's distraction and, using every ounce of force he could muster, slammed Shep with the post. There was a sickening THUD! Then a howl like none of them had ever heard. The guy ran for his life.

"Go get 'im, Shep!" commanded Sam. Shep took off in hot, albeit painful, pursuit.

"Lynn! Are you OK? What's going on?" yelled Sam as he rushed to his wife.

The man from the pick-up took off toward the creek behind Shep and the intruder.

"Is Manuel of church!" called Diego from the front porch, where he stood in front of his mother and sister, poker ready in his good hand.

Sully and Banks jumped from their car and joined the chase, their powerful flashlights sending beams dancing across the field.

Someone yelled in Spanish and Diego translated, "Is dark! No see man!"

A motorcycle roared to life on the other side of the creek and started up the hill. The folks at the house heard growling, cursing, and another thud as Shep caught up with the guy. The sound of the motorcycle began to fade in the distance; Shep's yelps did not.

"Shep!" cried Lynn, struggling against Sam's embrace.

"Get dressed. I'll get him."

Lynn quickly pulled on sweats and a T-shirt, slipped her feet into her good school shoes, and grabbed the flashlight. She could hear Shep yelping through the broken window. She ran past the Lopez family without a word.

"Sam!" she called. "Sam, where are you? Where's Shep?"

"Over here!" yelled Sam, "across the creek near the old Indian trail."

When Lynn got there, she saw that Sam had muzzled Shep with his handkerchief. He and the Mexican man were kneeling down next to the dog. The man appeared to know about animals and was examining the dog. He tried to explain something to Sam and indicated that Shep's leg was possibly broken close to the shoulder. Poor Shep was whimpering pathetically. The old hitching post lay on the ground beside him.

"S-S-Sam?"

Sam took his wife in his arms, and only then did she realize she was shaking uncontrollably. He held her for a long moment.

Shep struggled and finally got to his feet with the man's help.

"*Muchas gracias, señor*," said Sam over his wife's head. "*La casa.*"

They let Shep set the pace as he limped home, head down.

"Lynn, please tell me you're all right. I couldn't stay at that stupid seminar another minute, and you have my word that I will travel no more until this thing is over. Maybe never."

He kissed her on the top of her head as they walked slowly home, his arm around her protectively.

Lynn couldn't stop crying. It was so good to have her Sam with her. She was safe. Sam was home.

After looking around down at the creek, Sully and Banks reached the house about the same time as Sam, Lynn, Manuel and Shep. The Hispanic man helped Shep into the house and Maria showed him the blanket by the Bartholomews' bed. Ana was vacuuming up the last shards of broken glass, tears streaming down her face. Diego was putting the big pieces of glass into a box. He showed them the brick that had shattered the window.

When Ana saw Shep, she dropped the vacuum cleaner and ran to him.

"Careful," said Lynn. "Slowly. Stay calm."

Ha! Calm? She was one to talk. She was a basket case.

Shep lay down on his blanket, content to be home, though the pain must have been excruciating.

The officers came in and looked around at the decorations.

"Wow! Looks like somebody had a birthday," said Sully.

"Actually, this was supposed to be for Sam's welcome home party today," said Lynn. "Welcome home, Darling. Please let me introduce everyone.

"Diego, come and meet Sam. Sam, Diego."

"Nice to meechu," said Diego, glancing at Lynn.

"Nice to meet you, too, Diego." Sam was impressed by the boy's firm handshake.

Ana was hiding timidly behind her mother.

Be careful here, Lynn thought to herself.

But Sam took charge and turned on the charm.

"And you must be Diego's mother Maria. I've heard so much about you. *Mucho gusto*. I'm glad you are a part of our family now."

He gave Maria a big smile and shook her hand warmly. She understood his meaning even if she didn't understand his words.

"And Ana. Did you do all this decorating? Thank you so much. It looks great. And look, a *piñata*! Was all this for me?"

Ana smiled and nodded. "Diego make *piñata*," she said shyly.

"Thank you, Diego. I hope it has chocolate inside. I love chocolate!"

Within five minutes, Sam had put the whole lot of them at ease, just as Lynn had known he would. That was her Sam.

"Is Brother Manuel of church," said Diego.

Sam shook the man's hand. "*Mucho gusto, and muchas gracias*," said Sam.

"Hey!" cried Lynn. "I know you! You stopped to help me fix a flat tire the first day of school!" She shook the man's hand. "And, yet again, thank you." Manuel nodded his head and smiled hugely in recognition.

"Well, folks," said Sully, "now that we're all acquainted, we had probably better get on with the report. Good to see you, Sam. God sure put you in the right place at the right time tonight, didn't He? This is Banks."

Lynn started with Shep's growl and told everything. Everyone put in his two cents' worth in an excited, emotion-releasing jumble of English and Spanish. She hoped Sully got it all down—after all the talk, she wasn't even sure she got it right. By the time they were finished, they were all yawning.

The policemen left, saying someone would be back in the daylight to investigate the crime scene.

They went to check on Shep. "What do you think, Sam? Do we need to call the vet?"

"Diego, would you ask Brother Manuel what he thinks?" said Sam. "I don't know if the clinic here in town has emergency capabilities."

"Surely they do," said Lynn uncertainly.

Diego and Manuel talked quietly for a minute, and then Diego turned to Sam.

"Brother Manuel, he no is doctor to animal, but think Shep very bad. He rest, and tomorrow the doctor. Is a little hours, no?"

"OK, thank you," said Sam. "Now let's call it a night."

"Let's go to bed," said Lynn when she saw the confused faces.

Sam shook Brother Manuel's hand, ushering him to the door.

"*Gracias!*" he said again.

After everyone had settled down once again for the night, Lynn was lying with her head on Sam's chest, his arm encircling her. He prayed, thanking the Lord for safety and for His perfect timing. His amen ended in a *zzz*, but his wife never heard it.

"Mornin', Sarge," said Sully. "You pass that report about the vandalism at the Bartholomews' on to the Feds?"

Sarge just looked at him. Then he started shuffling the papers around on his desk.

"Don't exactly remember. It might still be here somewhere."

Sully's eyebrows lifted in surprise.

"Well, here's another one. Brick through the front window. Their dog almost got the guy, but... Well, it's all in the report. Pretty interesting read."

"Yeah, OK. Have a good day," said Sarge in dismissal.

Some kids really hate their teachers, thought Sarge. I hated my English teacher with a passion and used to dream about stringing her up on one of those stupid diagramming scaffolds. But I never actually did anything like this guy. Maybe he's got more guts than me. He snickered and shuffled the papers on his desk yet again.

Chapter 17

Lynn woke up with a start Tuesday morning. What time was it? Then she saw Sam lying beside her and the events of last night came rushing back. What a miracle! Thank You, Lord.

While Sam lay snoring, she quietly got up and got ready for the day. No way was she going to wake him. He was exhausted. She wasn't thinking too clearly herself, but she knew she had to go to work and teach two classes of ESOL students and try to make sense when she did. Thank the Lord she had planned the film for Bible class.

She knelt beside Shep. He didn't acknowledge her, so she didn't disturb him.

Just let him rest, she thought.

She showered, dressed, did her hair, and put on her face before she came out of the bathroom.

When she opened the door, she saw Sam on the floor by Shep. The dog was whimpering. Had he been hurt worse than they thought last night?

"How is he?" she quietly asked Sam. "Is he worse than we thought?"

"Must be. He's pretty unresponsive."

"My poor Shep," she crooned as she caressed the big head.

What would have become of them last night if Shep hadn't been around? Her tears washed her cheeks. So much for makeup.

"Can you stay with him a minute? I'm gonna take a quick shower and get him to the vet ASAP."

Sam disappeared into the bathroom as a knock sounded at the bedroom door.

"Come in."

Diego poked his head in and said, "*Mamita* say the breakfast..."

He saw Shep and knelt beside Lynn.

"Shep is very bad?"

"Yes, Sam is going to take him to the veterinarian this morning."

She dried her tears and continued, "Could you just bring me a cup of coffee? I want to stay with Shep until Sam is ready to take him. You three go ahead and eat."

Her phone rang and she dug it out of her pocket. Who on earth...?

"Good morning," came Pastor Juan's concerned voice over the phone. "I heard about last night, and I just wanted to check on everyone. Are you OK? Maria? The kids?"

"We're all good except Shep. He was injured when the guy tried to get away on a dirt bike. We don't know exactly what happened. My husband's taking him to the vet this morning."

"I'm so sorry. I know he means a lot to you."

"Not only that," said Lynn, "he may have saved our lives last night."

"Thank God he was there, then."

There was a pensive silence.

"Listen, I'm not sure it is wise to leave Maria there alone today," said the pastor. "Is Diego going to school? What do you think? Maybe she would enjoy spending the day with one of the families in our church. I could pick her up now and bring her back this afternoon."

"I think that's a terrific idea. She's had very little contact with her friends since she came here with me. Hold on and I'll ask her. Uh... let me give her the phone. I keep forgetting she doesn't speak English."

Lynn could tell that Maria was relieved and grateful.

But what about the kids? Ana was a nervous wreck, but again, Maria felt it would be better for her to go to school. If nothing else, it would provide a distraction.

Diego was terribly tired and a little shaky, but he wasn't comfortable with staying here without Shep, with or without his mother. Maria's friend had three kids under school age. What kind of rest would he be able to get there? Besides, he really wanted to go to school. He didn't want to miss Bible class.

They picked Shep up, blanket and all. Sam carried him in the front, and Maria and Lynn managed to get his back end into the Lexus. As gently as possible, they laid the dog on the back seat. Ana followed them out, tears streaming down her cheeks once again. She spoke to Shep soothingly in Spanish as she petted him, and he responded with a little lick on the hand. Maria handed Sam a travel cup of coffee and a toaster pastry. He detested toaster pastries, but he took it gratefully.

Lynn and Ana stood in the carport and watched the car disappear up the lane, and then Lynn checked her watch. Good grief! She would have to stop by the office with the kids to get a tardy slip.

They hurried back into the house to get their stuff. Maria had a travel cup and toaster pastry waiting for her too. Diego was already in the van.

Lynn sincerely hoped Officer Sully was not sitting on the side of the road looking for speeders this morning. They roared by Pastor Juan on his way to pick up Maria. She glanced at Diego, who was clearly enjoying the ride. He grinned.

"Not a word of this to anyone. Do you understand, Diego? Ana? Not one word!"

All she needed was a Jeff Gordon reputation on top of everything else.

Were her students wired today, or was it just her sleep deprivation? She didn't know, but they all made it through with the help of the Wheel.

Someone accidentally dropped a book during second hour, and Ana nearly jumped out of her skin. She looked at

Lynn, eyes wide, face pale. She was still trembling when she walked out a few minutes later.

As Lynn was coming out of her classroom with her arms loaded with the stuff she needed for Bible class, she fumbled her key while trying to lock the door and scattered her notes trying to retrieve it. Mr. Cline happened by right then and scooped up her keys and her notes.

"Good Morning, Mrs. B. How are you? How's Shep?"

"Shep is at the vet's even as we speak. Help me haul my stuff to the music room and I'll tell you all about it." She related what had happened last night as they walked.

Mr. Cline gave a low whistle. "Wow! Even I can see the hand of God in that.

"And," he added, "you are excused from staff meeting this afternoon. Go home and get some rest."

Lynn could have kissed his feet. Instead, she said, "Thank you."

During Bible class she showed part of the video series, *Incredible Animals that Defy Evolution*, by Dr. Jobe Martin. The movie was really interesting, yet she had to fight to stay awake during the first class but lost the battle and fell asleep during the second. Fortunately, she was in the back next to Mr. Cline, who let her snooze until time to wrap things up. The students enjoyed the video, so she decided to show more on Thursday.

Diego had planned to stay at school all day, but this was only his second day back, and after all that had happened, he was wiped out. He went home with Lynn after Bible class. There was no way Lynn was going to leave Ana there without Diego, so she got permission to get her out of class and take her home too. Without Shep and Maria, the house seemed cold, empty and silent as a tomb.

How depressing, she thought.

Diego went straight to bed, and after a cookie, so did Ana. Lynn made sandwiches and took them out to the porch with a pitcher of tea to wait for Sam. Surely he would be home soon.

She was checking the plastic they had hastily taped over the window last night when he drove into the carport.

"How's Shep?" she asked as he opened the car door.

Her husband looked ten years older and oh, so tired. He kissed her tenderly before he answered.

"His leg is broken. He was in surgery for much of the morning, and he will stay at the clinic for several days."

"How on earth did he walk up from the creek last night?"

"The vet marveled at that too, but he said trying to carry him could have been worse. Carrying him to the car was bad enough."

He flopped down into a chair on the porch, and she massaged his shoulders for a few minutes before they ate their lunch.

"I'll call the glass place and see about repairing the window while you take a nap," she said.

"Already done," he countered. "I called them while Shep was in surgery. Why don't we both take a nap? The window people will be here in the morning."

"Wonderful," she said as he pulled her to her feet.

Lynn did not usually like to take long naps, so after an hour or so she got up and left Sam snoring. She looked at him lying there, still incredulous that he was actually at home in his own bed.

Plans for the welcome home party had been shattered along with the living room window, and Maria had not been home to finish the meal she had started yesterday. What about supper? Soup was comfort food, so she made a big pot. Who cared if it was hot outside? A double recipe of cornbread ought to feed her crew with some left over for tomorrow. They could eat out on the porch and invite Pastor Juan to eat with them. Although she wasn't crazy about cooking, she enjoyed the opportunity to keep busy. Maybe they could save the *piñata* for the children to break after church Sunday night.

Wednesday was Diego's first full day at school. Lynn stayed all day so he wouldn't have to try to navigate the bus with his cast. He came to her room after school looking worn. She was locking her door when she heard, "Mrs. B! Hang on a minute!" She turned around to see Daniel Aimes rushing toward her.

"I need to talk to Diego."

"Oh, OK. I'll just go on out to the car and wait for him."

"Please stay," said Daniel.

He turned to Diego and took a deep breath.

"Diego, I want to apologize to you for my part in trying to hurt you. Do you understand?"

Diego nodded.

"I was very wrong. Will you forgive me?"

He looked at Diego with so much hope in his eyes that it almost hurt.

Diego glanced at Mrs. B. Then he stuck out his right hand. "Yes, I forgive," he said simply. "I… you… maybe… friends, OK?"

"Well, yeah!" said the astonished boy.

He hadn't expected Diego to be as quick to forgive as his mother. He pumped Diego's hand enthusiastically, a huge grin replacing the anxiety.

"Thanks!"

There was an awkward moment.

"Well, my mom's waitin' out front. See y'all tomorrow!"

There was a big box leaning against the back door when Lynn and the kids got home. Ken's cornet. Diego's fatigue evaporated as he began ripping off the tape and throwing out the Styrofoam peanuts. When he got to the case, he reverently lifted it out and opened it. His reaction to the horn was exactly what Lynn had hoped for. In spite of his excitement, however, his energy was beginning to wane, so he went to lie down.

He woke up later, and when Sam drove into the carport, the first thing he heard was Diego blatting away on the porch. The recorder was forgotten in favor of the "real" instrument.

"Sam..." Lynn's desperation showed in her eyes.

"Enough said. Just let me kiss my wife and change clothes. Then I'll take the boy to the barn and give him his first lesson and something constructive to practice. He really has a pretty good tone. Won't take long for him to get good, if he keeps practicing."

"Thank you, my love," she sighed. "I really miss Shep, but for his sake I'm glad he's not around right now."

Chapter 18

During Thursday's Bible class, the kids seemed to enjoy the film even more than they had on Tuesday. Some of the animals that Dr. Martin talked about made it abundantly clear that evolution simply could not be true.

On the way home Lynn stopped by to check on Shep. He was heavily sedated and barely acknowledged her presence. Poor thing!

"Guess what!" Sam said as he came in Thursday evening.

"I don't know. Tell me."

His grin meant it was something good.

"We interviewed a guy today that I think will be perfect for the traveling position. Retired military chaplain, international experience, speaks to crowds, grown children, mother-in-law lives with them so his wife wouldn't be alone when he travels, and he finished a bachelor's in business administration online before he left the service."

"Wow! Sounds like he was tailor-made for the job."

"Yep. Starts work Monday. He'll be here and in the Atlanta office until he learns the ropes. He sounds almost too good to be true."

Friday, Sam decided they needed a diversion. He invited Antonio to accompany the family to the high school football game. Even after only two lessons, Diego was doing really well on his trumpet, and Sam wanted the boy to see the marching band perform. Flanders County had one of the best bands in the state.

Antonio came home from school with Diego, and later they all piled into the van. Energy flowed through the kids like high-voltage electricity, and Spanish banter bounced between them like sparks. They were off to their first American football game!

On the way to the bleachers, Lynn waved to several of her Bible class students. Most of her ESOL students were conspicuously absent. Sam chose seats as close to ground level as possible for Diego's sake, unknowingly, directly in front of Jack Barrett and his buddies. Lynn greeted them enthusiastically, but as the family distributed themselves along the bench, the boys noisily stood up and moved away, flinging insults as they went. Sam heard, but ignored them and kept the Lopezes busy with a lesson on American football.

It was a great evening. County won, and Antonio decided then and there that he wanted to play football the next year. Diego was totally fascinated by the half-time show, just as Sam had expected. Lynn could see the wheels turning in Ana's head, as she watched the kids march and dance around the field. The girl was doing well on the recorder. What was she thinking? Was she interested in learning a band instrument?

On the way home spirits were high in the car. Everyone tried to teach Sam and Lynn one of the choruses from the Spanish church. Sam's big voice overpowered all the others put together. His volume, together with his lousy pronunciation, left everyone in stitches.

"What?" he asked innocently when the singing degenerated into peals of laughter.

Lynn heard his laughter but saw his wariness and watchfulness as he pulled into the driveway. He ushered everyone in and then unobtrusively checked around outside before joining the rest of the family.

Saturday the Bartholomew household slept in. It threatened rain but never actually did, so the day just became kind of a lazy, do-your-own-thing day.

Everyone was working on this or that project, but nothing that took much effort. Lynn worked on her lesson plans; Sam worked on his training materials; Diego practiced his trumpet;

and Ana helped her mom in the kitchen. They were preparing Sam's welcome home meal that had never been served.

"Sam," said Lynn.

"M-m-m," said Sam absently.

"Sam!" she said a little louder to get his attention. "I think you'll like the Spanish church tomorrow night. It's quite an experience."

"I'm looking forward to it. Did you mention the *piñata* to Pastor Juan?"

"No, but I'll call right now."

She called, and the pastor gave his enthusiastic approval for after church Sunday night.

"Speaking of fun things to do, could we bring the teens to your place next Saturday?" asked Pastor Juan.

She quickly checked with Sam.

"Sure! What time, and what can we do? There is a basketball goal, the creek, and lots of room for other games. I think we have our son's old football around here somewhere."

"You don't have to do a thing, but we would like you to join us. Will Sam be in town?"

"Yes!" she responded happily. "He has given up traveling and begins training his replacement Monday morning."

"Wow! That's fantastic!" said Pastor Juan. "We'll be there about 10 and stay 'til you kick us out."

"We have an old fridge that we keep stocked with soft drinks. It's out on the back porch, so folks can help themselves. There's also room to put anything that needs to be refrigerated and lots of ice in the freezer."

"Man! You're prepared, aren't you?"

"Well, we have lots of groups out here. Oh, and there's also a barbecue pit and a place for a bonfire, but you have to provide the wood."

Maria came into the room with Diego.

"Is Pastor Juan?" he asked, indicating the phone.

Lynn nodded.

"*Mamita* want talk, OK?"

She nodded again.

"This is really wonderful, Mrs. B! Thank you," said the pastor.

"You are most welcome, and please call me Lynn. I think Maria wants to talk to you. Hold on. See you tomorrow night."

Maria talked for a few minutes and then called Lynn back to the phone.

"Hello?"

"Hi, again," said Pastor Juan. "Maria and I were just talking. She thinks today might be a good day to go to the trailer and clean it out. What do you think?"

"I don't see why not. Let me check with Sam."

She talked with her husband a minute.

"Sam said fine. Would you like him to go along?"

"That would be great! How about right after lunch? I'll pick Maria and him up. OK?"

"Hold on again."

Pastor Juan could hear mumbling in the background.

"Sure, that'll be good!"

Maria sat on the edge of Diego's bed and smoothed the hair back from his forehead. "What do you think?"

"Now is a good time," said Diego, "but I want to go with you."

"Do you think you're strong enough?" asked his concerned mother.

Diego grinned. "If I can survive a day at school, I should be fine for a few hours at the trailer," he said.

Ana didn't even want to hear it. That part of her life was a closed book, and she never wanted to reopen it. Maria could hardly stand to see her precious daughter swallowed up by such bitterness, but there was nothing she could do.

The group drove slowly through the trailer park. Many of the residents recognized Maria, Diego, and Pastor Juan, but who was the big *gringo* in the back seat? *Policia*? Pastor Juan waved to reassure them.

They finally stopped in front of the last trailer. Maria just sat and stared at it for a minute. The weeds had grown up in the yard, and trash had blown in among them. Armando's clothes still hung limply on the line.

"Are you OK?" asked Pastor Juan.

He reached over and took her hand. Poor thing! That little act of compassion made the tears spring to her eyes and roll down her cheeks. She just looked at her pastor.

Finally she took a deep, though ragged, breath and nodded.

"*Vamos*," she said.

The four of them walked slowly to the kitchen door. Maria handed Juan the key and then followed him in. They kicked their shoes off just inside the door and started slowly through the little trailer. It was eerie. No one had been in there since the day Maria and Ana had packed up and left—the day Armando Lopez died.

A shiver ran down Maria's spine, and she again drew a deep breath.

"*Bien...*" she said, shrugging.

They all got to work.

Sam cleaned the kitchen. The trailer was furnished, so he only packed up the food items, wiped down the cabinets and checked the stove and oven. When he got to the refrigerator, he found some things that were still usable, but the leftovers and produce had to be thrown out. Diego worked in the bedroom he and Ana had shared, a curtain providing a little privacy for his sister. Since the clothes and things were already gone, there wasn't much to do, and his cast really didn't hinder him. Pastor Juan cleaned the tiny bathroom and went over the rest of the trailer. Because Maria was an immaculate housekeeper, it didn't take long.

The three of them all finished about the same time and went to Armando and Maria's bedroom to ask what else needed to be done. They found Maria sitting on the edge of the sagging bed beside a cardboard box of Armando's possessions, a piece of notebook paper in her trembling hand. She was as white as a sheet, swaying slightly, as if she were about to pass out.

Pastor Juan rushed in. "Maria, what is it?"

He knelt in front of her, looking earnestly into her face and spoke softly.

"What's wrong?"

Diego sat beside his mother and put his good arm around her. Sam went for a glass of water. Diego shifted so he could help his mother take a sip as Juan took the paper.

"May I read it?" he asked.

It was if she were in a trance, her nod barely perceptible.

Pastor Juan sat on the floor cross-legged. Maria leaned against her son.

What on earth? thought Sam.

Juan, his expression serious, finished scanning the paper and handed it to Diego. As the boy read, the blood drained from his face, as well. He took a drink from his mother's glass. Sam sat beside him and put his arm around him. He didn't have a clue what was going on, but whatever it was, he knew his family was in trouble. He also knew they would tell him when the time was right.

There was a heavy silence.

Finally, Pastor Juan bowed his head. "Father," he prayed quietly in Spanish. "We are frightened and alarmed by this letter. We know that You are our Defender, and so we claim Your protection now. You have promised to work all things together for good for those that love You. We love You, Lord, and we ask that we would recognize the good that this letter will bring. Because of Jesus, we pray. Amen."

It seemed as though they all gathered strength from the silence that followed the prayer.

Maria lifted her head. "*Gracias, Pastor*," she said, smiling shakily.

She stood up, and everyone stood with her.

"I want to go home."

Sam understood. They finished up and loaded the car as quickly as possible. He still had no clue what was on that paper.

The three Mexicans had been talking quietly.

"We will say nothing of this to Ana," Pastor Juan told Sam.

"That's probably a good idea. What about Lynn and me? Is it something we need to know about?"

The pastor consulted with the other two folks in the car for some minutes.

"The paper was a letter. Maria needs to process what it said and talk things over with Diego before she talks to you. It's pretty embarrassing for her. Can you trust us for a while on this?"

"I can," said Sam. "In that case I won't mention it to Lynn, either. She hates being left in the dark about anything."

He smiled at Pastor Juan. "Surely, you understand."

"Oh, I understand," said the pastor, returning Sam's smile. "I was married to a woman exactly like that."

Suddenly, he was sad again.

Sam reached over and squeezed his shoulder. What would my life be like without Lynn? he thought.

No! he admonished himself, don't even go there.

Pastor Juan reached for Maria's hand and held it. He wanted her to know that he was there for her.

Chapter 19

On the way home from church Sunday morning, Sam and Lynn stopped to see Shep. He was getting better and seemed to be a little more alert. He was ecstatic when he saw them, and it broke their hearts to leave him whimpering after them.

Sunday night the family carefully put the *piñata* into the back of the van and everyone buckled up.

The service was as animated as ever. Sam loved it. After church everyone went outside for the *piñata.* Sam watched as a couple of kids tried to break it and then stepped up and volunteered. Blindfolded, broomstick in hand, he started swinging. Every time he came near the *piñata,* the man on the other end of the rope jerked it out of reach.

Of course, Sam hammed it up and the people roared at his antics. Finally, it was someone else's turn and Sam came huffing to his wife's side.

"That's harder than it looks," he said.

A robust young man of about eleven grabbed the stick and submitted to the blindfold. He bowed to the audience and then took a mighty swing, catching the man on the other end of the rope off guard. The *piñata* burst open, spilling its contents everywhere. Kids dove in to get the candy, and Sam dove in with them—the only adult in the middle of the mass of children. Somehow, he came up empty handed except for one little Snickers bar. The adults shook his hand, laughing and making unintelligible remarks. He answered them all in English, having no idea whether he was saying the right thing or not.

Lynn noticed Ana talking with Pastor Juan and both of them looking her way. Wonder what that's all about, she thought.

Together they came to talk to her.

"Ana tells me you play the piano," said Pastor Juan. "Would you consider accompanying the singing whenever you are here?"

She felt honored.

"I would consider it a privilege," she said. "And Ana is learning to play the recorder. Before long she should be able to play in the service also."

"Really? That's terrific!" said Pastor Juan, beaming at the girl. "We'll look forward to hearing both of you."

Again spirits were high in the car. Until they pulled into the driveway. Sam slowed the van to a stop. There in glow of the headlights was his Lexus—with all four tires slashed.

The couple just stared. The family in the back couldn't see what was in front, but they knew something was wrong. Diego undid his seat belt and leaned forward.

"What...?" he asked.

Then he saw the tires and sat back slowly, quietly describing the scene to Maria and Ana.

Sam put the car in park and bowed his head over the steering wheel.

"Lord," he prayed. The others bowed their heads. Diego quietly translated as Sam prayed. "We don't know what's going on here or how we should react to it. Please guide us and give us wisdom. In Your Word You tell us to give thanks for all things, so we are thanking You now for this, another attack. We don't understand it but ask that You use it for Your glory. Protect us, Father, and help us to trust You. For Jesus' sake, amen."

He opened his eyes and turned to the others.

"Let's just go inside and get some supper and go to bed. Whoever did this could still be around to watch what happens. Let's not give him the satisfaction of seeing us upset or afraid."

I wish Shep were here, thought Lynn.

By the time Sam had gotten off the phone with the police, the ladies had finished heating the leftovers. There wasn't much conversation while they ate, cleaned up, and got ready for bed. Sully and Banks came but said an officer would be by in the morning to inspect the car and do a more thorough search for evidence. Sam called their insurance company.

Lynn could hear the Lopez family quietly talking together in Maria's room while she was putting her books by the back door. Diego came out, followed by Maria. They could hear Ana sniffling in the bedroom.

"Sam, Mrs. B," he said somberly, "*Mamita*, she want me talk for you. Say we go trailer tomorrow. The bad things is… because of we. We go. Will be b—"

Sam cut him off. "Ask your mother a question for me, Diego."

The boy nodded.

"If the boys who attacked Diego came after him again in your trailer, what would you do?"

Diego translated and Maria stood silent, tears pooling in her eyes.

"Would you make him move out because you were in danger?"

He waited for the translation and the response. Maria wagged her head and said something indignantly.

"No!" said Diego, echoing her indignation. "I am her son!"

"Right," said Sam. "You are our family now, and families don't abandon each other. We are all in this together, and together we will see it to the end."

He pulled himself to his full 6'3" and put one arm around Maria and the other around Diego. Ana came running out of her room, where she had been eavesdropping, and she and Lynn joined in the group hug.

Again Sam prayed. "Thank You, Father, for bringing us together, even though it was under circumstances we would not have chosen. Again we ask You to use all this for Your glory. In Jesus' name, Amen."

After everyone had gone to bed, Sam and Lynn lay talking in whispers. "Do you remember Fred?" asked Sam.

"Fred? Fred who? Oh, you mean that guy Liz dated a couple of times? Yeah, I remember him. Why?"

"Fred works for the FBI now, and he and I have emailed occasionally. He is their IT person for central Georgia, and he gives seminars for other IT people. He knows that a big part of my job is giving seminars, so he asks for my help sometimes."

"What's an IT person?"

"Information Technology, a fancy term for computer guy."

"OK. And you want to contact him because...?"

"Because hate crimes are Federal offenses. The FBI should have been here to question us by now. That means that somebody somewhere has not contacted them. I don't want to go to the police, because it was possibly somebody in their office that dropped the ball. Makes me wonder if someone on the force is kind of on the side of the bad guys in this."

"Hmm, you may have a point, but I hate to think it might be true. What can we do?"

"I'm going to call Fred in the morning and get his input. He's not an agent, but at least he can tell me who I need to talk to. Now, let's get some sleep."

A while later Lynn felt her husband get out of bed. She thought he was going to the bathroom, but he opened the bedroom door, instead.

"Sam!" she whispered loudly, "What is it?"

"Sh!" he warned.

He silently lifted the gun from the nightstand and tiptoed into the living room. She heard voices and got up to see what was going on.

"You go to bed now. I'll take over. I was getting up to check things, anyway," she heard Sam whisper.

"*Gracias*," whispered Diego. He quietly closed the door to his room.

"Sam?" whispered Lynn.

"It was Diego standing guard. He's been here since we all went to bed. It's my watch now, so go on back to bed. I'll see you in the morning."

How she wished Shep were here to stand guard so the bed wouldn't be cold on her husband's side again.

She managed to fall asleep, and the next thing she knew Sam was shaking her awake.

"Time to get up, Beautiful. The day awaits." He kissed her lightly.

"Now get up so I can sleep in peace. I've got an hour or so to rest before I get up and make a mad dash for the office."

"I'll wake you before I go," she said. "Should I call Pastor Juan about picking up Maria again?"

Sam didn't even hear her.

She went into the kitchen for coffee and found Maria working on breakfast. "Good morning!" said Lynn. "How are you?"

"Fine, tank you," answered Maria, "an' ju?"

The English classes were beginning to have an effect.

"*Muy bien, gracias*," said Lynn, showing off her recently acquired Spanish.

"Do you want to go to Angela's house again today? I can call Pastor Juan, if you like." She was speaking slowly, hoping Maria would understand.

"Jes, I tink jes."

"Uh... I just thought of something. Sam has no way to get to work. Do you think Pastor Juan would take him to town? If not, he can call somebody from his office to pick him up. He will send a wrecker here for his car."

Diego came into the kitchen.

"I think yes," he said. "May I can call?"

"May I call him?" corrected Mrs. B automatically. She tried not to correct the kids much at home. She hated to stay on their case all the time, but sometimes it just popped out.

"Yes," she said, "and ask him to take your mom to Angela's too."

She got ready to go and then woke Sam and told him Pastor Juan would be there in twenty minutes.

"Why?" asked Sam sleepily.

"How soon you forget, my dear. You have no way to work this morning. Remember?"

That woke him up.

He jumped out of bed and hit the shower. Lynn laid out his clothes and got her sweater.

"Bye, Hon," she called through the bathroom door.

He poked his head out, face covered in shaving cream, and kissed her good-bye.

"See you tonight," he said. "I love you!"

"I love you too. Have a great day!" she said, wiping the white lather off her chin.

Just as she was pulling out of the driveway, the police cruiser pulled in.

* * * *

Lynn was standing in her doorway watching the kids hurry by on their way to homeroom. Several of them greeted her as they passed.

"Hi, Mrs. B!"

"Mornin', Mrs. B!"

"How ya doin', Mrs. B?"

"Hey, Mrs. B!"

She returned all their greetings, pleased by their friendliness. The boys who had attacked Diego stopped at their lockers. Daniel had apparently asked for a different locker so that he wouldn't have to be around them so much. Boldly, she walked up to them.

"Hey, y'all! How's it goin'?"

They glanced at each other.

"Uh... hey," said Ben.

"Introduce me to your friend," said Mrs. B indicating the boy she felt had ordered the attack on Diego.

"Uh... this is James... uh... James Flanagan," said Ben.

"Nice to meet you, James. I'm Mrs. Bartholomew, Mrs. B for short."

She stuck out her hand, and the boy had little choice but to shake it.

"How are you liking Bible class?"

James just shrugged and scowled at Jack.

"Jack, I see you have on a basketball jersey."

She addressed the boy whose father had been the most aggressive at the meeting the other day.

"Are you on the team? This is my first year, so I don't know who does what yet."

Again the boys glanced at each other.

"He's our star player. Wouldn' have much of a team 'thout Jack," offered Frank Walenski, looking at the other guys for approval.

"My husband played in high school and college. He's an old guy now, but he still gets around the court pretty well. We have a goal out at our place. Come on out and shoot some hoops with him some day. He'll love it.

"Well, ya'll have to get to class. See you later."

And with that she headed to her room. Was that a motorcycle helmet she had seen in James's locker?

Sitting at her desk, she wondered about the helmet. It was a bright lime green color. Could James be the intruder? He didn't seem the type. Though he was very good at manipulating others to do his dirty work, she figured he was too big a coward to do anything dangerous himself.

After her classes Lynn straightened her room and got everything ready for the next day. Then she went out to the student parking area.

There it was! A recently washed and waxed lime green dirt bike. She walked on by at a pace that would make people think she was walking for her health. The vehicle's color matched the helmet, so she figured she was looking at James Flanagan's bike. Now what?

She looked around as she took another lap. The outside door closest to the student parking area was the one that entered by the teachers' workroom.

She went into the workroom and got a piece of paper out of the copier. She crumpled it up, and then dirtied it with lead shavings from the pencil sharpener and smoothed it back out a little. On her way back out to the parking area, she began picking up trash and had a pretty good armload by the time she got to the bike. She meandered behind it and "accidentally" dropped several pieces. When she picked them back up, one just happened to stay under the tire of a lime green dirt bike.

Rats! Now she would have to stay all day so she could retrieve the evidence. Oh, well, if that paper helped them catch the intruder, then it would be worth a few hours' thumb twiddling. If not… well, she had tried.

Back in her room, she got out her phone. First she called Sam.

"Hey, Hon, got a minute?" she said.

"Hi! What's up?"

"Did you call Fred this morning? What did he say?"

"As a matter of fact, I just got off the phone with him. He said he would contact some agents in our area and they would get right on it. He said they would probably not show up at our door in three-piece suits driving shiny black government-issue cars. They will try to be a little less obvious."

"Ooo, how cloak and dagger!" said Lynn. Then more seriously, "Listen, I might have found something."

She went on to tell about meeting James and seeing the helmet and then finding the bike and placing the paper under the back tire.

"If Sully took tire prints we can compare them, if I actually get some. If he didn't, we need to mention it to the FBI before it rains again."

"Whoa! Just call you Mrs. Holmes, as in Sherlock Holmes! Good job," said Sam. "I'm proud of you."

"I prefer Mrs. Bartholomew, but thank you anyway. I'm gonna call the vet now and check on Shep. I love you. See you tonight."

"Love you too. Bye."

"Wait! One more thing!" she yelled into the phone.

"Ow!" said Sam. "I'm still here."

"Sorry. Did you call somebody to fix your car?"

"Yes, and it should be finished by now. Thank the Lord for good insurance. Four new tires ain't cheap."

"OK, good. Well, I guess that's it."

"You're sure?"

"I'm sure. Bye."

"Bye."

She dug in her purse until she found the vet's card and dialed the phone number. After she had listened to the robot and punched all the right buttons, she finally got a real person.

"Yes, this is Mrs. Bartholomew. Shep, our German Shepherd, was brought in last Tuesday with a broken leg."

"Yes, Mrs. Bartholomew. How can I help you?" said someone in a nasally voice.

"Well, we are down to one car at the moment, so I don't think we'll make it in to visit today. I'm calling to see when you think he'll be ready to come home."

"If you can hold a minute, I'll check," said the voice.

"Thank you."

While on hold, she hummed along with two "oldies but goodies" that she remembered from her high school days before the voice finally came back on the line.

"Sorry for the delay. Shep can go home tomorrow. He will need to be kept quiet for several weeks yet, but being with his family will be good for him. Can you work out the transportation to pick him up tomorrow?"

"We'll do whatever it takes!" said Lynn, elated. "We've really missed him at home and can't wait to get him back. Thank you so much!"

She felt like letting out a whoop but restrained herself. She couldn't wait to share the news with someone, so she called Sam back.

"Shep's coming home tomorrow!" she shouted.

"Lynn, try to save some of my hearing for old age," said her husband patiently. "That's great news. Thank you for calling. Gotta go. Bye."

Next she called Dr. Benjamin's office and went through the same robot routine. She really hated those things. Finally, she got to talk to a human who said her name was Jean. After referring to her calendar, Jean said they had an opening for Diego at 4:00 the next Wednesday.

"That'll be fine. Thank you."

In the middle of last hour Lynn made her way to the teacher's workroom. She had made up some worksheets that needed to be copied. That little chore completed, she "just happened" to be facing the window when the final bell rang.

Students came pouring out of the building like angry bees out of a disturbed hive. She stood waiting while this student got into her car and drove away and that student got onto his bicycle and pedaled for the exit. Finally, James came sauntering toward the green motorcycle, helmet under his arm, backpack slung over one shoulder. He didn't even glance at the paper on the ground as he mounted his bike, backed out and roared away. She pumped her fist in the air like she'd just scored a touchdown, and then quickly looked around to see if anyone had seen her. Fortunately, she was alone in the workroom.

As nonchalantly as she could, Mrs. B walked out of the building toward that white piece of paper shining in the parking lot. She stooped to pick up a candy wrapper, a pop can and a torn piece of notebook paper. When she got to James's parking space, she barely managed to conceal her joy when she saw the perfect tire print on the paper. She carefully picked it up and carried it with the other garbage to her room. The trash went into the trashcan, but she tied *the* paper loosely in a grocery bag.

Once again she called her husband. "Sam," she said excitedly, "the tire print is perfect! Now, what shall I do with it?"

"Actually," he answered quietly, "the agent is here in my office even as we speak."

"Really?" said Lynn a little disappointed. "What happened to the cloak and dagger?"

"Well, you see, this is a consulting firm and he's here for a consultation. Since it's so near the end of the day, I've invited him over for supper. Ordinarily, I would take him out, but since Maria is such a great cook, I've asked him over and we can finish our conversation at home."

"Well, guess you can't get much more clandestine than that, can you? Do you think you could ride with him? I'll pick up Maria and see if she needs anything at The Store before we come home."

"The tire place already said they'd deliver my car here."

"Terrific! See you at home."

Chapter 20

When she called Pastor Juan to find out where Angela lived, she discovered that he was already there to pick up Maria.

"My husband just called and said he's bringing a client home for supper, and he's promised him some of Maria's marvelous Mexican food. Maybe you could take her to The Store and I could meet her there, get whatever she needs for tonight, and then take her on home."

Pastor Juan laughed. "Sounds like the name of a restaurant, 'Maria's Marvelous Mexican.' Hang on a second."

She could hear him talking things over with Maria.

"That's fine. We'll be there in a few minutes."

Lynn already had a shopping cart half full when Maria found her in the produce section. As they walked quickly from aisle to aisle, Lynn could feel the eyes of other shoppers on them. She could tell that Maria was aware of their stares, as well. Let 'em look, she thought. Maybe they would see that friendship comes in living color.

Of course, the checkout line was crawling, but they eventually got through, loaded the car, and headed home. When they got there, they saw two nervous teenagers sitting on the porch. It had never occurred to anyone to give the kids a house key because someone was always at home. Lynn had known they were cutting it close, but she really had expected to beat the bus home. She was not pleased with herself for leaving them in harm's way.

"I am so sorry, guys! I thought we would get here before the bus."

"No problem," said Diego, but his relief was obvious.

Maria told the kids about Sam's client and the supper plans. Diego was exhausted after standing guard last night and then a full day of school, so he went to bed. Maria and

Ana got to work in the kitchen as soon as the groceries were unpacked, and Lynn set about straightening the house in preparation for their guest. Sam came home, changed and went outside to pump up the basketball and make sure there was plenty of soda in the outside fridge.

A little after six a bright copper-colored PT Cruiser pulled into the driveway. A stocky forty-something man got out and waved to Sam. He looked like he could have been a Marine drill sergeant. His cargo pants and tennis shoes attested to the fact that Sam had told him to dress casually. A light windbreaker was open over a red ITALY T-shirt.

"Cisco," called Sam coming across the yard. "So good to see you, my friend. Let me introduce everyone. This is my wife Lynn," he said as he slipped his arm around her waist.

Maria and Ana were peeking out the back door.

"And this is Maria and her daughter Ana. And this is... Where's Diego?"

"He's resting," said Lynn.

"Oh, well, you'll meet him later. This is Francisco Bertonelli, everyone."

"Nice to meet you," said the newcomer to Lynn and, "*Mucho gusto*," to Maria and Ana. "My mother is Mexican and my father is Italian, thus the mixture of names. Just call me Cisco."

"Nice to meet you, Cisco. Won't you come in?"

"I'd like to show him around first, if you don't mind, Lynn. We don't want nightfall to catch us before he gets a chance to see the place. OK?"

"Sure! Y'all go ahead. I'll just help Maria get supper ready. After we eat, you two can go somewhere and talk shop."

The men ambled off in the direction of the barn and then disappeared into the woods by the creek. In a little while they were back. Cisco stopped at the car to get his briefcase.

"You've still got about twenty minutes," said Lynn.

"Good," said Sam. "After a glass of tea, let's see how good you are on the court."

"You're on," said Cisco. "Just let me go inside and empty my pockets."

Sam showed Cisco to the bedroom. When Lynn brought the men their tea, she noticed that Cisco was putting several zip-lock bags into his briefcase, along with his usual pocket stuff. He closed and latched the case before he took a long drink from his glass. "Hits the spot! Thanks!"

While the men played basketball, the ladies put the finishing touches on the meal. How Maria came up with such a grand feast in such a short time was beyond Lynn Bartholomew. Diego woke up and went outside to wistfully watch the men play. Every once in a while he would stoop to pick up a loose ball and throw it back in with his good arm.

When everything was on the table, Lynn called them. She showed Cisco the bathroom where he could wash up.

"Wow!" he said on his way through the kitchen. "It smells just like my mama's been cooking in here!" He said something to Maria in Spanish, and she gave him a wide smile.

"It's not fair," grumbled Sam as he shuffled dejectedly to the bathroom. "They have a full-sized gym at his office."

Uh-oh, thought Lynn. Somebody got beat.

After they had distributed themselves around the table, Sam explained, "It's our custom to thank the Lord for our food before every meal."

They all joined hands and he asked the blessing. When they had finally finished passing the refried beans, rice, Mexican spiced minute steaks and *tortillas*, they dug in. Of course, the hot sauce was on the table for anyone who wanted a little more fire.

At first Sam tried to make small talk, waiting for Cisco to reveal who he really was. Cisco was completely at ease conversing with the Lopez family in Spanish, and every now and then they would all burst out laughing at some joke he had told or comment he had made. Sam and Lynn looked at each other, feeling left out. This must be how Maria feels a lot, thought Lynn.

As darkness began to fall, Lynn closed the drapes and blinds in the house like she did every night. When he was sure no one could see in, their visitor finally began to talk seriously with the Lopez family. He tried to keep everything low-key, but Lynn could see the surprise on their faces when he told them he was an FBI agent.

When Cisco got up to get his briefcase, Lynn suggested they adjourn to the living room where it was a little more comfortable. She and Sam cleared the table, as quietly as possible. Cisco asked a lot of questions and recorded everything on his pocket device as the others told their story.

The Bartholomews were sitting at the island in the kitchen waiting their turn to be interviewed. They overheard Cisco's tone change when he asked one more question. Silence. Lynn looked up to see Maria twisting her hands in her lap. Diego reached over his sister and held his mother's hands. He spoke softly to her, and she got up and left the room. Lynn glanced at her husband, who just shrugged.

When Maria returned, she handed a piece of folded notebook paper to Cisco. He opened it and read silently for a minute. Not a word was spoken. Ana looked questioningly from her mother to Diego and back to her mother. Sam put down his coffee cup and sat up straight on his stool.

"I've seen that paper," he whispered to his wife, "but I don't know what's on it. Maria found it when we were cleaning out the trailer. She and Diego were really upset by it."

When he had finished reading, Cisco leaned back in his chair and just looked at the family. "Have you shown this to Sam and Lynn?" he asked.

"No," Diego answered. Maria just looked at the hands twisting in her lap as if they weren't her own.

"What?" said Ana, fear showing on her face.

"Listen," said Cisco, "I'm going to discuss this with Sam right now. You take Ana in the other room and explain it to her."

Cisco came into the kitchen and took the mug Lynn offered him. He sat on the stool opposite them and ran his hands over his crew cut.

"I need to question you about the hate crimes, but right now we need to deal with this."

He showed them what looked like a letter written in dull pencil on a dirty piece of notebook paper. In Spanish.

"It's from Armando Lopez's brothers in Mexico. It's a warning. Basically it says that if Armando ever stops running their drugs, he's dead. Then it says not only will he die, but they will kill his family as well. It also says that if the Cartel ever catches any of them in Mexico again for any reason, they will be killed."

Good grief! thought Lynn. No wonder Maria was wringing her hands. Her heart went out to the family once again. Was there no end?

"Lynn, Sam, did you know they were illegal when you took them in?"

"I guess we've taken kind of a 'don't ask, don't tell' attitude. From the circumstances, we figured they might be, but..."

"Well, they are. And you're guilty of harboring them." He ran his hand through his hair again.

"Ho, boy," said Sam. He also ran his hands through his hair.

Why do men do that when they think? Lynn asked herself.

"To be honest, I don't know that it would have made much difference. They were alone and destitute, Cisco. There was nowhere for them to go, and we had no way of knowing what Armando would do when he discovered them gone."

He took a breath. "And according to that letter, Mexico is not an option."

"Then when Diego got out of the hospital," continued Lynn, "he had to have a place to recuperate. What else could we have done?"

"Well," said Cisco, "now that you do know, what're you going to do?"

"I have to admit that I've wondered," said Sam, "so I've done some research on the Internet. I've found cases where the authorities allowed students who are already enrolled in school to complete the year."

"That may be true, but aside from that, the only way for them to become legal is to return to Mexico and go through the proper channels. Sometimes it takes up to ten years, I think.

"Ten years!" the Bartholomews exclaimed as one.

"What about that DACA thing that everybody's talking about for kids who came into the country illegally?"

"I think the Lopezes came in too late to be eligible for that," replied Cisco, his forheard wrinkled in thought.

"What if Maria were to marry an American?" asked Lynn.

"Look, this is not my area. I catch bad guys. You'll have to call in the paper pushers to sort all this stuff out. All I know is that now I'm in the soup. If I fail to report this to my superiors, I'm in trouble. If I report it, you could be in trouble, and who knows what will happen to the Lopezes."

He held his head in his hands.

"Can you turn in an explanation or appeal along with your report?" asked Sam. "I can write it so it will come from us instead of you, if you like."

Cisco considered for a moment, and then shrugged and said, "Don't know if it'll work or not, but it's better than nothing."

"Good! While I'm composing the appeal and Cisco's translating the letter, Lynn, why don't you get us another round of dessert?"

Both men went to get their laptops.

"Should we attach a copy of the letter with translation and maybe a picture of Diego in his cast?" asked Lynn as she was getting out the dishes to serve the mousse Maria had made.

"Go for it," said Cisco. "Can't hurt."

He snapped his fingers.

"Stan!" he exclaimed.

He took out one of his business cards and wrote a name on the back.

"Call Immigration and ask for this guy. Give him my name. Maybe he can tell you what to do. We'll make a copy of the letter and your appeal to give him."

"Thanks!" said Sam. "At least it's a place to start."

The Lopez family came out of the bedroom. Ana's eyes were red, and she was trembling. Cisco explained what was going on. They all breathed a sigh of relief that they wouldn't have to go—right then, anyway.

Finally, Cisco got around to interviewing Lynn about the attacks. She began with the first day of school and told everything she could remember. Cisco questioned her about a few of the details, but for the most part, he just listened. She showed him the tire track she had gotten at school. He put it in a zip-lock bag and labeled it. Sam really couldn't add much since he had come on the scene only a few days ago, but he told all that had happened since then.

"I do know it was a two-stroke engine," said Sam.

"Good," said Cisco. "With tire tracks and knowing it isn't a Honda, the field is considerably narrowed.

"How on earth can you know all that?" asked Lynn.

"Hondas are all four-strokes. The bike I heard Monday night was a two-stroke. The sounds are very different."

"Oh," said Lynn, knowing nothing more than she did a minute ago.

"You didn't by any chance see what kind of bike that kid has, did you?" asked Cisco.

"Uh… no," said Lynn, "but I can probably check tomorrow."

"We'll compare the tracks from here with the ones you got at school. That should tell us a lot."

Cisco reloaded his briefcase and prepared to leave, carefully including the plastic bags of evidence.

"I'll give all this information to our field agents and find the right person to receive your appeal. We'll be watching your place, but you'll never see us, and hopefully, neither will the intruder. His attacks seem to be spaced about four or five days apart, so we should have a little time to get organized. Your dog comes home tomorrow, is that right?"

"Yes, I'll pick him up around lunch time. Maria will go to her friend's house again tomorrow, but after that she'll be here with Shep. Is that all right? He won't be in any shape to protect her if anything happens."

"That sounds fine. Our men should be on the scene shortly. I'm not even going to mention them to the Lopez family, but you might want to tell the pastor that you won't be needing the men from the church anymore. Tell him the police are trying to catch the guy and one of his men might get in the way or be mistaken for the intruder."

Only later did Lynn realize that nothing had been said about the FBI receiving any report of the incidents from the police.

As she was turning down the bed, she stopped, "Sam, did I do the right thing in bringing Maria and the kids here? I wondered about their status but never asked. Now…"

"I know. I've been thinking the same thing. We've always believed in supporting the laws of our land. Been pretty adamant about people who cross the borders illegally. We even voted for David Todd in the congressional race in our district because of his stand on illegal aliens." He climbed into bed.

"The only scriptural principles that I know of that apply here would be the commands to feed the hungry and care for the poor and the widows and orphans. The Lopezes certainly fit those criteria."

"Well, like I told our Sunday school class, I don't believe God is finished with this situation yet."

They lay in silence for a minute.

Sam took her hand. "Let's give it to the Lord and ask Him to show us step by step what to do. Like we told Cisco, I'm not sure it would have made any difference if we had known. They were alone and destitute, and it was an urgent situation. We did what we had to do as followers of Christ, and now we are dealing with the authorities."

Chapter 21

Tuesday. English class. Bible class. Shep.

What was she forgetting? Oh, yeah, she was supposed to try to see what kind of bike James had. How on earth was she supposed to do it? If she was out there picking up trash again, someone was going to get the idea she was obsessive-compulsive or something.

Rats! Faculty meeting! She'd have to make another trip to school after she brought Shep home. At least she hadn't forgotten it entirely.

She decided to park near the student parking lot and go in the door by the teachers' workroom. She got all her stuff and opened the door to the carport. It was pouring down rain! Double Rats! Oh, well, she'd been wet before. She wouldn't melt between the parking lot and the school.

Wait a minute—if it was raining this hard, who would ride a motorcycle to school? Nobody. She would just have to wait until another day. Triple Rats!

She managed to stay calm enough during first and second hour, but Bible class was another story. Shep was coming home today! You'd think she was expecting the queen, for heaven's sake.

She got set up in the music room and greeted the students happily as they came in. After everyone was settled, she began.

"Who can tell me why Shep was here a couple of weeks ago?" she waited, hoping it wouldn't take long because she had a lot to cover.

"Everything reproduces its own kind," said several students more or less together.

"Good! Will Shep's wife ever in her whole life give birth to a duck?"

"NO!" came the emphatic reply, accompanied with guffaws and giggles.

"No way," said the teacher. "Mrs. Shep can only have a _____. Right! A dog or puppy. Everything reproduces its own kind.

"Returning to what happened during the week of creation. We stopped in the middle of the sixth day of the week when God created the land animals. Let's look at Genesis 1:26-28."

Here she flashed the verses in English and Spanish side by side on the screen and read them out loud.

"God's most important creation is Man—us. More detail about the creation of the first man is given in chapter 2, along with the account of the first woman. God named the first man Adam, and then Adam named the first woman Eve. God put the man and the woman in the Garden of Eden to live. This garden was a perfect place where Adam and Eve had everything they needed provided by God Himself. There was no worry or fear of any kind. No arguments, no stress—"

"No homework!" someone yelled. Laughter filled the room. Somebody hit the cymbal with a wayward drumstick that hadn't been put away. More laughter.

"You got it. Not even any school!" Cheers and whistles. The cymbal.

"And best of all, Adam and Eve had perfect communion with God Himself. Can you imagine? Walking and talking with *GOD*? Amazing!

"Let's look at Genesis chapter 2, verse 16. God says that He had given them every plant in the garden for food. Verse 17 is a continuation of verse 16."

She asked Antonio to read them in Spanish, and then she read the verses aloud in English. "'And the LORD God commanded the man, saying, Of every tree of the garden thou mayest freely eat: But of the tree of the knowledge of good and evil, thou shalt not eat of it: for in the day that thou eatest thereof thou shalt surely die.'

"God gave only one rule to Adam and Eve. What would your life be with only one rule?"

General mumbling.

"God placed two important trees in the middle of the Garden of Eden—the Tree of Life and the Tree of the Knowledge of Good and Evil. The Tree of Life was not forbidden to them at that time, but the Tree of the Knowledge of Good and Evil was. That was the only rule: don't eat of the Tree of the Knowledge of Good and Evil. Why do you think that was?"

She waited.

Finally Greg guessed, "Because it was poison?"

"Good guess, but no star on your chart. Anyone else?"

Again she waited.

"Because God's a bully!" James Flanagan snorted. Jack Barrett snickered.

"You have a motorcycle, right, James?"

For a split second, surprise and a little fear registered in James's eyes. Then they narrowed.

"Yeah, so?"

"Do you like your bike?"

"Of course," he said sarcastically.

"Do you put an energy drink in your bike to make it run better?"

James rolled his eyes. "Of course not! That's stupid."

"Why?"

"'Cause it'd mess it up!" He was getting a little frustrated with the line of questioning.

"That's exactly right, James.

"God loved His most important creation, and He didn't want them to know about anything bad. He knew it would mess them up. For that reason He prohibited them from eating of that particular tree. Remember, they lived in a perfect environment with no problems of any kind: no stealing, no murder, no rape…"

James started and turned white. His face hardened like flint.

She knew she had hit a nerve, but didn't know which one. She continued without a break.

"… no families arguing, no abuse, no parents abandoning their children…"

Jack's face was a carbon copy of James's—with an added dimension of deep pain and sadness. A variety of emotions registered on some of the other kids' faces.

Again she kept going.

"… no street fighting, nobody going hungry, no racism, no war. It was perfect, and God wanted them never to experience any of those things."

She pointed to verse 17 on the screen.

"What does God say would happen to Adam and Eve if they ate of the Tree of the Knowledge of Good and Evil?"

"They would die," said Donna.

"Right. God told them they would die if they disobeyed Him and ate of the Tree. We'll come back to that.

"Now, at some point, and the Bible does not specify when, God created millions of spirit beings to be His messengers and servants. Today we call these spirits angels. The chief of these beings was a beautiful and intelligent angel named Lucifer.

"The problem with Lucifer was his pride. The book of Isaiah tells us that he wanted to be like God. He wanted to be the supreme and sovereign one that everyone worshiped. He led a rebellion in Heaven to try and take over the throne and persuaded multitudes of angels to rebel with him. Of course, the rebellion failed because God *is* supreme, sovereign and all-powerful. God threw Lucifer and all his followers out of Heaven. Today Lucifer is known as Satan, and the angels that rebelled with him are called demons."

She waited to be sure they were absorbing what she was saying.

"Now, Satan knows that he has no hope of defeating the truly supreme and sovereign God, so he does everything he can to destroy God's most important creation, us. Satan hates everyone in this room and will stop at nothing to destroy us because he knows that is the only way to hurt the almighty God.

"Think about it. When you see beer commercials on TV, do they ever show people splattered all over the road because a drunk driver hit some car? Of course not. How many of you have been offered drugs here in this school?"

About half the hands went up, and she knew there were probably more that didn't want to admit it.

"Did the people offering them to you tell of the dangers or remind you of the consequences if you were caught?"

Guffaws and snorts.

"Why not?"

"They wanted us to buy their stuff," someone said.

"Right. They told you it would make you feel good, it would be fun, everybody's doing it, etc., etc. They weren't about to endanger their sale by telling you that it could ruin your life.

"That's called temptation, and Satan and the demons are pros. They never make rebellion against your parents appear abominable in the sight of a holy God or sex outside of marriage seem wrong. Satan might make you think that cheating is the only way to stay on the football team.

"Temptation comes from many different sources. Your friends can tempt you: 'just gimme the answers; she won't know' or 'I love you and I want you.' Things on TV can cause you to have improper thoughts or even tempt you to plan something like what you saw. Anybody been there or done that?"

A few hands went up slightly.

"The Internet. Now, I don't have to tell you that pornography is wrong. God gave you a conscience for that. But it's a huge temptation, is it not?"

Nobody moved.

"Horoscopes, fortune tellers, and Ouija boards are all Satan's attempt to get you to trust in something besides God for your future, even if they seem harmless.

"Temptation is all around us. Even billboards or commercials on TV use sex to sell their product, no matter what it is.

"Sometimes Satan tempts us to doubt what the Bible says. Maybe you've been questioning if the Bible account of creation is true or if evolution is the way it happened. Guess where those questions come from."

Time was running out. She hurried on.

"Satan and the demons can take on different forms. Since they're spirits, they don't have a body of their own and either take over the body of someone or something else or appear as someone who has died, or even come up with a monster-like form in your dreams or something. They're extremely tricky. Even the picture of Satan as a little red guy with horns and a pokey tail causes people to take him lightly or to believe that spiritual things are a big joke.

"Just one more reminder before the bell: God loves every single one of us. Satan, on the other hand, hates—no, despises—every single one of us. Think about that."

Finally, it was time to pick up Shep. Before she saw him, Lynn went to the business office to settle the bill. When she looked at the total, she about fell over. She knew it was going to cost a lot, but this was ridiculous.

"Is that negotiable?" she asked.

"Sure," said the redhead, owner of the nasally voice on the phone, "we can keep your dog and continue to charge the daily room and board until someone adopts him." She wasn't smiling.

Lynn gulped and asked meekly, "Do you take checks?"

"Of course," said Red, "Just make it out to Spencer Veterinary Clinic."

Lynn wrote the check with the sincere hope that the joy of seeing Shep well again would be worth it.

One of the vet's assistants brought him to the waiting room. Lynn's heart broke when she saw her dog hobbling on three legs with the broken one wrapped tightly in a pressure bandage. But when she saw the happiness and love in his eyes at seeing her, she simply melted into tears and sank to the floor to hug him. Without a doubt, it *was* worth it.

Lynn received the care instructions and asked almost the same questions she'd asked when Diego was released from the hospital. Now the two of them could recover together.

When they got home, Shep strained at the leash as Lynn tried to take him inside.

"OK. Let's go out in the yard for a while, but no running or chasing rabbits, doctor's orders."

They walked around for a few minutes, Shep exulting in the familiar smells he had missed so much. She let him roll in the grass as much as he was able and she could tell that a good head-to-tail shake made him feel better, in spite of the fact that it probably hurt his leg. But he was tiring, so she led him to the water bowl and then to the house. He settled onto his blanket by her bed, sighed a contented doggie sigh, and went to sleep. Man, it was good to see him in his rightful place again!

When the kids got home, Lynn met them at the door.

"Shep's home."

Before she could say more, Ana squealed, dropped her backpack in the middle of the floor and pushed past her on the way to the bedroom.

She never made it. The girl was attacked in the kitchen by a delirious Shep, who did his best to greet his Ana properly, just about knocking her over. After Ana, Shep danced over to Diego and greeted him a little more soberly.

It was as if he was saying, "See, we're in the same boat now."

Diego knelt and gave the dog a one-armed hug, which was a feat because Shep was wagging everything but his splinted leg.

Diego went to lie down and Ana took her books into the living room to do her homework. She sat on the floor, and Shep lay down practically in her lap. She read her history book with her hand on his neck.

Lynn tiptoed to the desk to retrieve the camera and take advantage of the Kodak moment.

Yikes! Faculty meeting! She had forgotten all about it.

"Sheila," she said when the secretary answered the phone. "This is Lynn Bartholomew. Has Mr. Cline already gone to staff meeting?"

"Hi! Yes, where are you?"

"I just brought our dog home from the vet's, and I simply forgot all about faculty meeting. Would you pass along my apology to Mr. Cline? I'll—"

"Uh-uh," said Sheila. "I have a hard and fast rule. I don't pass along kisses, hugs or apologies. Sorry."

"Oh. Well, OK. Guess I'll just talk to him tomorrow. Thanks."

The next morning, Lynn sat in the car after Diego and Ana went into the school. She watched James arrive, park his bike and disappear into the crowd of students entering the building. When she got out, she left her book bag on the seat and took several pictures of the school with her phone. One of those pictures just "happened" to show a shiny lime green dirt bike. Then she collected her stuff and went in the door by the teachers' workroom.

By the time she reached her room, she had only a couple of minutes before her first hour class. She texted Sam: Kawasaki, and sent him the picture.

Lynn stayed at school until the beginning of last hour. Then Ana and Diego met her at the office and signed out. They picked up Maria and headed to Dr. Benjamin's office, where they flipped through outdated magazines or fidgeted in the waiting room until they were at last ushered into the inner sanctum.

The nurse took Diego's vitals and asked all the appropriate questions, and then they waited some more. Someone came and took him to get his arm x-rayed. The ladies waited. The same someone brought him back. And they waited. Diego didn't look very comfortable on the examining table, but there he had to stay. There were two chairs in the room, one for the doctor and one for a visitor. Lynn sat in Dr. Benjamin's chair, Maria got the other, and Ana had to stand. Lynn began to doze in the close room. When Dr. Benjamin opened the door, she jumped up like she'd sat on a tack. The sudden burst of laughter bounced off the walls in the small examination room.

"You're fine," said Dr. Benjamin. "Stay where you are."

He shook everyone's hand and stuck the x-rays on the lighted board. They all crowded around to look. The pins were very obvious, and he pointed out the other breaks that were healing nicely on their own.

Dr. Benjamin was pleased with Diego's progress, but the others were sobered by what they saw. How could a father do that to his son? Dr. Benjamin noticed that the atmosphere in the room had suddenly changed.

"Listen, folks," he said. Diego translated. "I see cases like this and even worse every day. It's terrible, but we must not focus on the past. We can't do anything about that. We must focus on the future and on healing."

He looked from one to the other.

Diego was the first to speak. "I… yes… Doctor. Thank you. I forgive my father, and I thank you of help me."

A shocked Ana looked at Diego and then bolted from the room in tears. Poor thing. She was obviously having a harder time getting past the years of abuse.

"Let her grieve," said Dr. Benjamin. "She'll come around in time."

"Come around?" asked Diego.

Lynn explained that it meant that Ana would eventually be OK and forgive her father.

"When I can get off the cast?" asked Diego.

Dr. Benjamin chuckled at his mixed up syntax and said, "Let's give it three more weeks. The bones should be knit as good as new by then, and you can begin therapy to retrain and strengthen the muscles."

He started for the door. "Any more questions?"

"Just one," said Lynn. "Could you and your family come for supper Friday night?"

"Not Fridays. We're Jewish and our Sabbath begins on Friday night."

"When is it over?"

"At sundown on Saturday night. We could come then, if you like."

"Could we make it a week from Saturday? We have a big group coming this weekend."

The doctor wrote something on his prescription pad.

"Here's my home phone number. I'll talk to my wife tonight, and tomorrow maybe you can give her a call and set something up. Whenever we come, make twice as much as you think we'll eat. I have a teenage son with a hollow leg."

"Seth! I almost didn't recognize him. He's changed a lot since kindergarten."

"Yes," said the doctor. "He tells me about Bible class. Likes it a lot."

He scribbled something in Diego's folder.

"See you in three weeks to remove the cast. You can make an appointment on the way out."

Chapter 22

Everyone at the Bartholomews' house was excited about the Hispanic youth group's visit. They woke up early Saturday morning to finish getting things ready.

Rain. Not just rain, but thunder and lightning and rain. Kids can play in the rain, but not in this, thought Lynn. They listened to the weather forecast—thunderstorms all day.

When there was a break in the lightning, Sam called Pastor Juan.

"Right," he said. "I'm really sorry... OK, let's plan on that, then. Yes, two weeks from today."

They hung up and Sam turned to face his disappointed family.

"Last one back in bed is a rotten egg," he said racing for the bedroom. The Lopez family just stood there watching him.

"What he say?" asked Ana.

Lynn laughed. "Another pesky idiomatic expression. If you suddenly decide to race a group of people to do something, you challenge them by saying that the last one to complete whatever it is will stink... smell... like a rotten egg... uh... an egg that is too old... a bad egg."

She received three blank stares in return. Oh my.

"Sam was saying that since no one is coming today, we could all go back to bed. He challenged us to race him and said the last one in bed was a rotten egg. Understand?"

Nothing.

"Sam want we go bed, yes?" asked Diego.

"You don't have to, but since our work is all done, we could. You can do what you like. Sam chose to go to bed. Understand?"

Diego nodded a little uncertainly but explained to the others what he thought she meant.

Maria said something. Ana translated. "*Mamita*, she say you have... how you say... machine for...?" Here she made motions like she was using a needle and thread.

"A sewing machine!" supplied Lynn. "I do, but it hasn't been used in years. It's a little old portable. Where can we set it up?"

Was there anything this lady couldn't do?

"Ana, I'll need your help, since Sam's already sawing logs... uh... already asleep." No more idioms this morning, thank you.

Ana and Lynn made their way to the attic. Lynn moved some boxes and found what she wanted. It was dirty and maybe a little rusty, but she thought it would work. She and Ana hauled the old fashioned metal typing table down to the kitchen. She showed it to Maria, oiled the extension arms on both sides and left it for Maria to clean up.

Where on earth had she seen the sewing machine last? She had moved it around for years and couldn't remember where she had hidden it the last time. Would it still work?

Only one thing to do—start hunting. She began with Diego's closet. That sounded logical. Nope. She was pretty sure it wasn't in Ana and Maria's, but she searched there anyway. Nope. She didn't want to disturb Sam, so she went to the attic again. Ana went along to help but didn't really know what she was looking for. They shifted things around under the roar of rain pounding the roof directly above them.

Suddenly a disheveled gray head appeared at the top of the attic stairs.

"What in the world are you gals doing up here?" asked Sam huskily.

"Oh, no! I'm so sorry. We didn't mean to wake you!"

"It's OK, but tell me what you're looking for." Huge yawn.

"The sewing machine." She explained Maria's request and that they were going to use the old typewriter table.

"The sewing machine is on the shelf in the back of our closet," said Sam. "I put it there myself during your last Great Reorganization."

"Oh... yeah. Sorry."

"Forgiven. Now come on down and I'll get it for you."

A great clap of thunder crashed just over their heads.

"That was close!" said Sam. "We need to get downstairs and make sure all the emergency supplies are in place. We may need them before this day is over."

Middle Georgia has tornadoes, but there had been nothing in the forecast about that.

They climbed down and closed the retractable stairs as the thunder sounded again. Sam went to get the sewing machine while Lynn went to get the emergency kit out of the pantry. Bottled water, blankets, snack bars, flashlights, etc. were all there, but she began to put more of everything together just in case. It wasn't just the two of them anymore and she wanted to be ready. She asked Maria to cook whatever she was going to cook for that day and the next because they might lose power at any moment. Maria got to work.

There was a tiny storm cellar, but no one had been down there in ages.

Dog food! She couldn't believe she had almost forgotten Shep. He was always nervous during storms and would probably be even worse with a bum leg. When she went to check on him, Ana was already on the floor with him.

"Thank you, Ana. He hates storms."

"I too," said Ana. She was getting as much comfort from the dog as he was from her.

"We'll be fine," said Lynn. Reaching down, she squeezed Ana's shoulder with one hand and gave her dog a quick scratch behind the ear with the other.

The day slowly passed as each member of the household did whatever came to mind. The kids did their homework and practiced their instruments. Poor Shep. This time he couldn't escape the trumpet-recorder duo—none of them could. Lynn worked on her English, Sunday school, and Bible class lessons. Sam worked on the material for training the new employee. Maria cooked. It was almost dark when the storm finally blew itself out. Thankfully, they hadn't lost power, so all the emergency stuff went back into the pantry.

After supper Maria got the sewing machine set up in a corner of the dining room.

"Is OK?" she asked. She was losing her shyness, at least around the family.

"That's exactly where I used to put it," said Lynn. "There's lots of light there."

They tried the machine. It definitely needed oiling, but Sam quickly took care of that. Lynn pulled out the jumbled sewing basket that had not been touched in a very long time, except for occasional mending. They found some scraps of material and Maria went to work.

Lynn got out some board games, and the Bartholomews, Diego and Ana played everything but Scrabble all evening. They invited Maria to join them, but she preferred to sew. By bedtime, she had finished a new book bag for Lynn.

"Why, Maria, that is the cutest thing I have ever seen!" exclaimed Lynn when Maria gave it to her. "And it's really strong! I'm going to show this off at school and see if some of the other teachers want to order some. How much would you charge to make them?"

She was still examining the bag and found a cell phone pocket, places for pens, pencils or other things that migrated into women's purses and even a clip for keys. There was a zippered place for money. Maria had thought of everything, and she had used things like sequins and beads and odd buttons that had been rattling around in the bottom of the sewing basket for centuries. How on earth had she come up with something so cute and useful out of scraps?

"You're amazing!" said Lynn, giving her a hug.

Sam and Diego were mumbling over in the corner. The two had a calculator between them and were scribbling on a piece of paper.

"I think $20 should cover the materials and labor," said Sam.

"No way!" said Lynn indignantly. "These are one-of-a-kind handmade creations, and people will pay for that. I'd say a minimum of $35-40, and that includes a 'Made Especially for You' tag!"

* * * *

After her second hour class on Tuesday, Mrs. B drove quickly to the fruit stand and bought more than a bushel of beautiful apples. Then she pulled over to the side of the road and broke off a tree branch about a yard long.

With the help of the kitchen ladies, she hurriedly washed all the apples, grabbed some napkins and got to the music room just as the band kids were putting their instruments away. She stationed two kids by the door with apples and napkins, and everyone who entered got one of each. Then she got the computer set up. Thank the Lord Sam was home to help with her Power Point preparation now.

"Don't eat your apples yet," she admonished as the students took their places. This group hadn't had lunch yet, and those apples were oh, so tempting! She could see some of them smelling or even licking them.

She did a rapid-fire review of the last week's lessons. "Where did Adam and Eve live?"

"Good! The Garden of Eden. What kind of place was it?"

"Perfect. What did they eat?"

"Right, God said they could eat of every tree except one, the Tree of the Knowledge of Good and Evil. Why couldn't they eat of it?"

"Right again. God loved them and didn't want them to know about anything bad. What would be the consequence if they disobeyed God?"

"Yes. They would die.

"Look at Genesis chapter 3, verse 1." Then she read from the screen, "'Now the serpent was more subtil than any beast of the field which the Lord God had made...'" She continued the reading to verse 4. "'And the serpent said unto the woman, ye shall not surely die.'" She paused.

"What was the serpent calling God here?" No response. "Come on, if you say something and I say that's not true, I'm calling you a ___. What?" Still no response.

"Greg, what's your name?"

He looked like he wasn't following but finally said with a shrug, "Greg."

"No, it's not."

Everyone looked startled.

"What did I just call Greg?"

"A liar!" someone called out.

"Yes! The serpent was calling God a liar. Does God lie?"

"No!" they answered almost in unison.

"Correct. Remember, God is holy. That means perfect, without wrong, without sin, and everything He does is perfect. God can't lie because He's God. If He said they were going to die, they were going to die. Period." She put verse 5 on the screen.

"Verse 5 is really interesting. 'For God doth know that in the day ye eat thereof, then your eyes shall be opened, and ye shall be as gods, knowing good and evil.'

"In the first place, God never wanted them to know evil, so Satan was using the serpent to make something bad look good. He's a pro at that, you know. What does the phrase before that say?"

"And ye shall be as gods," the kids read.

"What did Satan want when he rebelled against God?" She waited for their response. "Exactly. He wanted to be like God.

"Now, was it possible for Satan to offer that to Eve if he hadn't been able to get it himself with a multitude of angels backing him up?"

"No way," someone said.

"This just emphasizes that Satan is a liar and will use every trick in the book to trip us up.

"Now, as we continue, you may eat your apples."

The kids all looked at each other, shrugged, and then one by one bit into their apples. Mrs. B continued the lesson to the sounds of munching.

"And now we come to the saddest verse in the Bible, Genesis 3:6." She read just the last part. "'She took of the fruit thereof, and did eat, and gave also unto her husband with her, and he did eat.' What fruit did they eat?"

"An apple!" most of the kids responded.

"Really, is it a sin to eat an apple? Did God prohibit them from eating apples? If eating an apple is a sin, then I just made all of you sin because I told you to eat an apple."

Some of the kids stopped mid-bite.

"No. He said they could eat of any fruit, including apples, except the fruit of the Tree of the Knowledge of Good and Evil. We don't have that tree anymore. We have to be careful that when we read the Bible we pay attention to what it says, not what some cartoon or book or tradition says."

She was almost out of time.

"What did God say would happen to them if they ate the fruit?"

"They would die," answered several students.

"But they didn't," said Greg.

"Look at this branch," she said, holding up the one she had broken off earlier. "Is it alive or dead?"

"Alive," most of them responded.

"Really? It looks alive, but tomorrow will it still look like this?"

"Dead!" called out some of the kids, quickly changing their minds.

"Actually, you're right. It is already dead because it has been separated from its source of life. It has the appearance of life because the leaves are still fresh and green, but there is no way that it could be alive. Adam and Eve still had the appearance of life, but they were already dead."

The bell rang.

Friday after third hour she went to the office to turn in her lesson plans for next week. When she got back to her room, she found a folded note on her desk.

"Don't use your back door," it read. There was a skull and crossbones on the other side of the fold.

What on earth? At any other time in her life she would have taken it as some student messing with her, but in light of all that had gone on recently, she wasn't taking any chances.

"Sam," she said when her husband answered the phone, "I think we have a problem."

She told him about the note. "We need to get either Juan or Cisco to call Maria and tell her to use the front door."

"Or not go out at all," said Sam.

"I'm leaving now." Lynn replied. "I'd feel better if she weren't there by herself, since Shep's out of commission."

"I'd feel better if you two weren't by yourselves!" He thought a minute. "I have a client waiting right outside my door, but if I have to, I'll reschedule. Let me call Juan to get hold of Maria, and then I'll call Cisco. We'll see what they have to say."

"OK. Call me when you know something."

She looked around her room as she continued to talk.

"I'm going to find something around here...

"The Wheel! Remember? The Wheel is too big to go in the back because of the washer and dryer. I'll take it home as an excuse to go in the front. If someone is watching, they won't know we were warned."

"Brilliant and beautiful—knockout combination. I'll call you back. Be careful!"

After she hung up, she realized that Sam had brought the Wheel to school for her. She wasn't sure she could handle the thing by herself. The tardy bell rang, signaling the beginning of fifth hour. She stepped to the door. Maybe she could snag someone to help her. The only boy still at his locker was James.

"James," she called, using her helpless-little-old-lady voice, "are you busy?"

"No," he said flatly.

"Could you help me with something?"

He swaggered reluctantly to her door.

"I need someone with your muscles to help me get this thing out to my car. Do you think you could do that? It's not too heavy for you, is it?"

Without a word the boy came in and shouldered the big wheel. She grabbed her stuff, locked her door and almost skipped down the hall after him. Oh, the irony of it all, she thought smugly.

"Where ya parked?" he asked gruffly.

"Right over here. I sure appreciate this." She led the way to the van.

When she was reaching to open the back, James said, "Be easier from th' side."

She stopped and thought a minute.

"You know, you're right. I never thought about it, but it really would be easier."

She opened the side door, and he simply rolled the Wheel in. She stuffed her book bag beside it so it couldn't move.

"Thank you so much, James. Do you need a pass?"

James just looked at her, turned on his heel, and walked away.

She was pulling out of the parking lot when it hit her: The note had not specified the back door of the house or the car!

As she reached for her phone, it rang.

"Juan is on his way to our place now. Cisco is communicating with his men and will get back to us. They are scanning the area for a high powered rifle that could hit someone coming out our back door long range," said Sam without even saying hello. "They said your idea to use the Wheel is a good one. They don't want me to come home right now because it would look odd to someone who—"

"Sam, wait a minute," she interrupted. "Something else just happened that you need to know about. First, did anyone call Maria?"

"Pastor Juan. He only told her he was picking up lunch and that y'all could eat on the front porch. He did tell her not to go outside but didn't mention the warning. What happened?"

"I asked James, the owner of the Kawasaki, to help me carry the Wheel to the car—"

"Good grief, Lynn! Why on earth did you ask *him*?"

"He was the only male in the hall. I thought it was kinda funny. Anyway, when we got to the van, he suggested putting the wheel in the side door instead of the back. Is that significant? Could've just been coincidence."

"Coincidence!? After that note on your desk? I don't believe in coincidence. I believe it was the protective hand of God. I'm calling Cisco right now. Until you hear otherwise, go with plan A, OK?"

"Of course, but lunch on the front porch? Is that safe?"

"It's in full view of our guardian angels with badges, and it's a beautiful day, so why not, right? Cisco suggested it."

"OK. I'm pulling onto the highway now. I should be home in about ten minutes. Anything else?"

"Not for now. If anything comes up, I'll let you know. Gotta go. I've kept my client waiting too long already. Love ya! Be careful."

"Love you too. Bye."

She turned onto the lane and then into the driveway right behind Pastor Juan.

Perfect!

"Well, hey!" she called to the pastor. She was trying to act surprised without actually lying and saying she was. "How are you?" They could hear Shep barking at the back door.

"Fine," he said. "I thought it might be a treat for Maria not to have to fix lunch, so I brought it."

"How thoughtful! That was really sweet!" said Lynn. "Hey, this is perfect. I'll carry lunch if you'll muscle that thing out of my car and in the front door. If you hadn't come along, Maria and I might have killed each other trying to get it into the house."

She took the bags from the Chinese carryout place and picked up her book bag so that he could get the Wheel.

They made it to the front porch.

"Silly me, my key is in my pocket. Maybe I can ring the bell. Never mind, Shep's already told Maria we're here."

In a minute, Maria opened the door. She looked greatly relieved to see the two of them. Shep pushed his way out and ushered them in, paying special attention to the food bags.

Her cell rang before she could even put down the bags.

"Hi!" said Sam in his there's-someone-with-me voice. "The people from the EPA are checking all the wells in our area. The guy will be there in about a half hour."

"EPA? Oh… OK, thank you."

"Love you too. Bye."

They were on the porch laughing over their fortune cookies. Shep was on his leash hooked to the clothesline. He had more freedom than with just the leash, but not enough to re-injure his leg running all over creation. A white van with an Environmental Protection Agency sign on the side pulled into the driveway.

Shep was doing his best to protect his environment, but how could he when his people had him tied to this stupid clothesline and had this stupid thing on his leg? He hobbled the length of the line and back several times while warning the intruder that he'd better behave himself!

A 50-something man with an ID badge hanging from his shirt pocket got out.

"Aftanoon, y'all," said the muscular African-American man. "Dis the residence of a Mr. Samuel Bartholomew?"

"Yes, it is," answered Lynn.

"He he-ah?" asked the man.

"No, he isn't. I'm his wife. Shep! Hush! Sam called and told me you were coming. What do you need?"

"Not a thing, Ma'am. Just need to check yo' watah. Is yo' dog dang'rous? Sho is a big un."

"Not unless you include licking you to death. Let me introduce you, and he'll be fine. What's your name?" she said, squinting at his badge.

"Name's George Sanders."

Pastor Juan stepped up, his hand extended, "I'm Juan, and this is Maria. I just stopped by for a bite of lunch. Have you eaten? We have some Chinese food left, if you're interested."

"Why, thank y'all!" said George with a wide grin. "Now I wish I had'na just eat my b'loney san'wich."

"George, come on over and meet Shep," said Lynn, taking the dog by the collar. "Shep, this is George."

George let Shep sniff his hand and then squatted down to dog level.

"Nice t' meet ya, Shep," he said, ruffling Shep's coat. "Looks like ya got a li'l banged up."

Shep decided he liked this guy and got so carried away demonstrating it that he knocked poor George right on his back side. Lynn had to drag the exuberant dog off before he really did lick the man to death.

"I see what y'all mean," laughed George. "Well, I betta git t' work."

He went to the back of his van and brought out some sort of equipment.

"C'n I start inside, since Shep is outside right now? I need t' take some watah samples from ever' place it comes in th' house."

"Sure. Do we need to stay outside too?"

"Not 'nless you plan t' push me down like he did!" said George with a grin.

George went to the kitchen and bathrooms and filled several small flasks. He then went to the washing machine, which was just inside the back door. While the flask was filling, Lynn could see he was very carefully checking the door.

"Now less go ou'side."

He took samples from all the outside spigots. On the carport he checked every square inch of the floor, even under her car. She could see he wasn't checking the floor as much as he was the back door of the house and minivan.

"Now, if y'all 'll show me th' well house, we'll be 'bout done."

She took him around back and showed him the little building that housed the well pump. He inspected it carefully.

"And las' but not leas', the septy tank,"

"Oh, my," said Lynn, "I don't remember where the septic tank is. Let me call Sam."

She pulled her phone out of her pocket and got her husband on the line.

"Sam, the EPA guy is still here. He needs to know where the septic tank is."

He told her as she walked out to the location.

"OK, we're there. Thanks. See you tonight."

The man took out a tape measure and measured from the septic tank to the well, looked at the landscape and made some notes on his clipboard.

"That'll do it," said George. "C'n we go inside and go ovah what I foun'?"

"Of course. Maria is just taking cookies out of the oven, and I have milk or tea, whichever you like."

When they were all seated around the table in the kitchen, the man dropped all pretenses.

"I'm Special Agent Sanders of the FBI, and there is no problem with your water. I did, however, find evidence that someone had tampered with your back door. Apparently, he was scared off before he could actually do anything. That's not to say that it was a false alarm, just that nothing has been planted yet. We found no evidence of any long-range weapon. I think it's safe to say that you're in no immediate danger."

Collective sigh of relief.

When George stood up to leave, he turned to Maria and Juan, "I just wanted to say to you folks that I am intimately acquainted with racial prejudice. My parents were very active in the Civil Rights Movement, and my grandfather was killed by a mob in Alabama. We will do our best to protect you and to catch the people responsible for these attacks."

Pastor Juan translated for Maria. She took George's hand and looked him in the eye.

"Tank you," she said sincerely.

Chapter 23

Saturday was a gorgeous day, with just a hint of October chill. Sam and the kids spent most of the day cleaning the barn in preparation for the Benjamins' visit and for next Saturday when the Hispanic young people would be there. Lynn also had them gather wood for a fire. She didn't know if the Benjamins were indoor people or outdoor people, but either way they could have a fire.

It was a perfect evening. Because it was already dusk when the family arrived, Sam showed the adults around the place and the kids ran down to the creek, while Lynn and Maria finished getting dinner on the table. Shep was on the clothesline again, wanting oh, so badly to be a part of the action down at the creek. Dinner was served buffet style and then everyone ate around the fire pit, plates on their laps. The fall nip in the air made the warmth from the blaze feel really good.

After dinner they sat around swapping stories and toasting marshmallows. The Lopez family had never seen toasted marshmallows before and ate a basketful.

Wait 'til they taste s'mores! thought Lynn.

Helen Benjamin spoke a little high school variety Spanish, so Maria wasn't left totally in the dark when the kids weren't around. Besides, with her English lessons, and just being around English speakers, she was beginning to understand much of what was said. In a mixture of English and Spanish, Maria showed the doctor's wife some of her book bags. Helen bought one on the spot and promised to mention the bags to everyone she knew.

After dinner the boys went to the barn to hang out, and the girls went into the house, taking Shep with them. Soon they heard the sound of Ana's recorder—and Shep singing along.

"Excuse me," Lynn said. She rescued the poor dog, taking him back out to his clothesline.

Helen met her at the door. "She's really good."

"Yes, thank you," said Lynn. "Let me get Shep staked out. I'll be right back."

Maria joined the ladies in the living room as they listened to Ana play. Soon they could hear her explaining the instrument to Ruth. The younger girl blew a couple of good notes and then squealed a couple. With a giggle, she gave the recorder back to Ana. Ana patiently showed her again. The next time she did better.

"Ana tomorrow play on the church," said Maria proudly. Lynn just looked at her. That was the longest speech she had ever made in English.

"How long has she been playing?" asked Helen.

Maria blinked and looked at Lynn to answer.

"Only since the middle of August, but she adores it and practices constantly, which Shep dearly loves."

Helen smiled and asked, "Do you think she could teach my Ruth? She's had a couple of years of piano, but she really doesn't like it. Maybe hearing Ana play tonight will give her incentive to try a little harder. Of course, we would be willing to pay."

"Why, that's a terrific idea!" said Lynn enthusiastically. "What do you think, Maria?"

"Is for Ana teach to Ruut?" said Maria. The English *th* was still a mystery to her.

"*Muy bien*... uh... very good."

"Her school is right behind Ana's. If it works for you, Ruth could come to my room after school on Tuesdays. I have to stay for faculty meeting, and Ana could ride home with me."

"I usually pick Ruth up after school, so I could just come a little later on Tuesdays. Maybe we should ask Ana what she thinks."

Lynn looked at Maria for approval. Maria had caught the gist of the conversation and nodded her consent.

"Ruth," called Helen.

When the girls came out of the bedroom, she continued, "Would you go get your father? We need to be going soon."

Both girls headed out the door, but Lynn said, "Ana, I need you in here for one minute."

Ruth went on out and Lynn said, "Ana, Mrs. Benjamin really liked your playing tonight."

"Thank you," said Ana, blushing.

"She would like you to teach Ruth to play. What do you think?" She explained the arrangements the ladies had talked over.

Ana looked from one to another of them in surprise and then turned to her mother. The two carried on a short conversation, and then Ana said, "Yes, very good. Thank you."

At that point the men folk came trooping in and said their good-byes. Helen wanted to talk things over with her husband before she mentioned the music lessons to Ruth. She never got the chance.

As soon as the car doors closed, Ruth started in on her dad.

"Did you hear Ana, Dad? Isn't she great? And she's only been playing a few weeks! Can I learn? Ana could teach me. OK, Dad?" She rattled on for a few more minutes. "OK?" If not for the seat belt, she would have been bouncing on the back seat.

Finally, Dr. Benjamin looked at his wife. "What do you think? You're the one who would have to endure the practice times while I'm at work."

Helen Benjamin just smiled. "I think it's a great idea. I'll talk it over with Lynn."

It had been an excellent evening. When they went back inside after seeing the Benjamins off, Diego said, "I like Seth very. He have many question of the Bible. I not know all answer. I need study."

"There are many Bible courses online. Maybe we could enroll you in one," said Sam.

"In Spanish?"

"Probably."

Diego was excited. "When we start?"

The silent observer had been watching all evening. Once when the kids had been roaming around down at the creek, they had come within a few feet of his hiding place. But with Shep tied up in the yard, they had not detected him. He was jealous of the good time they were having, and he was especially jealous of the warm fire as he sat shivering in his tree. Tonight, he thought.

Somewhere in the wee hours of the morning Lynn woke up. She couldn't identify what had awakened her, but both Sam and Shep were sleeping soundly. She was just rolling over to go back to sleep when she heard yelling coming from the carport.

"FBI! Stay where you are!"

Shep instantly set up an earsplitting racket. Sam grabbed the pistol and headed for the door.

"Get your robe on, Lynn! Quiet, Shep!"

They could hear quite a scuffle going on in the carport. Someone was using language she had rarely heard before and hoped she never heard again.

Maybe we got 'im! she thought.

The family came together in the kitchen, Diego with his poker. They all jumped when a fist pounded on the back door.

"Who's there?" shouted Sam in his deepest voice.

"It's Cisco!"

It was all Lynn and Ana could do to keep Shep back when Sam opened the door. She looked out and saw James Flanagan, handcuffed, with George Sanders on one side and Cisco on the other. The pungent odor of gasoline rushed in on a cold October wind and stung their noses. Shep sneezed. He was torn between staying here with his people and fleeing this hideous odor. His nose stung. He wiped it with his paws. He whined. Sam grabbed his collar, led the protesting dog to the bedroom, and returned quickly to the kitchen. Shep barked his opinion of the whole thing in no uncertain terms.

"Is everybody OK here?" asked Cisco seriously.

A five-gallon gas can lay in the carport, gas running out in an ever-widening circle. There was also gas on the walls, on the back door and on both cars.

Sam looked quickly back at his family. "We're all here. What's up?"

"Better close the door before the fumes get too strong in your house. Turn your furnace off. I'll meet you on the front porch," said Cisco in English, then Spanish. Sam carefully pulled the door closed.

Lynn was stunned. They all were. A cold chill ran down her spine. Questions flew through her mind in microseconds. What if the agents hadn't been there? Who would have been the first one to open the door? Who from this family would have died this morning? She moved closer to her husband. Sam put his arm around her protectively. His expression was grim, his skin a ghastly gray.

What would make someone hate enough to do something like this? She had seen James out there. His face was a mask, showing no emotion whatsoever.

The questions continued to go around and around in her head. She looked at those she loved. Would any of us have died this morning? Or be maimed for life?

They turned as one to do as Cisco had suggested.

Ana was clinging to her mother. Both of them were pale with fear. Suddenly, Maria sank to the floor. The shock had been too much for her. Because they had had their arms around each other, Ana was able to break the fall.

"*¡Mamita!*" she screamed. "*¡Socorro! ¡Diego! ¡Socorro!*"

Diego leaped to his mother's side, poker clattering to the floor, but there was little he could do with his cast on.

Sam quickly scooped up the unconscious woman.

"Get the front door! We've got to get her away from these fumes!"

He carried her to the far end of the front porch, as far away as possible from the gas. The rest of them followed. Shep was going crazy in the bedroom, throwing his big body against the door.

Ana was sobbing and shaking uncontrollably. "*¡Mamita! ¡Mamita!*" she cried over and over, on the verge of hysteria.

Lynn held her as they watched Sam gently lay her mother on the porch floor.

"We need to elevate her feet about twelve inches," said Sam. "Find something quickly!"

"This?" said Diego, struggling to drag a heavy flower box over. Cisco saw what was happening and quickly picked it up. They carefully positioned Maria's feet on it.

"Go get some blankets!" commanded Sam.

Lynn, Ana, and Diego hurried to comply. They each grabbed an armload and ran back outside. Cisco helped Sam spread a blanket under Maria to insulate her from the cold floor and then to cover her with more. Then he gave one to each of the others.

"It's cold," he said. "Wrap up in these."

The wind was picking up.

In a couple of minutes Maria began to come around, and Ana knelt by her side. The girl was terrified, and it showed. Diego knelt beside her and took his mother's hand.

"*¿Mamita?*" said the girl in a small, shaky voice. "*¿Mamita, estás bien?*"

Maria looked at her daughter, her cloudy eyes full of concern.

"*Si, estoy. ¿Y tú, mi hija?*" she said weakly. "*¿Diego?*"

"*Estoy bien, Mamita*," said Diego in as manly a voice as he could manage.

Ana was sobbing. She leaned down and kissed her mother. Maria struggled to get up to comfort her.

Lynn quickly moved to stop her. "Lie here for a few minutes, Maria. We are all fine."

Sam was afraid Shep was going to dismantle the bedroom piece by piece, if they didn't get him out of there. While the others were with Maria, he went in, armed with the heavy leather leash, and cautiously opened the bedroom door. His dog about bowled him over! He had to fight to get the leash clipped on. Shep even snapped at him, something he had never done before. Sam saw the room for only a split second before his dog literally dragged him to the front door.

The bedroom looked like it had been hit by a tornado.

Shep made a beeline for Lynn and Ana. So what if he was hobbling on three legs and dragging a 225-pound weight? His people needed him! He sent Lynn sprawling before he tackled Ana. He slowed down a little for Diego and then gave the still prostrate Maria a licking she would never forget—literally. His slobbery kisses and doggy breath went a long way in bringing his victim to full consciousness. She grunted, struggling to push him away.

Sam caught up with his dog and tied him on a short lead to the porch railing. Shep was straining at that leash with the power of a buffalo, whimpering, whining and barking short piercing barks. While Ana and Diego stayed with Maria, Lynn went over and tried to calm her dog. It was hopeless.

George had taken James up to the top of the driveway, away from the gas fumes, as well as away from the family. Now the boy was in leg irons too. They were taking no chances. Lynn could hear George reading him his rights.

The wind was blowing harder, cold for the barefoot family huddled on the porch but good for clearing the air. They couldn't go into the house yet because of the fumes, so they pulled their blankets tighter and tried to wrap their freezing feet.

The truck from the volunteer fire department pulled into the driveway, colored lights bouncing off the trees like a nightclub light show. The firemen jumped from the truck and went straight to work. Even these men, who were used to seeing all kinds of horror, looked solemn.

Sam looked questioningly at Cisco.

"We called them, number one, because of the fire hazard, and number two, to clean up the gas. They've got the equipment to take care of the carport safely and to get the fumes out of your house."

"Thank you," said Sam.

Then Sully and Banks arrived, more lights slicing the night.

An unmarked car pulled into the driveway. An agent got out of the front seat and opened the back door for James. It was as if the boy suddenly awoke from a dream. He started struggling with the agents and screaming obscenities at the top of his lungs. Another agent bolted from the driver's seat and joined the fray. Cisco sprinted to help. Sully and Banks were on alert. Maria stood up, leaning on her children, to see what was happening.

Shep went berserk, his furious barks echoing off the walls. He knew that guy! He had picked up his scent down at the creek. He had seen him at school. He had chased him away when he had tried to hurt his people before, and ever since, had had this stupid thing on his leg! Lynn's attempts to calm him were futile, and Sam pulled her away before the dog hurt her in his wrath.

If Shep got to James… Lynn refused to think about it.

The venom continued to spew from James's mouth as if he had been a snake, thwarted in his bite. He caught sight of Diego and turned into a raving maniac.

"I'll get you, Diego Lopez! Don't think I won't!" he screamed. His threats continued until the agents stuffed him into the back seat of the car and closed the door.

The silence that followed was deafening.

The car turned around and left, taking James into a future that Lynn could not even imagine.

The family stood huddled on the porch, Shep plastered against Lynn. She reached down to him without moving from her spot beside Maria. He was shaking like a leaf.

Cisco and George approached the group on the porch.

George spoke; Cisco translated.

"It's over," he said.

He took a deep breath and continued, glancing at Cisco. The next few minutes were not going to be easy.

"We've been tailing James ever since we matched the tire tracks that you got, Mrs. Bartholomew, to the ones Cisco took here. When we saw him fill that gas can this afternoon, we figured tonight might be the night."

Cisco took up the tale, translating as he went.

"We staked out your house from just behind those trees back there, a good place to see but not be seen. We had cleared a path to the carport so we could approach without a lot of noise.

"As soon as we saw what he was up to, we moved in." He paused.

"Why he...?" whispered Maria, swaying against Sam. "Why...?"

George grabbed a chair, and they lowered the lady into it.

"Put your head down between your knees," instructed Cisco gently.

Maria complied, and Cisco knelt in front of her. Diego sat on the floor beside his mother, his hand on her shoulder. Lynn pulled the shivering Ana inside her blanket with her.

Cisco continued.

"When we realized that James Flanagan was the perpetrator, we did some checking. We discovered some important facts that we think sent his prejudice over the edge.

"James's mother was from around here. She married a man from Macon, and they soon became financially successful. James was their firstborn. When he was a toddler, they were victims of a home invasion and robbery. The man killed James' father and assaulted his mother. She was five months pregnant with their second child, a girl, but was violated so brutally that she miscarried her baby. James witnessed it all.

"The man, a local migrant worker, was initially caught but later escaped and fled to Mexico. He was never seen again."

Cisco paused and looked down.

"His name..." said George as gently as he could, "was Diego Lopez de Vargas."

It was as if they were frozen in time. Even Shep was still. Maria slowly lifted her head, still dazed, and met Cisco's eyes. Everyone stared at George, trying to process what the man had just said.

"James's mother moved back to her folks' place here in Flanders County and was eventually able to get past it and get on with her life," he continued. "His maternal grandfather could not. He embittered the boy against all Latinos from that day forward.

"The fact that Diego was Latino was the first factor. The fact that he was physically weak was significant, because bullies look for easy prey.

"Then when James discovered Diego's name, apparently something snapped inside of him. An uncontrollable hatred took on a life of its own, producing an intense desire for revenge. He contrived the whole thing about drugs being in Diego's sweatshirt to manipulate his gang into attacking him," said Cisco.

Lynn heard what the man had said, but she just couldn't wrap her brain around the facts. What...? She tried to form a coherent thought but simply could not.

Chapter 24

The family had finally slept as dawn was staining the eastern sky—the fact that it was Sunday barely even registering. Late that morning, the family was sitting around the kitchen table listlessly eating the cereal Lynn had set out. No one had gone to church. She made another pot of coffee. Pastor Juan had left the Hispanic church before the end of the morning service and was there at the table with them. They had talked for the last hour, each one giving his or her perspective on the events of last night, Spanish and English all mixed together. The detail that one missed, another one picked up, each of them achieving at least some level of emotional release with the telling.

"What does it mean, *Pastor*?" Ana asked in Spanish. "Of all the Mexicans in the United States, why did a man named Diego Lopez have to be the one who murdered James's father? You always say God loves us. How could someone who loves me let all this happen? Why did James tell his gang to attack Diego at school? Why did he try to kill us last night?" Diego was quietly translating.

Ana wasn't crying; she wasn't whining; she honestly wanted to know.

Juan's hand moved to cover hers.

"Think with me, my dear. If your brother were not named Diego Lopez, James's gang might not have attacked him, revealing the abuse. Where would Diego be today?"

Ana's eyes grew wide.

"Dead," said Diego quietly.

Everyone was leaning into Pastor Juan's words, the truth dawning on each one in turn. Flickers of hope replaced the despair.

"And you. Where would you and your mother be?" continued the Pastor, "There would be no Mrs. B or Sam or Shep in your life."

He paused, letting the weight of what he was saying penetrate their overwrought minds and hearts, looking into the eyes of each one.

"According to the letter we found, you could not go back to Mexico. You would be stranded here in the United States with nowhere to go and no way to support yourselves. You would be alone; you would be destitute—not to mention illegal."

He looked at Maria. "Who named Diego when he was born?"

"Armando," she whispered.

"Do you see, Ana? God used your ungodly father to save your lives by giving his son the same name as another ungodly man.

"Coincidence? No way! God is supreme and sovereign. He allowed that name to be given to that tiny baby boy so that you could be sitting in this kitchen today.

It was silent.

Ana jumped up and started toward her bedroom. She whirled and pointed at Pastor Juan, crying, "But James tried to kill us last night!"

She wasn't ready to admit that God was good.

Maria went to her daughter and held her.

Juan spoke quietly. "Ana, look at me."

The distraught girl raised her eyes to him.

"Do you remember how sad I was when my wife died?"

Ana nodded.

"It didn't matter to James if he killed you last night. He just wanted Diego to hurt. He knew that if one of you had died or been severely injured, Diego would think that it was his fault and carry the pain of that for the rest of his life."

Maria lifted her daughter's chin and looked into her eyes.

"*Mi hija*," she said, "We need to thank God, not be angry at him."

After a second's hesitation, Ana tore herself away from her mother and ran to her bedroom. Shep limped after her, but she shut him out as well.

* * * *

"Good morning," said Cisco to the officer at the desk of the police station. Is Sergeant Johnson here?"

"Sure, can I tell him who wants to see him?"

Cisco handed him his card.

"Oh," said the young man, eyes wide.

He ushered Cisco to the first door on the right.

"Mr. Bertonelli," greeted Sarge, extending his hand. "What can I do for you?" He was doing a good job of hiding his nervousness. "Have a seat."

"Good morning, Sergeant Johnson," said Cisco. "Won't take but a minute. Just wanted to let you know we caught the guy that's been vandalizing the Bartholomews' place. You know, the *hate* crimes."

"Hate crimes! I thought it was just some kid acting out his feelings for a school teacher!" He tried to chuckle but didn't quite succeed.

"Just so you'll know, if we hadn't had the place staked out last night, that 'some kid' might have succeeded in killing his teacher, as well as a family of Hispanics."

He turned on his heel and walked out, leaving a white-faced police sergeant sweating behind his desk.

* * * *

Ana didn't want to go to church Sunday night. The rest of the family got dressed and prepared to leave, although they were moving rather slowly. Suddenly, it dawned on the girl that she would be at home alone. She was ready in ten minutes.

Lynn had noticed that since she had learned to play the recorder, Ana always seemed to pick it up when she was sad or pensive. Playing the instrument brought consolation. She had not played a note that day.

"Why don't you bring your recorder?" suggested Lynn. "Everyone has been looking forward to hearing you play."

Ana started to protest, but her mother stopped her and spoke to her in Spanish.

"It will be good for you. Playing always makes you feel better when you are sad. Besides, you are only accompanying the hymns."

Ana reluctantly got her recorder. The exuberance that Lynn had recently noticed had, in a matter of hours, reverted to discouragement and insecurity.

The people at church had heard the news reports, and they gathered around the family in loving support. Although Ana did not play very enthusiastically, kids of all ages crowded around after the service, begging her to teach them to play.

On the way home she asked, "Mrs. B, what I do? Everybody want play the recorder!"

Lynn had tried to get the kids to call her Aunt Lynn or even Grandma Lynn, but they just weren't comfortable with anything but Mrs. B.

"Teach them," interjected Sam.

"Yes," said Lynn, "I think it's a marvelous opportunity!" Thank You, Lord, she thought. Exactly the distraction she needs. "Do you think the families can afford to buy recorders and books?"

"They… how you say… discover moneys," said Diego.

Ana turned to her mother, and the two of them carried on a rapid-fire conversation.

Finally, Ana spoke again in English. "*Mamita* say only ten student. Only 10 or 12 year old. The kids no pay nothing at church."

"I think that is very wise," said Sam. "I will start looking on the Internet for cheap prices on recorders and books."

"Thank you," said Ana. She paused. "Mrs. B, you... I..."

"Do I think you're ready for this?" asked Lynn putting into words the question Ana was trying to voice.

"Yes. I not know. Only Ruth, okay, but much peoples..."

"You'll do just fine. I'll help you at home, and if you need me, I'll help with the group."

"Thank you," said a relieved Ana.

"You can tell the kids that if they practice hard, they might be ready to play in the Christmas program at church," said Lynn.

"Talk for Pastor Juan," said Diego. "Maybe he say Wednesday night and Sunday morning, and kids can... how you say... give you paper with the name on."

"Sign up," supplied Lynn.

"Thank you. Sign up Sunday night. You class maybe Sunday night behind church."

"And Wednesday!" said Ana excitedly. "Two class is gooder, no?"

"Yes, gooder idea," said Sam. He winked discretely at his wife.

It was nice to be able to come home and not worry about tires being slashed or paint on the house. It was also nice to have Shep, though still on three legs, giving them his hearty, sloppy doggy welcome.

* * * *

Mrs. B went to the lunchroom to look for Diego. Somehow, the clean P.E. clothes he had brought from home that day had ended up in her book bag. She had forgotten to give him the clothes in English class, so now she had to brave the cafeteria crowd to find him. She had some errands to attend to in town and had to leave ASAP.

There he was! He was at the head of a table of Hispanic students in the far corner of the room. They were engrossed in an animated discussion. Antonio was at the other end of the table. None of them even saw her approach.

"Hi!" she said. A couple of them jumped.

"Mrs. B!" Diego said in surprise. "What... Why you come? Is problem?" He jumped to his feet. "*Mamita* is OK? Ana?"

"No, no! Everything's fine. Your P.E. clothes were in my book bag, and I forgot to give them to you in class." She smiled and handed him the grocery bag. He blushed deeply under his brown skin.

"Thank you," he murmured, thoroughly embarrassed.

Mrs. B nodded, smiled at the other students and turned to walk away.

"Mrs. B!" Antonio called. She returned to the table and looked questioningly at the boy.

"Ever days in lunch, we talk Bible class." She tried not to let her surprise make its way to her face. "Me and Diego tries to say all that peoples no understands. Understand?"

"I think so. You and Diego try to answer any questions the kids have from Bible class. Maybe explaining in Spanish is easier for them to understand. Right?"

"*¡Si!* Yes! Yes!" said some of the kids at the table.

"That's terrific! How can I help?"

Diego began. "You say that behind Adam eat the fruit, God promise the Deliv... Delib... Pastor Juan tell me use name *Libertador*. Is good?"

"Perfect!" said Mrs. B, assuming it meant Liberator.

"Repeat, please," said a boy. "Why God promise a Deliver? What he deliver to Adam? He buy some thing on ebay? Pizza?" He looked around for the laughs that should have been coming. Nothing.

She recognized the boy from Bible class, but he wasn't in her English class. She caught his joke and chuckled a little. "Good question. What's your name?"

"Marcos."

There was an empty chair across from Marcos, so she sat down, errands forgotten. She happened to glance up at that moment and saw Jack Barrett a couple of tables away. He was scowling at her. Ben and Frank were with him. Apparently she had been the topic of conversation, because they were also staring at her. She smiled and waved. Jack sneered at her before he looked away. The other two weren't as rude; they just quickly found something in their lunch that needed attention. Mrs. B momentarily lost her train of thought.

"Uh..." She looked at Marcos' expectant face. Oh, yeah! "What does the word Deliverer or *Libertador* mean?"

The boy thought for a minute. "I think like liberate somebody of something. Maybe. I don' know."

"That's right!" said Mrs. B. "To liberate means to make free. Do you remember what the punishment for sin is, Marcos?"

"*Si*, death."

"God promised the Deliverer, the *Libertador*, to free Mankind from the punishment for sin, death. Understand?"

"Yes. Then God kill animals for make clo-thes to Adam and Eve, yes?"

"Right."

"Why?" asked Isabel. "Why no use cotton or other for animal no die?"

"What was the punishment for disobedience, Isabel? What did God say would happen?" She had taught all of this in class, but apparently some of the foreign students hadn't caught it.

"They die," repeated Marcos before Isabel could open her mouth.

"Yes. The covering of leaves that they had made was not sufficient. First of all, no blood was shed. Remember that the Bible says in the book of Hebrews that without the shedding of blood, there is no remission—payment—for sin. God is holy. The penalty for sin is death."

She waited for the explanation. Marcos was doing most of the translating because he was more advanced. She had no idea what he was saying but fervently prayed it was correct. There was a little discussion between Diego, Antonio, and him as they clarified some point. She would ask Pastor Juan to monitor them. Diego nodded at her to go on.

"Secondly, they were trying to make themselves acceptable to God by something that they did, apart from God. God does not accept our efforts to hide our sin. Only He can make a way for us to be accepted by Him."

Again she waited. "Do you understand?"

Some nodded slowly; some just sat there.

"Isn't that what religion does?" she continued. "Religion, no matter which one, is Man's attempt to make himself acceptable to God. It just doesn't work that way. Man can come to God only in the way God says." Again she waited.

"Don't worry. I believe it will become clear as we study more of the Word of God. Remember, we have just begun."

Everyone was surprised to hear the bell to end the lunch period. Antonio and Diego were trying to make themselves heard above the racket of high schoolers rattling trays, scraping chairs, and shouting above the din. Mrs. B could tell the kids were thinking as they crammed their unfinished lunches into their bags or hurried to return their trays and get to class.

"Wow!" she said out loud.

Word got around school about Ana's recorder class, and there were several students that wanted her to teach them too. She talked with Ruth and her mother, and they agreed to make her private lesson a group lesson at a reduced rate. Ana really wanted to teach more than one day a week, so Lynn agreed to wait at school for her on Thursdays also. Lesson plans had to be turned in on Fridays, so why not do them at school? Fourteen kids signed up, so she hung around to help.

Diego seemed to be really gifted on the trumpet, and soon he and Sam started accompanying on Sunday nights also. Not too many weeks passed before the recorders could play along on some of the hymns. With 2 guitars, 2 trumpets, 11 recorders, the piano, and the people singing at the top of their lungs, Lynn was pretty sure they could be heard all the way to her church on the other side of town. It was great!

Some of the older kids at church kept pestering Ana to teach them to play. Lynn decided that instead of sitting and twiddling her thumbs waiting for Ana after the services, she could teach the older kids. She had a group of about fifteen. Before long they had caught up with the younger group, so, with Maria's permission, they just all went with Ana. It was interesting to see the level of respect the older kids, even the guys, had for the girl. She was a born teacher and kept the kids in line. Lynn stayed nearby in case Ana needed help explaining something. Both the church group and the school group were getting really good.

One Tuesday Ana tore into Mrs. B's room between 5th and 6th hours. Out of breath, she said, "Guess! Mr. Randolph ask recorder group play on winter program. Bye!" And she fled to her next class.

"Wow!" said Lynn out loud.

On the way home she got all the details from the still excited Ana.

"Why don't you ask if the church group can play with the school group? They all go to school here too."

"Good idea!" crowed Ana. "Now, what we play?"

Bible classes were progressing well, but the kids were still having a little trouble accepting the fact that we who live today must die because of Adam's sin.

"Wait a minute, Mrs. B," said the guy with dread locks. "Are you saying that because one dude ate a hunk of fruit 6,000 years ago, I gotta die? That ain't fair!"

"Remember, *I'm* not saying anything. God is. Remember, too, that He is holy and will not tolerate sin in His presence. And just one more thing to remember." She picked up the branch that she had brought freshly broken from the tree a couple of weeks earlier. It was dry and brittle, with only a few leaves clinging for all they were worth.

"What was Shep here to illustrate?" she asked.

Several kids answered in unison, "Everything reproduces its own kind."

"Right! So as sinners, the only things Adam and Eve could produce were more _____."

Only a few responded soberly.

"Sinners."

"Yes, sinners. Listen to what the Bible says in Romans 5:12. 'Wherefore, as by one man sin entered into the world, and death by sin; and so death passed upon all men, for that all have sinned.' We decided this branch was dead because it was separated from its source of life, right?"

A few nods.

"What about these smaller branches up here near the end? Are they dead or alive? Obviously dead. But they're not separated from the main branch, so why are they dead?"

She waited just a moment before she continued.

"Because their ancestor was separated from its source of life, these little guys are also dead.

"And don't forget the promise that God made the same day Adam and Eve sinned. Who remembers?"

"*¡El Libertador!*" Antonio shouted. "Uh... the Delib... Delira..." He gave up and shrugged. Reiko helped him out.

"The Deliverer," she said in her quiet voice. "God promised to send someone to deliver mankind from the penalty of sin, which is death." She seemed to be grasping what the Bible was saying. Mrs. B was quite sure the Buddhist girl had never heard anything even remotely close to the teaching of the Word of God, but she was catching on.

* * * *

Jack Barrett stepped off the bus one afternoon after school, and immediately one of the guys who had been with him when he got arrested for DUI sidled up to him. He slipped him a small piece of paper. "From James Flanagan," he said and walked away.

Jack opened the folded note: "It's up to you now." He needed no explanation. He wadded the note into a ball and threw it into the gutter.

"Leave it to me, James," he whispered. "Leave Diego Lopez to me!

Since James Flanagan was no longer a factor, the tension between the Americans and the Hispanics had diminished significantly. It seemed that everyone relaxed and began to enjoy one another's company. Even the recorder groups from the church and the school had combined to make one large, multi-national group, and as the winter concert drew ever nearer, Ana asked if she could start meeting with them every day after school. There were almost 35 kids on shrill soprano recorders in the ESOL room. Lynn bought earplugs and asked Mr. Cline to move them to a larger room.

Only Jack Barrett appeared to be carrying on the feud.

* * * *

The semester continued smoothly with Lynn's English students making good progress and her Bible teaching still holding the students' interest. After several weeks she arrived at Exodus chapter 20, the Ten Commandments. It was the Tuesday before Thanksgiving, so she decided to wait until after the holiday to begin teaching the Commandments themselves.

She dedicated this class hour to the students to let them tell what they were thankful for.

The first session was pretty predictable. The high school group, however, held some surprises. At first it was silent, no one wanting to lead out. Then they began.

"I'm thankful for my family."

"My house."

"M' bran' new 2003 Mustang," drawled one boy proudly.

"Brand new 2003," someone muttered under his breath. The boy glared at him.

"My mom's new job."

Several others contributed, citing things for which they were grateful.

Frank Walenski spoke up a little shakily. "Uh, I'm thankful that... uh... Diego Lopez is alive and OK." He went from white to crimson to white again and sank down lower in his chair.

Jack Barrett snorted.

Silence reigned. Mrs. B waited.

"And I thank God for Frank and others of save my life," spoke up Diego.

"I am thankful for this Bible class," said Seth Benjamin. "Thank you, Mrs. B." A number of the kids agreed. Lynn started to tear up.

"And I am thankful to have the privilege of teaching you the Bible," she said.

"I have to admit," spoke up Mr. Cline, "that I was a little leery when Mrs. B asked if she could start a Bible class. But I also have to admit that I have learned an awful lot. Thank you, Mrs. B."

This was going a wrong direction. "Let's remember to Whom we must be thankful. The supreme and sovereign God is Who placed me in this school and allowed the events that gave birth to the idea of a Bible class." She waited. There didn't seem to be anyone else who wanted to participate, and it was almost time for the bell, anyway.

"Mr. Cline, do you think it would be OK if I close this time in a prayer of thanksgiving to God?"

"I think it would be appropriate," said Mr. Cline. "Would anyone object?" Everyone looked around, but no one raised a hand. "Go ahead then, Mrs. B."

Before she prayed, Mrs. B said, "In the Bible people prayed in many different postures. It is our custom to bow our heads and close our eyes. Why do we do that?" No one knew.

"When we bow our heads we are bowing in the presence of the supreme and sovereign God. I'm not sure where the practice of closing our eyes came from. I do it because I'm so easily distracted. When I talk to my God, I don't want to know what's going on around me.

"Let's pray."

* * * *

Pastor Juan wanted to reach out to the rest of his community during the Christmas season. Some of the young people of his church were beginning to build bridges in their relationships at school, but the majority of the Hispanics in the area were still regarded as outsiders. In all people groups there are good and bad elements, and it was no different in Perkins Grove, regardless of race or nationality. Juan wanted to plan something that would help the Hispanics look at things from the perspective of the Americans. Maybe Sam could give him some counsel. He had thought maybe he could invite everyone to a giant *Fiesta de Navidad* and try to encourage the less-than-desirables that the way to succeed in the United States was by being good, contributing members of the society in which they had chosen to live. Before he brought his idea to the church leaders, he talked it over with Sam one evening when he stopped by to bring more material for Maria's book bags. They were on the porch together hanging a string of Christmas lights. Sam was on the ladder.

"Could we have it here?"

Sam considered for a minute. "Everyone would have to know that there could be no alcohol on the property, absolutely no drugs, and smoking only in designated areas."

"Of course," said Pastor Juan, "and we would have to be in control of the music and make sure there were plenty of activities to keep everyone busy and out of trouble."

"Do you have a date in mind?"

"I was thinking of Saturday, December 17. What would be good for you?"

"Let me talk to Lynn. I'll get back to you."

* * * *

Ah, yes, the days between Thanksgiving and Christmas—the days when teachers had to draw upon the depths of their knowledge, experience, training, and creativity to keep the kids from driving them nuts. And just maybe, as a reward for the extra effort, the young scholars might even learn something.

Lynn had assigned Christmas-themed research projects for the ESOL kids to do on their notebook computers in class. They would present their findings orally as a part of their final exam. Reiko was Mrs. B's right arm. Her grade was already so high that she was excused from taking the final, so she circulated among the others correcting their English and working with them on their presentations. Reiko loved it and was learning far more than if she were studying just one aspect of this mysterious Christian holiday.

Bible classes would be even harder to control than her English classes because there were no grades involved. Lynn would have to catch the kids off guard.

The high school class came in like the surf pounding the beach in a storm. She did a quick review, depending on the visuals to help keep their attention, emphasizing the night Moses led his people out of Egypt, reminding the kids of the lamb that had died so that the first-born of believing families could live. Finally, she brought the Israelites to the foot of Mt. Sinai.

The kids were halfway paying attention. Then she asked a question.

"Who in here would consider yourself to be a good person?" The kids looked at each other, shrugged, and eventually, most of them raised their hands.

"May I give you a little test to see if that's true?"

More shrugs. "Go for it," said Bill.

"Have you ever told a lie?" Guffaws.

"Come on, Mrs. B, everybody lies," said Bill, who had appointed himself spokesman.

"That may be, but let's make it personal. If you have ever told a lie in your life, even a 'little white lie,' raise your hand." Eventually, almost everyone's hand went up.

"Thank you for your honesty," said Mrs. B. Snickers from those who caught it. "What do we call someone who has told a lie?" Nobody answered.

"Come on, y'all. It's not a hard question. If I told you a lie, what would you call me?"

"A liar," someone finally said.

"Right. Have you ever stolen anything?"

"What is this?" asked Bill, "An interview for *True Confessions* or *The Inquirer* or something? Or are you recording this to show our parents?"

"Just answer the question. If you've ever stolen something, even if it was small or even when you were a little kid, raise your hand." Hands went up a little slower this time, amidst lots of shrugging, mumbling of excuses and red faces.

"Come on, those of you who aren't raising your hands just finished telling me you're liars."

Nervous laughter, and then a few more hands went up.

"OK, now, what do you call someone who steals?" This time they didn't hesitate.

"A thief," several answered in unison.

Reiko's eyes were so big they were almost round. Mrs. B knew Japan had a save-face society; to admit to being wrong was a great dishonor. These next few lessons were going to be really hard on the poor girl.

"Now, here's a rough one. Are you ready?" She saw doubt and concern on their faces. She waited. Finally, Bill spoke for them all.

"Well, what is it?"

"Remember, I'm asking these questions to see if you're a good person, right?

"Have any of you ever thought sensual thoughts about someone? Even dreamed of having sex with this or that person? Maybe mentally undressed someone?"

"Yeah!" bragged one boy, whose hand shot up. He looked around for support and won a few snickers from a couple of the guys. But they quickly settled down when they saw that Lynn was serious. Everyone's eyes got big. Reiko's were about to pop out of her head. Nobody moved. You could've heard a pin drop.

"Or looked at porn on the Internet or shared dirty pictures with your friends?" she continued.

"Mrs. B," Bill whined.

"I'm not going to ask you to raise your hand, but you know in your heart if you've done any of those things." She could almost tell who was guilty by looking at their expressions, but she would never say so.

"The Bible says that if you have done any of those things you have committed adultery in your heart. If I asked for a show of hands and if you were honest, many of you would have to admit that you are adulterers at heart, right?"

Some kids were beginning to get a little nervous.

"Admit it to yourself, even if you don't have to raise your hand.

"Now, many of you have admitted that you are liars, thieves, and adulterers at heart. Do you still consider yourself to be a good person?" Not even Bill responded.

"Today we have been looking at three of the Ten Commandments found in Exodus 20. See, guys, one day we are going to stand before a holy God to be judged. The Ten Commandments are God's moral law. You know that these things are wrong because God placed within you a conscience.

"Let me ask you," Mrs. B said quietly, "if God judged you by just these three of the Ten Commandments, would you be found innocent or guilty?" Still nobody moved. Every eye was glued to her.

Finally, from way in the back corner came a subdued voice, "Guilty," said Mr. Cline.

At that moment the bell rang. The class went out a lot more quietly than it had come in. Mr. Cline ducked out without even a glance in her direction. Even Jack Barrett lost his usual swagger when he left the room.

* * * *

The Winter Concert was scheduled for Thursday the 8th. Ana's group would be playing *What Child Is This*, which was a traditional English melody, excellent for recorders. They had found a beautiful, lower intermediate three-part arrangement of the song, and the kids were doing an amazing job. The daily practices were paying off.

The Thursday before the concert, Ana complained to Mrs. B as she was getting into the car after rehearsal, "I no understand what is problem." She was frustrated, and it showed. "We practice and we practice. I know they play right note, but no sound good. Mrs. B, what is problem?"

Lynn thought a minute. "Have you ever tried to tune your recorders to each other?"

"Tune? What is tune? I think tune is melody, no?"

"Well, it is, but it has another meaning too. If two instruments are playing together and one is a little higher or a little lower than the other, even if they are on the same note, we say they are out of tune."

"What we can do for out of tune?" asked Ana.

"You have to adjust the neck of the recorder a little. I'll show you when we get home. Maybe Sam can leave work a little early one day and help you. He's better at it than I am."

"Tuesday is… how you say… dressed up rehearsal. He can do then?"

"Dress rehearsal. Yes, that would be the perfect time, and then he'll tune everyone again before the concert itself."

Sam's gonna love me for this one, she thought.

* * * *

Tuesday, Lynn decided to simply continue what she had started on Thursday in Bible class.

"Last week most of you admitted that you were liars, thieves, adulterers at heart, or maybe all three. Those are just three of the Ten Commandments. We also determined that if you were standing before the holy God today to be judged, you would be found guilty.

"Let's continue and find out what the rest of the Ten Commandments say. 'Thou shalt not kill.' You've heard that before, right? That word 'kill' is speaking of murder, assassination of another person—not stepping on a cockroach.

"I don't think we have any actual murderers in here today, do we?" Everybody chuckled nervously and looked around.

"How many of you have ever hated anyone? Maybe you're thinking of someone you hate, even as we speak." The smiles were replaced by scowls. Lynn saw Jack Barrett glowering at Diego. "Maybe a loved one betrayed you or a friend lied about you. Maybe a teacher treated you unfairly or someone broke your heart." She noticed tears in some of the kids' eyes. She spoke softly, sympathetically. "I know these things hurt, but hating is not the way to deal with it. In fact, the Bible says that if you hate someone, you've committed murder already in your heart." She paused, looking them in the eye.

"So now we can add murderer to your list. Do you still consider yourself to be a good person?

"Now, listen carefully to this next question. How many of you have *never* disobeyed your parents?"

A few hands went up, but were quickly lowered when someone around them repeated the question. She put the Commandment on the screen.

"Honour thy father and thy mother," she read. "This verse goes beyond simply obeying. Have you always *honored* your parents? You might have obeyed an order on the outside, but on the inside, you were seething… very angry," she amended for the benefit of her ESOL students. "Or maybe your parents never prohibited you from doing a certain thing, but you knew that if they found out, they would punish you. That's technically not disobeying, but it is dishonoring. What does the commandment say? '*Honour* thy father and thy mother.'" There it was in bold letters on the screen in front of them.

"Listen, guys, God didn't make a mistake when He placed you in your family, gave you your parents. He's the perfect and holy God. He doesn't make mistakes. If you feel that God placed you in the wrong family and are mad at Him because of that, come see me some time and let's talk about it.

"Now, I know that some of you are living in less than ideal situations. Maybe your parents are divorced. Maybe they're abusive. Maybe you're not even living with your parents at all. Maybe you find it hard to honor your parents because they're hypocrites. I understand all that. All I know is that God says to honor them, and honor them we must—warts and all."

Mrs. B was noticing an interesting phenomenon: the kids, including Bill, were being quiet, totally tuned in to what she was saying. She plunged ahead.

"Who knows what the word 'covet' means?" She waited.

"To want something?" asked someone.

"That's good, but let's say to really, really, really want something that belongs to someone else. To want something to the point of stealing it. Or to the point that you would lie to get it. Or to the point that you would dream of someone else's wife or of even killing to get what you wanted."

She flashed "Thou shalt not covet" on the screen.

"If we could just stop coveting, that would take care of several of the Commandments, wouldn't it?

"Now let's back up and look at the first Commandment. 'Thou shalt have no other gods before me.' This is God talking, and He is saying that anything in your life that is more important to you than He is has become a god to you. Has God always been in first place in your life?

"I think we all know people who have made money their god. Maybe some of you have made your girlfriend or boyfriend your god. Music has become a god to some people. Drugs can be more important in your life than anything else on the planet. Your cell phone. Anything that becomes more important to you than God has come between you and your Creator. It has become your god."

The bell rang, but nobody moved.

"Again, I just want you to think about these things, and we'll continue on Thursday."

She tried to smile at each one individually as they left. Some of them tried to pretend she wasn't there.

* * * *

Jack Barrett was slouched in the living room chair finishing his math homework. The only reason he bothered with homework was so that he could stay eligible for the basketball team. School was a necessary evil he had to endure until he was 18, basketball being the one reason he kept going. He glanced at his drunken father snoring on the couch.

Humph! He sneered to himself. Bet Mrs. B never had to put up with the likes o' him growin' up. Her momma and daddy were prob'ly perfect—easy to honor. How on earth am I s'posed to honor that? He jerked his thumb toward his dad, even though there was no one around to see. Not even God could expect me to honor that... could He?

Chapter 25

Thursday was the last study of the Ten Commandments. With very little introduction, Lynn put the Second Commandment on the screen. "Thou shalt not make unto thee any graven image."

"In your geography classes I know you have studied about other cultures that worship idols. Like the other Commandments, let's go beyond just the surface meaning.

"When we pray to God and ask Him for something, we are admitting that He is the One who is able to fulfill our needs. Does that make sense?" Shrugs and nods.

"Even asking God for something is an act of worship because we are admitting His supremacy and sovereignty. Now, if we pray to an image, are we not saying the same thing about that image?"

She could see Mr. Cline getting a little apprehensive.

"My church, have little... statues... of saints that we pray to," said one of the Hispanic girls. "Is the same?"

"Do you ask the saint for something?"

"Sometimes."

"Well, remember, I am not here to condemn any religion or to get you to believe like I do. I am simply teaching you what the Bible says. You can see it in black and white on the screen, and the rest is up to you."

Mr. Cline breathed a sigh of relief.

"Have you ever used God's name as a cuss word?" Mrs. B continued.

"Like how?" asked Bill.

"Now, Bill, do I really need to explain it to you?" Bill turned red.

"Have you ever called on God to damn somebody? Have you ever said 'oh, my ___?' Let's read the next

Commandment. 'Thou shalt not take the name of the Lord thy God in vain.' That means to use it as a cuss word or—"

"Mrs. B," interrupted Bill. "When I say that, I'm not using God's name as a cuss word; it's just an expression."

"What does the word 'vain' mean?"

"Proud?" asked Vicky.

"It can mean that, but another definition is worthless, of no value, or for no reason. That means, Bill, that if you are using God's name as just any ole common word, you are using the name of the God of the universe as if He had no value—in vain.

"Let's look at the rest of this verse." She read from the screen, "'Thou shalt not take the name of the Lord thy God in vain; for he will not hold him guiltless that taketh his name in vain.'

"One day we will have to stand before the supreme and sovereign God as judge. If you have ever once in your life used His name—in English, Spanish or any other language— in vain, you are guilty."

Once again silence fell over the room.

"There's just one more Commandment to look at. 'Remember the Sabbath day to keep it holy.' Other places in Scripture explain that one out of every seven days is to be used to rest. God rested after the six days of Creation, not because He was tired, but because He was finished with His work. We were designed to rest one day a week, but sadly, we Americans are addicted to work."

"Not me!" exclaimed Bill. "I like jus' goin' out in m' dad's boat and bein' lazy." General laughter.

"Let me ask you a question, Bill. Does your dad keep his boat in the water?"

"No, it's at our house. We pull it to the lake about thirty miles from here. Why?"

"What would you call getting that boat ready to go and cleaning up after you get back?"

"Work," admitted Bill, accompanied by the snickers of his friends.

"Come on, Mrs. B," sneered one of the scoffers from the back of the room, "get real. Nobody could keep all them Commandments. I've broke ever' one of 'em. I think ever'body in this room has. How can God expect us to do somethin' we cain't do?"

"Oh, no, Randy," said Mrs. B. "That's not what the Ten Commandments are all about. See, many people believe that we can make ourselves acceptable to a holy God by keeping the Commandments. He knew we could never do that. He gave them to us to show that we are *not* good people—that we could never be good enough on our own to earn His favor or to earn our place in Heaven."

General discontent.

"But," sputtered Bill, "that's not fair!"

"It'll make sense," said Mrs. B as the bell rang. "See you next Tuesday. I promise to explain everything before Christmas."

* * * *

On Tuesday Lynn began Bible class with a question: "What season is this?"

"Winter?"

"Yes, winter, but be specific. What are we celebrating right now?"

"Kwanzaa!" said LaKeesha.

"Hanukkah!" said Seth.

"Christmas!" said several of the other students.

"Yes, yes, and yes," said Mrs. B, "but let's concentrate on Christmas. What are we celebrating during Christmas?"

"Jesus' birth," responded several students.

"Really? Why would the whole world celebrate the birth of one baby? How many people celebrate your birthday?

Family? A few friends? Why was this baby's birthday so much more important than yours?"

"'Cause he was God's son?" ventured someone.

"What does that mean?" asked Lynn. They were not quick to respond.

"Obviously, it means that God was his dad," said Bill sarcastically.

"Explain, please," said Mrs. B.

"I cain't!" said Bill somewhat exasperated, "but I bet you can."

"Well, actually, I can't either, but the Bible can. Let's read Luke 1:26-35.

'And in the sixth month the angel Gabriel was sent from God unto a city of Galilee, named Nazareth, to a virgin espoused to a man whose name was Joseph, of the house of David; and the virgin's name was Mary. And the angel came in unto her, and said, Hail, thou that art highly favoured, the Lord is with thee: blessed art thou among women. And when she saw him, she was troubled at his saying, and cast in her mind what manner of salutation this should be. And the angel said unto her, Fear not, Mary: for thou hast found favour with God. And, behold, thou shalt conceive in thy womb, and bring forth a son, and shalt call his name JESUS. He shall be great, and shall be called the Son of the Highest: and the Lord God shall give unto him the throne of his father David: And he shall reign over the house of Jacob for ever; and of his kingdom there shall be no end. Then said Mary unto the angel, How shall this be, seeing I know not a man? And the angel answered and said unto her, The Holy Ghost shall come upon thee, and the power of the Highest shall overshadow thee: therefore also that holy thing which shall be born of thee shall be called the Son of God.'

"Mary was a virgin. She had never had relations with a man. A pure girl that God said would be the mother of His

Son. When she asked how that could happen since she was a virgin, the angel said in verse 35 that God's power would overshadow her humanity, her sinfulness as a descendant of Adam."

She let that thought hang in the air for a minute.

"Mrs. B," called out one of the kids, "What does 'espoused' mean?"

"It's the ancient Jewish equivalent to our engagement—a little complicated to explain right now, but if you want to know more, we can talk later. For now, let's just say they were engaged. OK?"

He nodded, and she continued.

"Remember the promise that God made to Adam and Eve on the day they disobeyed Him back in the Garden of Eden?"

Finally Seth answered. "Didn't he say something about a Deliverer that would free everybody from sin... or death... or the punishment for sin... or something like that?"

"*El Libertador*," said Antonio loudly for the sake of the Hispanic students.

"You remembered!" said Mrs. B with a big smile. She had only repeated it 10,000 times during the course of the semester.

"Yes, God said that if they ate of the fruit of the Tree of the Knowledge of Good and Evil, they would die, not only physically, but also spiritually. They disobeyed him and were separated from their source of life, just like that tree branch was dead as soon as it was broken off the tree. The promise was that one day a Deliverer would come to deliver them from the punishment for sin."

"I get it," said Bill, "Jesus was the Deliverer!"

"Exactly!" said Mrs. B. "Seth, you would know him as the Messiah, the One promised way back in the Old Testament."

"But how?" asked Bill. "How could a baby be the Deliverer?"

"We'll get to that. In many other places in the Bible, we are told that Jesus was God the Son. Remember, we studied that God is a Trinity, three in one, one God in three persons: God the Father, God the Son, and God the Holy Spirit. Jesus is God the Son. God, come to Earth in human form.

"Now, most of you are familiar with the circumstances surrounding the birth of the Christ Child. Let's just read again from Luke chapter 2." She read the verses that came up on the screen.

"'And it came to pass in those days, that there went out a decree from Caesar Augustus, that all the world should be taxed. (And this taxing was first made when Cyrenius was governor of Syria.) And all went to be taxed, every one into his own city. And Joseph also went up from Galilee, out of the city of Nazareth, into Judaea, unto the city of David, which is called Bethlehem; (because he was of the house and lineage of David:) To be taxed with Mary his espoused wife, being great with child. And so it was, that, while they were there, the days were accomplished that she should be delivered. And she brought forth her firstborn son, and wrapped him in swaddling clothes, and laid him in a manger; because there was no room for them in the inn. And there were in the same country shepherds abiding in the field, keeping watch over their flock by night. And, lo, the angel of the Lord came upon them, and the glory of the Lord shone round about them: and they were sore afraid. And the angel said unto them, Fear not: for, behold, I bring you good tidings of great joy, which shall be to all people. For unto you is born this day in the city of David a Saviour, which is Christ the Lord. And this shall be a sign unto you; Ye shall find the babe wrapped in swaddling clothes, lying in a manger. And suddenly there was with the angel a multitude of the heavenly host praising God, and saying, Glory to God in the highest, and on earth peace, good will toward men. And it came to pass, as the angels were gone away from them into heaven, the shepherds said one to another, Let us now go even unto Bethlehem, and see this thing which is come to pass, which the Lord hath made known unto us. And they came with haste, and found Mary, and Joseph, and the babe lying in a manger. And when they had seen it, they made known abroad the saying which was told them concerning this child. And all they that heard it wondered at those things which were told them by the shepherds. But Mary kept all these things, and pondered them in her heart. And the shepherds returned, glorifying and praising God for all the things that they had heard and seen, as it was told unto them.'"

She looked at the clock.

"Next week we'll look more at the life of Jesus and show how He proved He was God the Son. See you Thursday!"

It was the afternoon of the "dressed up rehearsal" in the auditorium. Ana had told the kids to wear black skirts or pants and some kind of Christmas sweater. They looked great. Sam came and started tuning the recorders out in the lobby.

While the band was warming up, Ana slid in next to Lynn, who was seated near the back of the auditorium.

"Mrs. B, help!" she whispered.

Mrs. B followed her out into the hall.

"What's wrong?" she said.

"I not know where we sit or nothing. We gonna play on the stage? When? How we go up there?"

The poor girl was almost in tears.

"I'll be right back," said Mrs. B as she hurried down to the front of the auditorium. Mr. Randolph was just calling the band to order.

"Excuse me," she said from the floor level. Mr. Randolph heard her, but couldn't find where her voice was coming from. "Down here!"

He finally spotted her.

"Yes," he said, somewhat irritated.

"I'm sorry to interrupt you, but could you show me where Ana's group is to perform?"

"Ana? Who's Ana? What group?" he asked, looking down on her from the high stage.

Oh, no! thought Lynn. "She's the girl that's been working with the recorders. You invited her group to participate in the winter concert several weeks ago."

"Oh, man," said the director slapping his forehead, "I forgot all about them. Uh… I guess they could just file up here and stand in front of the band. How many are there?"

"We narrowed it down to thirty."

"Thirty! I had no idea there were that many. Just a minute."

He called his student director over and told him to rehearse a number with the band.

Lynn could hear Sam tuning the recorders.

"Where are they now?" asked Mr. Randolph.

"Out in the lobby. My husband is tuning them."

"Tuning recorders? That's interesting," he said with a half smile.

They walked into the lobby to find three orderly rows of recorders, arranged in the standard semicircle, patiently waiting their turn to be tuned.

"Oh, wow," breathed the director.

"What else is on the program, besides the band?" asked Mrs. B.

Mr. Randolph whipped out a hand-written program. "Only small groups and solos that will perform standing in front of the band.

"Let's see… we'll fit the recorders in… here," he said, pointing to the paper. "What are they playing?"

She told him and he inserted it in the program.

"Do these kids have their music memorized?"

Ana overheard the question.

"No," she said.

"So they'll need stands too."

He looked at Mrs. B. "Any suggestions?"

"Let's go look at the stage." Sam was still tuning, so it looked like they would have a few minutes.

The two teachers stepped back into the auditorium and stood studying the stage area.

"There's still a lot of room on the stage," said Mrs. B. "Of course, the band has top billing and priority, but if we could skooch them all over just a little... angle them a little... maybe we could squeeze thirty chairs and fifteen stands up there. What do you think? The group could sit in the first rows on that side and it would take them just a minute to get in place. Maybe even while you're announcing them."

Mr. Randolph looked at the stage with squinty eyes for a minute, mentally calculating and staging everything.

"I think it'll work. Let me move the band over. Could you take care of the chairs and stands?"

"Of course! Where are they?"

"Backstage," called Mr. Randolph over his shoulder as he trotted down the aisle.

Finally, everyone was in place. The band went through their first numbers and really sounded good. Mr. Randolph was a good director.

He then stepped down from the director's box and went to the microphone. That was Ana's cue to get her group up on stage as quickly as possible. It took a few tries to get them in place without mishap, but eventually they got it.

It was beautiful to see. The kids were sitting up straight on the edge of their chairs, just like Lynn had taught Ana. Ana counted off, and they played almost flawlessly. Lynn stole a glance at Mr. Randolph when they started, and then again during the really complicated part. He was mesmerized, obviously shocked by what he was hearing.

When the group finished, there was total silence. Then, as if on cue, the whole band erupted into applause, hoots, and whistles. The group had been a hit!

When things had calmed down, Mrs. B approached Mr. Randolph again. "Why don't we have a reception after the concert?" she asked.

"My wife has been saying the same thing, so it must be a good idea. You're in charge," he said and turned around to the band.

Lynn, you're an idiot! she scolded herself. An absolute idiot!

Maria contacted the mothers from the church, and Lynn called the recorder moms from the school group. Mrs. Randolph took care of the band parents. Everyone would bring finger foods, sodas or paper goods. The gym was already decorated, and the maintenance staff would set up the serving tables. Mrs. B was merely the coordinator—the one to blame if something went wrong.

Chapter 26

Thursday, December 8. Concert day. Ana was running around like a headless chicken before school. There was nothing she had forgotten, she was just nervous. There would be no rehearsal that afternoon, but Mrs. B and anyone else she could recruit would be putting the finishing touches on the gym in preparation for the reception. Then she would dash home to collect Maria and the warehouseful of cookies she had baked. Normally, the winter concert was sparsely attended, but this year Mr. Randolph was expecting a pretty good turnout. Lynn knew for a fact that most of the Spanish church would be there.

She was a little nervous about the whole thing. Would the recorders do as well in front of an audience as they had at the dress rehearsal, or would they freeze up? Would the reception turn out all right? Surely there wouldn't be any trouble between the nationalities. Would the food hold out? Shep sensed everyone's stress and became nervous himself.

"What are you uptight about?" Sam asked the dog on the way out the door.

* * * *

During Bible class on Thursday, Mrs. B taught that the miracles of Jesus recorded in the gospels proved that He was God. No one but God could do what He did: He showed His power over the spirit world by casting out demons. He had created the water and the wind, so why would it be a problem for Him to command the storm to cease when He was out in the boat with His disciples? And He even demonstrated His power over death when He gave at least two people life again after they had died! Who but God Himself could have done all that?

* * * *

The concert was exceptional. The band outdid themselves, and the recorders were applauded all the way back to their seats.

At the reception, for the most part, the Hispanics congregated and the Americans congregated, but that was to be expected. There were, however, a few refreshing exceptions. Lynn noticed Helen Benjamin introducing Ana to several sets of parents as the recorder teacher. The girl handled herself gracefully, a tribute to her mother's training. Sam, Pastor Juan and Dr. Benjamin were talking with Mr. Cline. Maria and Mrs. Randolph were working the serving line together. Seth was introducing Diego to one of the trumpet players from the band, who in turn introduced him to Mr. Randolph. Mrs. B hadn't realized that Ben Gibson, one of the boys that had attacked Diego last fall, had a younger sister in Ana's group until she saw Mr. Gibson introducing his wife to Maria. The Gibsons didn't make the connection until Ana came to her mother with a question and was also introduced to the couple—the look on their faces was priceless.

* * * *

Her last Bible class was on Tuesday.

"Who can remember any of the Ten Commandments?" she began.

"Not that again," groaned Bill.

"Yes, that again. Remember, Bill, you were the one that said God was unfair because He gave us a bunch of rules we couldn't keep. And I promised to deal with that issue before Christmas break."

Bill blushed and slid down in his chair.

"Now, who can give me one of the Commandments?"

Different students answered:

"Don't kill."

"Good, but is that just talking about murder?"

"No, hating too."

"Obey your parents."

"Only obey?"

"No, honor them."

"Don't covet or steal."

"Very good. That's four. What else?"

"Go to church on Sunday."

"Well, not exactly, but we are commanded to take one day a week to rest."

"Put God first and don't worship idols."

"Don't use God's name as a cuss word!"

"Right, and remember that God will not hold guiltless the person that uses His name that way," added Mrs. B.

There was silence.

"The first one we talked about was lying. Remember? The second one was stealing, and the third one was adultery or even thinking impure thoughts about someone.

"I don't think we have to point out that we are probably all guilty of breaking at least some of the Commandments. 'Yeah, but just a couple of them. That's not so bad,' you might say. Listen to James 2:10. 'For whosoever shall keep the whole law, and yet offend in one point, he is guilty of all.'"

She drew a long line down the board.

"Let's say that this line is perfection. How far would someone have to be off the line to be imperfect?"

She made an X far to the right of the line. "Let's say this X represents murder. Far off the line, right?"

Another X closer to the line. "This is stealing. Maybe not as far off as murder, but still not perfection."

She made an X right beside the line. "This one represents a little white lie. A little sin perhaps, but still off the line.

"See, God is perfect. Heaven is a perfect place. If a perfect God allowed an imperfect person to enter into His perfect Heaven, it would no longer be perfect, would it?"

She paused.

"The only other place of eternal destiny after death is called hell. That's where all imperfect humans will end up."

She paused again.

"Wait a minute," said Bill. "So you're saying that everybody in this room deserves to go to hell?"

"No, I'm not saying that at all. The Bible is." She flashed some verses on the screen to prove her point: Psalm 9:17, "The wicked shall be turned into hell." Revelation 21:8, "... the abominable, and murderers, and whoremongers, and sorcerers, and idolaters, and all liars, shall have their part in the lake which burneth with fire and brimstone."

Finally she said, "You see, guys, we are lost. Hopeless. And the Bible says that there is nothing we can do to earn Heaven by ourselves. We've talked about that all semester. All of us have already admitted that we are not good people."

"What about going to church or being baptized or taking communion?" asked Susanna.

"Yeah," added somebody else, "my folks give a lot to charity. They do a lot of good. Are you saying that doesn't help at all?"

"Look at what the Bible says in Titus 3:5, 'Not by works of righteousness which we have done, but according to his mercy he saved us.' Isaiah 64:6 says that 'all our righteousnesses are as filthy rags.' And there are other verses in the Bible that show that religious acts do nothing to erase the sins we have committed."

She left those two verses on the screen.

"Have any of you have ever broken a law and had to go to court?" Every eye focused on Jack Barrett.

"OK, yeah," said Jack sulkily, "ever'body knows I been hauled in fer DUI. So?"

"What was your punishment?"

"Took m' driver's license," he said bitterly. "Twenty-four hours in jail, a $700 dollar fine, which I'm still workin' t' pay m' dad back, umpteen hours of community service, and a stupid kindergarten drivin' school."

He wasn't about to reveal that he was sitting in this Bible class because of that incident.

"Jack, did you try to tell the judge that down deep you really were a good guy? Did you tell him you helped little old ladies across the street or gave money for good causes?"

"That's stupid! Judge don't care 'bout none o' that. He ain't gonna change my sentence 'cause I done a good deed."

"You are absolutely right, Jack. So why do we think that when we stand before God to be judged, He would let us go unpunished because we did some good stuff?"

"Let's look again at Titus 3:5. According to this verse, why does God save us?" It took a while, but finally somebody got it.

"Because of his mercy?"

"Exactly," said Mrs. B. "What's mercy?"

Reggie, the big guy with tattoos answered from the back of the room, "Like if my posse is beatin' somebody up fo' dissin' us an' he begs fo' mercy, we might let 'im go."

"Well, sorta. Mercy means not giving someone the punishment he deserves.

"Let's look at John 3:16. 'For God so loved the world, that he gave his only begotten Son, that whosoever believeth in him should not perish, but have everlasting life.'

"See, God loves us so much that He doesn't want us to suffer in hell for all eternity, but His justice demands that our sin be punished. For that reason, the all-powerful, supreme and sovereign God came to Earth as a tiny, weak, totally dependent baby. He grew up, confronted every temptation that we confront, but did not sin. Because he was totally sinless and did not have any sin of His own to die for, He was eligible to die for ours. The innocent, who never broke even one of the Commandments, paid the price for the guilty."

She could see that some of them were beginning to understand.

"The best part is that three days later He came back to life again. He defeated Death so that He could offer us eternal life!"

"So that means that everybody's saved, right?" asked a girl on the right.

"No way," said Mrs. B. "Listen carefully. God completed His part. He did everything necessary for a person to be accepted by Him. But the only one He will acknowledge is the one that comes humbly to Him, admitting, confessing and turning from his sin. The Bible calls that 'repentance.'

"That person renounces any attempt on his own to try to make himself acceptable by good works, religious acts, or anything else. In hopelessness and desperation he casts himself on the mercy of God.

"He asks God to forgive him because he believes that when Jesus died on the cross, He suffered the punishment for his sin. And that when Jesus rose again, He conquered death and is now offering that person eternal life. This applies to every man, woman, and child on earth.

"God forgives the person's sin and transfers Jesus' perfection to him or her."

She glanced at the clock.

"In our very first Bible class, I told you that I choose to believe the Bible. Today's lesson is the key to the whole issue. It is up to you to believe it or reject it. Just remember, we have no guarantee that we will live to see tomorrow, let alone next year."

The bell.

* * * *

Her ESOL party was on the Thursday before Christmas break. Some of her students brought her gifts. She got four more mugs to add to her already large collection that kids had given her over the years, two very nice scarves, a couple of knick-knacks that would probably end up in the re-gifting box, a clay flower pot with a sleepy little Mexican coastal village painted on it, candy which she needed like she needed another hole in the head, a tooled leather purse from Mexico, and a beautiful Japanese kimono from Reiko. She felt it was too expensive to accept, but she could see that Reiko really wanted her to have it.

"My mother is very happy that you let me stay in your class even though I already speak English. She said it was good for me. We are Buddhists and don't celebrate Christmas, but we wanted to give you a gift anyway."

"Thank you, Reiko. Tell your mother thank you and that I'm happy you could stay."

After school as she was cleaning up from the parties, Seth and Diego came to her room. Seth's eyes were red, and Lynn was afraid to ask what had happened.

"I just stopped by to tell you I will be celebrating both Hanukkah and Christmas this year," said Seth.

"You will?" said Lynn, caught totally off-guard.

"I don't understand."

"Well, Diego and I were talking, and I finally realized that Jesus is the Messiah! Only the Messiah could keep all of the Ten Commandments. When He was dying on the cross, He was suffering for my sin, and then when He came alive again, He conquered death so He could give me life."

Tears of joy again filled his eyes.

"I have been accepted by God now, not because of my race or my religion, but just because of Jesus."

She was thrilled beyond words. She threw her arms around the boy, and then gave Diego, who was all but dancing a jig, a hug as well.

"I gotta run. My mom is waiting!" said Seth as he ran out of her room and took off down the hall. He turned around and waved, "Merry Christmas!"

Jack Barrett was still at his locker when Seth came out of Lynn's room, grinning from ear to ear. What was that all about? he thought.

Chapter 27

The semester was finally over!

On Friday night, everyone at the Bartholomews' was concentrating on personal plans.

Pastor Juan came over to talk to Sam about the Hispanic *Fiesta de Navidad*, scheduled for the next evening, Saturday the 17th. He and Sam went out to the barn to get away from the hubbub in the house. After they had worked out all of the final details, Sam turned to go inside.

"Uh… Sam…" stuttered Pastor Juan.

He was suddenly nervous and didn't seem to be able to get the rest of his sentence out. Eventually, he managed, and he and Sam talked for several more minutes.

"But they're undocumented."

"I know," said Juan miserably. "I am sure this is what God wants, so I am trusting Him to work it out." Sam shook his hand, and while he still held it, he prayed that God would, indeed, work it out.

Lynn noticed that the men had been outside for a long time. When they came in, Pastor Juan looked relieved, and Sam looked like the cat that swallowed the canary. What was that all about?

"What…?"

"Don't even ask," said Sam with a smug little smile. "Christmas is a time for secrets."

He knew his wife hated not knowing all the details, and he fully intended to squeeze every ounce of twisted pleasure out of this situation. He grabbed her, did a couple of waltz turns around the kitchen, gave her a quick kiss on the forehead, and swaggered away.

* * * *

Saturday night was Pastor Juan's *fiesta*, and Maria was again pouring herself into her cooking. Lynn did what she could to help, but she had her hands full with other things. Sam, Diego, and Ana pitched in wherever needed. Shep made a general nuisance of himself.

The *fiesta* drew a lot of people that Lynn had never seen before. She tried to meet everyone, and most of them were really nice. There were some that were a little standoffish and appeared to be mistrusting, but that was understandable. And then there were those that really wanted nothing to do with her or Sam.

Guess prejudice works both ways, she thought.

A *Mariachi* band was making the rounds, and several other men had brought guitars. She was surprised when Pastor Juan also took out a guitar. He played along with the men and was really quite good. They played traditional Mexican folk music and Christmas songs.

Every time the *Mariachi* band took a break, Diego cornered the trumpet player. Soon the boy had his horn out and was trying some new tricks the older man showed him. Diego's tone was good, but Ken's old cornet just didn't have much of a ring to it.

The Lopez kids and the Garcia kids had spent hours making "fringe pennant streamers," as Lynn called them, out of old catalog pages, to hang in strategic locations around the property. Tables were set up in the barn and were loaded to the groaning point with food and brightly colored decorations. Lynn recognized some of the common Mexican dishes like refried beans, rice, enchiladas, etc., but there were a lot of foods she could not identify.

There were bonfires in three different locations outside, and people were always crowded around them. It was a really mild evening, but who doesn't like to sit around the fire? The only contribution the Bartholomews made to the evening was The All-American Toasted Marshmallows. Everyone loved them. Who wouldn't?

Floodlights shone on the basketball court for the teens, and the younger kids chased each other or played hide-and-seek in the barn. Some of the men didn't seem to know what to do with themselves without booze, but the men of the church did their best to keep them occupied. There were checkers and dominoes, and Padre Rafael from the Catholic church played the Mexican version of dodge ball along with some of the teens. The Bible church kids did their part to include everyone in their games. Lynn's head was swimming from trying to understand the rapid conversational Spanish the folks used among themselves.

As it began to get late, Pastor Juan passed the word. "*La Piñata!*" Everyone gathered in the barn where the *piñata* had been hanging out of reach, but not out of sight.

When they were all inside, Juan jumped up on a picnic table and took the mike Sam had set up. He addressed the gathering in Spanish.

"Before we break the *piñata*, I would like to say a few words."

He called Sam and Lynn to the front.

"Most of you know what the Bartholomews have done and are doing for the Lopez family."

A few heads nodded slightly, but most people just waited for him to go on.

Sam and Lynn stood there in ignorance, an uncertain grin on Sam's face.

"I just want you to know that there are a lot more *Americanos* out there that are just as kind as they are. Most of them will accept our people, but we have to do our part."

"With all respect, Pastor," someone broke in, "there might be other nice *gringos*, but not many would take us into their home like the Bar... Barto... like the B's have."

The laughter helped everyone relax. Sam and Lynn took the opportunity to melt back into the crowd.

"You're probably right about that, but what do you think we can do to help the *Americanos* get along with us? What do you think our part would be?"

General mumbling and murmuring.

"Go back to Mexico," shouted someone bitterly.

"Friend, that may be the answer for some of us, but I'm talking about those of us who are staying here."

"It's complicated," said an older gentleman.

"Very complicated," agreed Pastor Juan, "but I was looking for just a few simple suggestions.

"Let me put it this way. If hundreds of thousands of *Americanos* migrated to Mexico, what would we want from them? How would we want them to behave?"

"Be clean!" hollered one lady. "Not dirty up our country."

"*Ay!*" said Pastor Juan as if in pain. "We're bad about throwing our McDonald's trash out the window, aren't we? What else?"

"Not get in trouble." This from a long-haired teenager.

"Great point," said Pastor Juan. "How many in our community have been arrested for drunk driving or possession of drugs or prostitution or petty theft or any of the other things we get ourselves into?"

The atmosphere was suddenly sober.

"I guess what I am trying to say is that, even though we aren't all citizens of the United States, we all need to act like good citizens.

"Basically, we need to follow the words of Jesus that He said in Matthew 7:12, 'Whatsoever ye would that men should do to you, do ye even so to them.'

"Can we do that? Not everyone will be kind in return, but you are not responsible for their actions, only yours."

Not everyone saw his point or agreed with it, but many of them did.

"Now, one more thing before we break that great big *piñata* up there. Christmas night you're all invited to our church for our annual program. We start at 6:00, and the church will be packed, so come early to get a good seat."

"And to Mass at Our Lady at 7:00 and 11:00 p.m. on Christmas Eve," broke in Padre Raphael.

"OK, who's up first?" asked Pastor Juan as Manuel handed him a broomstick.

Several kids raised their hands, wagging them in the air and jumping up and down.

"*¡Yo! ¡Yo!*" they cried, each trying to out yell the other.

"I think we should let *Señor Sam* go first, don't you?" asked the pastor above the din.

This was met with loud agreement, and Sam was drafted to be the first one to try to destroy the little donkey Diego had made.

He swung his heart out. If he had connected, he would have sent candy into the next time zone. Fortunately, the guy on the other end of the rope was a pro at keeping that candy-pregnant critter just out of reach. After Sam, several young people and kids tried until someone finally broke it, scattering its contents from one end of the barn to the other. Lynn was nearly run down by the rush of kids from behind her. She learned a valuable lesson that night: never stand in the front when there's a *piñata* to be broken.

* * * *

In the last week before Christmas, Maria was sewing frantically during the day when no one else was around. Diego was spending a lot of his free time in Sam's workshop. Lynn and Ana went their separate ways each time they drove to the mall. Sam seemed to be on the computer 24/7. He was sneaky enough to have everything delivered to his office where he conned his secretary into wrapping all his gifts. Actually, she was almost as excited as he was about the things he had chosen. He decided to add a little extra to her bonus this year. Christmas was coming, ready or not.

* * * *

Ken and Liz, the Bartholomews' adult children, and families felt that they already knew the Lopezes because Sam and Lynn had kept them so well informed on life in Perkins Grove. Liz's kids, Nathan and Maggie were just a little younger than Diego and Ana and both played in the band at their school. They would all get along fine. Lynn felt sure the girls would spoil Ken and Marj's baby Lisa rotten. Liz spoke a little Spanish, and Marj loved to cook. Lynn could already hear the laughter and giggles that would come from the kitchen when they all crowded in there with Maria. The brothers-in-law and Sam always had a good time together. Twelve people, two bathrooms, three meals a day—all things considered, she was expecting a great holiday. Oh, yes, and she had invited Pastor Juan and his family for Christmas dinner. That added five more. On the 26th, Sam was committing her to the asylum up the road.

Sam and Lynn, along with Ken and Liz and their families had all gone together to get Maria, Diego and Ana one big Christmas present each. Sam had spent hours on the Internet searching for bargains and had finally come up with some quality products for some really cheap prices. The items weren't new but were in excellent condition.

Ken's family arrived on Thursday. The baby took to Ana immediately, and Ana appointed herself Keeper of the Child. When Lisa tried to play in Shep's water bowl or eat his dog food, it was Ana that rescued her and gave the bewildered dog a pat on the head. Grandma Lynn could see that she was going to have to pull rank if she wanted to spend any time at all with her grandbaby.

Sam and Ken were dispatched to pick up Liz and Peter, and their kids at the Atlanta airport on Friday. It was happy bedlam when everyone got home, and the decibel level ebbed and flowed like the tide. Shep alternated between interrupting the activities of the different groups, taking refuge behind the

Bartholomews' bed, and begging to be let out. The quantity of gifts under the tree grew to ridiculous proportions, nearly engulfing the tree itself. When the kids started pulling out their instruments, Grandma banished them to the barn. Enough was enough!

Christmas Eve. Everyone was sitting around the fire after supper. Actually, the front door had been flung open and the kitchen window raised as high as it would go. The ceiling fan was going full-blast. It was pushing 80° in the living room, and every one in the Wisconsin contingent was barefoot, in shorts and T-shirts.

"But we have to have a fire to open presents," declared Liz, arms out, palms up. "It's tradition."

It was also tradition to act out the Christmas story from Luke 2 in the Bible. Parts were assigned, and as Peter read the well-known verses, the characters moved through the story. This year there were a few extra angels and shepherds. When the impromptu play was over, the family sat quietly for a minute while Sam reminded them that the Child in the manger came for one purpose, to suffer the punishment for our sin so that we could be accepted by a holy God. Maria understood most of what he said, and Diego filled in the blanks. After sharing, Sam asked if anyone else had anything to say. It was quiet, and he was about to move on…

"Thank You, God, for everythings that happen this year, for I can learn trust Jesus for Savior." It was Diego's voice that prayed quietly in the silence.

Maria prayed in Spanish, and Lynn thought she understood that it was along the same lines as Diego's prayer, although she heard her and Sam's names mentioned too. She was glad God was not limited to one language.

"Thank You for giving me cousins my age," blurted Nathan, "and that they like music!"

It was quiet for a long moment. Finally, Ken prayed, "Thank You, God, for coming to Earth as a tiny, helpless baby in the lowest of circumstances... and all because of Your amazing love for us." He paused.

"Now, Lord, as we open the expressions of love that we have for one another, help us to remember that it's all because of You. Amen."

"Amen!" boomed Sam. He, along with the rest of them, was sniffling and wiping tears. A box of tissues made the rounds.

A car passed slowly on the lane and turned around. Before it reached the Bartholomews' driveway, the driver turned off the lights and engine and let the car roll to a stop. He could see the scene around the Christmas tree through the picture window and the open front door, but he was just far enough back in the shadows that he could not be seen.

Baby Lisa had fallen asleep in her grandmother's lap, so Marj put her to bed.

"Traditionally," said Sam after everyone had settled in front of the fire, "we take turns opening presents so everyone can see what everyone else got."

He looked at the pile of presents that seemed to be taking up half the living room. "Any suggestions?"

Everyone had an opinion and gave it all at once.

Peter raised his hand high above the assembly.

"Peter," said Lynn in her teacher voice. Peter got the floor.

"Why don't we let the kids go first, then the ladies, then, if us guys are still awake, we'll open ours."

"I second the motion," said Maggie, jumping up to hand out gifts.

Ana and Diego's piles were considerably smaller than Nathan and Maggie's. They couldn't help but notice, but they were grateful for the new shoes. Ana also got some jewelry and Diego got some aftershave. Maria received a devotional book and some lotion.

Maria had sewn beautiful gifts for everyone, even the men; Diego had made wooden Scripture plaques with gorgeous wood-burning backgrounds for each family. The boy definitely had an artistic flare. Ana had used some of her recorder money to purchase appropriate gifts for each person.

Everyone was sitting there amidst their gifts when Sam, Peter and Ken disappeared into the bedroom and came back with several larger packages. The Bartholomew family's eyes were all shining at the Lopezes' reaction when Sam presented Maria, Diego and Ana their "real" presents.

Ana was first. She got three packages and began with the smallest one. An alto recorder! The middle-sized one was a tenor recorder, and the big one was a bass recorder. All three came with instruction books. She was flabbergasted. She didn't even know these instruments existed, and here they were, hers! Out came the tissues again.

When Diego opened his box, he found a full-sized Conn trumpet, with all the accessories and a new case. He couldn't believe his eyes.

"For me?" he whispered, caressing the instrument lovingly.

"For you," said Sam quietly.

Ken had put Maria's gift on the dining room table. It was by far the biggest and heaviest. Sam's secretary had packed it in such a way that the whole box just lifted off. He showed Maria how to do it.

Before the box was even halfway up, Ana screamed, "¡*Mamita*!"

"Sh-sh! The baby!" chorused the Bartholomew mothers.

When Maria saw the almost brand new sewing machine, her hands flew to her face and covered her mouth. She stood perfectly still, tears streaming down her cheeks unheeded. Her children flanked her on either side, arms across her shoulders. The rest of the family gathered around the table one by one.

"Tissue!" someone ordered.

At last Sam broke the silence. "Thank You, Father, for family. Thank You that You placed the generosity of heart within my own children to help with the purchase of these gifts for our newest family members. Thank You most of all for the gift of Life that You provide us through Your own precious family member, Jesus, in whose name we pray…"

Suddenly, Lynn lifted her head at the noise that didn't belong. Shep got up and padded to the front screen door, ears twitching. The car had started up and slowly moved away.

"Amen!" the family chorused.

The driver of the car was sad. He missed his mother and wondered if she was having a merry Christmas with her Hispanic family. As he slowly drove to the dismal alley behind the restaurant, his sadness turned to rage and bitter hatred.

It ain't fair! he thought, banging his fist on the steering wheel. Diego Lopez don't deserve all this—this happiness—when all I get 's a drunk dad, who's mad at me all the time for no reason. It just ain't fair!

He went into the filthy house without even a hint of Christmas to be seen.

"Merry Christmas," he whispered mockingly to the snoring figure on the couch.

* * * *

Christmas fell on Sunday that year, and the whole family, including the Lopezes, went to church with the Bartholomews. They took up two whole pews. What a blessing!

The music was glorious and the message just right for the occasion.

"Merry Christmas!" said everyone to everyone else.

After church Pastor Juan and his family came for dinner, bringing the total to seventeen. It took a while for the ladies to get everything on the tables, stepping around the men, kids, and dog. The teens had two card tables that they shared with the little guys. Baby Lisa cried until her high chair was placed at the end of the kids' table closest to her mother. It was a little awkward to hold hands around the tables, but they finally managed when they all stood up. Heads bowed, they waited for Sam to pray. The varied aromas wafting up from the dishes to the folks standing around the tables was delightful torture, and Sam mercifully kept the blessing short.

Everyone sat down expectantly and started passing platters and bowls. The star attraction was the enormous ham that Lynn had baked with pineapple rings and Maraschino cherries in their centers. Marj had put together a sweet potato soufflé with pecans and toasted marshmallow topping. There were mashed potatoes, green bean casserole, homemade rolls from Maria, and Liz had spent half of yesterday afternoon chopping vegetables for a big broccoli salad. Sam had begged and ultimately bribed Maria into making the same chocolate cake she had made for his homecoming party in September, but that would come later.

Shep kept trying to lick the baby's spoon—and the baby—until he was finally banished to the great outdoors.

When they finished eating, no one moved, not even baby Lisa. They all just sat as if in a stupor, feeling a little guilty for the seconds, thirds, and fourths they had eaten. Finally, the kids made their way outside, the men waddled into the living room, and Baby Lisa went down for a nap.

"Mom," said Liz while she was at the kitchen sink rinsing the dishes for the dishwasher, "thank you for taking in the Lopezes. They're great and have truly enriched our lives. This has been the best Christmas ever!" She gave her mom a big hug.

In just a couple of days it was time for the visitors to go home. No one knew what the future held for the Lopez family, but Lynn knew that Liz had been right, their lives had definitely been enriched by their presence.

Chapter 28

Second semester. Where was the time going? Mrs. B's English classes were doing exceptionally well. Unless a whole new crop of immigrants moved in next year, she was out of a job.

Several of her Bible class students transferred to other enrichment activities at the beginning of the semester, as Lynn assumed they might. Jack Barrett was still coming, although she couldn't quite figure out why. Ben Gibson and Frank Walenski continued, but they seemed to have drifted away from Jack. Daniel Aimes had sought out different friends, and his new buddies came to Bible class, so he stayed too. All but one or two of the foreign students still came. Mr. Cline and Mr. Philips continued, and the principal seemed satisfied that things were still going smoothly.

Between Christmas and New Years Day, Diego had hardly put his new trumpet down. He went to Mr. Randolph as soon as school started.

"Mr. Randolph, may I can join the band?" he asked.

"Now?" asked Mr. Randolph, "in the middle of the year? What do you play?"

"Trumpet."

"How long have you played?"

"I start in September."

"You've only been playing for four months, and you want to join the high school band in the middle of the year?"

"Yes, sir," said Diego.

"I don't think…"

"Please, sir, you will listen me play?" asked Diego hopefully. "You listen and say no, if I no play good. OK?"

"Fair enough," said Mr. Randolph.

He pulled out a Sousa march and gave it to the boy to sight-read. "This is a pretty fast piece, but you can start slowly, if you like."

Diego studied the music for a minute, raised his horn and played. He missed a few notes, but actually, did very well. Mr. Randolph was impressed.

"Are you sure you've only been playing since September? Who's your teacher?"

"Yes, sir. Sam Bartholomew teach me all days. I have a brok-ed arm at first, so was little more hard, but I practice and I practice. I get this trumpet for Christmas."

Mr. Randolph took the horn and examined it. "Very nice!"

Diego's proud grin spread from ear to ear. "Thank you!"

"Do you have any music with you that you've been working on?"

Diego took out a duet piece that he and Sam had been practicing to play as an offertory at church.

Mr. Randolph looked at it. "Are you sure you can play this? Hang on just a second," He went to the closet and came back with his own silver cornet. "Let's play it together. Which part do I play?"

The two of them played together, and a couple of students poked their heads in the door to see what was going on.

When they were finished, spontaneous applause broke out in the hallway. "What do you have fourth hour?" asked Mr. Randolph.

"Today, study hall. Tomorrow, band, yes?"

Mr. Randolph laughed out loud.

"Yes! See you tomorrow fourth hour."

* * * *

Sam was slumped down in his desk chair, tie loosened, half-asleep, reading yet another site on the Internet. He'd never mentioned it to Lynn, but he had been searching the

Net for several days after work, trying to find a way for Maria and the kids to get visas. He had already spoken to the man Cisco recommended and learned that the family could stay in Perkins Grove at least until school was out this year.

He had jumped from site to link to site, *ad infinitum*, and frankly, he was getting discouraged. Suddenly, he sat up straight, wide awake! Could this be it?

It seemed there was a provision for people in danger—refugees, if you please.

Why hadn't he thought of that before? He was excited. Religious, racial and social persecution were the only motives usually allowed for a refugee or asylum status visa to be issued, but he knew of cases where people fleeing natural disasters and wars were granted entrance also.

This site said that people who had offended a criminal organization were not eligible, but what if those people had had no knowledge of the offence? Could a case be made?

"Juan!" he said when the pastor answered the phone. "I think I've found it!" He then read the paragraphs.

"Praise God!" said the pastor. "Now what?"

"Well, I'll call Stan, the guy Cisco told me about. I've talked to him once, but he wasn't too helpful as far as permanent status goes. Maybe this will build a fire under him."

"Go for it!" said Pastor Juan.

Sam immediately made the call. He got through the robots only to discover that Stan was in a meeting. He tried again a few minutes later. Closed! The robot just told him to leave a number. He didn't.

There was nothing to do but wait until the next day. He consulted his schedule on the computer—jammed until noon, and the afternoon wasn't much better. He would call over lunch.

He would have to be careful when he got home. Lynn could read him like a book and would want to know what was going on. He needed a diversion. It was Tuesday. He checked the school calendar. His wonderful wife could be an airhead sometimes, so he kept the calendar to remind her if she had something coming up.

Yes! That'll do!

"Hey, Hon!" he greeted her over the phone. "What're you doing tonight?"

"Nothing that I can think of. You're the Keeper of the Calendar. You tell me what we're doing." She sounded tired. He would have to convince her that tonight's game would be a good idea.

"Do the kids have their homework done? Have they been to a basketball game yet?"

"Don't know and don't know, but I'll ask. That's a great idea! Is there a home game tonight?"

"Yep. Just checked the calendar. We'll invite Juan and his crew and Antonio. Do you want me to pick you up or meet at the school?"

"Hang on and let me ask Maria if they would like to go."

He could hear mumbling. He smiled, visualizing the phone against his wife's tummy where it always was when she didn't want the caller to hear.

"Great! Why don't you pick us up? What time?"

"Let's see. Says here the girls' game starts at six. No JV tonight. Varsity boys are right after the girls, so you name the time. I'm ready to go. I'll just come home and lose the tie, and we'll take off. How's that?"

"Sounds good. We'll be ready. Hot dogs at the game for supper?"

"Yuck!" said Sam. "But I'll gag one down for the sake of family unity." He loved to make his wife laugh.

He called Juan.

"Can't reach Stan until tomorrow. Do your kids have their homework done? Can you pick up Antonio and meet us at the basketball game tonight? Our treat. I had to have something to keep Lynn from noticing my excitement. She knows me too well." He waited for Pastor Juan's response.

"Great! See you there!"

The girls gave the other team a beating they would be ashamed of for a while. Unfortunately, the tables were turned for the boys. Although Jack Barrett was the star of the team and usually made twenty to thirty points a game, when he saw Diego and crew in the stands, he got so distracted he couldn't buy a basket. County lost 82-48. Ouch! Yet another reason to despise Diego Lopez.

By the time they got home, the family was worn out, and everyone went straight to bed.

Whew! thought Sam, dodged that bullet!

In the morning he got up and left a little early. "Gotta make an early phone call," he said as he kissed his wife good-bye. It had occurred to him as he was falling asleep last night that government offices open at 8:00. His office opened at nine.

"This is Stan," said the official after Sam had finally reached his office.

"Stan! Sam Bartholomew here. How are you?"

"Good," said Stan. "What can I do for you?"

"You remember our conversation about the illegals living with us? I think I've found something."

"I remember," said Stan. "What ya got?"

Sam told him what site to go to and then the section and paragraph. Stan read over it quickly.

"Do you think that would apply to threats from a drug cartel?"

He then reminded Stan of the letter and everything he had told him during their earlier conversation.

"Usually, they wouldn't be eligible, but your case is not usual," said Stan. I'm sorry I didn't think of it earlier. Email me a copy of the letter and the translation, along with a brief description of the situation. I'll take it from there and get back to you."

"Can they stay in the States while they're in process?" asked Sam.

"Well, we've already established that they can stay until school is out this year. Seems reasonable that they wouldn't have to go where their lives are in danger."

"Terrific!" said Sam. "Thanks much, my friend!"

"Hope it works out for you," said Stan.

Sam hung up and leaned back in his plush desk chair, hands clasped behind his head.

"Thank You, God!" he prayed out loud.

* * * *

Ana's group was invited to play in the spring concert the last Friday night in April, so they started practicing in earnest right away. With the addition of the alto, tenor, and bass recorders, which some of the other kids had bought after Ana had introduced them, the sound was much richer, fuller. Lynn was proud of the girl. What had started as a distraction to keep her mind off the prejudice against her people had turned into a project that had blinded the eyes of the participants to cultural, national or racial differences. Perhaps that attitude would spread to the rest of the town.

Chapter 29

Mr. Tucker, the high school science teacher, had planned a field trip combining all three of his science classes for the last Friday in January. They were going to Perkins Gorge to study the plants and animals in winter. An outdoor field trip at this time of year was risky, but how else could they see things firsthand? It was all Diego talked about for days.

The day of the much-anticipated field trip finally arrived. Diego jumped out of bed, got dressed, ate breakfast and was ready to go before Lynn even had her coffee.

"What's this?" she asked, filling her cup.

"How you can forget?" asked Diego. "Today my science class go to the Perkins Gorge for the field trip."

"That's right!" She was happy to see the boy so excited. "Do you have your lunch, water bottle, dry socks and rain poncho? Are you dressed warmly enough?"

"Yes, I am use layers, like you say, and here is everythings I need," said Diego, patting the daypack Sam had loaned him. "I have the cookies *Ma*... Mom... made to share." He was trying to use Americanisms whenever he could.

"Do you need anything else?"

"Nope," said Diego, again trying to sound more American. "When we come to home, Antonio, Daniel, and me, we gonna know every trees in the gorge. We gonna make the presentation in the class. Gonna win first place in science fair!"

She had also forgotten that the boys were going to stay overnight with Diego to work on their project. Ana was to spend the night with Gloria.

Lynn had never seen Diego so excited. In the car he chattered like a middle school girl the whole way. Ana couldn't get a word in edgewise. Lynn chuckled at his enthusiasm when he left her at her door and went, almost skipping, down the hall.

Over sixty kids were making the trip, plus parents. Besides Antonio and Diego, two girls were missing from Lynn's first hour class. With only seven students in the class, having four out made it impossible to have a normal lesson. Mostly the remaining three chatted with their teacher about this and that, Mrs. B gently providing correction, when necessary.

Perkins Gorge was amazing, and Diego was loving every minute of the field trip. When the bus passed the location of Armando Lopez's accident, Diego felt Antonio lean over him to look out. Diego kept his face to the window while he searched his heart to try to identify any emotion. There was no sense of loss, no loneliness, no bitterness, hatred or regret. All he could find was an unfathomable sadness for his father's rejection of God.

After a morning of exploration and discovery, the group stopped to eat their bag lunches at a picnic site near the edge of the gorge.

Even in the dead of winter, the view was amazing. The colors were not the riotous colors of autumn, the light greens of budding spring, nor the dark variations of summer. They were the muted browns and cold grays of winter, accented by dark evergreens.

Because the deciduous trees had lost their leaves, the panorama was actually better than during the other seasons. The kids saw trees growing straight out of the rocks and water glistening in the sun as it trickled down the sheer faces of cliffs to the river. They could see clearly the trails on the other, less-visited side of the gorge. At one point, Mr. Tucker made everyone be quiet and listen to the water flowing rapidly far below. They could hear the thunder of the waterfall in the distance. Diego drew a deep, contented breath, savoring the smell of the crisp, fresh air.

After the kids had disposed of their trash and policed the area, they shouldered their backpacks and started up the trail where it followed the precipice. Daniel, Antonio, and Diego had fallen back to the end of the line, and Jack Barrett was last, behind Diego. When Diego stopped to examine one of the trees and make a rubbing of its bark, the rest of the group disappeared around a bend in the trail.

This was the moment Jack had been waiting for! Suddenly, he ran up to Diego, pushed him and stuck his foot out to trip him. Both boys went down.

Jack crashed through the split-rail fence and slid toward the gorge, head first!

"Aaaagh!" he screamed. "Help!"

He was scrambling to get back on the trail when the ground gave way beneath him! The whole ledge he had just been on was suddenly gone!

Diego swung one arm and caught Jack's ankle as he slid downward with the landslide and hooked his other arm around the tree at the edge of the trail.

"Help me! Don't let go! Don't let me fall!" screamed Jack, struggling to grab anything within reach. There was nothing to grab on the steep slope.

"Diego, don't let go! Don't let me die! Please!"

"No moving!" commanded Diego.

He was losing his grip as Jack kept kicking and twisting.

Antonio and Daniel heard Jack's screams and looked at each other. Hesitating only a split second, they sprinted back around the bend.

"Mr. Tucker!" yelled Daniel. "Mr. Tucker! HELP!"

Antonio threw himself on his stomach to try and reach Jack. He was too short, so he scrambled to his feet.

"Put your legs around tree and hold my legs," he ordered Daniel.

The taller boy flopped down on his back. He locked his legs around the tree, wrapped his arms around Antonio's legs, and laced his fingers, forming a human chain. Now Antonio was over the precipice too.

"Jack!" yelled Daniel, "shut up and stop kickin'! We can't get you if you keep kickin' us! Jack! Stop kickin'!"

Daniel's words finally penetrated Jack's panic and he stopped kicking. His screams turned to whimpers, "Please... please... please!"

Antonio managed to grab Jack's other leg just as Mr. Tucker gripped his pants on Diego's side. Everyone crowded around to see what was going on.

"Get back!" ordered Mr. Tucker. "Move down the trail. This whole rim could go! Brad, Stuart, you may stay. The rest of you, go! Mrs. Mason, you're in charge!"

The girls were staring, wide-eyed and pale. Some had started crying. Mrs. Mason herded everyone to a wider, safer place on the trail.

Less than two minutes had passed since Jack and Diego had fallen, but it seemed like an eternity.

"OK, let's get 'im up here!" yelled Mr. Tucker.

He, Antonio and Diego dragged Jack's legs toward them until half his body was back on the trail. The other two boys helped pull him all the way back on the trail and then helped Antonio and Daniel up.

For a while, all they could do was sit there panting.

Jack needed several minutes to stop crying before Mr. Tucker supported him down the trail to where the others were waiting and lowered him to rest against a boulder.

The boy was still shaking badly. Someone passed him a water bottle.

Diego, sitting a couple of feet away with Daniel and Antonio, was pale, in spite of his naturally olive skin, and was rubbing his bad arm.

"Jack, Diego," said Mr. Tucker when they had calmed down. "What on earth happened back there?"

Silence. Then Jack spoke in his whiny, bitter voice. "This idiot tripped me!" he accused.

"Diego?" said Mr. Tucker.

Diego looked at him and shook his head. Then he looked down.

"What happened?" demanded Mr. Tucker.

The boy again shook his head without looking up.

"I tol' you he tripped me! He was tryin' to kill me 'n' just about did!"

"Didn't look like that t' me," snapped Daniel. "When we got there, looked t' me like he was tryin' to save your life, not end it."

Mr. Tucker took off his ball cap and scratched his head. He was shaken.

"Well," he said finally, "All I can do is cut our trip short and get back to school so Mr. Cline can deal with you."

The bus was quiet on the ride back. Diego felt awful, but what could he do? It wasn't his fault, but who would believe him?

"Lord," he prayed silently, "show me what to do. Please, show me what to do."

Lynn had planned to stay all day to wait for the boys, so she worked on bulletin boards, which she hated with a passion, and the never-ending lesson plans. Next week, progress reports were going out, so she also had to average everyone's grades, another job she could do without. If only she could just *teach* without all the other stuff.

Oh, well, guess it comes with the territory, she thought.

"Mrs. Bartholomew, please come to the office. Mrs. Bartholomew."

Lynn nearly jumped out of her skin when she heard her name come over the speaker in her room.

"Coming!" she said, not knowing whether anyone heard her or not.

She headed for the office at a gallop, thinking all the way. This has to be an emergency. Why else would they call me? Who died? Who's hurt? Sam? What's going on? Lord...

Finally, after what seemed like a 5k run, she hooked a left into the office.

"Sheila?" she asked breathlessly.

"Go right in," said the secretary, looking concerned.

When she opened the door, she saw Diego and Jack Barrett sitting across the desk from the principal.

Oh, no! Her heart sank.

"Come in," said Mr. Cline solemnly. "Have a seat."

As she sat down, she looked at Diego. His jacket was torn, he was filthy, and he was wearing one tennis shoe and one very dirty sock. He was looking at his hands, so she couldn't see his face nor read his body language.

Jack was fidgeting. He also was dirty and scratched up.

She waited for Mr. Cline to speak. "It seems we have a problem here," he finally said. He was speaking as if it grieved him to have to tell her whatever it was he was going to say.

He hesitated.

"It was his fault!" Jack shouted. "He jumped me when nobody was around!"

Mr. Cline waited. Diego didn't move a muscle. Jack fidgeted. Mr. Cline still waited.

"What could I do? I hadda defen' m'self!" yelled Jack, almost in tears.

Mr. Cline waited.

Lynn knew what she was hearing couldn't be true, but she had to let Mr. Cline take the lead.

"Lord, help him," she prayed silently.

"Diego?" said Mr. Cline.

Diego didn't respond.

"Diego, is that the way it happened?" asked Mr. Cline.

Diego kept staring at his hands. Finally he lifted his head and looked Mr. Cline in the eye. "No, sir," he said.

Jack jumped up screaming, "It is too, you filthy spic! That's exactly what happened!"

"Sit down, Jack!" ordered Mr. Cline sharply. "We'll have no more of that in this office. Understand?"

Jack sat down, sulking.

"No one more was there," said Diego. "Jack know he is lie, but is only what I say and what he say. Who gonna believe a filthy spic?" He said it without bitterness—more like hopelessness.

"But I would like to hear your side of the story, please. What happened?" asked Mr. Cline.

Diego looked at Jack. Jack looked at Diego.

"Why won't you b'lieve me?" cried Jack, jumping up again.

The tears were spilling out of his eyes now. He dashed them away bitterly.

"Look at 'im. He won't even say nothin'! That should prove he's guilty!"

"Sit down, Jack!" demanded Mr. Cline again.

The room was silent, except for Jack's sniffling, while Mr. Cline tried to figure out what to do. The boy ran a sleeve under his nose, leaving a smear of mud across his face.

"You boys wait in the secretary's office while I talk to Mrs. B," said the principal.

Jack jerked himself out of his chair and bolted for the door. Diego stood up slowly, and with his shoulders hunched dejectedly, walked to the door. He didn't look at Lynn.

Mr. Cline took a deep breath and let it out slowly.

"So, what do we do?" he asked Lynn.

"I don't know what to tell you. But I do know that I don't believe Jack's story for an instant. What happened?"

"According to Mr. Tucker, Diego saved Jack's life. The two boys had fallen behind the others. Mr. Tucker heard someone yelling for help. By the time he got there, he saw Diego on the ground with one arm wrapped around a tree. He was holding on to Jack's ankle with the other hand. Jack's whole upper body was hanging over the edge of the gorge. Antonio and Daniel were making a human chain to reach

Jack's other leg to pull him up. Mr. Tucker and the other boys helped, and somehow between them, they got everyone back on the trail.

"Mr. Tucker said both boys were as white as sheets, especially Jack, but as soon as he realized he was safe, he started cussing Diego out for jumping him. Diego wouldn't say anything then either."

"What did Antonio and Daniel say?"

"Same thing. They heard Jack and Diego yelling. When they got there, they saw Diego holding on to Jack's ankle and made the chain to help pull him up. We don't know what happened before that, but like Diego said, it's his word against Jack's."

"And none of the other kids saw anything either?"

"No, they were all further along the trail."

They sat in silence.

"What are you going to do?" asked Lynn.

"I don't know yet. The boys are obviously both suspended until we can get to the bottom of this. But I can tell you one thing…" He stopped and looked at her seriously.

"What?"

"Mr. Barrett is not going to take this lying down."

Lynn just looked at him. She took a deep breath and let it out slowly. Great.

"I don't imagine it will occur to him or Jack to thank Diego for saving his life."

"I don't imagine it will."

"What do you suggest I do?" asked Lynn.

"I don't have a clue, unless you can somehow convince Diego to tell you the truth."

He stood up. "Now if you'll excuse me, I have a very unpleasant phone call to make. I don't share your faith, Mrs. B, but if you would pray for me while I call Mr. Barrett, I would really appreciate it."

Lynn had also stood up to leave, but when Mr. Cline said that, she dropped her head right there in his office and prayed for him and all the others involved.

When she finished, Mr. Cline said, "Wow! I've never had anybody do that for me before. Thank you."

She could see he was moved.

"And you can be sure that I'll keep praying for you until this is resolved," she said as she started out.

She stopped with her hand on the door. "Actually, I pray for you regularly anyway. I know I wouldn't even try to run a school like this without God's help."

After a quick stop at his locker, Lynn took Diego to her room. She didn't try to question him on the incident; she would ask Pastor Juan to do that. They got there just before the final bell rang. She wanted to wait for the halls to clear before they started for the car. Diego went to the back corner so no one could see that he was there, but people kept peering through the door window, just the same. The rumor mill was well oiled and running at full throttle.

Ana slammed the door open, a look of horror on her face.

"Diego!" she cried. She had heard the rumors.

Lynn went behind her to close the door on the mob in the hall. The girl ran to her brother and threw her arms around him, sobbing. What on earth had she heard?

A few minutes later Daniel and Antonio appeared at her door.

Good grief! She'd again forgotten they were supposed to come home with her tonight. Now what?

"Mrs. B," said Daniel, "do you still want us to come to your house tonight?"

"Yes!" interrupted Diego emphatically, breaking Ana's embrace. "We no gonna let Jack control!"

He grabbed his backpack and started for the door. "Let's go!"

"Whoa!" said Lynn. "Daniel, Antonio, do y'all still want to come over?"

The boys looked at each other. "I, yes," said Antonio.

"Me too," put in Daniel. "I agree with Diego. We can't let bitter people like Jack Barrett control us. And we need t' win this science competition to prove it!"

"Good!" said Mrs. B. "Daniel, check the hall."

Daniel poked his head out.

"Only a couple o' kids down the hall at their lockers."

"Nobody between the door and you car," said Antonio, looking out the window.

"Then let's go."

She grabbed her stuff and headed for the door.

"And I?" asked Ana. "I miss the bus for go to Gloria."

She looked like she was going to cry again.

"We'll drop you at her house."

"No! I want go home!" she cried. "Cisco said was over! You said when James went for jail was over! No is over!"

She was sobbing, and Lynn couldn't blame her.

Would this never end?

Chapter 30

Lynn called Pastor Juan on the way home and asked him to come over. Diego had tried to talk her into not saying anything to Maria about what had happened, but she had not agreed. The boy's mother deserved to know what was going on.

The decision, however, was taken entirely out of her hands.

As soon as the car stopped in the carport, Ana jumped out and ran to the back door crying and calling out.

Maria, instantly alarmed, met her daughter just inside the door.

Lynn had no idea what the girl was saying, but her story must have grown with the telling, because her mother's eyes grew round. Maria turned to Diego with... Lynn couldn't discern the look on her face.

Diego went to her, put an arm around her shoulders and tried to play down the whole thing, straightening out some of the details and minimizing some of the exaggerations.

While the boys were showering, Lynn explained what she knew. She was probably creating more questions than she was answering because of the language barrier, but she did her best to at least let Maria know there was a problem. Pastor Juan could fill her in after he talked to Diego.

Not long after they got home, the pastor arrived. He was solemn as he talked with Maria. He knew all too well what could happen when news of this got out.

The boys had their stuff for the project spread out all over the living room floor and the dining room table. While Daniel and Antonio kept working, the pastor took Diego to his bedroom to talk.

Lynn could hear the murmur of voices but couldn't discern anything. It seemed they were back there for a really long time. She prayed Pastor Juan was getting some answers.

Sam was at a company-wide meeting tonight in Macon. How did he always manage to be somewhere else when she needed him most? He didn't answer when she called, so she left a quick message just to let him know not to hang around after the meeting.

The phone rang. "Hello?"

"Lynn," said Mr. Cline urgently, "turn on Channel 5 right now!"

Click.

She was stunned that he had used her first name, but went immediately to the TV.

"… show that again," the reporter was saying.

There followed a fuzzy video clip of a group of teenagers on the edge of a deep gorge. Somebody focused the camera.

"Boys! Everybody!" she yelled, "Get in here! Juan!"

They all came on the run.

"Hey! That's us!" exclaimed Daniel.

"Sh!"

The reporter was narrating the scene.

"It looks like these two are lagging behind. The others go around the bend, and then it appears that the last one purposely trips and pushes the other boy. They both fall, the alleged aggressor breaks through the barricade and starts sliding toward the gorge. As the ledge breaks away, the victim grabs the ankle of the other one when he goes head first into the gorge.

"If you listen carefully, you can hear their cries for help."

The reporter was silent for a moment, and they barely heard Jack's screams.

"Two other boys arrive on the scene. Risking their own lives, they form a human chain and grab the other leg. A man rushes to catch the leg where the first boy is losing his grip. A large group of teenagers follows the man, but he apparently sends them further down the trail, except for two bigger boys who help drag everyone to safety."

The picture returned to the TV anchorman.

"You have been watching a video that was caught by two cinematography students from the University this afternoon at Perkins Gorge. They were filming the winter landscape for a project, when they captured this dramatic footage from the south rim.

"If you have any information about the teenagers you have seen exclusively on WVMG, the Voice of Middle Georgia, please call 555-WVMG as soon as possible."

He cut to a commercial.

Lynn punched the off button.

Everyone stood there looking at each other.

"Praise God!" Pastor Juan shouted suddenly, dancing around and pumping his fist in the air. "Yes! Yes! Yes!"

The pastor and Diego were grinning from ear to ear, high-fiving each other.

"That's exactly what Diego just finished telling me, and now it's not just his word against Jack's!"

Lynn put her arm around Maria, who was still staring at the screen.

Diego came to her. "*Es OK, Mamita. Es todo OK.*"

The phone rang again.

"What do you think of that?" asked Mr. Cline. "I've already called our lawyer. I don't want to get involved with the media until we know where we stand legally. Has Diego said anything about all this yet?"

"Not to me," said Lynn. "He and Pastor Juan were still talking when you called the first time. Apparently he had just revealed the whole story."

"Yes, I met Pastor Juan at the winter concert. May I speak to him?"

"Sure. Hold on."

Pastor Juan had been talking quietly to Maria, his arm around her shoulders. Lynn called him to the phone but then stuck around to hear what he had to say.

"Hello, this is Pastor Juan."

He was silent while Mr. Cline talked.

"Yes… Yes, sir… Yes, when Jack pushed and tripped him, Jack lost his balance too, and they both went down. Then… well, you saw the rest."

He listened a minute and then said, "Of course, I'll be happy to—anything I can do."

He hesitated. "Mr. Cline, there are some things you need to know. This is not the first time Jack has accosted Diego. Apparently he has been tormenting him all year."

He paused again.

"Yes. Once Jack stomped on Diego's foot so hard during P.E. that he almost broke it. I think he went to the school nurse that day but just reported it as an injury in P.E. He was limping for days."

I remember that, thought Lynn. She could never get a straight answer about what had happened.

"Another time Jack 'accidentally' dropped his lunch tray on Diego's head."

Lynn remembered that day too. Maria had scolded him for staining his good shirt.

"And there are several other less dramatic examples of Jack's harassment that I'll let Diego tell you later."

He listened again.

"No, he didn't want to report them. You see, from our perspective, the Hispanic community is just beginning to be accepted by the townspeople. Diego was afraid to jeopardize that delicate balance by raising a ruckus. Now, I guess the ruckus has been raised for him."

"Wow!" whispered Lynn to herself. "We've got some young man here."

Somebody saw the news story and called in the identity of the young people.

The phone started ringing off the hook. Her cell rang again and again. Daniel's cell rang, and Lynn had to speak to his mother and assure her that he was fine. Pastor Juan's cell rang—Gloria calling to tell him their home phone wouldn't stop ringing. What should she do?

"Turn off the ringer and turn on the answering machine," he told her.

As Lynn was going by the living room window, she noticed a van pulling into the driveway. When it turned to park in front of the house, she saw WVMG-TV NEWS emblazoned on the side.

Oh, no! she groaned.

She texted Sam. "Get home. NOW!" it read. Then she turned off her cell.

Pastor Juan and Daniel put their phones on vibrate. Unless it was Gloria, Pastor Juan wouldn't answer. All the kids from school were calling Daniel, and he wasn't about to get into it with them.

Lynn thought better of her text and turned on her phone long enough to call Sam. He would be in a panic if he got that message with no explanation. There were four missed calls on her phone, three of them from her husband. She groaned again. When he found out she was OK, she was not going to be OK; he was going to kill her.

"Lynn!" he yelled when he answered. "Don't you ever do that to me again!" She could hear not only the panic, but also the anger in his voice. She deserved it.

"I'm so sorry, Sam," she started. "It's been a madhouse around here. Where are you? When will you be home? A…"

"Is everyone OK?" yelled Sam.

"Yes," she said, "we're all fine. Please don't have an accident trying to get here. A few minutes one way or the other won't matter. There's no threat. It's just that a WVMG News truck just pulled into the drive, and they're unloading equipment even as we speak. And all our phones have been ringing off the hook."

You will not cry, she told herself. "What should I do?"

"Let Shep out. I'm flying down I-16 right now, and I sincerely hope some cop doesn't have his radar pointed my direction. What in the world is going on?"

"Jack and Diego got into it on the field trip today, and it made the evening news. The phones are going crazy, and the news people are ringing the doorbell."

You will NOT cry, she repeated to herself.

"Pastor Juan's here."

"Oh, boy," sighed Sam. "I'm slowing down to a sane speed, but I should be home in about 45 or 50 minutes."

"Please be careful," said Lynn. "I'm sorry." She pushed the red button on her cell, but before she could shut it off, it rang. Mr. Cline.

"Is your place as crazy as mine?" he asked.

"Worse," she responded. "What should I do?"

Shep was barking his head off at the news truck, adding to the general confusion.

"Shep!" she yelled. His deep-throated barks simmered down to nervous whines and snorts of frustration.

She could hear Mr. Cline's dogs putting up a fuss at his house.

"Well, I'm turning my phone off as soon as we hang up. I already turned the house phone off, and so far, it shows nine messages on the answering machine.

"Mr. Weston, the lawyer, is going to call the police. He feels we should report it as an attack, a hate crime."

Here we go again, she thought.

"Lynn," said Mr. Cline. She thought his voice sounded sympathetic. "The media is probably going to show up at your place yet tonight or tomorrow. Your response is 'No comment' until we can better figure out what to do. OK?"

"They're ringing my doorbell right now. I'm not going to open it... Uh-oh, Pastor Juan just opened the door. I'd better go."

She groaned yet again. She had never had to deal with reporters before. Where was Sam?

"Pastor Juan!" she yelled as she hurried to the door. "No comment! No comment!"

Shep accompanied her and set up a racket worthy of praise.

The reporters backed off, and the door was soundly closed.

Sam hung up after talking with his wife, but a few seconds later his phone rang. Cisco, the FBI agent.

"Cisco, my friend," said Sam congenially. "How are you?"

"Sam!" said Cisco, "didn't you see the news tonight?"

"Nope. I'm on the road, but my wife told me a little of what's going on. I should be home in about forty minutes. "What should we do?"

"Just say 'No comment' to everything and everybody. We'll be in touch."

"Thanks," said Sam. "Any advice for keeping our sanity?"

Cisco chuckled. "I just catch the bad guys. Staying sane is on your own plate."

Sergeant Johnson sat at his desk with his head in his hands. There was no way he could have shuffled this report to the bottom of the stack. He had done his duty and would let the chips fall where they may.

"This is exactly why I wish these people would just disappear!" he muttered to himself.

* * * *

The next day when Sheila buzzed Mr. Cline and told him who was on the line, he took a deep breath and picked up the phone. "Mr. Cline here." He had been dreading this call since last fall and was frankly surprised that it had not come sooner.

The publicity the school had received because of the Gorge incident probably precipitated it now.

"Mr. Cline," came the serious male voice. "This is Walter Sweazy from the National Association for Individual Liberties." Mr. Cline said nothing, and finally the voice continued.

"We understand you are having your middle and high school students to take a mandatory Bible class. I'm sure—"

"Well, you understand wrong," interrupted Mr. Cline.

He was neither angry nor disrespectful, just emphatic.

"We offer a voluntary Bible study during our activity period, which is perfectly within our Constitutional rights."

"That may be what you have been led to believe, Mr. Cline, but if you do not deal with this matter immediately, I can assure you there will be repercussions.

"I believe the name of the school board chairman in your district is… let's see… Mr. Alan Smith. Is that correct?"

"That is correct," said Mr. Cline.

"Just so you will know, I will be calling Mr. Smith as soon as our conversation here is finished." Mr. Sweazy was keeping his voice serious, but not antagonistic.

"Would you like his phone number? Be happy to give it to you." Mr. Cline's tone was friendly, as well.

Mr. Cline spoke into the intercom. "Sheila, would you bring me Alan Smith's phone number, please? Give me his cell phone too." He had the numbers right in front of him on his computer, but he was stalling, trying to anticipate his opponent's next move.

Mr. Sweazy ignored him and continued, "When NAIL goes after something like this, not only is the school district sued, you personally are sued, as is every single board member. When we finish with you, Mr. Cline, not only will you be out of a job, but we will also go after your home, your car, your savings, as well as those of every board member." The man was not shouting, didn't even sound like he was delivering a dire threat. Just stating the facts.

Mr. Cline shuddered but kept his cool. "We are well aware of NAIL's bullying tactics, Mr. Sweazy. I am also aware that you have *lost* your case in the Supreme Court. A Bible class is no more against the law than a chess club.

"Our lawyer's name is Mr. Weston, and any further contact will be through him. And by the way, Mr. Weston has already briefed all our board members, so you will not be able to bluff them either. Good-bye, Mr. Sweazy."

He hung up the phone and put his hands behind his head. His chair squeaked when he leaned back. He had followed Mr. Weston's advice in dealing with NAIL and knew he had nailed them.

* * * *

Diego especially, but also Antonio and Daniel, were touted as heroes. They made no comment to anyone about the affair. And of course, Jack and his dad could not say anything, which drove the news media crazy. Reporters from as far away as Atlanta interviewed everyone at school and in the community. Everything that had happened since the beginning of the school year came to light.

Finally, Mr. Weston had to agree to a press conference.

He stood before the assembly of reporters, including one from CNN.

"Good morning, ladies and gentlemen."

He introduced himself as spokesman for the school and the families involved in the Perkins Gorge incident and restated the fact that none of them wished to comment.

"This is your opportunity to ask questions concerning what happened at the Gorge last Friday. You have all seen the video, so it would really not advance anything to ask questions about what you plainly saw.

"As to the why, why does any person bully and seek to injure another? We—"

"Mr. Weston," shouted out one of the reporters. "We've been told that this Jack Barrett has been harassing Diego Lopez since last August. Could you elaborate on that and tell us why nothing has been done about the bullying in the high school?" Several grunts and murmurs of agreement rose from his colleagues.

"Let me start at the beginning and tell what we know of what has occurred in the high school."

With that he outlined all that had happened since the boys attacked Diego in August, Armando Lopez's death, the intruder at the Bartholomews' place and the subsequent arrest of James Flanagan, and the other incidents between Jack and Diego.

"Maria Lopez, Diego's mother, chose not to press charges after the first attack because the doctor had told her that Diego might not have survived another beating. If the abuse the boy was suffering had not been revealed, he might be dead by now."

The reporters began shouting questions all at once. Mr. Weston did not know them by name, so he just pointed to individuals and took their questions with as little confusion as possible.

"What about the school?"

"If you'll bear with me a minute... I was just getting to that.

"The principal followed the procedure spelled out in the handbook for punishment for aggressive behavior in school after the first attack. The boys were all suspended and received zeros for all work during that time period.

"Why didn't Diego report Jack's continued aggression?"

"There are about 90 Hispanics in this area. For the most part they are decent people. The majority are either citizens or legal residents, who want to get along with their American neighbors. You may not be aware that some folks in the Perkins Grove area still harbor bad feelings against the Latinos, and—"

"Why?"

"I don't know why," said Mr. Weston, beginning to get a little irritated by the constant interruptions. "Why is there racism anywhere? Why is anybody intolerant of someone different from himself or herself? I can't answer those questions."

He held up his hand to ward off further interruption.

"Some people accuse them of stealing our jobs. We have peach orchards, pecan groves, and peanuts in this area. There is a chicken processing plant and a peanut processing plant. I do not have to tell you that many Americans do not like to do the kinds of labor associated with those products. The Latinos are not taking anyone's job, at least here in middle Georgia. They are filling the hole left by Americans who refuse to work in those positions."

"What about the undocumented aliens?"

"I don't know how many or which ones are illegal. It is not something talked about. Nationwide, there—"

"What about the Lopez family?"

"Mrs. Lopez and her children were forced to come to the United States illegally by Mr. Lopez. Since he was killed, they have obtained permission to stay legally at least until the end of the school year."

"Why didn't she press charges against the boy that attacked her son at the Gorge?"

"As I was going to say earlier," and here he glared at the man who kept interrupting, "some in the Hispanic community are up in arms about the affair. They want her to press charges—want retaliation. But what would be served? Jack is a minor, so there would be no prison time. The Hispanics would come out looking like the bad guys."

"Who is this Bartholomew couple? Why are they involved in this?"

"Mrs. Bartholomew is the high school ESOL teacher. She invited Mrs. Lopez and the children to stay with her when they were left destitute as a result of Mr. Lopez's death."

"Why? Didn't she know that folks might not like it? Wasn't she afraid?"

"Look, I personally would not advise people to take in just anybody. There are immigrants, both legal and illegal, who hate America. Some hold a life philosophy of violence toward those who disagree with them.

"The Bartholomews are Christian people who live their faith instead of just talk it. They felt that as Christians they could not turn this poor family away to fend for itself. They believed that God would protect them, and from where I stand, He has. Besides," He paused. "Have any of you been out to the Bartholomew place?"

The room erupted in loud laughter.

"Yes," said Mr. Weston, smiling. "I'm acquainted with Shep too. Need I say more?"

"What about this Bible class at school? Is it mandatory?"

"Of course not," answered Mr. Weston. "That would be illegal. After the initial attack on Diego last August, some of Mrs. Bartholomew's students started asking questions. She wanted to answer those questions from the Bible, so with Mr. Cline's blessing, she began the class during the enrichment period at school."

"Is NAIL aware of this class?"

"Yes, and they know as well as we do that we are within our Constitutional rights."

"Really?"

"Where have you folks been? There are hundreds of Bible classes in public schools in this country, and the US Supreme Court has declared them perfectly legal."

He answered more questions and then concluded the time by reading a prepared statement:

"'You have all seen the video of what happened during the field trip. There is no reason to continue imagining more. If you have questions about the incident, watch the video again. Neither the school nor the families wish to comment further, and if the harassment continues, charges will be filed. Thank you for your cooperation.'"

As it unfolded, no hate crime could be proven. The video showed one boy attacking another, but no motive could be established. Jack was expelled for endangering the life of a student and was finally accepted in a vocational school in the next town.

But the repercussions continued in ever-widening circles.

Chapter 31

The tension between the Hispanic and Anglo communities that had just begun to ease returned with a vengeance. Lynn was afraid something terrible was going to erupt between the two groups. Even relations at school were strained, but she couldn't get her English students to talk to her about it. She felt she was caught in the middle, as both sides were suspicious of her. She prayed constantly about the situation. Though she was continuing her study of the life of Christ during Bible class and showing how He fulfilled so many of the Old Testament prophecies, the stress was affecting her students there as well. The underlying mistrust was drawing their attention away from the things they needed to learn.

Many Latinos were agitated about the whole thing, demanding justice. They were not at all pleased that Maria would not press charges.

Pastor Juan called a meeting of community leaders, including Padre Rafael of the Spanish Catholic church. He asked Diego and Antonio to come as representatives of the student population. The men and women talked over several plans of action. The idea of calling the whole community together to discuss the problem was quickly thrown out. Number 1, the townspeople could misconstrue their intentions. Number 2, there was the potential that the meeting could go the wrong way and turn into a violent, vengeful mob that could take out years of frustration on tiny Perkins Grove.

"This situation is ripe for interference from the Conference on Hispanic Rights. Do we want them involved?" This from a lady who had been a high school teacher in Honduras but now worked as a maid in the motel out on the highway.

"Absolutely not!" said Padre Rafael with feeling before anyone else could answer. "I have dealt with them ever since I came here from Mexico. I'm sure they have their place, but we really don't need them here right now. What could they do? How would their involvement improve our lives in Perkins Grove? Most of their people are probably trying to help, but some of their leaders are just glory hogs looking to see themselves on TV. This problem is tailor-made for that type of individual."

"Are we agreed on that?" Pastor Juan asked the assembly. The consensus was affirmative. "So, how do we proceed?"

"Let me handle the outsiders," said the padre. "Often they will listen to a priest, when someone else would be ignored."

"We are also going to have to persuade the others here in our community to keep it local," put in Manuel.

"Good point," said Pastor Juan. "Let's do our best to be sympathetic and open to what our people have to say, and maybe they won't feel the need to involve outsiders."

The discussion went on for some time until the representatives were sure they had looked at the problem from every possible angle. Finally, they assigned each man and woman the job of speaking to the people under his or her influence and persuading them to let it go—that nothing would be served by retaliation. Diego and Antonio were given the task of trying to cool down the hotheads at school, which was not going to be easy.

"Anything else?" asked Pastor Juan as they were winding down. He waited a moment.

"*Amigos*, we are going to need wisdom to deal with each person's concerns. I know some of you do not claim to be Christians, but I think we all can see that we are going to need God's help in this thing. Manuel, would you pray and ask God to direct us and give us the words to say?"

Pastor Juan spoke to the men in his church and then visited several places where he knew the Latinos worked. "Look," he told each group or individual, "some of us are here illegally. We simply cannot afford to draw attention to ourselves. The quickest way to get the Feds down here checking papers would be to try to take the law into our own hands and do something stupid."

Most of his compatriots agreed, but there were still a few that tried to hold out.

"The reporters are already calling attention to us," someone shouted. "We need to show them we will not accept this treatment!"

"And what would that accomplish except get us thrown in jail or sent back to our own countries?" countered someone else. "Then we become the bad guys."

"I agree!" another responded. "We need to show them we are peaceful, not vengeful. Pastor Juan is right. Some might be deported. Is that what we want?"

The heated discussions continued. Although the majority remained on their side, Pastor Juan and the other leaders that supported him lost favor among some of the people.

The pastor often found himself defending Maria's decision not to press charges. And every time he did, he had to work at being dispassionate. The first time he stood up for her, he surprised himself by realizing that he had fallen in love with her. Yes, he had admitted that she could be a fantastic mother for his children and that there was a strong bond between them, but he had not acknowledged that he loved her. He was surprised, but he also felt a happiness and a deep contentment that he had not experienced since his wife died. He couldn't wait for this mess to be over so he could ask her to marry him. Whenever her name came up in the discussion, he had to tamp the glow that he knew would light up his face if he wasn't careful. The smile that kept wanting to sneak out had to be replaced by a set jaw.

Padre Rafael was no help at all.

"Why don't you just marry her and get it over with?" he asked behind his hand after one of the meetings. His eyes were twinkling, but he too was trying not to let Juan's situation show on his face and thus detract from the business at hand.

If the old priest can see through me, Juan asked himself, can everyone else?

He longed to tell his children, her children, his church, Sam and Lynn—the whole world!

But there were a couple of problems with that. First, he hadn't declared his love to Maria. He figured she was at least as insightful as Padre Raphael, but he longed to tell her and look in her face to gauge her reaction. Second, if he let people know how he felt before the present crisis had blown over, he was afraid that they would think that his love was blinding his reason. He sighed.

Folks just could not understand that a long drawn-out court case and the resulting media attention would only make matters worse. Sure, they would probably win, and Jack might be sent to juvenile detention, but how would that improve their lot? One by one, some of the opposition saw Juan's point and took a less aggressive stance. Others remained firm, even trying to circumvent Maria altogether by hiring their own lawyer. The lawyer met with Mr. Weston but soon came to the conclusion that without Maria's consent, there was nothing they could do.

The situation at school was a microcosm of what was happening in the larger community. Diego and Antonio discovered that they had to watch themselves not only around the Anglos, but also around their own countrymen. The black students tried to remain neutral. With the history of prejudice against their race, they did not want to get involved in this fight. It was not an easy time for any of them. Lynn just tried to keep a low profile not only at school, but also out in the community.

Fortunately, the furor eventually died down, and, although relations were not what they had been before, at least there was a truce.

Finally, it became old news, and life got back to normal—whatever that meant.

* * * *

This year the Bartholomews' Sunday school class was planning the church Valentine banquet, but because of the uproar caused by the Perkins Gorge incident, they had decided to postpone it for a couple of weeks. Sam and Lynn were their Sunday school teachers, and they were embroiled in the affair. There was no way they could enjoy a banquet until the dust settled. The kids quietly moved the date to the end of the month.

"Bless you!" said Lynn, when they told her.

Finally, the night arrived. The banquet was to be a semi-formal to formal affair. The college-aged kids had foregone having dates of their own so that they could do the whole thing—decorate, cook, serve and clean up. They wouldn't let Mrs. B help at all.

Sam designed a fancy invitation on the computer and gave it to his wife with a single rose. He could be so romantic. He had mentioned the banquet to Pastor Juan, and since the Spanish church wasn't planning anything special, Juan invited Maria to be his date for the evening.

Lynn decided to wear the dress Maria had made her for Christmas. It was dressy enough, but not so dressy that it would make Maria uncomfortable. Ha! She needn't have worried. Maria made an absolutely gorgeous red velvet outfit for herself that made her look… what… incredible! That was it, absolutely incredible!

Juan's not gonna be able to take his eyes off her, thought Lynn. She knew he was crazy about her and wished he would just get on with it. From Lynn's point of view, Maria was just as crazy about him. She just hid it better.

The Garcia kids came to the Bartholomews' house so that the older ones could baby-sit the younger ones there. The girls loved helping the ladies add the finishing touches to their outfits. They felt like the fairy godmother getting Cinderella ready for the ball.

The weather was spectacular, and this year's banquet was a rousing success.

Sam took the long way home and chattered the whole way. Lynn just looked at him. What on earth was his problem?

Juan, on the other hand, sat in the back seat with Maria and barely said a word. Had the two men had a fight or something?

Finally, Sam pulled into the fast food place on the outskirts of town.

"Who wants a milk shake? Maria? Juan? No? Well, I do." He jumped out of the car and ran around to open the door.

"Lynn, come with me." He grabbed his wife by the hand and dragged her inside. "We'll be right back, y'all."

"Sam! For heaven's sake! We just finished a four-course feast, and you want a milk shake? What on earth is going on? You haven't shut up since we left the church!"

"You ninny! You mean you haven't figured it out yet? You're even more naïve than I thought."

"What?"

"Sorry. You'll just have to wait 'til we get home."

He fended off her blow and grinned wickedly, savoring the moment.

"What?!" Lynn asked a little more emphatically, her frustration showing in her red face.

The girl at the counter just looked at them as she handed Sam his shake. Old people are too weird, she thought.

When they got home, Maria called Diego and Ana into her bedroom. Juan took his children to the kitchen. Sam and Lynn sat on the couch. He was smiling smugly; she was scowling.

"You still don't get it, do you?"

He drew her hand to his mouth and kissed it tenderly. "I love you," he said.

She harrumphed and jerked her hand away.

In a few minutes everyone came back into the living room. They all looked really happy, but poor Lynn still had not guessed what was going on.

Juan dropped to one knee in front of Maria and took out a small box. Shep thought he wanted to play and immediately jumped him. When Sam grabbed the dog's collar, he had an "aw, Dad" look on his face but sat like a good boy.

Lynn's hands flew to her mouth to keep the scream that was forming in her throat from coming out.

"Maria, I have prayed much about this moment, and I believe I am following what God wants me to do." (big gulp) "Maria, will you marry me?"

He took the ring with the tiny diamond from the box and slipped it onto her finger.

Maria pulled him to his feet and threw her arms around her new husband-to-be, surprising everyone, including herself.

"*¡Si!* Yes! *¡Si!*" she cried.

Lynn's scream refused to be held back any longer. She rushed to the happy couple and gave them both a big hug. Suddenly, everyone was hugging everyone else—except, of course, for Diego and Gloria, who shook hands—the fact that they would soon be brother and sister not yet sinking in. Shep didn't know why everyone was so ecstatic, but he was sure it had something to do with him. He got his share of hugs too.

Chapter 32

Pastor Juan had an idea that might bridge the chasm that had opened up between the Latinos and the locals after the incident at the Gorge. What if they planned a big *Cinco de Mayo* party and invited all the Hispanics in the area plus the whole town? Maybe if *they,* the Hispanics, initiated the good-will gesture, the Anglos would see that they meant business about trying to get along. Pastor Juan would talk to the Hispanic groups, and the Bartholomews could get support from the non-Hispanics. Plans for the *fiesta* became the main topic of conversation every time the families got together.

* * * *

The end of the year was coming up fast. Interest was beginning to wane in all the classes, and Bible class was no exception. Mentally the kids were already on vacation. Mrs. B had to think of something that would not only grab their attention, but also get the point across.

Hmm, maybe that would work. She sat perfectly still as she thought it through.

She needed to run the idea by Sam. He was her rock, the one that kept her feet on the ground, so to speak.

"Talk to Don Burton from our Sunday school class," he said after he'd gotten over the initial shock. "He goes up all the time. If the cost isn't out of sight, it's not a bad idea."

He stopped to think a minute.

"Actually, my dear, it's a very good idea. Go for it!"

She called the airport and got all the information. Then she called Don Burton before she approached Mr. Cline.

"Sure!" said Don. "In fact, it won't cost you a dime. We're getting ready for a show, and my group was planning a practice run anyway. They can go on home, and I can stay for your class."

The next day she had her nose on the door when Sheila unlocked the office.

"Tell me you're kidding," said Mr. Cline when she asked him.

He looked at her face.

"You're not kidding." He took a deep breath and let it out slowly. "I assume you have some logical reason for wanting to do this, some legitimate point to make."

"Of course," said Mrs. B.

She did not expound.

"How much will it cost?"

"Not one red cent."

"Now you've got to be kidding! How did you pull that off?"

"Let's just say I know the right people."

Mr. Cline sat thinking for a minute.

"OK, let me check with our insurance agent. There've been a lot of accidents involving airplanes, so we might have to get parental permission or something."

"Just to watch?"

"I don't know. Let me get back to you. When do you want to do it? Could we invite the rest of the student body to watch the demonstration?"

"I was looking at May 2. If they could come during third hour, Don could be finished and ready to speak in class when the lunch rotations start."

"Good. I'll call our agent right now, and then bring it up in faculty meeting this afternoon."

She stood up to leave. "Mrs. Bartholomew," said Mr. Cline. "You see this gray hair right here above my temples?"

She nodded.

"That wasn't there until you started working here."

* * * *

Spring concert was approaching, but Ana's group was not doing as well as they had before. Since it was a mixed group of Americans and Latinos, the Perkins Gorge incident had really affected them. There just wasn't the unity they had had before. Some had even dropped out.

"What I do, Mrs. B?"

The poor girl was always sad, bordering on depression. Her grades had gone down, as well. Her heart was not in leading the recorders anymore.

"Would you like me to take over the leadership for a while?" asked her teacher gently.

"Please," begged Ana.

Mrs. B talked to Sam, asked permission to be excused from staff meeting for a few weeks, and stood in front of the group for the first time. Ana sat in the first chair position, her usual spot when the group played.

"OK, y'all. Let's hear what you've been working on for the concert."

They played, not too enthusiastically. It was abundantly obvious that they were just plain discouraged.

"Now," said Lynn. "That really wasn't your best, was it? What can we do to fix it?"

Nobody said a word, but their body language screamed, "Let's just give it up!"

Sean, one of the older students who played the bass recorder, spoke from the back of the room, "Come on, guys, we can do this!"

"Thank you, Sean. You're absolutely right. Let's name the problem, shall we? Before the incident at Perkins Gorge, this group was excited about playing together, and you were *great*!"

The kids glanced at Ana, who was fiddling with the recorder in her lap.

Mrs. B cleared her throat to get their attention.

"What happened?" she asked gently.

Nobody spoke.

Lynn waited.

Finally, one of the younger Hispanic girls spoke up.

"The *Americanos* no like us. How we can play with them?" She was close to tears.

"We like you," countered a boy.

The vast majority of the other kids agreed.

"Do you know what Diego said after the incident?" asked Lynn.

None of them did.

"He said he was not going to let the prejudice of one person control him. Diego has carried on, in spite of what happened. If he can do that, don't you think we could? None of the people in this room attacked Diego, and none of you Latinos have tried to retaliate. I commend you for that."

She stopped and waited until every eye was focused on her.

"We need to make a decision here today, right now. Are we going to let the actions of one bitter person cause us to throw away everything that this group has accomplished together?"

She let them consider that for a minute.

"If you want to continue playing together, get behind your leader—the Mexican girl that taught every single one of you to play and gave you such great success at the winter concert—and get past this, stand up right now."

Sean stood immediately, followed by one, then another until they were all on their feet. The blonde behind Ana gave her a hug.

Sean began to clap. Mrs. B joined him, as she called Ana to the front with her. The applause swelled, until all the recorders had been laid aside, and everyone was cheering.

Ana breathed a sigh of relief, smiled, and took her place.

"Number 152!" She said firmly.

The students quickly took their places and found the number, instruments at the ready.

"One, two, ready, play!" counted Ana.

Wow! What a difference! The group sounded like itself again.

Mrs. B gave them a thumbs up and walked out. They didn't need her anymore.

Concert day arrived. Before they left the house, Ana came to Lynn while she was reading her Bible.

"Thank you, Mrs. B," she said. She didn't need to say anything more. Lynn knew and gave her a nod.

"You'll do great!"

The concert went well, and the recorders really did do a good job. After the final number all the musicians stood and took a bow as the audience applauded. Someone ran on stage with a bouquet and thrust it into Ana's hands, and the wave of applause surged again. She didn't know what to do, so she bowed slightly and sat down with the rest of her group, her face blazing.

"Encore!" yelled Sam. The cry was immediately taken up by others. Lynn had never seen this strong a reaction at a school band concert. Mr. Randolph stepped to the microphone. The audience settled in for more.

"Would you like to hear more from the band or from the recorders?"

Some people yelled band, others recorders.

"Both!" bellowed Sam above the din.

Mr. Randolph went over to confer with Ana. Sean made his way to the front and spoke to her also. Apparently she wasn't too sure about his suggestion, but she turned to the recorders and relayed to them what Sean had said. They all grinned and opened to the page. Lynn had overheard the exchange.

Yep, she thought, that'll blow 'em away.

First the band played Sousa's "The Stars and Stripes Forever." It was great!

After the applause died down, Ana counted off. The audience roared when they heard the first strains of the group's rendition of "Old McDonald Had a Farm," complete with geese honking, horses neighing, and several other farm animals making their recorder debut.

Maybe this was the beginning of restoring unity in Perkins Grove.

* * * *

May 2, the day Don Burton was to be her special guest in Bible class. Mr. Cline had gotten the necessary clearances and everything was a go. It was a beautiful spring day. The whole middle and high school student bodies were allowed to go outside, and they filled the bleachers, waiting expectantly. But the teachers had been sworn to absolute secrecy, so nobody knew what they were waiting for. Didn't matter. Any excuse to get out of class would do!

At 10:25 Mrs. B started looking up. Was that spot in the distance a plane? Or were her 61-year-old eyes playing tricks on her? The spot grew bigger. It was! It was *the* plane! She got Mr. Cline's attention and they started yelling and pointing skyward. The kids soon caught on and saw the spot growing ever closer. She stole a glance and saw that almost everyone was looking up.

Just before the plane roared overhead, there was a communal gasp and a few screams. "Somebody fell outta th' plane!" they yelled. That person was followed by another and then another. Lynn thought she counted eight in all.

"They're skydivin'!"

"Look! They're skydivin'!"

The bleachers shook with stomping, cheering, shouting, whistling, hooting teens. Every time the divers changed formations, the kids oohed and aaahed appropriately. The things the divers did during their freefall defied description. Turning flips, joining hands, forming a circle, and then back-flipping away from each other again. They seemed to be playing around up there forever, cavorting like a bunch of puppies. Lynn's heart was in her throat. Weren't they ever going to open their 'chutes? Did she call the whole school out here to watch eight people self-destruct before their very eyes?

Finally the team broke apart, and the sky suddenly filled with brightly colored parachutes, the kind that could be guided. She breathed a sigh of relief.

"Hey! They're comin' down near here!"

"No they ain't! They're comin' down right here in th' football field!"

The first jumper hit right on the 50-yard line on this side of the field. The next two on the 30s, then the 10s, back to the 30s again on the other side of the field, and the last one on the 50 in front of the opposite bleachers, forming a diamond. The kids went wild while the jumpers gathered their parachutes. Coach Michaels ran a bullhorn out to the leader.

"Let's hear it for the Middle Georgia Skydiving Club!" said the leader, indicating his team. They all took a bow as the bleachers erupted again. He introduced each team member by name. When he got to the next to the last one, the helmet came off and a full head of long auburn hair tumbled out over the jumper's shoulders. The girl stepped forward waving both hands, as the applause roared on.

"And last, but definitely not least, your own Don Burton!" Don had graduated a couple of years ago, so many of the kids knew him. He was the hometown hero of the day.

"We want to thank Mrs. Bartholomew for inviting us here today, and—" He was interrupted by more cheering. She waved. "—and we want to invite you all to the Middle Georgia Air Show on May 13, where we'll be performing again. Thank you!"

The team members gathered their gear while the kids continued to cheer. They were pumped! Mr. Cline finally took the bullhorn and called everyone to order. He addressed the team.

"Thanks, guys... and gal."

The girl waved. More cheering.

"I think you can tell our students thought you did a phenomenal job today!"

Cheers and whistles.

"But, unfortunately, now it's time to get back to class."

No cheers and whistles, only moans and groans. He dismissed the students by section, and Mrs. B heard their excited comments as they passed by. Some of them ran down to the field to speak to the jumpers, a small crowd gathering around Don Burton. After a few minutes, Mr. Cline shooed them all inside.

Lynn went down to get Don and meet his team. Mr. Cline invited them all to lunch in the school cafeteria, but they declined saying they had to get back to the real world and go to work. Her special guest got everything packed up and followed her to the music room.

As the first group of students came in, they were virtually silent, awed by the presence of the great Don Burton who had just jumped out of an airplane at 15,000 feet. The high schoolers, however, felt they were above hero worship. But they couldn't fool Lynn Bartholomew. She could see it in their eyes. They were just as star-struck as the younger kids.

Don was outgoing and friendly and greeted everyone as he or she came in. Mrs. B introduced him as the speaker of the day.

"First, I want to show you my gear," said Don.

He showed them each piece and explained its use. The kids were focused.

"Now, let me ask you a question. What would happen to me if I jumped out of the plane without my 'chute?"

The kids looked at each other.

"You'd die," said Bill matter-of-factly.

"So I'd be pretty foolish to jump without it, right?"

"No!" said Bill, "You'd be downright stupid!"

Bill got the laughs he was seeking.

"You're right. Now, how do I know this piece of nylon is gonna take me safely to the ground?"

They were stumped.

"Because it's been proven to work?" asked a girl.

"Good answer," said Don, "but how do I know it'll work this time?"

"I guess you don't," said someone.

"So what would make me trust my parachute?"

He waited, but nobody seemed to know.

"OK, let me tell you. It's a little word that I'm sure Mrs. B has taught you. Faith.

"When I jump out of that plane, I'm putting all my faith in that little piece of cloth. Yes, I have all the facts to back up my decision, but I *choose* to put my faith in my 'chute." He took a drink of water. "When I jump, I'm completely at the mercy of my parachute. There is absolutely nothing I can do to save my life without it.

"Guys, that's how it is with life. Everyone in this room will die someday. No use ignoring it or trying to deny it. All of us are going to die. It's that simple.

"Let's say Jesus Christ is like our parachute. Just as I'd be 'downright stupid' to jump out of a plane without a parachute, you will be downright stupid to die without putting your faith in Jesus as your Savior. We call Him the Savior because he saves us from eternity in hell—what the Bible refers to as 'the second death.'

"OK, so how do you do that? I strap my parachute on, but how do you 'put on' Jesus?

"When I was a junior in this school, someone talked to me about these things. I thought he was some kind of religious wacko, but I couldn't get what he said out of my head. It haunted me for about a year. I thought about it, asked a million questions and read the Bible for myself. If what this guy said was true, it was too important to ignore.

"Finally, just before I graduated, I stopped fighting God. I turned from my sin and asked Jesus to save me, putting my faith in Him alone. Since then, my life has been amazing. If for some reason one day my parachute doesn't open for real, and I go *splat* on the ground, I have no doubt that I will go to Heaven.

"It's really pretty simple. Do you know you're a sinner?"

Everyone chuckled a little.

"Yep," said Bill. "Mrs. B made sure of that."

"Actually, all Mrs. B did was tell you what the Bible says, right?"

Nods and shrugs.

"So OK, it's been established that if you had to stand before God when you die, you would be found guilty, right?"

A few nods.

"So what's your sentence, since you've been found guilty?"

Nobody wanted to say it.

"The Bible says you will go to hell," Don said softly. "Does that concern any of you? Aren't you even a little worried that all this stuff Mrs. B has been teaching is true and that you're on your way to hell?"

The students were deathly silent.

"When Jesus came, He took your punishment for you on the cross. Then when He rose again, he defeated Death and now offers to you eternal life.

"So what's stopping you from putting on your parachute? Why not admit your sin to yourself and to God? Why not stop trying to save yourself by being good enough to get to Heaven? You're just kidding yourself and you know it. Why not put your faith in Jesus as your only hope? Why not ask Him to save you today? It's your choice."

The bell rang.

When Lynn got to her classroom Friday morning, she found a folded piece of paper on the floor where it had been slipped under the door. Her mind instantly went back to the note with the skull and crossbones—the note that had alerted them that James Flanagan was about to do something desperate.

She opened the note and read, "I put on the parachute."

There was no signature, just a big happy face drawn on the bottom. She had no idea who it was from, but she did notice one thing: The handwriting was the same as the warning note.

Chapter 33

Lynn sat up in bed and stretched. Today was the day! Saturday, May 6th. *Cinco de Mayo,* Mexican Heritage Day had fallen on Friday, but the big celebration was scheduled for Saturday, so everyone could come. Pastor Juan, Padre Rafael, and the other Hispanic community leaders had planned a huge *fiesta* for the entire Latino community, Mexican or not, and had invited the whole town, as planned. The annual spring Super Sidewalk Sale would be going on downtown at the same time, and Lynn wasn't sure how that would affect the crowd—it could take people away from the party or draw more. The hope was that by inviting the whole town, the Latinos would be showing their desire to get along. They really wanted this event to take out several more bricks from the wall of distrust between the two groups.

Besides posters in store windows, word-of-mouth advertising, radio spots, and fliers, she and the others had extended special invitations to everyone they could think of. Mr. Cline had accepted and promised to bring his family. Lynn had invited all the teachers at faculty meeting and had given a special invitation to the lunchroom ladies and maintenance staff. Of course, she encouraged her Bible class students to come and bring their families. Sheila had been so excited that she had mentioned it to everyone that passed through the office and had invited the whole African-American community.

Sully was coming and possibly even Banks, after he woke up. He didn't seem to function as well as Sully after an all-night shift. Sarge had reluctantly accepted Sully's invitation but was still very much in favor of sending all the Latinos to somebody else's jurisdiction. He didn't exactly hate them, just didn't want them around, convinced that his world would be a better place if they were sent back to wherever they came from.

Sam had invited his associates at work and Mayor Claxton, who had then extended the invitation to the city council. Diego had invited Mr. Randolph and the band, as well as Dr. Benjamin and family, who would come in the evening because of the Sabbath. Ana had invited her recorder students. She had even gone out to the cars after rehearsals to personally invite the parents. Lynn's Sunday school class had invited all their friends from the community college, and Don Burton had invited the skydiving team and everyone else at the airport. The ESOL students had invited the Americans from school. Pastor Juan and Padre Rafael had made sure that the whole Hispanic community knew they were invited to the Bartholomews' place, just like at Christmas. Some of them, in turn, had asked their American employers and co-workers.

It promised to be quite the melting-pot event!

Lynn jumped out of bed and peeked out the window. Glorious! The sun was just beginning to shine in all the brilliance of a spring morning, and there was not a cloud to be seen. Thank You, God!

She could hear Maria rattling around in the kitchen. Maria, Ana, and Lynn had been filling the freezer for weeks, and they had worked feverishly the last couple of days on the food that didn't freeze well. All the ladies from the Bartholomews' church, the Catholic church, and the Spanish Community Bible Church had also been cooking like fiends, and now it was time to pull it all together.

"Get up, Sleepy Head!" Lynn said as she shook Sam. He lifted one eyelid and closed it again. "Come on. There's work to be done, and we need your muscles to do it."

"Let Diego do it," mumbled Sam. "He has two good arms now."

"Yes, but he's no match for my big, strong husband. You gonna let some kid 10 inches shorter and a hundred pounds lighter, not to mention fifty years younger, show you up?"

"Yep," he said without shame.

She laughed and punched him playfully in the arm."

"How can you sleep? This is a huge day, the day we've been working toward since the whole thing with the Lopezes began."

"OK. You're right. Just five more minutes," Sam said flopping over on his tummy.

"Five minutes. I'll get the first shower. Then you have to get up."

She didn't linger in the shower like she sometimes did. She was too excited.

She dressed and then shook Sam again. "Your turn," she said, "and no soaking."

She kissed him and left him to get up on his own.

"Good morning, Maria! How can I help?"

"Good morning!" said Maria. She handed Lynn a knife and, smiling wickedly, pointed to a bag of onions.

"How many?"

"Every," said Maria.

"The whole thing? Thanks a lot! But you won't see me crying over a bag of onions. No, ma'am!"

On her hands and knees, she reached into the very back of the cabinet in the corner and pulled out a food processor. She had actually forgotten she had it, but a whole bag of onions had a way of making one remember things like that.

"Let me get a cup of coffee and a muffin, and then I'll get to work."

She swallowed her breakfast quickly and started peeling onions. Though the processor did the chopping, she cried real tears just peeling and cutting processor-sized pieces.

"Good morning!" said Ana.

She was already dressed and ready for the big day. She got her breakfast and sat at the bar as far away from the onions as possible.

Diego came in from outside with Shep at his heels.

"I think all sports equipment is out in right places," he said as he washed his hands at the sink. He snagged three muffins and a glass of milk and also sat at the bar.

Shep sat between brother and sister looking from one to the other with soulful eyes, hoping some crumb would "accidentally" fall in his direction.

Finally, Sam came out scrubbed squeaky clean and dressed like a coach, complete with whistle around the neck.

"Good morning!" he boomed. "Happy Independence Day!"

Diego looked at him strangely.

"I thought was 4 of July."

"No, Mexican Independence Day."

"Mexican Independence Day is 16 of September," put in Ana.

"Really?" said Sam, looking confused. "Then why are we celebrating today?"

"*Cinco de Mayo* is Mexican Heritage Day in the United States. It isn't celebrated much in Mexico."

"Oh. Thanks for setting me straight before everyone gets here. What's to eat?"

Since Lynn's hands were all oniony, Maria handed him a plate with a couple of muffins. He got his favorite mug and poured his coffee, then sat down near his wife. Almost immediately, however, he got up and joined the kids at the bar.

"Sorry," he said. "I can't smell onions and enjoy blueberries."

He bowed his head and silently thanked the Lord for his food.

"Diego, what has to be done outside yet?" asked Sam after he had prayed.

"I make the signs for parking, but we still need put up the ropes to mark the area and put the signs. I put sports equipment outside, but you can check for be sure I did right. Oh, and the tables no are... are not... out."

"And the decorations," added Ana. "And the *piñata.*"

"That's all yours," said Lynn to the girl. "As soon as people start arriving, you can ask them to help."

"And the barbeque pit," said Sam. "I never got around to that. Oh, and the sound system."

"I can help," said Diego, "but I don't know to do by myself."

"I listen radio yesterday," said Maria. "Say maybe rain. Later only."

"I looked outside, and it's beautiful," said Lynn. "Not a cloud in the sky. Maybe the rain will hold off until after the *fiesta.*"

"Yes," said Diego, "is beautiful outside."

Pastor Juan and his family with Antonio in tow were the first to arrive, followed by a carload of Lynn's Sunday school students. Everyone delivered the food they had brought to Maria. Then Lynn, ever the organizer, put them all to work. Even Pastor Juan's younger kids each got a turn helping Sam scrape the grill with the wire brush—great fun for kids. The guys hauled the picnic tables out of the barn and arranged them around the yard. The girls taped down the paper tablecloths in the colors of the Mexican flag. There were four big folding tables that would hold the food, another for the drinks, and a game table for plates, napkins and silverware. Gloria and her brother worked well with Ana to get the streamers up. Diego had made a big *piñata* to climax the event, and he and Antonio hung it high in the tree, where it would later be lowered to break. The boys got the ropes and signs up to mark part of the field for parking, using trash barrels at the corners. Since Pastor Juan had brought a big washtub, and four giant ice chests full of ice, he got the job of moving the sodas from the outside fridge to the tub to make room for more food. And Shep, true to form, ran from one group to the other, getting in the way. When more people got there, he would be banished to the inside. Miraculously, the jobs were all completed more or less at the same time.

All the helpers met on the porch for a cooling glass of tea, and Pastor Juan committed the day to the Lord in prayer, thanking Him for whatever result it would bring. As they all said "Amen" together, Manuel and his family arrived with the meat, a whole cow that everyone had pitched in to buy and have butchered, plus countless chickens. The beef and the chickens had been perfectly cut and were marinating in great plastic bins in a Mexican spice mixture, ready to go. He pulled his truck up beside the grill so he wouldn't have to unload everything. The tailgate became his table—and he had never even heard of a tailgate party.

Padre Rafael had put together a committee to make a display of Mexican history in the United States, and they had done a bang-up job. It was set up on the porch out of the fray.

People were coming and going all morning. The Bartholomews enjoyed renewing acquaintances with people they had met at the Christmas party and introducing them around. Lynn couldn't have asked for things to go more smoothly.

Folks were engaged in soccer, football, basketball, volleyball, splashing in the creek, and all the other activities that had been planned for the day. The Latinos challenged the Americans to a soccer game that would take place after lunch, and the Americans reciprocated with an invitation to play basketball. Lynn remembered some of the Mexican games the younger kids were playing from Christmas, and the older folks enjoyed just sitting around in lawn chairs talking, watching, and yelling their encouragement to various players. Some of the Mexicans arrived decked out in their brightly colored native costumes, and cell phones and cameras were snapping, videos rolling. There was even a reporter from the newspaper in the county seat taking pictures and interviewing people. The *Mariachi* band in full regalia was making the rounds from group to group. As far as Lynn could tell, everyone was having a good time, and even though the American and the Latino groups were still somewhat segregated, there seemed to be good will between them.

Reiko and her mother came but stayed only a little while. Their quieter Asian culture made them a little uncomfortable among the outgoing south-of-the-border crowd. Mayor Claxton and his wife were there doing a little politicking, getting a head start for the election in November. They decided to stay for lunch, although they really hadn't planned to. Sam and his colleagues from work and some of the taller Mexican guys were shooting hoops. Manuel had been at the grill all morning, where people were constantly stopping by to cheer him on.

Chapter 34

As it got closer to lunchtime, the crowd grew. Lynn didn't even know this many people lived in Perkins Grove. And that didn't count those who either refused to associate with the Latinos or those who went to the Sidewalk Sale instead. By 11:00 it looked like the whole Hispanic community was in the yard, along with at least half the American population, black, white, and brown mixing without reservation.

It's a good thing Perkins Grove is tiny! thought Lynn.

About 11:30 Maria and some of the ladies began putting the food out. When everything was ready, Sam and Pastor Juan used the sound system on the porch to call everyone in. Sam prayed first in English, and then Pastor Juan prayed in Spanish, both thanking the Lord for the food and for the success of this day.

A couple of times, Lynn heard thunder in the distance and saw the lightning, but nothing right where they were. The wind was picking up. She sincerely hoped the predicted showers would hold off at least until after lunch.

Four long lines formed, and everyone began filling plates from the bounty on the tables. As soon as one dish was emptied, it was replaced by a full one. Refried beans, tortillas, and rice were prominent, but scattered among them were the traditional American potato salad, baked beans, casseroles and veggie plates. Two extra tables had to be set up just to hold the desserts. What a feast! Manuel stayed at his post, chatting with everyone who stopped by to get a portion of meat.

Lynn heard the thunder a little closer now, and could actually see the rain falling not too far away. Although the sky was getting darker and the wind stronger, she still hoped it would pass them by. In the tree the *piñata* danced merrily.

Finally, everyone was served and was either still eating— or sitting, trying to recover from their lack of self-control at the table. A few were going back for more, and of course the kids were already back at their games. Lynn noticed how perfectly still it was. Good! Nothing to worry about yet. She went into the house, carrying some of the empty dishes. Shep, who was locked in her bedroom, began to bark a bark she had never heard before. Just nervous with so many new people around and not being allowed outside to wreak havoc in the middle of everything, she thought. She opened the door to give him some attention, but he pushed by her and continued to bark with renewed urgency.

At that moment Maria opened the back door to bring something else in. Shep darted past her, barking for all he was worth. He ran from one group to another, scaring the daylights out of everyone on the property. Lynn called him. Sam called him. Ana and Diego ran after him.

"Sam, what is it? What's wrong with him?"

This wasn't like Shep. Something was terribly wrong.

Then she noticed the stillness again.

Oh, no!

She quickly, but quietly, spoke to her husband.

"Sam, did you notice how still it is? Doesn't that usually happen before a tornado?"

They both looked up and saw the greenish sky just over the trees.

Sam jumped up on the porch and grabbed the mike. His voice boomed over the sound system.

"Everyone into the house quick! Storm coming!" Pastor Juan repeated the instructions in Spanish.

Lynn started directing people inside. It was the best they could do. The storm cellar was useless for this many people.

"Maria, open the front door so people can come in that way! Help me translate! Close the curtains! Push all the furniture against the walls to make more room! Women and

children in the most protected places, men around them. Put
people in the bedrooms first. Hurry!"

And then they heard the tornado siren wailing in the
distance.

"Hurry!" she repeated.

Shep, true to his breed, was herding everyone toward the
house. The tornado was coming. They could hear the roar.
Debris was swirling in the ever-strengthening wind.

In the house, people were on or under the furniture, on the
counters and tables, in closets and crammed in everywhere
else as tightly as they could. Mothers shoved toddlers under
beds or inside cabinets. The bathtub and shower stall were
full. The pantry was jammed. Kids were on top of the washer
and dryer. Fathers held their little ones to make room for
more.

"Juliana! Juliana! I no find Juliana!"

A frantic mother was trying to push her way out the door
to find the toddler she had thought was already inside with
her other children. Two of the men stopped her and kept her
inside. Manuel, Sam and Pastor Juan were bringing up the
rear, and Lynn was struggling to hold the door open for them.

"Shep!" she shouted above the roar. "Where's Shep!?"

"I don't know!" yelled Sam.

He pushed her inside and slammed the door.

"What about Shep!?" she cried, trying to get past her
husband and open the door.

"Lynn, stop it! It's too late. Listen, this lady's baby girl is
out there. Shep is a dog. I know—"

The rest of what Sam said was lost in the roar of what was
happening outside. Lynn buried her head in his chest, and he
encircled her with his strong arms.

Children clung to parents and wives clung to husbands.
Everyone, black, white, brown, native and foreign-born,
huddled together in the dark, hoping and praying they would
live to tell about this day. Some were screaming, some crying
and some praying out loud, but the cacophony of things

crashing against the house and of the tornado itself was drowning them all out.

It seemed to go on for an eternity, but in reality it was all over in a few minutes.

Sam slowly opened the back door and looked out on a scene horrifically different from the one they had left only minutes before. The funnel had missed the house, but just barely. Lynn's eyes followed a path of destruction that went through the parking area, across the field and up the hill on the other side of the creek. Trees looked like toothpicks scattered at random. Twisted tables and chairs were scattered everywhere. Broken dishes and remnants of food were strewn and splattered on everything. The barbeque pit had disappeared, but the soggy *piñata* still hung in the branches of the tree where it had been left. Manuel's truck was on its side.

Juliana's mother pushed her way out the door screaming out the name of her child.

"Juliana! Juliana!"

"Listen up!" called Sam over the heads of the people. "I know there are many of you who are concerned for your families."

He paused and swallowed hard. "I just looked at the road. There is no way to get through yet. Please help find the missing child, and then we'll work together to get everyone home."

Some of the people emerged from the house slowly, as if in a daze. Others pushed their way out, mouths falling open in shock at what they saw.

Most of them spread out, calling the little girl's name. But some crowded into the cars that weren't demolished and tried to leave, only to be stopped at the top of the driveway by one of the huge sentinel oaks that had fallen there. They jumped from the cars, confusion and anguish written on their faces. Mayor Claxton was frantic. His town had been hit by a tornado, and he was stranded out here!

"Mrs. B, where Shep?" Ana was running toward her, tears washing her stricken face.

"I don't know, Ana, but I do know that right now it's more important to find Juliana."

She took the girl by the shoulders and looked her in the eye.

"Do you understand?"

"Yes." She turned around and slowly began to walk toward the back of the house.

Lynn couldn't stand to see her so dejected. She hurried after her and put her arm around the girl.

"Let's look together," she said.

They began to work their way over broken limbs and folding chairs that had been blown into their path, slipping on potato salad or refried beans.

In a little dip behind the barn was the rotting stone foundation of the carriage house that had once stood there when this property was part of the cotton plantation. They slid down the muddy bank, still calling the child's name.

Suddenly Ana stopped.

"Did you hear?" she asked.

"Hear what? I didn't hear anything," whispered Lynn.

She stood perfectly still, listening.

Then she heard it—a child's whimper. It sounded like it had come from the old carriage house ruins.

"Call her, Ana! Talk to her in Spanish!" They slowly went forward in the direction of the sound—but the whimpering had stopped.

When they reached the carriage house area, Ana called and called.

Suddenly, Lynn saw a slight movement under the leaves of a fallen tree over in the only corner of the old foundation that was still somewhat intact. She grabbed Ana's arm and pointed.

It was the tip of Shep's tail. They ran forward and tried to get to the dog but found it impossible.

"Ana, run as fast as you can and get the others! We heard Juliana. She has to be here too. Hurry!"

Ana took off like a jackrabbit, yelling at the top of her lungs.

"Shep!" Lynn called. "Shep!"

She was rewarded with a weak whine from the dog. And then she heard a human baby cry. They were together! At that moment she understood how much more important was a human life than that of a dog—no matter how much she loved him.

"Juliana! *¡Tu Mamá está llegando!*"

She tried to reach the child by climbing down through the branches of the fallen tree, talking to the baby in a mixture of English and broken Spanish, but she was afraid she might make matters worse. She couldn't make it. She realized she was crying.

"Lynn, we're here! Climb back up. We're going to have to get this tree out of the way!" Sam called.

Lynn sagged with relief.

"Diego, go get the chain saw from the tack room! You men, let's see if we can move the tree without dragging it. Try to roll it off."

"Juliana! Juliana!" called the toddler's father.

The sound of her father's voice must have roused the child.

"*¡Papá! ¡Papá!*" she cried.

It was heartbreaking to hear the fear and desperation in her little voice and not be able to go to her. Maria had her arms around Juliana's mother. The men were positioning themselves.

"OK, we have only one chance."

Pastor Juan was translating Sam's instructions. "On three, lift and push. Keep working your way down until we get the tree rolled out of the way. We dare not let it roll back. Where's the dad?"

He spoke to the father and some of the men.

"As soon as you can, jump down with Juliana and push from down there. OK?"

The father nodded, willing to face any danger to save his little girl.

"OK. Ready? One, two, three. Lift! Push!"

Women, muscles hardened by working in the fields, were helping, and everyone was putting everything they had into it. Lynn, Maria, and Juliana's mother joined forces with the others.

The tree moved slightly and the father jumped down with his daughter. Everyone held their breath.

"Wait!" he called.

They were straining to hold the tree in place.

"Shep, he is here over Juliana. The tree, she is hold him."

Sam looked at Lynn. There was no choice.

"Let's get this tree out of the way!" yelled Sam.

A few men jumped down with the father to push from there. They all gave one more mighty heave, and the tree rolled over, dragging a limp Shep with it, flinging him in a heap onto the rubble.

Juliana's mother jumped down with her baby and her husband.

"Don't move her!" yelled Pastor Juan, who had been a medic in the Army.

He went to Juliana and quickly examined the bloody child.

"She's OK! Just a big bump on the head."

Everyone cheered and clapped.

To Sam he said quietly, "The blood must be Shep's."

Sam and Lynn knelt down by their dog.

It was obvious he was dying. He had been impaled by a branch and was losing blood rapidly. He was conscious and seemed to know his life was coming to an end. He didn't try to stand up or bite anyone and submitted to Manuel's examination without reaction.

Manuel slowly shook his head.

Ana came, and Sam and Lynn made room for her between them. Both put an arm around her.

"Good-bye, my Shep," she whispered.

Juliana's father came to him, his daughter in his arms, his wife and other children clinging to them. He knelt by the dog, not even trying to keep back the tears.

"*Gracias, Shep, gracias!*"

"*Grashiash,*" repeated the baby around her thumb. She popped it out of her mouth and offered it to Shep. He gave it a little lick.

Then he looked lovingly at Lynn, Ana, and Sam and closed his eyes.

Seconds later he stopped breathing.

As hard as it was for Lynn to believe, when she glanced at her watch, she saw that only about eight minutes had passed since they had come out of the house.

After a few seconds, Pastor Juan put his hand on Sam's shoulder.

"Sam, we have to go. The Sidewalk Sale… Will you go with us to assure the community of our good intentions?"

"I go," said Juliana's father, handing the girl to her mother.

"Of course!" said Sam standing and dashing away his own tears. "Lynn, I have to go. Will you be all right?"

"Yes," said Lynn, sniffling. "Maria and Ana and I will bring food and coffee for the workers."

"Good idea. I wish I could stay with you."

"No. Human lives are at stake, and Shep's gone. Go!"

She gulped down her own sadness.

"Go!" She waved him away.

Sam turned and jogged up the hill to catch up to the other men. He threw open the tack room and his workshop and let the men help themselves to the tools they thought would be helpful.

As soon as they had seen that they didn't need the chain saw to free Juliana, several of the men had taken it and cut away the big tree that had fallen across the driveway. They almost had a passageway cleared by the time the rest of the folks got there. Six men gathered around Manuel's truck, and with a lot of grunting and not a little swearing, righted it. Miraculously, it started when he turned the key! So what if there was no windshield or driver's side window!

Many of the cars in the field had been destroyed by debris from the tornado. Two cars had tumbled over and over, half way to the creek. A little red convertible had been smashed flat when an old sedan had landed crossways on top of it. Sam's Lexus had come through without a scratch because of a large limb that had blocked the entrance to the carport. That same limb, however, had shattered the back window of Lynn's van. About half the cars had received little or no damage. All colors and nationalities were forced to share rides, but no one seemed to notice, all vestiges of prejudice or resentment blown away by the tornado.

Maria started making coffee to fill the big thermoses. The power was out, but fortunately Lynn's stove was gas and still worked. When she was young, Maria had learned to boil the coffee in a pan and then pour it through a cloth filter. Her friends fashioned a filter out of a dishtowel and secured it while Maria carefully poured the coffee through. Some of the ladies pitched in to help make sandwiches, while others started organizing the children.

Not knowing the condition of their homes or anything else in town, Juliana's mother and a couple of other Hispanic mothers joined forces with some of the town women to stay at the Bartholomews' farm with the children and anyone else unable to help with the rescue efforts. Lynn showed them where the emergency supplies were, including the candles and lanterns. Who knew when she would be home again. They could help themselves to whatever food they could find. The ladies assured her that they would be fine and would try to clean up outside as much as they could.

Ana and Lynn got a tarp to throw over Shep. They could bury him when the emergency was past. Ana was inconsolable.

"You know, Ana," said Lynn, "Shep is the hero of the day. He's the one that first gave the tornado warning. A lot of people could have been hurt or even killed if he had not done what he did. He could have come into the house and saved himself, but instead he sacrificed his life to save Juliana. It looks like he dragged her to the safest place he could find and stood over her to protect her. If he had not been there, Juliana would have been killed."

"Yes," said Ana, drying her tears.

They stood looking at the tarp for a minute.

"Mrs. B, we need go to town and help."

"Yes, there's nothing more we can do for Shep."

They started walking toward the house.

Suddenly, Ana stopped. She looked at Lynn, her eyes filled with wonder.

"Mrs. B!" she said excitedly, "I understand! I finally understand!"

Her words came out in an excited rush.

"See, Juliana was supposed stay with her big sister, but she disobeyed and ran away. When the storm came, she was lost. Shep found her. There wasn't no way she could save herself, and the only way he could save her was to die for she live. He hadn't done nothing wrong. He was innocent, but he die protecting her from death."

She paused to take a breath.

"That's what Jesus did for us, for me… I believe, Mrs. B! I believe!" She gave Lynn a big hug.

"I must tell *Mamita*!" And with that, she took off running.

Lynn was stunned. "Thank You, Lord," she whispered. As she approached the house, she saw Ana call her mother outside and tell her what she had done. She watched when Maria gathered her daughter into her arms, a huge relieved smile on her face. Lynn caught her eye and gave her a satisfied nod.

The ladies made sandwiches from everything they could think of until the bread ran out. Lynn went outside to see if she could find anything usable. Though the tornado had passed right in front of the house, the house itself had received only minor damage from flying objects.

It was amazing that, in spite of all the destruction in front, the back was virtually untouched. The fridge on the back porch was still full of food that had not been put on the tables yet, and the washtub beside it still held a lot of sodas. There were several packages of bottled water standing ready. The ladies filled a big ice chest with food and sandwiches. There were still plenty of paper goods and plastic tableware in the house that had been put back for the later crowd. Lynn went to the medicine cabinet and got all the gauze, bandages, ointments and anything else she thought might be useful.

Ana and Gloria taped plastic over the opening left by the broken back window and swept all the glass out of the van. They helped Lynn wrestle the back seat out, and throw in a large tarp, some ropes and a wobbly table they had pulled down out of a tree. When everything they could think of was in the car, they left for town.

The silence was eerie. Maria's hand stayed fixed over her mouth. Ana's eyes were like saucers. Lynn, concentrating on maneuvering around all that littered the roadway, wore a scowl of disbelief at what she saw. All the way to town they passed through trees that the men had cut great sections from and moved to the sides of the road.

When they got to Main Street, they could plainly see the tornado's path. It had demolished the entire three blocks of businesses—like a village that a small child had constructed of blocks, only to be destroyed by a kick from his big brother. Like a war zone. Like someone had driven a giant bulldozer down the street. Like King Kong had come through, ripping buildings from their foundations.

Like the town had been hit by a tornado.

This year's Sidewalk Sale had been advertised as Bigger And Better Than Ever, which meant that the crowds were now somewhere within or under the bricks, boards, merchandise, and debris that had once been shops, boutiques, and restaurants.

A deputy sheriff stopped the van at a roadblock.

"I have food and water for the workers," Lynn told her.

The officer directed her to a spot in front of what was once Mandy's Boutique, which had already been searched.

Lynn helped Maria and Ana set up shop. They had planned to tie the tarp up, but there was nothing left to tie it to, so they just left the back of the van open and put the food onto the table. She took a thermos of coffee and her backpack full of water and went to the workers. She was serving men with cuts and bruises, who had been digging people out of the rubble without a break.

Sam, the guys from the Sunday school class, and the Hispanic men, some still in their Mexican costumes, worked feverishly alongside the police and rescue squads from surrounding areas to reach any survivors. Sully and Banks were directing another group of volunteers across the street. Pastor Juan and Dr. Benjamin, who was still wearing his *yarmulke,* were working on the casualties lined up on the sidewalk, waiting for the ambulances. Some of Lynn's Sunday school girls were trying to console injured, lost, scared, or almost hysterical children. Behind the yellow tape that separated the onlookers from the volunteers and rescue squads, people were crying and calling, desperately hoping for word of loved ones. Firemen were everywhere. Some ambulances were leaving, some were loading patients, and some were arriving from hospitals in neighboring towns. Diego and Antonio were nowhere to be seen.

"There's food in front of Mandy's, when you get a chance," she repeated again and again.

Dr. Benjamin asked her to leave water for the injured.

She turned around from handing someone a cup of coffee and saw Diego speeding her way.

"Mrs. B! Mrs. B!" he called.

"Over here, Diego! What is it?"

"Is Jack Barrett. He and his dad are trapped in basement of the house! He say his dad is pinned and hurt bad. All the mens are work on other peoples. What we can do?"

At that moment they saw the National Guard trucks rolling in. They ran toward them.

"Help us! Help us, please!" called Lynn as she ran.

The troops were already jumping off the trucks and running toward the concentrated rescue area. She finally caught up to one young man and managed to grab an arm.

"Can't you come with me before you join the others? We have a man trapped in the basement."

"I can't go without letting someone know, ma'am," said the young man. "My orders are to stay with my company. Come with me and we'll find someone to help you."

"Diego, go back and stay with Jack. Tell him and his dad that help is on the way." She ran to catch up with the young soldier.

When they reached the action, she saw Sam and the Hispanics backing off to let the Guard take over. "Thank You, God!" she sighed.

"Sam! Over here! Sam! Bring the men over here!" she hollered. The sounds of portable generators, power tools, hand tools, shouting, crying, and orders from those in charge drowned out her calls. Without stopping to think, she yodeled.

Sam heard and knew that sound could come only from his wife. He led everyone her way. They looked awful. Manuel, who had obviously been bleeding from a deep gash, was holding a bloody rag to his shoulder. He seemed a little dazed, but determined to keep going.

"Diego found a man pinned in the basement of his house! There's no one left to help him!"

"We go!" said Manuel. "Where?"

Lynn realized she didn't know where the house was exactly, but she led them in the direction Diego had been coming from when he found her. Sam passed around the rest of the water from her backpack as they walked. It was late afternoon, and they could see big generators and floodlights being set up in strategic locations.

Diego met them on the way. "I forget tell you where is the house."

He led the group quickly toward a tiny house on a dead end alley.

They heard Jack trying to calm his father, but his father was yelling obscenities and cursing his son and everything else. Antonio was working on the pile of debris.

"He may not let us help him," said Lynn quietly when she heard the man's anger. She told Sam and Pastor Juan that this was the man that had threatened to sue her when she had pulled his son off Diego last fall, father of the boy that had tripped Diego on the field trip.

Some of the men were already helping Antonio uncover the stairwell.

"Doesn't matter," said the pastor. "We can't just leave him there. We can deal with his attitude later."

He and Sam turned to help the other men.

"Call the boy, Lynn!" said Sam. "See if he can get out."

"Jack!" she called.

No answer.

"Jack, this is Mrs. B. Are you OK? Can you get out?"

Silence. She tried again.

"The men are here to get your dad out, but you need to come up here out of the way!"

Silence.

"I ain't leavin' m' dad!" Jack yelled.

Then she heard the dad say something to the boy but couldn't make out what it was.

Jack's head appeared out of the mess on the ground. He was shaking so much he hardly managed to climb out. He had a gash above his temple that was bleeding badly. Diego whipped off his T-shirt and Lynn fashioned a bandage around the boy's head. She took off the windbreaker she had grabbed on the way out the door at home and handed it to Diego, who threw it around Jack's shivering shoulders.

"We need someone small to go down and see how he's pinned," said Sam.

Before anyone could stop him, Diego wiggled down through the opening Jack has just left. He yelled up in Spanish.

"He can't see how the man is pinned," said Pastor Juan. "It's too dark."

"Lynn!" said Sam, "go get the flashlight out of the van."

She took off as fast as she could go. Sergeant Johnson intercepted her just before she got to the van. Since the Guard had arrived, he had taken a break and stopped for a quick bite to eat.

"Mrs. B, what is it?" he called.

She was gasping for breath and could hardly speak.

"Light... Come... with... me!"

She snatched the flashlight from the glove compartment and started to run back.

"Wait!" called the sergeant.

He jumped on a PGPD motorcycle.

"Get on! Which way do we go?"

Lynn straddled the bike and pointed, still too winded to say anything. They wound their way back to the house around uprooted trees, overturned vehicles, downed power lines and lawn furniture.

When they pulled up to the house, Sam grabbed the flashlight and ran to the stairs. Lynn and the sergeant followed.

"Diego!" called Sam.

Diego poked his head out and took the light.

"Take this one! It's stronger," said Sergeant Johnson holding out his department-issue flashlight. He had a strange look on his face. The boy took it and headed back down the stairs. He started calling out information. Pastor Juan told him what to do to stop Mr. Barrett's bleeding.

Diego saw what needed to be moved in order to open the way enough to get the injured man out and called that information up also. The pastor directed the men, and even Sarge joined the effort. He had radioed for reinforcements, but there were still none available.

Lynn went over to Jack, wishing she knew what to say. He was standing to the side, watching the action as if it were a scene from a movie.

"If we only had a couple more men," Pastor Juan mumbled.

When he heard that, Jack shuddered and kind of woke up. He and Lynn looked at each other.

"Can we help?" he asked, jumping over the broken boards. The pastor told them what to do, and they got to work.

Diego yelled something again.

Pastor Juan looked at Lynn.

"I understood."

She dropped the board she had just pulled from the pile and started running as fast as her shaky legs would carry her to—

CRACK!

Screams rang out from the basement.

"Dad!"

Sarge had to wrestle Jack to the ground to keep him topside.

"Diego!" called Pastor Juan. "Diego!"

They heard Mr. Barrett's muffled voice, but not Diego's. Antonio sprinted for the stairs. Something hit the basement floor, and Pastor Juan grabbed the boy before he could go down.

"No one's going down there until it's stable!" he said.

"I okay!" came Diego's pain-filled voice.

"Go, Lynn!" said Sam.

This time she had enough sense to pace herself. She heard a siren behind her and turned to wave down an ambulance returning for more victims.

"We've got a seriously injured man over here!" she panted up at the driver. "Can you help us?"

"Git in," said the driver.

Lynn showed him where to go and once again started to the house on the alley. She and the other EMT had to get out and move debris twice so that the ambulance could get through.

When they pulled up, Sarge told them to help the men move a heavy piece of the roof. If they could shift it just a little, Mr. Barrett would be free. The EMTs took their places beside the Hispanic men, Jack and Lynn.

"*Uno, dos, tres!*" yelled the pastor.

The roof moved an inch or two.

"Again! *Uno, dos, tres*! Again!"

The process continued until the roof was finally out of the way.

"OK!" hollered Diego, obviously still in pain.

He worked his way up the stairs to give the EMTs room to work. The medics grabbed their gear and gingerly scrambled through the debris.

Diego's face was white with pain. He turned around, and Lynn gasped when she saw his back.

"Something over us move. I jump over Mr. Barrett head so no hit him."

Lynn examined him. Across his shoulders, his back was swollen and turning purple. There were abrasions and lacerations, and the whole area would have to be cleaned before she could see how badly he was hurt. Thank God his back had not been broken!

Finally, Mr. Barrett was maneuvered into a rescue basket and several hands reached down to help haul him up the stairs. They got him into the ambulance, and with lights flashing and siren screaming, he was taken to the hospital. A disconsolate Jack stood watching his dad being taken away.

Diego, bare from the waist up, scars from his beatings and surgeries light against his dark skin in the front and blood drying on his bruised back, put his arm around the boy.

"He will be OK, Jack. He will be OK."

Jack's lip started to quiver and Sam went to him. The boy collapsed into the big man's arms, sobbing.

After the torrent of emotion had passed, Diego spoke again.

"Jack, where you sleep tonight?"

The boy looked at him like he didn't understand what he was asking.

"You cannot stay here. You come at our house, OK?"

"Great idea, Diego," said Sam. "We'll take you to the hospital and see your dad, and then you can come home with us and stay as long as you need to.

"Sergeant Johnson?"

Sergeant Johnson looked down, unable speak for a minute.

"Go," he finally managed to choke out.

"Lynn?" said Sam.

"Y'all go on. I need to get back to the van and see how Maria and Ana are doing. We'll probably be home before you are. And please get someone to look at Diego's back."

Sam, Diego, and Jack left on foot for Sam's car. Pastor Juan asked them to take a couple of the men to the Hispanic sector to check on things there.

"The rest of us are going back to help," he said.

"Need a lift to your van?" Sergeant Johnson asked Lynn when the others had gone.

"Please!"

She was beginning to feel every single one of her 61 years, but she knew that rest was still a long way off.

"I need to say something first," began the sergeant, clearing his throat. "Your folks were some of the first ones on the scene today, in spite of having to clear the road from your house. I know they saved many lives, and they risked their own to do it."

He looked down, but Lynn instinctively knew there was more.

"I have to admit I was wrong about the Hispanics as a whole... I... I'm sorry.

"Sure, they have their bad apples, but so do us rednecks and our black brothers down the road. And Diego's attitude toward the guy that has been tormenting him all year... I don't know what to think. Thank you for all you and your husband have done."

Lynn was amazed.

"Forgiven!" she said with a huge smile.

Thank You, God, she thought for the umpteenth time that day. She put out her hand to the man who had shown such prejudice against the whole Hispanic community. He took her hand and then threw his other arm around her for a quick hug. Amazing!

They reached the van, zigzagging around the Red Cross, National Guard and various other service groups that had arrived while they were with Jack. There were news trucks and reporters setting up their cameras and sound equipment. Some of the more zealous news people tried to stop Sergeant Johnson for an interview. He waved them away and kept going. When they got to the van, Lynn was not surprised to see that it was already full of passengers.

Maria approached her before she even got off the officer's bike.

"The Red Cross, they tell us take the childrens. No can find parents, and place in school no is ready. They have the names."

Lynn looked in the van and saw a half dozen disconsolate children staring back at her from the tarp in the back.

"Hi, guys! I'm Gramma Lynn and I have a bunch of kids at my house that want to meet some new friends. I know y'all will have fun there."

"I want my mommy!" cried one little toddler, tears streaming down his chubby face.

"I know you do, Sweetheart. Come here."

She hugged the grimy little towhead to her until the sobs turned to sniffles.

Ana stepped up, leading Reiko by the hand.

"Reiko's mother hurt, but not bad to go to hospital. Their house is..." She pointed up the street to where the Yakomoto home had stood just beyond the business district. Even in the waning daylight, Lynn could see the hole in the landscape.

She poked her head into the van and rearranged some of the children. Then she helped Reiko and her mom into the middle seat. Mrs. Yakomoto had a big bump on her head and her arm was bandaged from the elbow to her fingers. Her left eye was swollen shut and glowed a bright purple. Reiko sat beside her, scraped and bruised and dirty, but not really hurt. Both of them looked lost.

"Try not to worry," said Lynn. "We'll take good care of you."

She smiled reassuringly.

She noticed that the Mexican restaurant owners were serving the food they had prepared for the sidewalk sale crowds. Since the *El Tecolote* was tucked away on a side street, it had received little damage. They had a portable generator to keep the coffee pot going and had found something to string white Christmas lights on so they could see what they were doing.

"Please," said the restaurant owner, "take this to help feed the childrens."

He handed her several bags of food. She wasn't sure what was in them, but they sure did smell good. Her tummy rumbled. When had she eaten last, anyway? In another lifetime, she thought.

Just as she was pulling out, Sergeant Johnson came up with a screaming baby in his arms.

"Mrs. B!" he yelled. "Can you take one more? We don't know who this child is or where her parents are. The shelter still isn't set up."

"Of course," she said jumping back out of the van and taking the infant. "Send the parents too, when you find them."

She passed the baby in to Maria, who passed the toddler she was holding over to Ana.

"Think, Lynn," she told herself as she was driving home. She had no idea how many people would be staying at her home or how long they would be there.

I guess we'll just have to spread everyone out on the floor, she thought. She started mentally counting bedding.

They had their own well, but the pump was electric. Thankfully, Sam had taught her to use the portable generator when he had been traveling, so they would have lights and water. She thought through the other details and had the towels, blankets, and clothes questions pretty much worked out by the time they got home.

But what about the baby? She glanced in the mirror and saw Maria was thinking as hard as she was. In the ragbag she had a couple of old, soft dishtowels that they could use for diapers. She and Maria would have to put their heads together and come up with some kind of formula. Getting the formula into the baby would be the trick.

"Lord," she prayed silently, "we need some creativity here."

Maybe one of the mothers at the house would have a bottle.

Pulling into the driveway, she stopped, then eased into the carport. Thankfully, it was dark so they couldn't see the mess they had left this afternoon.

Was it only a few hours ago? Did everyone feel like she did?

And there was no Shep waiting to greet her in the candlelit house.

Someone came out with a lantern and helped get the children inside. Lynn and Maria maneuvered the generator to the back of the carport by the light from the high beam on the van.

Her cell rang. Thank goodness they still had that!

"The boys and I are going back to town to help. Jack's dad is stable, but they can't do surgery until tomorrow because of all the other casualties being brought in. They've set up a shelter in the school gym and they need help over there. That's probably where we'll be for a while. How's it going at home?"

"Just about to fire up the generator. I'll probably take a load of mothers and children home—if they still have one— to the shelter, or back here if they don't. How's Diego? Do they need me in town for anything?"

"He'll be really sore for a while, but he's OK. And I think you're doing your part, but I'll ask. I love you."

"I love you too. Thanks for all you're doing. Bye."

Lynn ran a shuttle most of the night. She took people to town and brought other people back until she could hardly keep her eyes open.

Wake up, Lynn! she admonished herself. We don't want to deal with an accident right now.

Chapter 35

The men returning from Jack's house had heard cries for help from a building that had already been searched. They finally found a man behind the trash dumpster, where he had lain unconscious since the storm. The man had been confused and unable to give them any information. He had a gash on the back of his head that had soaked his hair with blood and stained the back of his sport coat. Pastor Juan had finally gotten him calmed down and had gotten the bleeding stopped. When a wall collapsed across the street, injuring some of the rescue workers, everyone had run to help. Pastor Juan had left the injured man resting against an overturned car, but now no one could find him.

Around three or four in the morning, the exhausted pastor drove by his house and found that a tree had fallen on it. It was damaged, but not destroyed. Maria was at the Bartholomews' and so were his kids. He just wanted to be where they were, where she was. He would go there for what was left of the night and deal with his own losses tomorrow.

He was almost to the Bartholomews' lane when he saw someone staggering across the road. The man stumbled and fell right in front of him. Pastor Juan slammed on the brakes and jumped out. It was the guy he had left by that car! He was conscious, but that was all. If he didn't get help soon...

"Come on, fella, get up," said the pastor, "You're too big for me to get in the car by myself. How on earth did you get out here?"

He helped the man to his feet and supported him until he got him into the car. Now what? The already overcrowded hospital was on the other side of town with miles of detours between here and there, and this guy needed help now. Sam and Lynn's driveway was much closer. The man kept mumbling and calling out incoherently.

Pastor Juan headed the car into Sam's spot in the carport and opened the back door of the house without knocking. "Maria, Lynn! I need help here!" Together the three of them managed to get the man as far as the kitchen. Lynn quickly spread a beach towel on the floor. There was not another inch of floor space left and not one single blanket. If anyone else showed up they would have to sleep on the porch in the hammock.

Pastor Juan quickly examined the man. "Lynn, do you have a blood pressure cuff?"

"I have the wrist kind," she answered, hurrying to get it. The man's blood pressure was low, but not dangerously so, thank goodness. Since all the medical supplies had been taken to town, the pastor cleaned the wound and then bandaged his head with Sam's handkerchiefs and duct tape.

"We need to get him out of his wet clothes. Lynn, can you find something of Sam's for him to put on? Maria, help me get his coat off." Pastor Juan looked for some identification and found the man's driver's license.

Justin Todd, it said.

After he was dressed in one of Sam's sweat suits, they helped him sip some water. Then they laid him down and made him as comfortable as possible.

Justin Todd finally began to come around. He was still pretty incoherent and kept desperately calling the names of two women. How horrifying! thought Lynn. He doesn't know where his loved ones are. Maria kept giving him liquids while Pastor Juan checked on his head. He really needed stitches, but that would have to wait. Finally, he either passed out or went to sleep. Lynn wasn't sure which, but at least he was quiet.

Maria went back to her bedroom, carefully stepping over sleeping children and adults. Pastor Juan stretched out in Sam's recliner. Reiko and her mother were in Sam and Lynn's bed, and some of the older kids were on their bedroom floor. Lynn lay down in the living room on the air mattress she had reserved for herself and her husband.

She tried to sleep but kept waking up every few minutes to pray for Sam, the boys, and the town in general, and to check on Mr. Todd. A couple of times she got up and walked through the rest of the house, but everyone seemed to be sleeping calmly.

Just before dawn, Sam and Diego came home, bringing Jack with them. The boys flopped down wherever they found a spot and were out in seconds. Sam was about to lie down when he happened to shine his flashlight on the man in the kitchen.

"Good grief, Lynn! Do you know who that is?" he whispered.

"His driver's license says Justin Todd. Why?"

"That's Justin Todd, Congressman David Todd's son. The whole town has been searching high and low for him! His picture's been passed around all over the county. I have to call someone and let the authorities know he's here. Is he OK? How on earth did he end up at our place?"

She quickly told him everything she knew. Then she woke up Pastor Juan. Sam went outside, dialed 9-1-1 and told the dispatcher that Justin Todd had been found and that he was resting comfortably at their house.

Yes, he could hold... Yes...

He gave the phone to a somewhat out-of-it Pastor Juan who described Todd's injuries and condition, and then handed the phone back to Sam.

Yes, Mr. Todd could stay the night here. Yes... Yes, an ambulance in the morning would be fine. Hang on...

"Do we have a baby girl here, Lynn?" Sam asked.

"Last count, I think there were three baby girls. We know who two of them are—their parents are all in the hospital. Sergeant Johnson gave the other one to us just as we were leaving town. Why?"

"Justin Todd's daughter is missing. He and his wife had split up at the sidewalk sale, and the baby was with her."

He listened to the voice on the phone for a couple of seconds.

"Two months old, dark hair and eyes, pink 'Grandma loves me' T-shirt. The mother is pretty beat up, but she'll be OK. She's beside herself with worry for her daughter and her husband. Could we have a look at the unidentified baby? She has a birthmark on her right thigh."

"Let me wake Maria. She's the baby person. They're all in her room. I'll need the flashlight. I'll go first and find the right one, and then you can come."

"We're checking," Sam said into the phone. "Can you hold? We have a lot of people here. It may take a minute."

Lynn carefully stepped over and around the sleeping forms between her and Maria's room. She tapped lightly on the door.

"Maria!" she called softly. "Maria!"

The door opened quickly. Maria was still in her clothes but had obviously been asleep.

"Yes?" she whispered.

"Where's the unidentified baby? We may know who she is. Sam's here and would like to see her."

"Is here. The first in the floor."

Lynn motioned to Sam and shined the flashlight so he wouldn't step on anyone.

"Thank you, Maria," he whispered. "Where is she?"

"There," said Maria, indicating the sleeping child.

Sam knelt down and tenderly turned the infant toward him. Hair and T-shirt were right. He moved the edge of the dishtowel *cum* diaper and saw the birthmark.

"It's her!" he whispered loudly.

The child stirred in her sleep. Sam spoke softly into the phone.

"I believe it's her. Hang on and let me go outside so I won't wake anybody."

He went back outside to talk to the dispatcher and was put through to Congressman Todd himself.

"Yes, sir, they're both here and are resting well. The baby doesn't seem to have a scratch on her. Maria Lopez, the Hispanic lady whose family lives with us, has taken exceptional care of her, as well as a whole houseful of other children."

Sam paused to listen. "Yes, sir, your son was injured and was found by Pastor Juan Garcia of the Spanish Community Bible Church. Pastor Juan was an Army medic in the Middle East and knew exactly what to do for him."

Pause.

"Yes, sir. We can have the baby ready to go in the morning when they come for her father. Thank you, sir. Good night."

Sam came in, put down the phone and crashed on the air mattress. Lynn lay down beside her husband, who was already snoring, thinking she would not be able to sleep at all because she would be working out the logistics of feeding a houseful of people when she had no clue what was in her cabinet. Maybe as tired as they all were, they would sleep in a little, while she checked out the situation.

Ha! she thought. Nobody sleeps in with babies in the house!

The next thing she knew, there was a baby crying somewhere, and the sun was streaming innocently through the kitchen window as if it had not betrayed them only yesterday.

The ambulance showed up early to take Justin Todd to the hospital, and Congressman Todd and his wife followed it into the driveway. Justin was still lying on the kitchen floor. When he heard his father calling his name, his personal fog began to lift, and he immediately asked for his wife and daughter.

"They're fine," said the Congressman. "Jean is in the hospital with a broken bone or two, and your mother is rocking baby Patty right here in this house."

Mrs. Todd came to her son, knelt beside him and showed him his daughter. She laid the child beside the father, who was lying on his side because of the gash in the back of his head, and then leaned down to kiss her son on the cheek.

The baby's cooing accompanied her father's sobbing like a sweet violin.

After a minute, Mrs. Todd again took the baby and the EMTs moved in to get Justin loaded up.

"How can I ever thank you?" said Congressman Todd sincerely, the strain of the last eighteen hours showing on his face.

"Maria Lopez is the one you should thank," said Lynn. "I was running people back to town while she took care of little Patty and the others. Would you like me to call her? She speaks English pretty well now."

"And Pastor Juan Garcia is the one that found Justin. He's already gone back to town to help," added Sam.

Congressman Todd had been quite vocal in his opinions about foreigners in general and illegals in particular. Sam wanted to be sure he got the message that it was Latinos that had saved his family members.

Lynn remembered it was Sunday. After breakfast, which had to be eaten in shifts, Sam held a brief impromptu church service for everyone at the house. Then he and the boys went back to town to check on Jack's dad and to help wherever they were needed.

Reiko used Lynn's cell phone and was finally able to reach her father. He had been on business in Atlanta and had been frantically searching for his family. Mrs. Yakomoto had a sister in Macon, and the family was going to stay there until things were straightened out.

Mr. Yakomoto arrived that afternoon. "Thank you for all you have done," he said. "I am sure we will be fine now."

"Please, if there is anything at all that you need, do not hesitate to let us know." Lynn looked especially at Reiko, who nodded her gratitude.

Phone calls were flying thick and fast between the Bartholomews, the Red Cross and Sarge. They were trying to locate the parents of the children who had gone home with Lynn last night and giving updates to the mothers who had stayed to help. Sam delivered a vanload of people when he and the boys went back to town to help.

Lynn didn't know what to do about Jack. She and Sam were not approved as foster parents, but she hated to just turn him over to DFCS and let him get lost in the system. According to Sam, it would be a really long time before his father would be able to live on his own.

She called Sergeant Johnson and talked to him about the boy. "We would like to keep him, if there would be any way," she said. "We've never been officially approved as foster parents, so—

"Good grief, Mrs. Bartholomew!" interrupted the sergeant, "I think you've more than demonstrated your trustworthiness. I'll put in a word for you at DFCS. They're so stretched right now, I'm sure they'll be tickled to death to have you."

Later that morning Ana and Gloria took the little ones outside, and they all started cleaning up from the storm. Lynn looked in the tack room for a shovel, but all she found was a hoe that the men had left behind. Without Ana seeing, she slipped down to the old carriage house to bury Shep. Fortunately the ground was soft from the storm, but it still took a long time to dig a grave deep enough to bury the big dog. She piled some of the stones from the foundation on top of the mound to keep any hungry critters from digging him up. Too tired to shed any more tears, she said a quick, but sincere prayer of thanksgiving to God for her wonderful pet.

Now she was really exhausted. She dragged herself to the house, took off her muddy shoes, and crashed onto the bed. She never knew when Sam came home and crashed beside her.

It seemed that the tornado had taken out its wrath on the Perkins Grove downtown business district. It had touched down there and then followed a path east to the Bartholomew farm. After passing Sam and Lynn's place, the funnel had dissipated and eventually blown itself out. Most of the downtown businesses had been leveled, and the few residences on those blocks had been destroyed, as well.

The rescue had continued through the night and into Sunday. Aside from the National Guard and Red Cross, volunteers had come from miles around and continued the search for victims. By mid-afternoon, everyone had been accounted for, as far as anyone knew. Miraculously, only two people had lost their lives. The number of injured that were hospitalized had risen to 243, and there were countless less serious wounds. Stories of heroism began to surface.

By Monday morning power had been restored to most of the outlying areas. There was nothing left downtown to restore power to, but generators were still in place to do whatever needed to be done with electricity until the buildings were restored. The high school had sustained some damage, but the gym was still being used as a shelter for those who needed it.

Most of the downtown businesses had to be razed and rebuilt from scratch because they had been totaled. As the clean up continued, the Hispanics were involved in every aspect of the work. Some were hired by the city to haul away the debris and to help repair the buildings that had been damaged by the tornado. Others were hired by the county to repair the school buildings. Construction companies employed them, and of course, the farmers desperately needed them to clean up and replant the fields. The few who weren't employed volunteered.

The Tuesday after the storm, Mayor Claxton called. "May I come by to see you and Sam Thursday night?" he asked Lynn.

She thought a minute but couldn't think of anything else going on.

"Hold on a second and let me ask." She and Sam compared notes. "Sure, what time will you be here?"

"Around 7:00 OK?"

"Perfect! See you Thursday." She hung up wondering what in the world the mayor wanted with them. Sam couldn't imagine either.

"Guess we'll just have to wait and see," he said.

When their guest arrived, Jack and the Lopez family were introduced to him but then made themselves scarce by going to their respective bedrooms. Lynn served coffee and Maria's homemade Mexican cookies. The ladies had had to drive about twenty-five miles to find groceries and gasoline. Their reserves had pretty much been wiped out after the storm.

When they were settled in the living room with the refreshments, the mayor began.

"The town council and I have been talking. After the storm and the way the Hispanics jumped in to save the lives of people who hated them—often putting themselves at risk—we have realized what a tremendous contribution they have made here. And that has been largely because of what you two have done."

Lynn gulped, just about choking on her steaming coffee, and glanced at her husband.

The mayor continued, "I have been sent by the council to express our thanks."

Sam opened his mouth to respond.

The mayor held up his hand. "I'm not finished. As a sign of victory over the destruction, we're going ahead with the Memorial Day parade. Congressman Todd from this district is the Grand Marshal, and he would like you to be Co-Grand Marshals and ride in the car with him."

Lynn's mouth dropped open, and she didn't seem to be able to close it. Sam had been setting his mug on the coffee table but stopped in mid-air.

"Would you repeat that, please," he said.

The mayor smiled and said slowly, "We want you to drive a classic 1956 Cadillac convertible in the Memorial Day parade, while Congressman Todd and his wife ride on the boot. You will be Co-Grand Marshals and wave to the crowd." He gave a parade-style wave to illustrate.

Sam and his wife looked at each other, speechless.

"Furthermore," said the mayor, we're inviting the Latino community to take part in the parade. We've already spoken to the owners of the Mexican restaurant, and they're going to have a float or something and then have a booth in the park with the others. We want you to invite that *Mariachi* band, the one that was here at your house, to play in the parade if they want to, or just up and down the street if they don't want to march. I understand your Diego plays in the band at school. They were practicing for the parade before the storm."

The mayor scooted to the edge of his chair, warming to his subject.

"Can you think of anything else?"

Lynn was mulling something over in her mind. Then she spoke up.

"Uh... What about a flat-bed truck for all the volunteers who helped after the storm? That would include Hispanics, whites, blacks, and any others—even people like Jack, who were rescued themselves but then stayed and worked."

"Great idea!" exclaimed the mayor. "The police and fire departments are already represented. Maybe the National Guard and the Red Cross could enter something."

"Maybe all the news people that were here during the storm would like to come back and cover the parade," said Sam.

The mayor was writing everything down in a pocket notebook.

"Excuse me a minute. I'll be right back," said Lynn standing up.

She knocked on Diego's door and then went to Ana's room.

"Come in," called the girl.

"Ana," said Lynn excitedly, "You won't believe what the mayor just asked us."

She quickly explained what he had said. Diego listened from the doorway.

"Do you think you could have your recorder group ready to march in the parade?"

This time Ana's mouth dropped open.

"March? With recorders? In the parade? Is this possible?"

"Well, I admit I've never heard of it before, but why not? Sam could work with you; he's an old marching band guy. What do you think?"

"Do it!" said Diego. "I help too. Is very good because not all the kids are Hispanics. The town will see us work together. School is… how you say… stop for rest of year, so have more time for practice."

"Maybe I help," said Maria. "I and friends make clothes."

"Then I can tell the mayor we've got another entry in the parade?"

They all agreed excitedly.

Lynn returned to the living room, grinning.

"Mayor Claxton, I think I have an idea."

She explained her plan. Sam was incredulous at first. A marching recorder band? Whoever heard of such a thing?! But as the idea grew on him, he became excited about it too.

"Well," said the mayor, "it will certainly be unique."

He stood to leave.

"Thank you so much for everything you two have done. We'll be in touch."

"Let me walk you to the car," said Sam.

When the two men were far enough away to talk without being heard by the folks in the house, Sam said to the mayor, "I know the Hispanics will really appreciate all you are doing to honor them," he began, "but there is something they would appreciate even more."

"What's that?" questioned the mayor, matching Sam's serious tone.

"Well, as you know, a few of them are here illegally. Except for Maria and the kids, I have no idea who nor how many, but if there is something you or Congressman Todd could do to encourage real immigration reform, it would show your gratitude far more than riding in a parade."

"Actually, the men and I kicked around some ideas along that line, but nobody wanted to go near that can of worms. As you know, Congressman Todd has been very outspoken on the issue of immigration into this country, legal and illegal."

"I know, but I'm hoping that since the Hispanics played such a big part in saving the lives of his son, daughter-in-law and granddaughter, he might look at things differently."

"That's a thought. I'll see what I can do."

"Thank you," said Sam. "All we can ask of anyone is that he do his best."

The mayor got the point.

Sam came in, praying that God would do what only He could do in this situation.

When he had shut the door, Lynn ran to meet him. He said nothing of his private conversation with Mayor Claxton.

"Can you believe it?" asked Sam, grinning. "They actually want to *honor* the Hispanics!"

He grabbed his wife by the waist and swung her around. "Woo-hoo! Thank You, Lord!"

The others came tearing out of the bedroom. They all joined hands and did a little dance around the living room laughing and being silly. They tried to pull Jack in, but he just watched with his arms folded. He had never seen anything like this before.

"We call Juan?" asked Maria.

They called, and the pastor was as excited as they were.

Maria got out more cookies, and they sat around the
kitchen table chattering until they wound down enough to go
to bed.

Jack sat at the table with them, watching, listening and
thinking. What is it with these people? They call themselves a
family, but they ain't even all from the same country.

Jack had never seen people live together like this without
fighting and screaming. He had been in this house for five
stress-filled days. When were they going to crack and start
fighting and yelling at each other? They couldn't be for real.
They couldn't keep up this goody-two-shoes front forever. He
knew they were just being nice to each other for his benefit—
always laughing or smiling or joking around. Maybe it was
because they hadn't lost everything like he had, but
somehow, he didn't think so.

And what about Diego? Now that Jack thought about it,
he realized that Diego had never tried to get back at him for
bullying or belittling him or trying to hurt him. He had
thought it was because he was a wimp, but now he could see
a strength of character that he had never noticed before.
Looking back at the Perkins Gorge incident, he realized that
Diego really had saved his life. He would never openly admit
it, but it was, nevertheless, true. Diego didn't even seem to
hate James Flanagan, who had tried to burn this house down.
What was up with that?

Oh, Jack couldn't put all those thoughts into words; they
were just things swirling around in his head.

But the one question he could form was…why?

Was it because they were religious? He'd known other
religious people who went to church all the time, but they
weren't like this. He just didn't understand. But he would
bide his time. He knew eventually they would slip up, and
then he would see them as the hypocrites they had to be.

Chapter 36

Things were coming together fast for the Memorial Day parade, and excitement was building. The parade route would follow the tornado's path through the middle of town. The weather forecast was for a hot, sunny day, typical for this time of year in central Georgia.

On the big day, Lynn fussed with her hair and her clothes, as did everyone else in the household. After changing three times, Sam finally decided on a blue dress shirt, open at the collar like he had just taken his tie off. Diego had on his marching band uniform for the first time—very impressive. Ana's long flowing teal dress with a wide green stripe running from the right shoulder to the left hemline, front and back was gorgeous. All the girls in the recorder band would be decked out the same. The boys in the group had black pants, teal shirts and a cummerbund that matched the stripe in the girls' dresses. The effect was remarkable.

Even Jack was excited, but he did his best to hide it. He also dressed with extra care in a new pair of jeans and the T-shirt that Maria had embroidered with the parade theme on the front and his name on the back. She hoped he got the message.

The family gathered around the breakfast table. "Lord," prayed Sam, "this day and all it represents is of You. We can say nothing more than thank You. We ask You for grace and wisdom to maintain the unity in the future. In Jesus' name, amen."

UNITED WE ARE STRONGER THAN THE STORM! read the banner carried by the high school cheerleaders to start the parade. Behind them came the solemn military color guard, a sergeant calling out the cadence. Spectators removed their hats or respectfully placed their hands over their hearts as the flags passed. This year, for some reason, it seemed a little more important to salute.

The high school band was next. Every once in a while the band would stop and play and march in some fancy formation for the crowd. The on-lookers showed their appreciation with loud applause. Then the band marched double-time to catch up with the color guard.

Next came Congressman Todd with his wife and the Bartholomews. The Todds waved and greeted folks from the boot of the baby blue 1956 Cadillac convertible. Sam was crazy about classic cars and proudly drove this beauty with Lynn by his side. They waved and smiled and called to friends that lined both sides of the street in front of the skeletons of new construction. There was Mr. Cline with his family, and across the street stood Sheila and her brood. They waved, jumping up and down in their excitement. Lynn waved to her fellow teachers and to some of the parents of the recorder kids. Sam waved to their pastor and his family and to his colleagues from work.

"Mrs. B! Mrs. B! Hey, Mrs. B! Over here!"

"Sam, stop!" said Lynn urgently.

Sam hit the brakes, thinking something was wrong. The Todds nearly pitched into the back floor.

"What—?" Sam tried to ask.

"Keep going. I'll catch up!" Lynn jumped from the car before her husband could say another word and ran over to a large group of her Bible students who had gathered to cheer her on. Several of them got hugs, handshakes, or at least a squeeze on the shoulder.

Even the guy with the dread locks gave her a bear hug that about crushed her. Frank Walenski shook her hand enthusiastically.

"I am so glad to see y'all! Did everybody come through the tornado OK? How about your families? Houses?" Everybody was talking and laughing at once, trying to recount their tornado experiences. Greg was sporting a shoulder brace, which he proudly showed off to his teacher. Bill held up the cast on his forearm.

"Too bad it wad'n' his mouth!" someone shouted. Bill swatted the speaker with his good hand.

"I gotta run! Y'all come on down to the park later and let's talk." With that, Lynn took off at a trot to catch up to Sam and the Todds. She greeted several people on the way and would have been just as happy to walk the rest of the route talking to folks. Ah, the price of fame, she thought.

After the Grand Marshall's car came a huge VFW float honoring all the branches of the military with veterans from WW II, Korea, Vietnam, the Gulf War, and the conflicts in the Middle East all on board. Patriotic marches blared from speakers hidden somewhere within the bowels of the vehicle.

The Red Cross, National Guard, Ambulance services, Police and Firemen's Associations were all dispersed among the floats, ear-splitting sirens blasting from time to time. The excited rescue dogs that had been used to find victims after the storm dragged their owners down the street, noses to the ground. Sergeant Johnson rode his motorcycle, and Sully and Banks were behind him in their cruiser.

Wonder who's minding the town, thought Lynn.

In the flatbed truck full of volunteers who had helped in the rescue, Pastor Juan and Maria were waving from where they stood just behind the cab. Dr. Benjamin was beside them. The Bartholomews' Sunday school kids, Manuel, and the Hispanics were scattered among the other volunteers. Jack was in the back corner, not scowling, but not quite smiling, either. Lynn had noticed his excitement this morning, as well as his feeble attempt to hide it. He was softening; he just didn't know it yet.

Since Memorial Day was initiated to remember the soldiers who had died in the War Between the States, there was a large group of costumed re-enactors, battle flags flying, musket fire reverberating along the parade route, just for effect.

The Chamber of Commerce's peach float, a mainstay in every parade in Perkins Grove, carried the mayor and town council members, who were throwing out candy to children and adults alike.

Ana's group was one of the last entries, far enough back that the Bartholomews, Diego, Pastor Juan, and Maria were able to get to the stands in time to watch them perform. The kids had worked really hard to learn to march in less than one month. There were missteps, yes, but overall, they were great! They played a pretty fast Celtic number, but marched in a slow cadence. The girls gave their skirts a little kick with each step, which made them look full and flowing. It was beautiful, and the crowd roared their appreciation.

The next-to-the-last entry was four clowns passing out helium balloons imprinted with the theme: UNITED WE ARE STRONGER THAN THE STORM!

At the very end of the parade Mr. Barrett, Jack's dad, drove a Scooterchair flanked by a nurse on one side and a doctor in surgical scrubs on the other. He still had a bandaged head, a back brace, a cast on his right forearm, and a medical boot on the opposite foot. It was a tribute to modern medicine that the man was still alive. He was pulling a little trailer with a banner on each side that read simply THANK YOU!

* * * *

Maria and her friends had set up a booth in the park at the end of the parade route and had their machines ready to embroider names on the backs of T-shirts with UNITED WE ARE STRONGER THAN THE STORM! on the front. Proceeds would go to help the families who had lost everything in the storm. The *Mariachi* band filled the park with music, strolling around playing and singing all day long. In the decorated gazebo, Mayor Claxton and Congressman Todd made speeches.

The Mexican restaurant had a booth on one side of the park, and the aroma of Mexican spices permeated the air. On the opposite corner, Mama's Kitchen filled the air with the smell of hot grease from the fried chicken, catfish, hush puppies, and French fries—enough to send anybody's cholesterol over the moon!

The Bartholomews were meandering around the park hand-in-hand, listening to tornado stories and talking to everyone. Just before lunchtime, Sam got involved in a pick-up basketball game on the park's outdoor court. He was in his dress pants and shoes, shirttail hanging out, sweat stains beginning to show under his arms.

"Dignity, always dignity," muttered Lynn, quoting from an old Gene Kelly movie. She went to Maria's booth and bought her husband a T-shirt. Then she marched right onto the court.

"Time out!" she called.

"Lynn! What on earth are you doing?" Sam said, trotting over to her. The other players gathered around to see what was going on.

She didn't say a word. She offered him the T-shirt with one hand and held out the other for his dress shirt.

"You want the shirt off my back? Fine, but first I get a hug." He grabbed his wife before she could get away and gave her a sweaty, stinky, pick-her-up-off-the-ground hug. The players cheered. Then he took off his shirt and handed it to her.

"Gotcha back," he grinned with a wink, as he trotted back into the game.

Lynn carried the damp shirt carefully back to the Maria's stand. She borrowed a hanger that the ladies were using for their display and hung Sam's shirt where it could air out. Glad I caught him before it was too late, she thought.

She wandered over toward the Mexican restaurant's booth. The tamales the owners had sent for the gang at her house on the day of the storm were delicious, and she decided to see if they were on today's menu. Maria's were every bit as good, but Lynn had never gotten the opportunity to thank the restaurant owner, so she decided to seize the moment. Besides, she had not the least desire to tempt a heart attack by eating at Mama's Kitchen. She signaled Sam and made her way to the *El Tecolote* booth with purpose.

"Mrs. B! Mrs. B!" She heard her name but couldn't locate the speaker. Finally, she saw Isabel waving to her from the tables surrounding the restaurant's booth. The girl appeared to be waitressing. She was dressed in a mid-calf, white traditional Mexican dress with colorful ribbon trim. The top was made to be worn off the shoulders, but Isabel's was firmly in place on her shoulders, making little cap sleeves. Lynn couldn't help but notice that her face was devoid of all make-up except for a little lipstick. The girl's natural beauty was much more enhanced by a little make-up than by a lot.

"Isabel! Is that you?" she called. Isabel ran up and gave her a quick hug and then took her by the hand and led her to a table.

"Sit here, please. I no can stop now, but I want talk, OK?" She looked so happy and excited about something that Lynn couldn't help but laugh and nod in agreement. "You want menu?"

"Yes, please... well, actually, I already know what I want. Are you serving tamales?"

"Of course, yes! What you would like to drink?" She was writing on her little order pad, while that happy smile lit up her face like a Christmas tree. Even with the other customers, her obvious joy just spilled over. Lynn couldn't wait to hear what she had to say.

Lynn asked Isabel to introduce her to the restaurant owner after the lunch rush had passed. When things slowed down a bit, Isabel came to the table, followed by a man who obviously enjoyed his own cooking.

"Mrs. B, I like you to meet Mr. Perez, my boss," said Isabel.

"*Mucho gusto*, Mr. Perez." She extended her hand. Mr. Perez took it and smiled broadly.

"*Mucho gusto!*" Then he fired off a round of Spanish fast enough to launch a rocket. Lynn thought she could actually feel the G-force. She just looked at him and then turned her bewildered gaze to Isabel, who laughed out loud.

"No, Mr. Perez, you have to speak English! Mrs. B no speak Espanish. She only know '*mucho gusto.*'"

Mr. Perez laughed heartily. "OK, sorry. Nice to meechu!" he said, shaking her hand again. "You like the tamales, yes?"

"Yes! I loved them! And I wanted to thank you for the food you sent to help feed the children on the day of the storm."

"Is nothing... uh... you welcome. My wife and me, we want go to *Cinco de Mayo* party, but have to work. We plan go after, but..." He shrugged.

"I understand. A lot of plans changed that day."

"Mr. Perez, I can go there and talk for Mrs. B a little?" asked Isabel. There was no one waiting to be served, so the restaurant owner nodded and waved them away.

Lynn and Isabel went and stood under one of the old oaks that had survived the storm. It still amazed Lynn that a tornado could totally destroy everything in its path, while disturbing very little on either side.

Isabel could contain her joy no longer. "Mrs. B, I do... did... what you say!" She was so excited that she had to stop a minute and regroup. "I choose to believe the Bible. I repent for my sin. I believe that Jesus suffer the punishment for my sin when He die on cross. I have life eternal now because He rise from the dead and give it to me." The girl was so happy and excited she could hardly stand still.

"I wash my face and put on this clothes—only good clothes I have. I no go with mans... men... or boys more, no! Then I see Mr. Perez in The Store. 'Isabel?' he say, "You look wonderful! You come work in my restaurant, OK?'" She did a little twirl. "I say OK. I go talk to my father. I very happy!" She stopped, out of breath.

Lynn threw her arms around the girl and praised God with her, shedding more than a few tears.

Just then Isabel saw some customers approaching her tables. "I go now." She gave her teacher a dazzling smile and a wave as she ran over to do her job. Lynn happened to glance at Mr. Perez. The jolly restaurant owner gave her a thumbs up and a grin. Lynn waved and ran to find her husband. News this great was too good to keep to herself.

* * * *

Toward evening, Maria disappeared from her workstation. A little while later Sam, who had washed his face, combed his hair, changed back into his dress shirt and added a tie and sport coat, made his way to the gazebo and called for everyone's attention. He asked them all to gather around. He was joined by Diego, who had traded his band uniform for a coat and tie, and the two of them began to play a trumpet voluntary. Pastor Juan appeared on the right, decked out in a suit, looking expectant. Gloria and Ana proceeded from a curtained area behind the T-shirt booth and walked to the gazebo in time with the music, a single rose in their hands.

A murmur arose from the crowd as little Melissa Garcia toddled to Gloria's side, dropping rose petals as she went.

"Aww! How sweet!"

Everyone looked askance at everyone else and shrugged. What was going on? A wedding? Looked like it.

Suddenly the music stopped. When it began again, Sam stood alone playing "Here Comes the Bride." Maria appeared in a mid-calf, cream-colored lace dress, and Diego escorted her from the booth to the gazebo. The pastor of the Bartholomews' church faced the crowd on the top step. Diego passed his mother's hand to Pastor Juan and then stood between him and Sam.

"Ladies and gentlemen," began the pastor, "we are gathered together this day to join this man and this woman in holy matrimony…"

At the end of the short ceremony Sam took the microphone. "Just one more thing, Mr. and Mrs. Garcia," He looked at someone in the crowd. "Congressman Todd."

The congressman came up and took the microphone. "Congratulations, Mr. and Mrs. Garcia. I know you will be very happy together." He stopped and looked down for a second before he continued.

"Most of you folks know where I have stood on the immigration issue, but these last few weeks have caused me to take a fresh look at things.

"Many lives were saved in Perkins Grove because of the unselfish acts of heroism by the Garcias and the Hispanic community. We applaud your courage." His applause was joined by the onlookers in the park.

"For the sake of national security and in an effort to be fair in granting the privilege of living in this great country, our government must be very careful to whom we award visas. I believe you have demonstrated your worthiness, and so I had my office contact Immigration on your behalf. The outcome was very positive, so here, Diego…" He handed Diego an envelope. "Ana…" Another envelope to Ana and then one to her mother. "and Maria, is permission to stay in the United States while your visas are being processed." There was a startled intake of breath, followed by more and louder applause.

Sam addressed the crowd. "Ladies and gentlemen, many of you do not know the story of this family. They were brought here by force illegally and then were stranded with no way to go home. The whole story truly is amazing. Maybe someone will write a book about it some day."

He turned to the still-stunned family. "Welcome, Diego, Ana, and Maria to the United States of America!"

Acknowledgements

I never started out to write a novel; I was just filling the hours while recovering from an illness. The book was written on two different continents, in airports, going down the Interstate, in waiting rooms of doctors offices, at the edge of the Amazon jungle, in the mountains of north Georgia, in hotel rooms, guest rooms, buses, on three different laptops and on the desktop where I now sit. To say that it is a miracle is not an exaggeration, which is why I thank my God for the whole thing. Thank You, Father.

There are dozens of people I would like to thank in this section, but I will name only a few: Cindy Brown, Jane Haase, Pamela Hendrickson, my wonderful sister-in law Rita Buice, my musician son Johnny Larrabee, my daughter Christine Augustine, my brother Ed Buice, and last, but far from least, my wonderful husband John. Big hug to all of you. Couldn't have done it without you!